RED STARS

RED STARS

The CASE of VIKTOR and NADYA'S NOTEBOOKS

DAVIDE MOROSINOTTO

DELACORTE PRESS

English translation copyright © 2020 by Denise Muir
Original Italian text copyright © 2017 by Book on a Tree Ltd.
Jacket art and interior graphic layout copyright © 2017 by Mondadori Libri
S.p.A., Milano

All rights reserved. Published in the United States by Delacorte Press, an imprint of Random House Children's Books, a division of Penguin Random House LLC, New York. Originally published in Italian as *La Sfolgorante luce di due stelle rosse* by Mondadori in Milan in 2017, and subsequently published in English in the United Kingdom by Pushkin Press, London, in 2020.

Delacorte Press is a registered trademark and the colophon is a trademark of Penguin Random House LLC.

Translated extract from Alexander Pushkin's *Ruslan and Ludmila* on page 366 copyright © 2020 by A.D.P. Briggs 2020. Used by permission of A.D.P. Briggs. All rights reserved.
Image credits are located on page 432.
The font used on page 402 is Shortcut Regular and was created by Misprinted Type.

Visit us on the Web! rhcbooks.com

Educators and librarians, for a variety of teaching tools, visit us at
RHTeachersLibrarians.com

Library of Congress Cataloging-in-Publication Data is available upon request.
ISBN 978-1-9848-9332-1 (hc) — ISBN 978-9848-9333-8 (lib. bdg.) —
ISBN 978-9848-9334-5 (ebook)

Illustrations on pages 38, 102, 120, 340, and 420 by Simone Tso
Jacket design by Bob Bianchini
Interior design by Tetragon, London

Printed in the United States of America
10 9 8 7 6 5 4 3 2 1
First American Edition

Contents

NOTEBOOK 6 – THE LONG WINTER

List of Maps

On the day of my thirteenth birthday, I became a hero.

I knew right away. Not as soon as I arrived in the city but almost, as I trudged up the icy river, dragging my sled – and her – behind me.

It was afternoon, somewhere between half past four and five o'clock, darkness had fallen, like a coat of thick, black paint. It was twenty degrees below zero.

I remember the bodies on the banks of the Neva. They'd appear suddenly, here and there, like waxen mushrooms. I also remember an old woman, in a threadbare coat, clasping a bucket and dragging herself along the ice in the middle of the river. She stopped, suddenly, pulled out a long nail and hammered it into the ice with the swing and force of a woodcutter. She lowered her bucket into the hole she'd made and pulled it through the water below. Then she saw me. She stopped. I took one step, just one, but she dropped everything and ran, ignoring my shouts to stop, that I wouldn't hurt her.

I felt bad. I knew how precious water was, the bucket and nail even more so, but I was too weak to go after her. I put my wrist to my forehead to adjust my hat and moved off again. A bridge. Another bridge. Then I saw it. The Hermitage Museum. It was different from how I remembered it. Darkened windows boarded over. No more gold or statues; rubble everywhere. But it was still the museum.

The Hermitage was where it had always been. It had resisted.

So that was me. A hero.
I had made it, after travelling so far, to save the city.

Viktor, are you mad?

Why?

You know you can't write stuff like
that. You'll get us into trouble and I think
we've been through enough already.

Listen, Nadya. This is my story. I want to tell it my way!

We've already told it. Our way. Back then. We
just have to wait for someone to read it. Trust me,
please. Let the notebooks speak for themselves.

CCCP
PEOPLE'S COMMISSARIAT FOR
INTERNAL AFFAIRS

ATTENTION

The pages enclosed herewith did not
pass the censorship inspection and have
therefore been classified NON-COMPLIANT and
DANGEROUS.
   Adequate clearance is required to read
on.
   All breaches will be prosecuted to the
fullest extent of the law.

CCCP

PEOPLE'S COMMISSARIAT FOR
INTERNAL AFFAIRS

REPORT FOR INTERNAL USE

The attached document was recovered during
a search of the residential unit at 8
Stolyarny Alley and obtained by the Ministry
of Justice as evidence in the investigation
into Soviet citizens:

* Viktor Nikolayevich Danilov; born
  Leningrad, 17 November 1928;
* Nadya Nikolayevna Danilova; born
  Leningrad, 17 November 1928.

The accusations levelled at the afore-named
citizens concern events which took place
in the period from June to November of the
year 1941.

This document, more specifically referred
to as "the notebooks" by the accused,
comprises a variety of materials, including
loose sheets, notes written on scrap paper,
leaflets, old postcards, drawings and
photographs. It is presumed that some of the
pages were originally joined by wire spirals
but were later tampered with to allow the
order to be changed.
  This order also appears to have been
changed by the accused at a separate time,

in all probability to reconstruct the proper
chronological order of events.

The folder was entrusted to the People's
Commissariat for Internal Affairs /NKVD/, to
the undersigned Officer in Charge, for the
purpose of determining the fate of the two
young people named above.

Accompanying the document were two
regulatory rubber stamps which I have been
authorized to use, at my sole discretion, on
completion of the inquiry.

They are identical, both bear the star
and two ears of wheat, but have different
wording - one says INNOCENT, the other says
GUILTY.

There will be only one sentence.
Only one justice.
Glory to the Party.

Signed:

COLONEL VALERY GAVRIILOVICH SMIRNOV

Col. Smirnov

NOTEBOOK 1

The notebook has been
split into chapters and,
where necessary, I have
added annotations in the
margin, written in my
own hand.   —Smirnov

Leningrad, 22nd June 1941

It's Sunday today and Viktor and I have been to the museum.

Of all the places in this city, I like the Hermitage Museum best. It occupies a whole row of palaces along the embankment of the Neva, although the biggest one is the Winter Palace, a beautiful royal residence that is brick-red on the outside, with a thousand golden statues that light up the sky like stars.

The Winter Palace was once home to the Tsar. I can't imagine what he found to do in a house with more than a thousand rooms. Luckily, the revolution came and the Winter Palace stopped belonging to the Tsar and became the people's, so it's a little bit mine now too, and Viktor's.

I've been to the museum lots of times and I know all the paintings and statues in its endless collections off by heart. I even gave a lesson on them at school once, for the whole class, and I was so good they all clapped. When we got home, Viktor told me not to boast because I shouldn't take credit for the fact that our parents work at the museum and let us visit them on school holidays.

Today is a "visit the museum day."

Yesterday was 21st June and we celebrated the summer solstice, when the sun sets really late and the light never leaves the sky. Viktor and I spent the day in the park with our friends from the Young Pioneers. We had a picnic on the grass, played football and tug-of-war, then in the evening Papa took us to the ballet and after that to a late-night street concert . . .

> Get to the point. It doesn't make
> any sense otherwise!

. . . So we woke up late this morning. Papa had gone out already and Mama said, "Get ready, I'm taking you to the museum today."

I flew out of bed so quickly I didn't notice Viktor was still sleeping down below, lying on his tummy with his face squashed into his pillow. I sent him flying with a kick.

"What's up?"

"What's up is we're going to the museum. Get up!"

We had rye bread and butter for breakfast then waited for Mr. Berezin to finish in the bathroom.

He took for ever, he always does, and came out an hour later with his big wool underpants pulled up to his armpits and the *Pravda* under his arm.

"If you're thinking of going in there, I'd wait a bit, ha, ha!"

Viktor and I looked at each other, wondering what we might find. Papa says the Red Army could use Mr. Berezin as a chemical weapon, but we were in a hurry so we went in anyway, noses pinched, and to save time, we brushed our teeth as well, squeezed together over the sink.

Viktor started making faces and it was really funny because, although we're not completely identical (I am a girl, after all!), we did look the same in the cracked bathroom mirror, and it was like being teased by a short-haired version of myself.

I burst out laughing, and to laugh you need to breathe in, so I breathed in and, like I said, Mr. Berezin is a human chemical weapon, I very nearly died from the stink!

> Stop it, Nadya! You're not supposed to put silly things like that in a diary.

Natalya Zhirov was waiting when we came out of the bathroom (the Zhirovs are the other family we share the apartment with, along with the Berezins), and she had no idea why my brother and I were braying like a pair of donkeys (something else Papa always says).

Anyway.

It was a lovely day outside, so warm it made you want to go swimming in the river. Mama always says the sun in Leningrad is the most beautiful sun in the whole world. It hides during the winter but when it comes out in summer, there's no beating it, she says, and I agree with her.

Good weather always puts Mama in a good mood, me too, that's why we decided to walk to the museum instead of going by tram like we usually do. ←

Viktor started fussing right away that it would be quicker on the tram, but Mama reminded him a good communist is never lazy. That shut him up right away. No one cares more about being a good communist than Viktor.

It's a nice walk from our flat to the museum and the streets were empty. Nearly everyone stays up late on Midsummer's Day to "make merry," Mama says.

When we got to the square outside the Winter Palace, a guard greeted us and asked Mama, "Are these the famous twins, then?"

5. — The Danilovs' apartment is in Leningrad. 8 Stolyarny Alley, top floor.

I tutted, what other twins might Mama have? Although my brother and I look very alike, we're chalk and cheese really. For example, at that moment, I was looking up at the sky, admiring how the dome of the Admiralty seemed to pierce the sun, while Viktor couldn't take his eyes off the guard's rifle and shiny uniform!

Anyway, we went inside the Winter Palace and Mama said, "Remember our rule. Eyes down and off you run!"

Viktor and I yelled yes as we dashed up the stairs and into the rooms full of statues. Mama always tells us to run at the museum, partly because it's so big and takes ages to get around, and partly because, if you stop to look at everything, you never have enough time to see it all.

Mama took us to see the statue of a crouching boy today. He looks so perfect you almost expect him to stand up any minute. Mama said an Italian artist called Michelangelo made the statue. Then she said Papa was waiting for us in his office and we were all going to eat together there.

Mama and Papa are both assistants to Dr. Iosif Orbeli, the director of the Hermitage. I love the office they share with all their colleagues, it used to be a ballroom, so you can imagine how big it is!

Even though it was Sunday, lots of people were at work. When they saw us, they all rushed over to greet us and announced that it was "time for a break!"

A lady turned on the radio for some music, Papa opened a drawer and pulled out some sandwiches, Viktor sat down on a gold chair, and I perched on a wooden crate.

"That crate you're sitting on," Papa said. "Look inside it, Nadya."

I did what he said and inside I found some notebooks, including the one I'm writing in now! There were loads of them in the crate, each with a hard, red cover and a rectangle at the top, like a label, to write your name inside.

Anyway, the best thing about the notebooks is that the pages and the front cover have holes down one side and a wire spiral holding them together.

"They're new," Papa explained when he saw how delighted I was. "They were sent here by mistake but Dr. Orbeli thought they might be useful and asked if we could keep them."

"Oh, do you think I can have one?" I asked straight away.

Mama said no, Papa said who do you think will notice, that's not the point Mama said, so Papa said he'd already started writing in one but didn't like it because the spiral got in the way (Papa is left-handed like me, whereas Viktor and Mama are right-handed).

And with that, he ripped his notes out (he'd only used three pages!) and handed the notebook to me and Viktor.

"You can both use it," he said, "keep a diary together."

"Two people can't write a diary," one of Papa's colleagues said. I don't agree. I think it's a fantastic idea.

I took the notebook and wrote my name on the front cover, Nadya that is, and Viktor wrote his. I used a blue fountain pen and Viktor a red pencil.

The true communist colour!

After that, I started writing about all the amazing things that happened today.

I don't agree that spiral notebooks are no good if you're left-handed, I actually like them because the spiral tickles my hand.

Papa obviously made the whole story up as an excuse to give me the notebook. I only hope Mama isn't too angry with him, she gave him such a nasty look!

I'm going to attach a photo I found in one of the hallways at the Hermitage, to show what the building looks like inside.

Done.

That's enough for now, Papa has laid out the sandwiches and I'm hungry. The grown-ups have a bottle of vodka and things are livening up. Two young clerks are dancing on the other side of the office, one of the women's pleated skirt is whirling around like a spinning top.

The frames are all empty because the room's being renovated.

A man with a red nose (I think he's called Garanin or something like that) is singing away to himself but his voice is awful. It's so bad a woman tells him to stop, "Quiet, Vladimir, quiet."

"Why, what's wrong?"

"The radio! Let me hear what they're saying on the ra

"Citizens of the Soviet Union!

At four o'clock this morning, German troops attacked our country and their planes bombed our cities!

This attack upon our nation, launched without warning, is perfidy, unparalleled in the history of civilized nations and violates the treaty of non-aggression between Germany and the Soviet Union.

. . .

The Soviet Government has ordered our troops to repulse the predatory assault and to drive German troops from the territory of our country. This war started today has been forced upon us, not by the German people, not by German workers, peasants and intellectuals, whose sufferings we well understand, but by the bloodthirsty fascist rulers of Germany who have enslaved Frenchmen, Czechs, Poles, Serbians, Norwegians, Belgians, Danish, Dutch, Greeks and other nations.

. . .

It is not the first time that our people have had to deal with the attack of an arrogant aggressor. At the time of Napoleon's invasion of Russia, our people's reply was war for the Fatherland and Napoleon suffered defeat and met his doom.

It will be the same with Hitler.

The government calls upon you, citizens of the Soviet Union, to rally still more closely around our glorious Bolshevik Party, around our Soviet Government, around our great leader and comrade, Stalin. Ours is a righteous cause. The enemy shall be defeated. Victory will be ours."

We heard this speech on the radio today, at 12 o'clock, in our parents' office at the Hermitage. I rushed to grab the notebook out of Nadya's hands so I could write it all down to remember for ever.

Unfortunately, the speech was very fast and there are bits (where the dots are) where I couldn't keep up.

It's difficult to describe what happened afterwards but, as Papa said, this is a Terrible Moment in History, and our memories must be preserved for Posterity.

The person who spoke on the radio was the People's Commissar for Foreign Affairs of the USSR: Comrade Vyacheslav Mikhailovich Molotov.

He sounded very concerned on the radio. One woman in the office cried during the speech, Nadya too.

"It's strange that Molotov addressed the nation," Mr. Garanin commented. "Comrade Stalin should have made such an important announcement."

"So what?" another woman said.

"Well, it must mean something. Maybe the radio's not telling us the full story."

"Shut your mouth!" the woman snapped.

I think she's right: Mr. Garanin can't go around saying whatever he likes just because we're at war.

At war.

Hitler, the dictator who rules Germany, has launched a surprise attack on us and we must now defend ourselves.

S. – Vladimir Garanin. Employee at Hermitage. Investigate further.

Everything is going to change. Maybe I'll be allowed to fight, I'm nearly thirteen after all, and I'm a Young Pioneer.

I have to ask Papa.

The thing I liked most about Molotov's speech was when he said the Russian people had defeated Napoleon and it would be the same with Hitler. I bet we will.

Poets will write about this war for centuries. It will be the most glorious war in the whole wide world!

My brother Viktor writes some really silly things.

There is nothing wonderful about being at war and (I admit I cried when I heard the speech on the radio) I'm really scared.

We don't know what's going to happen but there's no doubt it's very serious. The radio said that the enemy has already bombed many Soviet cities, including Kiev and Sevastopol where our cousin Anna lives. We don't know if she and her family are still alive.

Everyone is scared, especially because Leningrad is so close to the border, as one of Papa's work colleagues was quick to point out.

I looked for a map when I got home and I've stuck it in here.

The Soviet Union is enormous and Leningrad is on the far left, close to Europe. The fascist Enemy is bound to attack us first.

After Molotov's speech, the announcer on the radio said more news would be broadcast shortly and the music came back on, only it had changed to patriotic songs, not the happy music we'd been dancing to earlier.

Dr. Orbeli came out of his office. He looks like Grandfather Frost, the old man who brings presents to children in winter, because of his long white beard

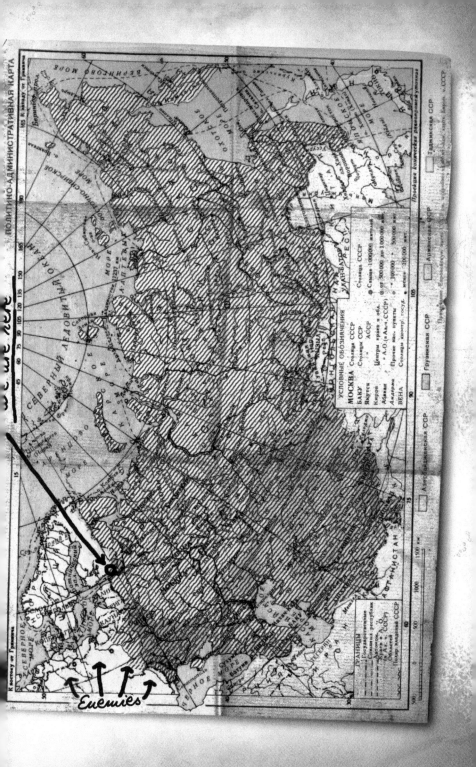

(although he has a black moustache!) and wrinkled forehead.

Mama and Papa say Dr. Orbeli is the best director the museum could ever have, he can foresee problems before they happen.

He did it this time, too. "It's here then," he said, as if he'd known all along that war was going to break out.

He began handing out typewritten sheets and when my father asked what they were, the director replied, "The evacuation plan. It is our duty, now, to save the Hermitage's many treasures and make sure they are not destroyed by the enemy."

My brother Viktor sometimes forgets his place – he jumped to his feet and blurted out that, at such a tragic time, there are more important things than paintings.

Dr. Orbeli silenced him with a look.

"There is nothing more important than culture. Men may die but art lives for ever. Young people in the future will thank us for what we are about to do."

Everyone went back to work and Mama came over to Viktor and me, "Do you two feel up to going home alone? Mrs. Berezin can make you something for dinner. Papa and I will be along shortly."

I've never really liked Mrs. Berezin, much less her husband, but it didn't seem like a good time to be difficult.

When Viktor and I left the museum, there were people everywhere, the whole city seemed to have poured onto the streets. It was even worse on the tram and we saw long queues outside the shops on our journey home.

People were talking all around us, I've never heard the word "war" so often.

Back home, we asked Mrs. Berezin if she could make us dinner and she said okay, then Viktor told her the shops

S. – Interesting. Find out if Orbeli has gained access to classified information?

were open, so she rushed out with the whole family's ration books to stock up.

Maybe we should do the same; there might be shortages because of the war so it's best to get as much of everything as possible. But Mama has all the ration books.

Since there was nothing I could do, I stayed here to write.

We ate with the Berezins this evening and there was only one topic of conversation at dinner. The Zhirovs ate in their room, but we heard their voices from behind the door. They must be very worried. Their son, although I hardly remember him, is a soldier somewhere.

After a while, I couldn't stand it anymore and went off in search of some peace and quiet. I fell asleep reading my book and I've only just woken up. It's nearly midnight. Viktor is snoring his head off, Mama and Papa aren't here.

Their bed is right next to ours and it's empty.

They didn't come home.

24th June

The radio says we're winning the war.

The Nazis (another name for the fascists) have invaded the Motherland but they weren't expecting the proud resistance of the Red Army and are now in retreat across the Russian front.

What I don't really understand is, if we're winning, why is everyone behaving as if we aren't? The queues outside the shops are so long they fill the streets, people line up outside the closed shutters from four o'clock in the morning.

We've been told we need to be ready for when the enemy arrives. I keep asking how he's going to get here, if we've already beaten him back at the border, but no one answers.

Young Pioneers like us are also expected to contribute to the war effort. That's why Viktor and I had to attend an excruciatingly boring drill yesterday – Mr. Yashkin (the leader of our section) made us carry bucket after bucket of water up to the top floors of the apartment buildings in our district.

"What are they for?" I asked.

"To put out fires in the event of an air raid," Mr. Yashkin replied.

The drill was so boring and really hard work! Luckily, it wasn't just me and Viktor, there were other children with us, like my friend Darya who lives in the building opposite ours, she's in my class at school and my squad at the Young Pioneers. We carried the buckets up and down stairs together and even managed to spill one on Boris's head. He's a bit weird. He goes to our school but he never speaks to anyone and is big and burly as a bear.

When the water landed on his head he just stared at me. I felt a bit sorry for him, but then Darya started laughing so I laughed as well.

Too bad Mr. Yashkin shouted at us for wasting water. We had to do extra trips as punishment.

Anyway.

My parents haven't been home since the war started, not until Mama arrived this morning. She had those black shadows under her eyes she gets when she doesn't sleep.

"The director gave the order to evacuate the Hermitage. That means there are trains just waiting to be loaded, and your father and I have to get all the exhibits, label them, pack them up, put them into crates . . ."

"Does that mean there will be no more paintings in the museum?"

"We're putting them all away somewhere safe."

"Who will put us somewhere safe?" I asked before realizing it was a stupid thing to say. So stupid that Mama turned away without replying.

"Mrs. Berezin can't look after the two of you all the time," she said instead. "Today you have to go to Uncle Dmitry's."

Uncle Dmitry is a labourer and he lives in a barrack-hut near the Bullet Factory. He's not a real relative, but

S. – Dmitry, surname unknown. Bullet Factory. No record of this person in our archives.

Mama told us to call him "Uncle" (she wouldn't say why when I asked).

Anyway, I wasn't in the mood to go to Uncle Dmitry's and I said so. Viktor did, too, but it didn't get us anywhere.

We put our things in a bag (all I took was this notebook) and went out to wait for the bus. Mama fell asleep on her feet, head resting against the window.

I gazed out at Leningrad.

Viktor and I were born here. We're so lucky. It's such a beautiful city. It was founded centuries ago by a Tsar and stands at the point where the River Neva flows into the Gulf of Finland.

That means the city is surrounded by water – it's actually made up of lots of islands connected to each other. The surrounding area is full of lakes (some small, others bigger, like Lake Ladoga, which is so big it could be a sea).

Leningrad is also the city in which communism – the idea that people should all work together and share everything – originated.

The Father of our Nation, Lenin, was exiled to Europe by the Tsar, but sent back to Russia in a train with lead-sealed windows for fear he might speak to someone and infect the whole world with communism. Where did Lenin's train journey end? Right here in Leningrad, which is now named after him!

I'd better stop now or this diary will end up like a history book, but honestly, Leningrad is a very important city and it's now in danger: there were trucks full of people with sad faces when we got to the suburbs.

"Who are they?"

"Soldiers," Mama answered. "They're going to the front."

"Where you fight the enemy," Viktor added.

"Shouldn't they be wearing uniforms?"

Mama said they didn't need uniforms and I thought, well, a rifle at least would be useful. Maybe they'll be given one when they arrive.

Anyway, there's no point in worrying . . .

The wooden huts the labourers live in have small vegetable plots beside them. Each hut has a main door on the short side, and it opens onto a long corridor which runs to the other end of the building where the kitchens and shared bathrooms are located. There are lots of doorways down each side of the long corridor, one for each family living in the hut.

The strange thing is that when you knock on a door and go inside, there's just one big communal space behind it, not separate rooms. If a family wants to mark off their own area, they have to hang up a tablecloth or use a piece of furniture, if they have one.

The great thing about the barrack-huts, though, is that the inhabitants live together like one big family, like when Viktor and I sleep at the Young Pioneer House.

The bad thing about the barrack-huts is that you can never find anywhere to be alone.

To give you an idea of what they're like, I've drawn a plan of one and stuck it here.

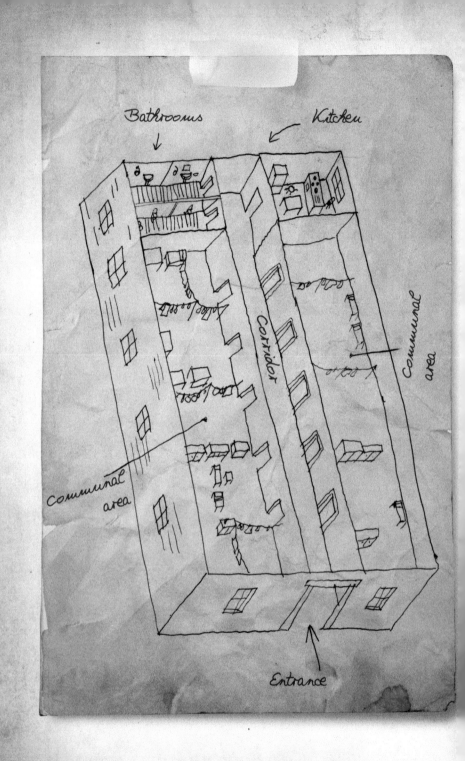

See? Something happened while I was sticking in the drawing and it made me really angry.

Before I write about it, I have to explain that Uncle Dmitry wasn't here when Viktor and I arrived. There were no grown-ups around either because all the men and women labourers have to work continuous shifts because of the war.

We stayed with Grandma Olga who looks after all the children in the hut. First of all, there's Viktor and me, we're the oldest (nearly thirteen), then four or five children who go to the same school as us but one year below, and a lot of small children, even a few babies.

I was sitting minding my own business in a corner, writing in my notebook, when Grandma Olga came over and asked me what I was doing.

"Well, it's like a diary that Viktor and I are writing together," I replied. "I do most of it, though. I write down everything that happens. All my thoughts. Secrets, too."

I've no idea why, but Grandma Olga got really angry when I said that. She started yelling that secrets are supposed to be kept secret and that one day I'll lose the notebook, someone will read it, and Viktor and I, our entire family, will be in big trouble.

← S. – Suspicious. Investigate further.

"Is my name in that notebook? And Dmitry's?"

"Of course not," I said.

"I don't believe you. Show me."

I didn't want to show her so I ran away.

I'm hiding in the vegetable garden, no one knows I'm here, not even Viktor.

I have to admit my brother can be odd sometimes: since war broke out, he hardly speaks to anyone anymore, not even me.

Anyway, I've decided I'm not going back into the hut until Mama comes to get us.

There's no way I'm letting anyone get their hands on my notebook.

26th June

Yesterday, the 25th of June that is, we went back to the barrack-hut, but with Papa this time.

I didn't want to risk Grandma Olga taking my notebook again so I left it at home. I worried about it the whole time, terrified someone (the Berezins, for instance) might find it.

Grandma Olga was right about one thing, secrets should always stay secret.

There was this student, once, a boy with blue eyes who used to live on the floor below us. The police came and arrested him one night. I asked Papa what the student had done wrong, but he wouldn't tell me. Later, I overheard the women on the first floor say he hadn't known how to keep his mouth shut.

It must have been a very serious crime because the student never came home.

I don't know if my notebook will contain many secrets or not, but I've decided to do whatever I can to protect it.

Sis, you're turning this diary into a really boring read. We're living through the most exciting times and you're wasting time talking about Grandma Olga?

Just as well I'm here to write something interesting every now and then.

Starting with the events of last night: our first shift on fire watch!

Papa came to get us at the hut. He said Mr. Yashkin had summoned us.

"Summoned us for what?"

"For your turn on fire watch!"

This is how it works: the enemy might send planes to bomb the city so squads of Young Pioneers are deployed on roofs every night to scan the sky and raise the alarm if they spot a plane or a fire.

Each group is provided with:

* binoculars
* a hand siren
* a map of the city
* buckets of water and sacks of sand to put out any fires.

Unfortunately, due to a hitch of some kind, our district didn't receive any binoculars or maps.

Mr. Yashkin made do with sheets of paper to write notes on and three pairs of binoculars (one pair of which was his own, which he uses to go birdwatching in the forest because Mr. Yashkin is an ecologist; the other two were theatre glasses that ladies use at the ballet).

He then split us into three groups.

Each group needed:

* a Lookout, to scan the sky with the binoculars
* a Notetaker to record the location of enemy planes
* Relays, to run and raise the alarm, or put out fires.

S. — Sabotage?

I was appointed lookout because of my razor-sharp vision. I tossed up with the other two lookouts to see who should have the good binoculars but I lost, unfortunately, and ended up with a pair of the tiny opera ones.

I appointed Nadya as my notetaker (obviously, she never stops writing!) and Mr. Yashkin saddled us with Darya, her brother Stepan and a boy called Boris as relays. Boris is strong as an ox but a bit slow and doesn't try very hard, that's why I don't like him.

"Where should we station ourselves, sir?" I asked Mr. Yashkin.

"Come with me," he said.

He took us to the building across the street, up ten flights of stairs and out onto the roof, where women hang their washing; we couldn't move for sheets.

The people who live in the building complimented us for being so brave and brought us pillows and old blankets. One woman left us a small stove and a kettle to make tea. They all urged us to keep our eyes open.

"It's not a game," Mr. Yashkin said before he left.

We were well aware it was not a game. The fate of Leningrad was in our hands!

The first thing to do was explore. The second was to build a shelter, it gets damp at night and our watch was until eight the next morning. We were going to be there for a long time.

We inspected every inch of the roof and eventually decided that the best place was the northern corner. There was a chimney pot I could climb up to get a good view of the sky. The others could easily wait down below it.

Nadya and Darya laid out the blankets and Boris lit the stove. Stepan tied a sheet between two washing lines to make a sort of shelter, and when it was all ready, I climbed up to my spot on the chimney.

"Ready, Viktor?" Nadya asked.

"Yes, you?"

"You tell me where the planes are and I'll write!"

"Great."

I got into position with the binoculars.

"What can you see?"

"The sky," I replied. "Sky, sky and more sky."

"Anything else?"

"There's something over there!"

It turned out to be just a cloud.

"There's something tiny right there!"

This time it was a swallow.

"Anything else?"

"Sky, sky and more sky."

"Oh well," Nadya said. "The important thing is to keep your eyes open."

The binoculars were mother-of-pearl with a handle on the side to make them easier to hold. They were very pretty but you couldn't see much with them.

Not that there was anything to see!

Just sky, all pearly grey even though it was the middle of the night. The flat, empty sky. Away in the distance, on my right, I could see smoke from the factories. A few birds in flight. The cloud I'd spotted earlier. Nothing else.

"Can I have the binoculars for a bit?" Nadya asked.

"I'm the lookout."

It was my duty, I couldn't give them away to a mere notetaker.

Hey, I'm not a "mere" notetaker! I'm your sister!

It was pretty boring, though.

Nadya and Darya started talking about girls' stuff. Stepan had curled up in a corner and fallen asleep.

I was tired, too, but I couldn't fall asleep with the fate of the city on my shoulders!

"Do you want some tea?" Boris asked.

It was the first time he'd ever spoken to me.

Boris is odd, he's always by himself at school, gets terrible marks, and whenever we pick teams for football, he gets left out. He could be the best player of the lot though, he's so big.

"No thanks," I said.

"It'll keep you awake."

I decided to come down from the chimney. The two of us moved to the edge of the roof, near the eaves, so I could continue to keep watch as I drank my tea.

"It's good."

"I make it all the time at home," he replied.

That's unusual, I thought, Mama and Papa never let Nadya or me make the tea.

"Why do you make it?"

"My mother can't cook, so I do it."

We stood in silence. My sister and Darya joined us after a bit.

"Where's Stepan?"

"He's sleeping."

"Can we have tea, too?"

"Here."

"Any sugar?"

"I don't have any."

"It's okay, it tastes fine without sugar."

"Great, thanks."

"What's going to happen now?"

"They say we're winning the war."

"Bull," Boris muttered.

"What do you mean?"

"We're not winning. We're losing. Do you remember what Molotov said on the radio? Hitler and Stalin had made an agreement, but Hitler betrayed us and attacked anyway. We weren't ready, the Germans had surprise on their side. And they have the best army in the world. Everyone knows that."

"The Red Army is the best army!" I answered.

"We don't even have rifles!" Boris said. "We're not a real army, just peasants and labourers sent to fight. The Nazis are elite troops."

I jumped to my feet. "What you're saying, that's . . . that's . . . treason!"

"It's the truth," Boris said. "The Nazis use the blitz-krieg method, lightning war it's called. They'll be here in a few days and they'll attack the city. That's why your parents at the Hermitage are evacuating the museum. That's why we're here on this roof. To raise the alarm when the enemies arrive."

Boris was far too full of himself for my liking, I wanted to punch him.

S. – Boris. Surname? Patronymic? Include in the investigation.

45

Instead, I turned to walk away.

"Where are you going?" Nadya asked.

"To the toilet," I replied. "I must've drunk too much tea."

The truth is, I didn't want to get into a fight. But I did need to go to the lavatory. I opened the roof door and stepped down onto the stairs.

It was dark, so I started to feel my way down. The bathrooms weren't on the top floor, or the next floor down, so I went down yet another level. I started to think I should just have gone on the roof.

I finally came across an open door and realized I'd found the bathrooms. I went in and did what I had to do.

VIKTOR!

It wasn't actually Nadya's voice I heard. In truth, it wasn't anyone's voice, more like goose bumps, a tingling feeling warning me that my sister needed me.

Give me a break!
I was only wondering where you'd gone!

Mama says it happens sometimes to twins. They have a very special bond because they're born at the same time and grow up together. I've always wondered how she knows that, considering she's an only child.

In any case, I raced up the stairs, taking them as fast as I could, and when I burst out onto the roof, Nadya was shouting, "Planes! Over there, look! Are those planes?"

I grabbed the binoculars. I saw them, too.

They were dots, no bigger than insects. Flying in formation. I adjusted the binoculars slightly. I couldn't see if there were any markings on the wings, but they might be enemy planes.

"Nadya," I said, calm as can be. "Take a note of their position. If I'm not mistaken, Haymarket is over in that direction and the planes are heading northeast. Towards Nevsky Prospect."

"Haymarket. Nevsky. Got it."

"Come on, then," I cried. "Let's raise the alarm. Planes flying over the city!"

While Darya ran to wake up her brother, Nadya, Boris and I dashed down the stairs.

We started yelling and knocking on doors, then went out into the street and ran all the way to Mr. Yashkin's house.

He opened the door in his nightshirt and by the time he got into the street and looked up at the sky, the planes had already gone.

"Are you sure?" he asked.

"Definitely," I replied.

"Umm," he said. "Well, we had better submit a report. I'll take care of it, you go back to your positions." He said nothing for a few seconds then added, "I bet those devils were on a reconnaissance mission. When they come back to Leningrad, they'll meet their match, you can be sure of that!"

We thanked him, I even did the military salute.

I hope Mr. Yashkin tells everyone how heroic we were. They may even give me a medal.

27th June

The city soviet declared martial law today, Mr. Berezin told us at breakfast.

"What does that mean?" I asked.

"It means Leningrad is officially at war. The old laws no longer apply and there are lots of new ones which we all have to abide by from now on."

In effect, there are an awful lot of new laws. For example, it's now forbidden to go out at night, and if the police stop you and you don't have a special permit, you could be arrested. It's called a curfew.

"Does that mean we won't be able to do fire watch anymore?" Viktor asked.

"No, that's different. You'll be given a special permit for that. But be careful you don't lose it."

Another of the new laws is that all men and women aged over sixteen have been called up to fortify the city. Mama and Papa already spend nearly all their time at the Hermitage and, from now on, they'll also have to do special daily shifts to dig trenches, build barricades, put up barbed-wire fences and other things like that.

Viktor is really annoyed that the new law is only for people who're already sixteen because he wants to take part.

**ЗА РОДИНУ,
ЗА ЧЕСТЬ, ЗА СВОБОДУ!**

One of the leaflets they were handing
out in Leningrad today!

On the plus side for him, we have lookout duty again tonight.

I'd much rather be asleep in my own bed.

28th June

About our flat: when you come in, there's a long corridor piled high with the Zhirovs' old furniture (this flat used to be theirs when they were very rich, before the Communist Revolution and before I was born).

The corridor has a doorway on the right into the Zhirovs' room, and a doorway on the left that takes you into the room we share with the Berezins. It used to be one big living room but now it's split into two by a wooden partition that almost touches the ceiling.

Our room is nice because it has my parents' bed and the bed where Viktor and I sleep, a stove, a small wardrobe and piles of books everywhere – on the floor, on top of the wardrobe, around the edges of the room, there's even a pile of them, like a wall, between our bed and Mama and Papa's, giving us somewhere to put things, like a night-light or an alarm clock.

Back out in the corridor, there's another doorway at the bottom. That's the kitchen. It's really small but has a long table and a window. The bathroom is off the kitchen.

Mama always says we're lucky to have an inside toilet.

Anyway, there are four of us in the Danilova family, three Berezins (Mr. and Mrs. Berezin plus Anastasia who's twenty-two), and five Zhirovs (the grandparents, Natalya and her husband, and Yulian, who's one and a half and cries all the time. I haven't counted Natalya's brother, as he's a soldier and hasn't lived here for ages).

I'm writing all this to explain that, with so many people in the flat, there's always someone around and always noises to be heard – voices, people cooking, the Zhirovs' stove whistling, someone in the bathroom, someone waiting their turn to go into the bathroom, and so on.

It's a nice home because you never feel alone.

Until this morning, that is, when Viktor and I got back from our lookout shift at eight o'clock.

"We're here!" Viktor shouted.

"We're back!" I said.

But all was still in the flat.

The Zhirovs' door is shut and we can't hear any voices behind it, not even Yulian crying. The Berezins have gone out. The kitchen light is off and the bathroom door is wide open.

It's so quiet I can almost hear the blood in my veins, thank goodness I've got Viktor with me.

I wonder how people who don't have a twin manage.

30th June

They're sending us away.
I can't believe it.
They're sending us away.

1st July

I couldn't bring myself to write anything yesterday. I cried nearly all day.

Everything seemed to be going fine.

It was Sunday the other day, so Viktor and I put on our uniforms, red neckties and star badges and went to the Young Pioneer House.

All our friends were there, along with Mr. Yashkin, who hasn't been called up to fight because he's old.

"We need to be ready for the hard times ahead," he said. "So, today we're going to do gas mask drills!"

A gas mask is a rubber cap that covers your face, it has two big eyes to see out of and a funny-looking trunk with a filter at the end to clean the air.

"If the enemy drops a gas bomb, you could choke to death. A gas mask could save your life because it lets air in but keeps the poisonous gas out."

"Ooh," we gasped.

"But it must be worn and used properly, and the instructions followed carefully."

Mr. Yashkin spent about half an hour showing us how to put the mask on but when I tried it later, I'd forgotten everything he'd said.

"It smells horrible!" I cried. It was difficult to breathe and I could hardly see a thing out of the big eye pieces.

"You'll get used to it," Mr. Yashkin replied. He took a photo of us.

Viktor is first from the left, wearing a checked shirt, I'm in the middle. We look funny, don't we?

It turned out to be a fun day. At night, we did another lookout on the roof and this time we were better organized. Darya brought an elastic band to play *rezinochki*. My brother and Boris agreed to put the elastic band around their knees so Darya and I could jump over the stretched bit and do lots of acrobatics.

We didn't see any planes.

Anyway, we were tired when we got back to the flat on Monday morning (yesterday) and thought that there would be nobody home, but Mama and Papa were waiting for us.

You could tell right away something was wrong because they both looked so serious.

"What's wrong?"

"Come here," Papa said. "Let's have breakfast."

They'd laid out a proper feast in the kitchen. There were cheese pastries, fried eggs and ravioli, which are my favourite.

But instead of being happy about all the delicious things to eat, I was scared, because Mama's eyes were red, and it was like there was a black cloud hanging over the kitchen.

"What's wrong?" Viktor asked. "You're scaring me."

That's when I realized he could feel it, too, so I went over to him and squeezed his hand. Papa said, "Sit down, eat."

"Tell us what's wrong first."

Mama said, "Later."

"Now."

So they told us . . .

It's probably better if I take it from here.

It was obvious that Papa didn't know where to start, so he pointed to the band he was wearing around his arm.

54

He explained that it was the symbol of the People's Militia, a voluntary citizens' army, set up so that Russia would be protected by its own inhabitants!

"Does that mean you've signed up?"

"More or less."

"So you'll be going to fight? Like the soldiers in the Red Army?"

"I have been ordered to and it's my duty," he replied. "For our country."

At that point, my sister Nadya erupted. "But Boris said there aren't even any rifles for real soldiers! What will you fight with?"

"With whatever they give me. You don't always need a rifle to fight." He said it really quietly, under his breath. As if it were something he'd thought long and hard about.

"If you fight, you could die, couldn't you?" Nadya asked.

I pinched her. Of course, he could die. That's what happens in war.

"I promise I'll try not to," he replied.

He smiled. He seemed proud, but also a bit tired. Or maybe something else . . .

It was resignation.

"Papa will be leaving in five days," Mama explained. "We don't know where he'll be sent."

"But the radio said we're winning!"

"You need to fight to win."

"But the radio said . . ."

"Nadya, what you hear on the radio is not always the truth," Papa said.

He stopped and looked at Mama.

It was like he was asking for help.

and she took over, "Papa will be gone in five days. I'll be staying at the Hermitage. They need me. We have to protect all the artworks, and like Orbeli said, the museum must be evacuated. It's my duty. Just like it's your father's duty to fight."

Mama and Papa looked at each other.

That's when they told us.

Nadya and I have to go away.

The city soviet council has prepared special trains, "children's trains" they call them. They're going to take us far away from Leningrad.

"It's for your own safety."

"We want to stay here with you!"

"You can't stay with me," Mama said. "It will be dangerous, and I have to work in the museum."

"And I won't be here anymore," Papa said.

That's when I realized there will be no more Us.

"You can't send us away."

"The city will come under attack. It's going to be bombed."

"But the radio says we're winning, that can't be a lie as well."

"Nadya . . ."

"You can't send us away. Please . . ."

"You have to go. You'll be safe. The trains will take you as far away as possible from the front, near the Ural Mountains, where the enemy will never get you. It'll be like a holiday. Then when you get back, we'll all be together again."

"The war won't last long," Mama said. "If you ask me, you'll only just have got there and it'll be time to come back."

"You and Viktor probably won't even get off the train."

"Mr. Yashkin will be with you, as well as all your friends from school and from the Young Pioneers."

Papa smiled. "The Urals are wonderful at this time of year. Maybe they'll let you camp out and Mr. Yashkin will take you climbing. I'm sure it'll be great."

"You'll have fun."

"And we'll have a big party when you get back."

Oh!

I don't know why I'm even writing down all the stupid things Mama and Papa said. I know it's all lies. Lies, lies, lies. You could tell from their faces and their red eyes, it was all fibs, fabrications and fairy tales.

What a pack of lies!

The truth is, they've decided to send us miles away, and it's not true the war will be over quickly, and it's not true we'll be home really soon and that we'll all be together again.

There is no more Us.

Papa's going to fight, Mama's staying in her beloved museum, Leningrad is going to be attacked, and my brother and I will be alone.

Alone.

ALONE!

"Nadya, Viktor," Papa said, "you need to be strong and brave and get on that train. It's the right thing to do, it's your duty, just like I have mine and Mama has hers. Make us proud."

That was a lie, too.

My parents had to work today, so Mama left for the Hermitage and Papa for the suburbs to build barricades.

They promised to be back for seven, but they didn't come so Viktor and I had breakfast leftovers for dinner and waited for them to come home, the flat like a cold, empty shell.

We fell asleep together on the big bed. I couldn't stop shaking I was so anxious, but with Viktor by my side, I managed to sleep.

I woke up all of a sudden, a little before midnight, and saw Papa sitting on the edge of the bed, his head in his hands.

When he realized I was awake, he smiled and pretended nothing was wrong.

"Papa," I mumbled, "tell me what's going on."

Viktor had also woken up by then, so all three of us sat up together on the bed.

"Okay," he said, "I'll try."

He heaved a deep, worrisome sigh. "The next few days, perhaps even months, will be extremely difficult. We have to separate. I don't think I'll be able to sleep at night thinking of you two so far away, and worrying about your mother. I will pray every single second that you are safe. Terrible things happen in wartime. I know you think you already know that, but you don't. But . . ." He let out another heavy sigh. "Compared to everyone else, you two are lucky. You are twins, you look out for each other and you can always stay together. That will make things so much easier."

Papa stood up and pulled a canvas bag out from under the bed. He opened it and there were five exercise books inside, just like the one I'm writing in now, all with the same red cover and spiral.

"Dr. Orbeli let me take them for you. You can write about everything that happens to you while we're apart. Then when we meet again, your mama and I can read them and find out what you got up to. It will be like we never separated." He picked up the books and gave them to me, solemnly. "Promise?"

"Of course, we promise," I said.

Then Viktor added, "We promise to stay together, always."

He took my hand.

And I squeezed his as tight as I could.

S. – Further theft of State property (perhaps). Art. 89.

2nd July

We're leaving tomorrow at dawn. We don't know where they'll send us, but Mama says the city soviet has thought of everything and will tell us where we're going when the time's right, but most importantly, they'll tell our parents, so they can write to us.

Mama thinks one hundred thousand children have already left Leningrad, a lot of them very young, so we shouldn't worry.

I know she's right and I wish I wasn't so scared, but the truth is I am, a lot. I've never been away from Leningrad, I've never been away from home, and I've never been to the Ural Mountains.

I'm scared I won't be happy there, and I'm scared I'll want to come home but won't be able to. I'm also scared something bad will happen to Mama and Papa.

Viktor is pretending everything's all right, but I know he's just as worried as me. I saw him looking at the atlas earlier, trying to work out where the Ural Mountains are. He was tracing the course of rivers and the crests of mountains, his forehead all wrinkled, the way it is when he's about to do something difficult.

Anyway, we're going whether we like it or not.

Mama woke us at five o'clock this morning and asked us to come with her. Since it's been raining for two days solid, she had us put on our coats.

"Are we going to the museum?" I asked, still half asleep, but Mama replied chirpily, "No, I asked for the day off to spend it with you two. We're going shopping."

We went to our district shop and even though it was still closed, scores of people were already queuing up outside, more than thirty, their umbrellas like a row of black flowers.

Most were women, and they all carried straw baskets or fabric bags for their groceries, one even had a wheelbarrow and a thick stack of ration books.

As soon as they saw us, it was one long chorus of "Oh, what lovely twins, oh my aren't they sweet," before they started grumbling.

"The shop didn't open until noon yesterday," one lady said. "And there was nothing left."

"I know. People are buying up everything."

"The storerooms are empty."

"It's all gone."

"It's awful."

Their conversations were a little depressing, so we stopped listening and started chatting to Mama. She wanted to know everything we'd been up to over the past few days, including the fact that I'd argued with Grandma Olga about my notebook, down at the barrack-hut, and that Viktor had been in the lavatory when I saw the planes.

In the meantime, it was getting late, the rain was getting heavier and the shop still hadn't opened. Viktor started huffing and puffing.

"Why do all three of us have to queue? You could have left us asleep at home then woken us when you'd finished the shopping."

"We don't have much time left together," Mama replied. "I couldn't bear to leave you alone even for a second!"

She asked if we could give her the biggest present ever – would we write her a letter before we left, so she would have something to keep while we are away and not miss us so much?

(I've written mine already and put it beside her bed.)

The shop finally opened, and we went in, although only a few people at a time.

Unfortunately, there was nothing left inside. The shop assistant, a kind girl who lives at the end of our road, told Mama she had nothing to give her and that she should come back another day, but Mama leaned over the counter and said, "Please."

Again, the girl said, "I would if I could, but there's really nothing left."

Mama insisted, "I'm begging you, they're leaving tomorrow, I can't send them away with nothing to eat."

The girl stopped to think for a second then gestured to us to follow her into the back room.

It was all dark and musty but there were several big boxes, a few baskets of rye bread and some shelves of tinned food.

Mama gave the girl our ration books and bought all the bread she could, as well as some tins, a bag of flour and one of sugar. We left the shop loaded up like packhorses.

We took all the food home, but Mama kept half a loaf of bread and some tins in her bag and we went out again.

"Where are we going now?" Viktor asked.

"To buy some more things," Mama replied.

We always do our shopping at the same district shop where we're registered. I didn't know you could buy things elsewhere.

"Trust me."

We took the tram to the suburbs then Mama asked some people, whispering in their ears, for directions, but they all shook their heads until one woman eventually pointed us to a park with lots of trees. We went into it and saw some tarpaulin sheets hanging over trees to provide shelter from the rain, blankets were laid out on the muddy grass and people stood with their backs against the tree trunks.

"You two wait here," Mama said.

She went over to a fat man in a leather jacket (in the summer! I suppose it *was* raining!) and said something to him. She moved away from him and went over to someone else, then to someone else and to someone else again. When she'd spoken to them all, she went back to the start and spoke to them all a second time, this time showing them a black velvet pouch.

I know that pouch well, it's where Mama keeps all her "gold," namely a necklace Papa gave her when they got engaged and a pair of silver earrings with a shiny stone.

In the end, the fat man took the necklace in exchange for a fabric bag filled to the brim and Mama came back over to me and Viktor, smiling.

"What did you buy?" my brother asked.

"Some things for you," she said, opening the bag and pulling out a bar of chocolate wrapped in shiny paper. "It comes from abroad," she explained, "and it's really, really good. I also got some other things you'll need for your trip."

We got the tram home but stopped at the museum on the way. Mama took us into a giant hall covered in frescoes and we sat on the floor and had a picnic with the bread and tins Mama had put in her bag. She'd obviously planned everything.

S. – Black market.
Location: Vdulnaya?

S. – Purchase of contraband
goods. Art. 78.

"I wanted to eat in the park," she said, "but it's too wet."

"It's much nicer here," I said.

We came home after lunch and she's in the kitchen now, making biscuits, because she says it'll be a long trip tomorrow and we'll be hungry. Viktor and I are in our room packing our bags.

I don't feel like doing it. I tried to put it off until the last minute by writing the letter for her, then describing everything we did today, but I can't put it off any longer, I have to do it now.

Later

I packed my bags, or rather, I put all my things into a blue checked haversack, and Viktor did the same.

Stuff in my bag:

- my favourite dress—the smart, polka-dot one
- two hair ribbons
- my Young Pioneers uniform, with the red necktie and red star badges
- the notebooks Papa gave me
- Papa's fountain pen and seven or eight ink cartridges (he said I could take them!)
- four red pencils, Viktor likes to write with them
- the biggest book I could find in the flat, which is *Anna Karenina* by Leo Tolstoy
- a photo of Mama when she was young.

In his bag, Viktor put:

Let me have a turn to write.

I thought about it, then decided to stick the photo in here, so I don't lose it! Mama is really pretty, isn't she?

My bag contains:

- a clean shirt
- my favourite book—*Russian Endgame* by Ilya Rabinovich, the chess master (he's from Leningrad like me, I'm going to be a chess master someday, too!)
- a bear's tooth.

My turn now.

Mama asked to see both our bags and she said we'd done a good job, although she took out my favourite dress and put in some foot-cloths, a heavy wool jumper, some gloves and a hat. She did the same for Viktor and said that we should wear our heaviest clothes and coats to travel.

I asked why, given that it's summer now and they say the war will be over really soon, but she said it's better to be prepared.

I said she must think we'll be away for a long time and can't bring herself to tell us.

I got really angry and scrunched up the letter I'd written for her.

Later, at night

We had our last dinner here at home and I'd like to say it was a nice, happy meal but it wasn't. Viktor and I shouted and cried all the way through it.

To begin with, they told me my friend Darya WON'T be leaving with us tomorrow, or her brother Stepan, or Mr. Yashkin.

Apparently, Mr. Yashkin thinks leaving Leningrad is for cowards and has decided to stay, while Darya's parents want her and Stepan to stay with their family for a few more days.

"That means we could stay a bit longer, too!" I cried.

"Yes, but it's safer to leave now," Papa replied.

"Papa has to join the Militia, it's better if you two are already away when that happens."

That's when Viktor got angry. "You want rid of us!"

"I'm not leaving!" I screamed.

We started arguing and didn't stop, not even when the Zhirovs came into the kitchen. Mama jumped to her feet at one point and ran into the bathroom, and when she came back in again you could see she'd been crying.

I feel really sad for her, but I'm really sad for me, too.

Why can't we leave in a few days with Darya?

Or why can't we stay at home with Mama, to keep her company when Papa leaves?

Why, why, why?

It's three o'clock in the morning, Mama and Papa's bed is empty but I can hear them speaking in hushed tones in the kitchen, so the other people in the flat won't hear.

I get up, tiptoe down the hall and stop just before the door, which is slightly ajar, clutching my notebook to my chest.

"You'll see, it will all be okay," Papa says.

"I'm scared," Mama says. "For them and for you."

"We'll manage," Papa replies, "and they'll be fine. You'll see. They'll be together. Nadya has Viktor to rely on, and Viktor has Nadya."

I hear Mama start to cry and I go away, although I realize Papa is right. I have my brother, that's why I'm not so scared at the thought of leaving tomorrow.

Dear Mama,

    You asked us to write you a letter for when we'll be far away. Here it is. I don't know where to start, though... I asked Viktor to help me but he's studying his atlas and told me not to bother him. If you ask me, he's worried about leaving tomorrow. You know what he's like when he's scared – he goes all hard, like a rock.

    Never mind, I've thought of what I can write.

    Since you'll probably be sad when you read this, I'm going to make a list of happy things you can do until we're all back together again.

    Don't you think that's a fantastic idea?

    So, here's Nadya's list of fun things to cheer you up:

- Have a sauna in the public baths but stay away from the fat lady who does the massages (do you remember the time she nearly broke my arm? It was so sore!!!)
- Sit on the banks of the Neva, throw a stone and try to make it bounce three times across the water.
- Have a glass of vodka! I've never tried it but Mr Yashkin says it works wonders, and he should know, he always has at least three or four glasses.
- Make cheese pastries and eat them all yourself.
- Skip down the corridor in our flat, only stepping on the black tiles.
- Read Pushkin's fairy tales and do all the different voices.
- Lie on the big bed with your arms and legs out to take up all the space and imagine you're the blanket fairy.

- Imagine you're giving us one of your really big hugs.
- Write Viktor and me a letter every day until we arrive in the Urals. Then maybe I'll have something nice to think about if I feel sad because you're not there.

I love you, Mama. Viktor does too. We don't want to go.

Don't forget us.

Yours, Nadya

CCCP

PEOPLE'S COMMISSARIAT FOR INTERNAL AFFAIRS

REPORT FOR INTERNAL USE

End of first notebook, to be used as evidence in the investigation into citizens:

* Viktor Nikolayevich Danilov;
* Nadya Nikolayevna Danilova.

The accused have confessed to the following crimes:

* theft of state property /notebook with metal spiral/: punishable with 10 years' imprisonment under Article 89 of the Penal Code;
* neglecting compulsory wartime duties and violation of patrol rules /engaging in children's games and other distractions during fire watch/: punishable with 1 + 15 years' imprisonment under Articles 82 and 257 of the Penal Code;
* purchase of contraband goods /miscellaneous foodstuffs/ on the black market: punishable with execution by firing squad under Article 78 of the Penal Code.

* Substantial evidence implicating third
  parties has also been obtained and
  will be the object of several further
  official investigations.

For the most part, the information in this
notebook has been found to be detailed and
reliable.
   The last page appears to have been written
on a separate, crumpled sheet of paper which
was added to the notebook at a later date.
   Said sheet bears the "farewell letter
to mother" to which the accused, Nadya
Nikolayevna Danilova refers in her commentary
on the events of the 2nd of July 1941.
   I shall continue my investigations.

            Signed:

         COLONEL VALERY GAVRIILOVICH SMIRNOV

            Col. Smirnov

Train 77

S. - chapter 8
-No date

Nadya's clearly the writer in the family.

I've been staring at this empty page for an hour now and haven't a clue what to put on it.

The problem is, I said I'd write about everything that happens to me. I promised Nadya when we said goodbye.

But are promises actually worth anything?

I also told Papa I'd look after my sister.

That I wouldn't leave her.

And look how that went . . .

When I woke up on the morning of the 3rd of July, I could hardly believe it.

Nadya and I had never left Leningrad before, except the time we went camping. But we were just children back then and the campsite was only a few miles from the city.

This time we were about to set off on a long journey alone. Where would it take us? Where would we sleep that night? Would I be called upon to fight?

All kinds of thoughts spun around in my head, like a turbine.

Our parents were already awake and waiting for us, sitting on the bed beside our haversacks, one for me and one for Nadya, all packed and ready to go. They were plumper than the night before because Mama had filled them with bread and chocolate, biscuits, cheese and eggs, and other foodstuffs.

There were also two rolls of banknotes with an elastic band around them. Oh, and a pair of earrings for Nadya and a religious icon for me.

"But we're not religious, Papa," I said. "It's anti-Soviet!"

"I know, but this icon has been in our family for generations, it belonged to your grandfather who received it from your great-grandfather. It's valuable because it's made of silver. That means it's worth a lot of money."

"And what use would that be to me, the money I mean?"

"I don't know, no one can know. But I'd like you to have it anyway."

We left the flat, Papa on one side, then Nadya, me and Mama on the other. Mama took my hand and I was about to wriggle free (I'm not a baby anymore!) when I felt Nadya jolt me. I realized I should let Mama's hand stay where it was. Not because I needed it. Because she did.

I looked up and tried to take in every detail of our street, the tall buildings, wondering when I'd see them again. Would they be the same or would they all change?

"What station are we leaving from?" I asked.

"From Sortirovochnoya," Papa said. "All the children's trains are going from there."

I'd been so sure we'd be leaving from one of the important stations, like Moskovsky or Finlyandsky. Certainly not Sortirovochnoya, I'd never even heard of it.

"It's on the outskirts of the city," Papa explained.

This meant we had to get a bus. It was jammed full of people, mostly parents and children. I saw two friends of mine from school – Kostya and Anatoly. And that Boris boy I argued with the night of our first patrol (he was

76

alone, staring out of the window). There were hundreds of children and a lot of them were very young.

It was nice to see Kostya and Anatoly. I would've chatted to them but our parents kept us glued to their sides, like we were on a leash.

The station really was on the outskirts, it took ages to get there. When we finally got off the bus, there were hardly any buildings, just the odd factory, some bare dusty fields and row after row of labourers on foot. Some were digging with shovels, some were rolling out barbed wire, others were shunting massive blocks of concrete.

"Is this what you do when you're with the Militia?" I asked Papa.

"Yes," he said. "Barriers and trenches."

Sortirovochnoya station was small and ugly, and the number of people gathered outside was unbelievable.

We joined the line and Mama kept hold of my hand, squeezing it tight, until we'd almost reached the door and the cordon of soldiers wearing helmets. They were barring the way.

Papa spoke to one of them then turned to Mama. "We have to say goodbye here. Only children may enter the station."

"Why?" Mama protested. "Can't I take them up to the platform?"

"Orders," the soldier replied. "Only those who are leaving may enter. However, madam, if you give your name to the official under the tree over there, you will be contacted in the next few days with the children's destination and details of where you can write and send parcels."

Mama shouted, even though she always says never raise your voice to the police or soldiers because it's dangerous. Instead of reprimanding her, the soldier actually apologized.

That's why there was so much commotion everywhere, so many children crying and parents shouting – because the families arriving were having to say their farewells in a rush in front of the soldiers.

Papa hugged Nadya tight then put a hand on my shoulder and said, "Promise me, Viktor."

"Of course."

"We have to live apart for a while but you and Nadya will be together. You must never, ever separate."

"Of course."

That's when Mama scooped me into her arms and gave me two kisses on the cheek. Her face was wet, she must've been crying.

I felt numb. Like a stone. "We'll be fine," I said. "Come on, Nadya. Let's go."

Taking my sister's arm, I pulled her past the soldiers, inside the station.

I didn't turn around but then I remembered I hadn't told Papa I hoped nothing bad would happen to him in the war.

When I tried to get back to him, there were so many people behind us pushing forward that it was impossible. I had to give up.

I didn't get to see him one last time.

The station was just one big hall with a waiting room, some ticket offices which were all shut, and a double door on the opposite side that led out onto the platforms.

We were all just standing waiting, squashed together in the stifling heat. If they knew we were going to have to wait so long, they could've left us outside in the open air.

I looked around for my friends but couldn't see them anywhere. Some children were pushing each other, others were crying. The soldiers stared out at us from under their helmets.

An elderly clerk with a moustache climbed up a wooden ladder at one point, holding a megaphone in his hand. "The first train of the day is nearly ready," he said. "I'll be passing amongst you to count you. We request your cooperation."

A few minutes later, he and a soldier began to make their way around the room. He carried a writing box around his neck laid out with a bundle of papers, a large bottle of ink and a fountain pen. The clerk was asking everyone for their names and their identity papers, then he'd write something on the paper, dip the handle of his pen into the ink (not the nib end) and write a number on the back of their hands.

When he got to Nadya, he said, "Papers."

She handed them over, he wrote her name at the bottom of a page crammed full of names, almost in the margin, then quickly wrote "76" on her hand.

He pulled out a fresh sheet of paper, asked me for my papers, took note of my name and then wrote my number on my hand: "77."

We waited a few more hours, the time it took the clerk to get around to everyone, checking their papers one by one. It was midday by the time he finished.

He went back up his ladder and announced, "The first train is ready to leave. All those with number seventy-six please step forward. Form an orderly line!"

The doors to the platform were flung open and two soldiers and another clerk stood guard in front of them. Everyone had to file past them, one by one.

"I'm number seventy-six," Nadya said.

"Me too," said a boy.

"Me too," said a mother holding a newborn.

That's when I noticed all the people who had the same number as my sister. Whereas I didn't. My number was different.

"What does it mean?" I asked.

"I don't know but stay near me."

I got into position behind Nadya and put my arms around her so that our haversacks were tucked between us. This also meant that no one could steal our things – I'd seen some suspicious-looking faces in the queue that I didn't like one bit.

Everyone started to push. Some children fell over. The man with the moustache eventually climbed back up his ladder. "Stay calm, one at a time! Only those with number seventy-six!"

Since no one was listening to him, more soldiers appeared, wielding truncheons. The pushing stopped. Nadya and I were still stuck together, I didn't want to lose her in the crush.

When we made it to the doors, I saw the train sitting at the platform, dark and gloomy looking, hundreds of children hanging out of the windows. Some were crying, some were waving goodbye. Who knows who to.

I thought I recognized a girl from our school, her father was someone important, in the NKVD, I think. That stands for People's Commissariat for Internal Affairs. But she was on her own now as well.

When our turn finally came, we stepped forward to go past the soldiers. The clerk at the door looked at the number on Nadya's hand and said, "Forward."

Then he grabbed my hand and said, "No, not you."

My heart stopped. It felt like the station, the crowds of children, the soldiers, everyone, had come thundering down on my head, like an avalanche.

"What?"

"Train seventy-six passengers only. You are on the next train."

"But she's my sister."

S. – This must be Anna Akhm999999 Tesehenkov. #3 12 years old at the time.

80

"Sorry."

"There must be a mistake . . ."

The clerk gestured to the soldiers and they barred my way, planting themselves between me and Nadya. One grabbed me by the shoulder and said, "Clear off, kiddo. You're on the next train."

"But that's my sister!"

"You'll see her when you get there."

Nadya had started shouting too, and I was suddenly jolted backwards. I don't know what happened, maybe the soldier punched me. I fell.

All I remember is a boy with a spotty face leaning over me afterwards. "Are you Viktor?"

I said yes and he handed me this piece of paper.

For Viktor: come to the third window!

The only windows in the room were near the doors to the platforms. They were tall and narrow, made up of lots of small pieces of glass held together by strips of lead.

I counted them to find window number three and saw Nadya on the other side.

Pushing and shoving my way through, I managed to get over to her and press my face against the glass. Nadya did the same. She was crying. She pointed to one of the glass sections at the bottom. It was broken and there were shards of glass on the floor. That's how she'd got the note through.

"Viktor, I can't leave without you."

"Don't worry. You go and I'll be right behind you. I'm on the next train and we're all going to the same place."

"Viktor!"

"Nadya, don't be afraid! I won't leave you alone. I promised Mama and Papa."

She nodded, tears streaming down her face, realizing we had no choice.

She opened her haversack, pulled out three notebooks and a bundle of red pencils and said, "Write down everything that happens to you. Do it for me, promise?"

"Of course I will," I replied. "We're not going to be apart for long. No more than a few hours."

Nadya still had tears in her eyes, her face was ashen.

"Viktor, don't lie to me. Not now. Just promise, will you?"

I promised.

I took the notebooks and the pencils.

Then I stood and watched as a soldier took her arm and made her get on the train.

The train whistled.

It started to move.

And took Nadya away from me.

I don't know how long I stood there, face pressed against the glass, staring at the empty platform. It didn't feel real.

If only I could turn back the clock. See the scene again. Change it.

I could accept the war, Papa in the Militia, Mama at the museum on her own, even Leningrad attacked by the enemy.

Anything at all – except being separated from Nadya.

My sister is a real pain in the neck, she says "anyway" all the time, can be a proper pest and wastes hours on all sorts of nonsense. But we've always been together. We sleep in the same bed, are in the same class at school, the same section at Young Pioneers. And now she's gone? On a different train?

I couldn't really take it in.

A hand touched my shoulder and I heard a voice say, "Viktor?"

It was my friend, Kostya Bighead, we call him that at school because his head's so big and round it looks like a ball about to roll off his neck.

Seeing a familiar face in all the chaos made me feel dizzy.

"Where's Nadya?"

I couldn't answer.

Kostya's head wobbled, deflated, like a punctured football.

"I get it. Train seventy-six. Anatoly was on that one, too."

Anatoly is his best friend.

"What now?"

"Do you have anything to eat?"

That's when I realized everyone around us was eating, producing all sorts of provisions from their bags. If Nadya's train left around midday, it had to be two in the afternoon by then.

"Yes, I've got some food."

I immediately regretted saying that because Kostya is famous for his appetite, but it was too late to take it back.

I handed him a hunk of bread, a boiled egg and two squares of chocolate. He wolfed them down before I had time to look up.

"Got any more?"

"Maybe later. We don't know how long we'll have to make it last."

"Surely they'll give us an afternoon snack on the train? Or dinner at least?"

"I don't know. Didn't your parents make you anything?"

"Yes, but I've eaten it all. I always eat when I'm nervous."

It was stifling in the station – there were so many children you couldn't move. The tiny ones were screaming. The platforms were empty.

My sister would reach our destination and I'd still be waiting here.

I told Kostya to follow me and I pushed my way through to the official who'd given out the numbers, the one with the moustache. He was standing in the corner, smoking a cigarette.

I hated him because he'd taken Nadya away from me. But he was probably my only hope of ever seeing her again.

"Excuse me," I said. "When's the next train?"

"I don't know. Some time. Don't you know there's a war on? We're transporting thousands of people. And they all have to come through this station."

"Where are we going?"

"I don't know that either. Far away from here. And trust me, child, it's for the best. It won't be long before Leningrad falls." My eyes opened wide. "This city is doomed," he said.

"How dare you?" I shouted, in the voice Papa sometimes used.

"And who might you be? NKVD? It wouldn't matter anyway, even the secret police can't do anything now. The Germans will take care of that, they'll kill us all. Just a matter of days."

"I . . ."

"You'd do well to listen to someone who's a few years older than you, son. I've been through a World War, the October Revolution and the Winter War against Finland. I know what I'm talking about. They've tried to kill me a hundred times and failed. This time will be different. There's no hope. Hitler will get us all."

Kostya grabbed my shoulder.

"Just ignore him. He's clearly off his head. Comrade Stalin won't let the enemy get to Leningrad."

Comrade Stalin is the father of our nation, our beacon of light in difficult times. I'd never heard anyone speak in such a defeatist way before.

We went back into the crush. Two girls were playing *rezinochki*, jumping over an elastic band. All the children around them looked like rabbits in a cage.

S. – Preposterous. Find this official.

85

Hours went by.

Some children fell asleep.

More and more people were arriving outside the station, shouting and demanding explanations when the soldiers wouldn't let them in..

Mama and Papa had insisted we go there early in the morning. In hindsight, it would have been better to arrive late, then me and Nadya would still have been together. I hated my parents for what they'd unknowingly done.

A train eventually arrived. A huge, black locomotive spewing coal fumes and pulling a long line of windowless carriages. Cattle wagons.

The children around me began to stir, the clerk got on his megaphone again and told us to stay calm. Another seemingly endless wait ensued before the announcement finally came, "Number seventy-sevens on the platform."

Kostya was seventy-seven like me so we made our way together to the doors and waited our turn. The queue was going really slowly but they finally let us pass and we made it out to the platform. It felt almost cold after being squashed inside with so many people for so long.

The soldiers opened the doors of one of the wagons and told us to climb in. Inside there was nothing but hay on the floor and the stink of cows.

"When are we leaving?"

"Where are we going?"

"How long will it take?"

The usual questions. All ignored.

Kostya and I climbed inside and went to sit in the corner beside two wobbly planks we could look through that also let us get some air.

The wagon filled up. Someone shut the door from outside. More time passed. Ages, it felt like.

Kostya asked me for something to eat, I gave him some more bread and also had some myself.

Finally, the train squealed and rattled into motion.

Out of sheer relief, we all laughed and clapped our hands. Kostya and I squeezed our faces up to the gaps in the planks to look outside – at the iron rails, the street-lights, the buildings of Leningrad.

We passed through a number of junctions then heard another whistle – our train was overtaking a passenger train sitting in a siding, its locomotive stopped. Hundreds of children were looking out the windows.

"That's train seventy-six! They left before us but they're still there, ha!"

The general mood had lifted when we'd finally started moving and people were poking fingers through the chinks in the walls to wave at the other train.

I nearly got a splinter in my eye craning to see Nadya. But there was no sign.

Someone behind me said, "You could've been over there with them, Mikhail, can you believe it? What a disaster that would've been!"

I whirled around and found myself looking at two boys my age. The one who'd spoken was small with big ears, the other one had bright blond hair, light-coloured eyes and a gentle, girlish face.

The blond one, Mikhail, said, "What a nightmare that would've been. I definitely had a narrow escape," and started laughing.

I don't know why but he really rattled me. Maybe because he was celebrating not being on train seventy-six when I would've done anything to be on it.

Without stopping to think, I lunged and grabbed him by the shirt. "What do you mean by that? That you had a narrow escape?"

"Hey, get off me," Mikhail protested, trying to get away.

That's when I saw it. His hand. There was a spindly "7" then an ink stain where the second number had been.

I knew right away.

"You were number seventy-six, weren't you? They gave you seventy-six but you rubbed it out."

"What if I did? It's none of your business."

"Why did you do it?"

Mikhail jerked free and for a brief second something flashed in his eyes. He was wondering whether to hit me. Luckily, he realized he'd probably come off the worst and took a step back.

"I didn't like the kids on that train," he mumbled.

"No, of course you didn't, ha," his big-eared friend cackled. "So dull – *deadly* dull, you could say – ha."

Kostya pulled my elbow. "Calm down," he said. "What's got into you?"

I went back to the corner, near the gap in the planks.

"You can't just jump on people like that," Kostya continued. "And what's it all about anyway?"

This I did know. I hated that blond kid because he'd had the brilliant idea that I hadn't. It hadn't occurred to me to rub out the number on my hand to get past the guards and stay with Nadya.

I should've been smarter.

Then we wouldn't be in this mess.

There were hundreds of kids in our wagon. Almost all of them were my age. Not a single adult. It was weird, there'd been so many at the station, especially mothers and grandmothers looking after babies.

Maybe all the mothers had done the same as me and Kostya and gone into the same wagon together to talk about women's things. Who knows? There wasn't a lot of conversation in our wagon.

A boy broke into song at one point. Then another boy punched him in the mouth. The singer stopped.

"Where do you think we're going?" Kostya asked.

"I don't know. My father said they're sending us to the Ural Mountains."

"That's miles away. Do you think they'll bring us dinner?"

"I don't know."

They didn't bring us dinner.

The train rattled on and on until it suddenly came to a halt. Around us there was nothing but open fields, clumps of scrawny-looking trees and a river winding, snake-like, through the grass.

The train lurched into motion again and travelled for about half an hour before it stopped once more.

The sun was setting, it had to be around ten or eleven o'clock at night. Some of the kids who hadn't thought to bring any food with them were starving and beginning to protest. I stood up, "Hey, calm down, everyone."

"I'm hungry," a girl said.

"Me too," said a big, lanky boy whose shirt was open, showing a filthy neck.

The lanky boy went over to one of the smaller kids and grabbed his collar. "Looks like you've got quite a feast there, eh? I saw you scoffing in secret earlier."

"Leave me alone!"

"Only if you give me something to eat. I wouldn't say no if I were you."

"But it's mine!"

"The only thing that's yours is the punch coming your way."

"Hey, hey," I said. "We're all good communists here, right? There's no need to steal food from each other. Anyone who's got something, dig it out and we'll share it between us."

The lanky kid let the child go and headed over to me, dragging his feet on the straw. "So who are you to be dishing out orders?"

"Viktor Nikolayevich Danilov," I replied. "With whom do I have the honour of speaking?"

He spat on the floor, just missing a girl. "I'm someone who could teach you a lesson if I felt like it. You say you're a good communist. If you ask me, you look like the typical communist who says he wants to share everything but keeps his chocolate to himself."

Oh, so that's how it was. He'd seen the chocolate.

"Kostya," I said. "Open the bag, take out whatever's left and split it equally. Make sure everyone gets a piece."

"But there are a hundred of us in here!" Kostya whined. "There won't be enough even to dirty our tongues with!"

"We get what we get," I replied.

I felt strangely calm. Instead of being scared with all those eyes on me, I felt energized. The boy with the filthy neck was taller than me but I was stronger. And if he wanted a fight, that was fine too. Better actually.

"So," I said. "What have you got to share with the people?"

He shrugged. "Nothing. Just some bread."

"That'll have to do then. Who else has got something?"

It turned out that there *was* more. Cheese, dried sausages, kasha. Pies filled with salmon or meat. Apples. I appointed Kostya treasurer and told him to collect all the food and split it evenly. But he got stuck with the numbers. A skinny girl called Klara stepped in to give him a hand.

"You be treasurer and I'll work out how to divide it," she suggested. "We could keep some for breakfast."

It was a good idea. We put it to a vote, everyone agreed.

"So," I said when the portions were ready. "Everyone happy now?"

Not really, not everyone, but we had to make do. Kostya and Klara dished out the meal and all I got was a crust of bread with a little butter, a piece of sausage and a curl of chocolate that was just enough to get a taste, no more.

It wasn't easy giving up the cake that had cost Mama so much, but the tall kid was right – talking was easy. Actions were more difficult.

"Lev," he said when dinner was over.

"Is that what you're called?"

"Yes. I live in the barrack-huts. I saw you there a few days ago. The other kids say you're from a high-ranking family."

"Oh really," I said. "Where I come from is none of your business."

"Why were you at the huts?"

"I went to see someone," I replied.

Mama says not to talk about the people we know to strangers. But Mama's rules seem to belong to another world at the moment.

"Dmitry," I added.

"I should've known."

"Known what?"

"That I can trust you."

He gave me a crooked smile and spat on the ground again, this time hitting the trousers of the boy in front of us. He stuck his hand out.

I shook it. Now that I'm alone, an ally could come in handy.

The train rattled on through the night, regularly stopping and starting. Like an old man with hiccups.

I tried to sleep but it was impossible and I didn't know why. Then I understood. It was because Nadya wasn't there. I'd never slept without her.

At one point during the night, I realized I wasn't the only one awake. Klara, the skinny girl, had her head against the side of the wagon. She was trying to read in the light filtering through the chinks in the wall.

"What are you doing?"

"I'm trying to work out where we're going," she replied.

She showed me a piece of paper: it was a map of the Soviet railway network showing all the stations joined by lines, like wires in a circuit diagram.

"And where are we going?"

"Moscow."

"Really? How do you know?"

"Because I've been watching the stations. We've just gone past Chudovo. The line goes straight to Moscow from here."

92

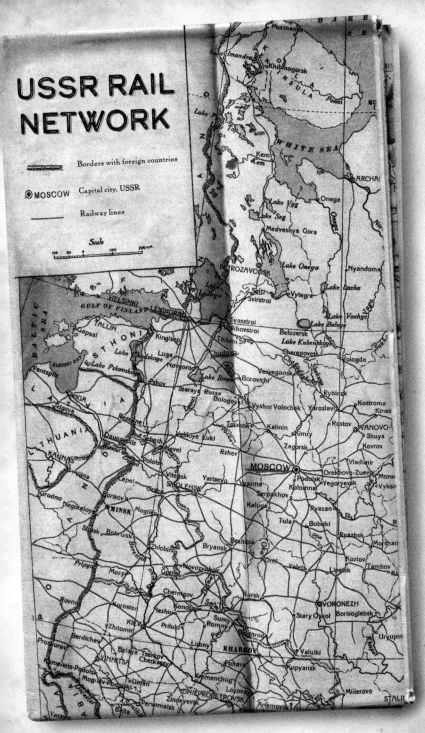

USSR RAIL
NETWORK

Borders with foreign countries

◉ MOSCOW   Capital city, USSR

Railway lines

Scale
100 50   100   200 K.M.

I studied the map and pointed to a junction a little further up the line. "Well, we could go that way as well . . ."

Klara looked at me, deadly serious. "I hope not. That leads west, towards the front."

"My father had to sign up for the Militia. What about yours?"

"No, mine didn't."

"Why not?"

She didn't reply.

I went back to my spot in the corner and laid my head on my hands, to see if I could drop off. I couldn't, obviously.

Going to the toilet – which was just a hole in the floor – was a problem in the wagon. When you stood over it, you could see the track flashing past below you. The hole was all right for us boys but since it was a bit trickier for the girls, we tied some coats and clothes together to make a curtain of sorts.

We couldn't hide the smell or the noise.

The train stopped in a tiny station. We tried to knock on the walls but no one came to open the doors.

It set off again.

We had breakfast, split everything equally like the night before then chatted to pass the time. We're all from Leningrad. A lot of the kids go to the same school as me. Mikhail, the blond guy who rubbed out his number, and his big-eared friend, Yury, actually live quite near us.

Only one boy isn't Russian. His name is Flavio and he's from Peru. He has tight curly hair and dark skin. His parents are communists, they'd been fighting the state but lost and fled to the Soviet Union.

The time passed and at four o'clock in the afternoon we arrived in Moscow.

I've always dreamed of seeing the Kremlin and the many other places in Moscow that Papa has told me about. Instead, all we could see was a desolate crisscrossing of train tracks surrounded by tall, grey buildings.

Someone finally came to open the doors – soldiers and a few guards wearing the People's Militia armband. They'd brought water and loaves of bread which were handed out to everyone but they wouldn't let us get out.

"You'll be leaving again shortly, so pipe down."

"Not too much further."

"Don't worry and don't eat it all right away. That's all there is so make it last."

I ordered everyone to hand over the fresh provisions to Kostya, who would be treasurer again.

"Oh, look at them," one of the guards said. "What good little communists!"

The other guards laughed. All I felt was tired. I asked if they had any news of train seventy-six but they said no.

The doors of the wagon were closed again and a few hours later, our journey resumed.

Klara looked at her map and said we were now moving east, towards the Ural Mountains.

We passed through Moscow and, peering through the same chink in the wall, I saw houses and tall buildings, trucks and soldiers. The tracks were full of trains, some of which had armoured wagons that looked like fortresses.

Then the city was over and we were back to countryside.

We ate. We slept.

The next morning we arrived at the city of Kazan, in the Republic of Tatarstan.

You have arrived, they told us.

Mga, 7th July

Dear notebook, do you want to know where Mga is?
It's here!

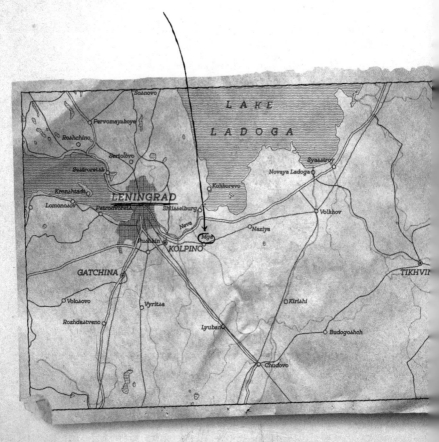

Basically, we're just outside Leningrad. In all this time, we've only come about seventy kilometres. And believe it or not, we've stopped again. The train is sitting on the track, as still as a dead animal.

If Viktor were here with me, no doubt he'd have argued with everyone already and come to blows with the train driver (Papa always says Viktor can be a bit of a hothead).

I have to admit though, even I'm getting sick of it now.

They won't let us off the train and as for escaping, well, even if we were to try, we'd never manage because there are soldiers – Red Army and Militia – everywhere. The latter are easy to recognize because they're not wearing a uniform, just the armband like Papa. It occurred to me that Papa might even be with them by now. It's beginning to feel like we've been away for a lifetime when we only set off four days ago.

It's so boring. I read to pass the time. Thank goodness I brought a big book with me, it'll take me ages to get through it.

The book I chose, *Anna Karenina*, has a beautiful opening:

> *Happy families are all alike; every unhappy family is unhappy in its own way.*

Isn't that beautiful? The first time I read it I cried, it's so true. We were a happy family once, or at least I thought we were. I was happy.

But now . . .

One of the young women is called Irina, she has her baby boy, Pyotr, with her. A few hours ago she hung out of the window to speak to one of the soldiers guarding the tracks.

He told her the front is now at Pskov, four hundred kilometres from Leningrad. It's hard to believe the enemy has made it so far since the war started.

Irina asked if there's a risk the enemy might reach Mga but the soldier said no, although you can never know for sure.

I wonder how long they'll leave us here on this train.

I wonder if Viktor has already arrived in the Ural Mountains.

I hope so, I hope he's all right.

I hope he's thinking about me as well.

Monday 7th July

It's nearly dawn and it's hot already. The others are still asleep in the barn but the mosquitoes were bothering me so I got up.

I'm sitting on a tree stump now, trying to write, my feet in the mud.

There's mud everywhere here.

"Here" is a kolkhoz, the farm I'm living on now.

I had to stop writing last time, just when it was getting exciting. We'd arrived at Kazan station.

I think I'd better start from there.

"Get off."

"Everyone in line."

"Toilets are over there. Then everyone assemble in front of the station."

"Quickly!"

It was the first time we'd seen the sky in days, we were confused and tired. It took a while to herd us all back together.

There were soldiers and railway workers outside the station. And a clerk with a list. He asked everyone for their name then told us to get into the trucks lined up on the other side of the road.

"Fyodor."

"Angela."

"Natasha and Gavriil."

Each time, the boy or girl or mother and child would hand over their passport before they climbed into the truck.

I waited with Kostya and the others which is how we all ended up on the same kolkhoz. It's fifty kilometres from the city, on the banks of the Volga which is the longest river in Europe.

Basically, it's like a rural village here. There are roads, houses, cow sheds, wells. But all the fields are collective: the peasants work the land together, tend each other's cattle then split the products of their labours.

From the outside, I'd say it's a good communist idea. On the inside, it's a little more complicated, like the Young Pioneers only less fun.

On our arrival, we were split into brigades and assigned a supervisor. We got Mr. Garayev. He speaks mainly Tatar, which sounds sort of like Arab, and when he tries to speak Russian, no one understands a word.

"Who know farm work?"

Lev was the only one to raise a hand.

"Who know other work?"

Only Lev again.

"Is good," Garayev said. "Here work hard, need much strength. Kolkhoz grow all food for Moscow. And for soldiers now war on. If harvest not enough, no food for us here. You understand?" We understood. "So I has work quotas to meet, if you no meet quota I has big problem. You not city children anymore, not nice boys and girls. You learn quickly or see what I does!" After this reassuring introduction, he pointed to the large barn. "You here sleep," he said. "On Saturday you rest. Tomorrow rest. Monday work very lot. Understand?"

S. – it's not supposed to be fun!

He left. We ventured inside the old barn.

One of the girls started to cry, most of us were feeling pretty miserable. The place was full of rats.

"What are we doing here?" asked one of the younger boys called Ilya.

I had no idea but I couldn't say that. People were starting to look upon me as the leader of the group, which was great but also a responsibility.

"Lev, do you know how to fix things? Like cutting wood and hammering nails? Stuff like that?"

"A bit."

"I have a fair idea," said Flavio, the Peruvian boy.

"Well, you can teach everyone how it's done. Klara, take someone with you and have a look around the place, find what needs doing most urgently. Kostya and I will split everyone into teams and each one will be given a job – fixing the windows, cleaning up, etc. Agreed?"

We all set to work, everyone except Mikhail, the blond boy. Of all the children in our brigade, he's the only one I can't stand. Whenever Garayev shouts at someone, he seems to enjoy it. Whenever any of the younger ones hurts themselves, he laughs. He wouldn't dare with Lev, because he's so big, but with Ilya he keeps playing nasty jokes. He hangs out with Yury all the time. The two of them will do whatever they can to shirk the difficult jobs. Luckily, I keep an eye on them. And I have ways of making them do their fair share – whether they like it or not.

8th July

It's evening and I've just finished my second day of work. I wanted to write something last night but I couldn't. The truth is I was too tired – my back aches so much

I can't move and it's not easy to hold my pencil because my hands have been rubbed raw.

I started at five o'clock this morning when Garayev came into the barn banging a spoon on a metal bucket. *CLANG! CLANG! CLANG!*

"Wake up, wake up, lazy children! There is cows waiting for milking!"

We went to milk the cows.

"There are wood waiting to be chopped!"

We chopped wood.

"There is hens waiting for grain!"

"There are ditch must dig."

"There is trees must cut!"

And so on.

Us repairing the barn.

Drawn by Klara.

The worst job was digging the ditch, there was so much mud.

It's completely different here in the country – there are no cars, buses or trams, people travel everywhere on foot or by horse. The children on the kolkhoz speak only Tatar and don't seem to like us. Me, Lev and Flavio nearly got in a fight yesterday.

That aside, I think a lot about Mama and Papa and wonder if everything is all right at home.

I'm especially worried for Nadya. Why isn't she here yet?

I'd like to ask someone but Garayev wouldn't know and there's no one else.

But I have an idea, I just have to work out how to make it happen.

11th July

I put my idea to Kostya, Lev, Flavio and Klara, they're probably my closest friends here.

We came up with a plan.

This morning, Garayev came in to wake us up at five o'clock as usual.

He took us to the cattle sheds, which are long, low buildings with hundreds and hundreds of animals inside. The cows have wet eyes, rough, pink tongues and they swing their tails to swat the flies away.

"Lev, Viktor, you open door!" Garayev ordered. We did as instructed. Just like every morning, the huge truck from the city had arrived and was outside the shed, reversing to get the trailer as far inside as possible.

The job here was to grab a bucket, milk all the cows, empty the full buckets into the big milk churns, then load the churns onto the back of the truck so it could take them back to Kazan.

"Quickly, quickly," Garayev urged. "By now you learn how do. Three squads, fastly. Buckets, churns, truck, go!"

Everyone usually makes a dash for the buckets because although milking might sound disgusting, it's actually quite fun: you get to sit down on a stool under the cow, pull the udders which go *PFFTT* and watch the warm milk spurt out.

But this time me, Lev and Flavio pretended to trip up so we would be put in the third squad, the one that loads the full churns onto the truck. The most difficult job.

"You too asleep this morning," Garayev cackled. "I wake you louder with bins next time, faster, faster."

I would normally have answered back but not today. Me and the others set to work in silence, climbing on and off the truck.

Klara went to speak to Garayev to distract him. Kostya whistled to signal the coast was clear.

I jumped onto the trailer and hid down at the bottom.

Our plan worked to perfection. After a bit, the truck drove away with me hidden in the back. It rumbled out of the kolkhoz and made its way through the fields on its way back to the city.

I crouched in the back and enjoyed the ride.

I was surprised to see Kazan was such a big city, not on the same scale as Leningrad but still big. It has a castle on the hill, a port on the Volga, and lots more.

I needed to get to the train station but the milk truck turned in a different direction so I ended up having to jump off. I asked around for directions and a passer-by told me which way to go. Then I asked another woman, then another, going from person to person until I finally reached my destination.

It was utter chaos at the station, with trains arriving

and departing constantly. I approached a station official and asked if I could speak to someone important.

"Get lost," he said.

I didn't give up, I kept asking until eventually, to get rid of me, he took me to an office on platform one.

There was a woman railway worker inside, wearing a beret on her head and a worried look on her face. She was filling out forms. "Who are you?" she said when she caught sight of me.

"I am Viktor Nikolayevich Danilov. A citizen of Leningrad. I arrived here last week on train seventy-seven."

"Ah. The children's train. Show me your papers."

"I can't, they were taken from us when we arrived here in Kazan."

"They must be here with the others then."

The woman pulled open a drawer full of passports. She rummaged around a bit until she pulled out mine. It had a piece of paper on the front with lots of stamps on it.

"Here it is. You have been assigned to the kolkhoz of Anton Abramovich." She looked at me and added, "You shouldn't be here."

"I know."

"So why are you here?"

I explained that it was to do with my twin sister, Nadya Nikolayevna Danilova. I said she'd been assigned to train seventy-six and I didn't know if she was coming to Kazan as well but, if by any chance she'd been assigned to another farm, could I at least know which one so I could visit her?

"Oh," the woman said. "That's not good. It's also not proper procedure. Siblings should never be separated." She looked through the passports again but didn't seem to be able to find Nadya's. "Bad news," she said eventually.

"I'm afraid train seventy-six never arrived in Kazan. It must've been sent somewhere else."

"Do you know where?"

"I can send Leningrad a telegram to ask . . . but don't expect a reply. There's a war going on up there, you know."

"I know," I said. "My father's in the Militia."

The look she gave me seemed to say she was sorry.

"Does the kolkhoz know you're here?" she asked.

"No. I ran away."

"That wasn't very clever. The Commandant is a good man, he would've brought you here. Actually . . ." She lifted the receiver on her telephone and, without dialling a number, spoke into it. "Excuse me, Comrade, is Anton Abramovich Khasanov still there with you or has he already left? Ah, he's still there. Well, tell him not to go, please. Yes, there's one of his charges here."

She replaced the receiver and smiled at me. "The Commandant is here today. He'll take you back to the kolkhoz. I couldn't find your Nadya but at least I can save you a long walk."

So that's how I ended up travelling back to the kolkhoz in Commandant Khasanov's car.

To tell the truth, he wasn't very happy to see me there, in the station office.

"Who might you be?" he barked. "And what are you doing here?"

The railway lady told him everything, the Commandant muttered and went gradually redder and redder in the face. You could see he was getting angry.

He asked me why I'd done something "so incredibly stupid" and I replied that I had to know what had happened to my twin sister. He calmed down a bit then.

"Do not do it again," he said. "I am responsible for you and all the others on the train. Your loved ones will want you back in one piece when the war is over, and I will be held responsible if anything happens to you. So you must never pull a trick like this again."

I agreed and Khasanov said we could draw a line under the escapade.

When we got back to the kolkhoz, he sent for our brigade leader, Garayev, who had spent the day looking for me.

The two men spoke for a long time and when Garayev came back, he had a face like a thundercloud.

"I keep eye on you, Viktor Nikolayevich," he said.

In the meantime, I've been removed permanently from milking duty.

At least it means I'll get a bit more sleep in the morning.

Mga, 14th July

The train's still stopped, still in the same place. It hasn't gone any further and I don't know if it ever will.

Why aren't we moving? No one knows. Maybe there's a blockage on the line ahead. Or maybe it's the enemy. Or maybe they don't know where else to send us.

Since I last wrote, the train was shifted to a derelict piece of track just outside the station, beside the depots, sheds and other railway buildings. We were allowed to get off but told to stay nearby.

"You can't keep us all cooped up like this!" Mrs. Burova lamented. "There are small children here!"

"We are awaiting orders, Comrade. . . ." said Bok, the People's Commissar who'd been assigned to our case. "I'm trying to find out, asking around . . ."

"Well, do it quicker!"

"And while you're at it, try to find us clean sheets . . . and some soap would come in useful as well," Irina added.

Of all the women travelling on train seventy-six, Mrs. Burova and Irina are the nicest. Mrs. Burova is very tall and quite strict, she must be about forty years old, whereas Irina is much younger, she looks almost like a girl.

The two of them have set up a kind of committee, the "Mothers' Soviet" they call it, and every day they get together to take their grievances about this place to Bok.

To be honest, it's not that bad. There are lots of trees and it's like being at a Young Pioneers camp. We young ones have taken control of the train and turned carriage four into a play area for the younger children. We all sleep together in carriage eight, or even outside when it's not raining.

I've made a new best friend, too. Her name's Anna.*

She has raven black hair and I think she's really pretty. Until last year she went to the same school as us, but then she was sent to a college for special children.

You wouldn't believe how clever she is, she knows so many things. She can speak several languages, like Latin and French for example, and plays chess at the same level as me. That's how we made friends.

Anna brought a beautiful inlaid wooden chessboard with her and a book of famous chess matches to read. Since there's nothing to do here except get bored, the chessboard has become one of the most important things on the train and we got a tournament going right away.

Anyway.

I couldn't sleep the other night because of the heat and a baby crying, so I eventually decided to get up.

I took the chessboard and practice book and sneaked off to one of the empty carriages where I could sit quietly with an oil lamp.

To pass the time, I studied this one game:

* S. – Anna Terechenkov again. Viktor saw her boarding Train 76 a few pages earlier.

Black wins in six moves.

White surrenders in ten moves.

As I sat poring over it, someone said, "What a game that was!"

I turned around and Anna was there, peeping through the compartment door.

"What are you doing here?"

"I woke up and saw you leave the carriage. I wondered what you were doing."

"Oh," I said. "I was just trying to get myself back to sleep."

"Chess sends you to sleep? It has the opposite effect on me."

"To be honest, me too, and as you can see, I'm wide-awake." I thought for a second then added, "Why did you say, 'What a game that was' before?"

Anna laughed. "Because it was a great game. I remember it, I was in the audience when they played. Last year. Ragozin versus Botvinnik. Botvinnik was black.

We played a game after that and she won. We played another game and I won. Then I won again then she won again. By that time it was dawn and I asked her, "Are you a big Botvinnik fan?"

"Oh no," she said. "I support . . ."

". . . Olga Rubtsova!"

We said it at the same time which wasn't much of a surprise because Olga Rubtsova is Russia's most famous chess champion. But it was funny nevertheless and we burst out laughing. We've been best friends ever since.

It makes me happy because I've been feeling lonely without Viktor around.

Things might be better now.

Mga, 16th July

Mrs. Burova went to speak to Commissar Bok again today and he said they're sending us home! Since the line to Moscow is blocked, we can't continue our journey so they're taking us all back to Leningrad on trucks.

Yes!!!

Papa and Viktor will be miles away by now, but at least Mama and I will be back together. She'll be so happy to see me! If they don't let her know she has to come and get me, I think I'll get the bus to the museum by myself. I wonder if she's missed me as much as I've missed her. I can't wait to see her face when I throw myself at her!

Mga, 17th July

The trucks didn't come yesterday.

We don't know if it's because the enemy is getting closer or not. As usual, there's a lot of confusion and everyone's really wound up. Anna and I tried to play chess but we couldn't concentrate so we gave up.

Mrs. Burova says we should be ready nevertheless. The order to leave could come any minute.

I don't think we should hold our breath waiting.

26th July

It's been three weeks and I still don't have any news of Nadya.

I went back to see the kolkhoz commandant, Comrade Khasanov. He was reading the newspaper on his veranda, I asked him if there was anything about my parents, about the Hermitage Museum or battles involving the Militia.

"Ah, my dear boy," he said. "The newspapers never tell the little stories, the personal ones, only the big ones about all the people."

"What do you mean?"

"That you have to decipher the language of newspapers. It's like a code. Take this article, for instance. It says that there was a 'proud battle.' Do you know what that means?"

"I . . ."

"It means we lost many men. Here it says, 'heroic resistance' which means we tried to resist but were crushed by the enemy."

"So the newspapers tell lies?"

"Oh yes, all the time. They also tell the truth, but it's hidden and you have to dig to find it."

"So what's really happening in Leningrad? Has the enemy invaded the city? Are we losing the war?"

Khasanov lit a cigarette and stopped to think before replying.

"I don't know," he eventually said. "The German troops are commanded by General Leeb, an officer of vast experience. He fought in France and has always been victorious. But . . ."

"What?"

"Russia is not France. The enemy might've taken us by surprise, but the longer the fight goes on, the slower they'll get. They're not used to our plains, our rainy seasons. The cold weather will also be here in a few weeks and that will make it even worse for them."

"So there's hope?"

"I definitely think so. But there are also hard times ahead, young man. Very hard. For all of us."

4th August

I realized right away that something was wrong.

We were all sitting in the sun. I was eating a piece of bread, when Kostya said, "Isn't that Garayev?"

"Yes, that's him," Lev confirmed. "Looks like he's in a hurry."

I had a bad feeling and wasn't surprised when Garayev halted in front of me and said, "You run big house. Comrade Commandant wait you."

"Ah!" Mikhail exclaimed. "There goes Viktor skiving again!"

That boy really gets on my nerves. I would've punched him but Garayev was sweating and hopping from foot to foot. That's what alarmed me.

If it had been good news he wouldn't have been in such a hurry for me to hear it.

When I arrived at the Commandant's house, there was no one on the veranda.

I knocked on the door.

The sound of scurrying feet, then Mrs. Khasanova let me in.

"Are you Viktor? Poor boy," she said, squeezing me as tight as Mama did back at the train station in Leningrad.

Khasanov appeared from behind her.

"Come this way," he said.

He led me into the sitting room, keeping a hand on my shoulder, and gestured to the elegant sofa. From a sideboard he pulled out a bottle of vodka and filled up two glasses. One was for me. He handed it over solemnly. The liquid inside was as crystal clear as water.

"Drink," he said. "It will do you good."

I've never tasted vodka. Papa always says it's bad for children and alcoholism is one of Russia's biggest problems.

That's probably why I was so curious to try it, but I lost my nerve because of the expression on Khasanov's face. He was scaring me.

"What's going on?" I asked. "Do you have news . . . ?"

I didn't make it to the end of the sentence.

"Yes, dear boy, it's bad news I'm afraid."

Khasanov knocked back the vodka in a single gulp.

Then he pushed a crumpled newspaper over to me – the *Pravda*, dated 19th July.

It said . . .

Oh, I'll just stick it in here, it'll be quicker.

MGA - The despicable cowardice of the fascist beast will stop at nothing, not even at crimes which would revile any human being. The latest attack on our people fills us with unimaginable horror.

Our heroic correspondents in the city of Mga, not far from Leningrad, have sent reports of a monstrous attack on one of our "children's trains" — the convoys which depart Leningrad daily, carrying the hopes of our youth and the pride of the Motherland.

Yesterday, one of these trains, number seventy-six to be precise, was targeted by enemy planes as it travelled through Mga station. The bombs destroyed both the locomotive and the carriages, resulting in the tragic deaths of all the young passengers on board.

The soldiers and railway workers who fought heroically to save them have been plunged into a profound state of shock.

But our children, slaughtered in an act of perfidious betrayal by the fascist Leviathan, have not died in vain. Our valorous troops are poised to retaliate and courageously avenge this horrific crime!

"What does it mean?" I stammered.

"It means your sister's train was bombed by the enemy. There were no survivors."

"But that's impossible," I said. "There must be a mistake. Maybe we need to interpret the news differently, like that thing you said about the 'proud battle' and 'heroic resistance.'"

Khasanov poured himself another vodka. "No mistakes,

young man. *Pravda* can be terribly accurate when it wants. I'm sorry."

"But it says here that train seventy-six was in Mga. It left Leningrad on the third of July and the article is dated the nineteenth! After all that time, my sister can't still have been so close to the city!"

"You said that when you left, her train was stationary on the track. It must have been held up."

"Or maybe there are several trains numbered seventy-six. Maybe every week they go back to number one again."

"That occurred to me, too," Khasanov said, "so I asked my friend in Kazan, the woman you met, for more information. But no, it's not like that. To avoid any chance of error, the children's trains have all been given a different number. So the number seventy-six in the article is the one your sister Nadya was travelling on. I'm so sorry."

Khasanov hugged me, spilling his vodka all over the carpet. But it didn't seem to matter.

"Is there anything I can do to help? I'll tell Comrade Garayev to give you the afternoon off. If you want, you can sleep here tonight. My wife will make a bed up for you in the kitchen."

"Oh no," I said. "There's no need. Thank you."

I said goodbye, as politely as I could, and went back to the fields, to the others.

A wind was blowing outside and it made me feel a bit better.

Train number seventy-six.

Bombed.

No survivors.

Yet, deep down, something tells me it can't be true.

My sister Nadya is still alive.

I know she is.

No, it's more than that. I'm certain she is.

I listened to the rain pounding on the roof all night.

I worked in the mud all day.

I tended cattle. Repaired a fence. Raised the embankment of a canal.

I was so tired by the time night came, I collapsed, face down, onto my bed. Then when I turned around, they were all there.

Kostya, Lev, Klara, Ilya, Flavio. My friends here at the kolkhoz.

Klara spoke first. "We know," she said.

"What?"

"About your sister."

"Damn fascist pigs," Lev snarled in his man's voice.

"Bombing children," Ilya mumbled.

"How do you know? Who told you?"

"After work tonight, we heard two men talking about the seventy-six tragedy . . ."

"Fascist pigs," Lev said again.

"I remembered Anatoly was on train seventy-six," Kostya added, "along with your sister, Nadya."

"That's why you were so odd yesterday," Klara said. "We wondered why you kept to yourself all day."

"What about it?"

"Nothing." She touched my shoulder. "I'm so sorry, Viktor."

I shook my head. "There's no need."

"What do you mean?"

"You don't have to be sorry. My sister is fine."

"But train seventy-six."

"The newspapers are wrong. My sister is still alive."

"How do you know?"

117

There it was. The question I'd been expecting. This was the difficult bit.

"I just know."

"That's not much of an answer."

"But it's the truth. If my sister were dead, I'd know." Klara squeezed my arm.

It's always so hot in the barn, my shirt was sticking to my skin. Yet her fingers felt ice cold.

"Viktor, don't be like that. It's not right that . . ."

"You don't believe me."

"How can we believe you?"

"Nadya and I . . . we're twins. We were born barely minutes apart. Until the 3rd of July, we'd never been more than a few metres or a few hours away from each other. Sometimes it's like . . . like I can feel . . ."

"Whoa!" Lev said.

"Whoa!" echoed Flavio. "Are you trying to tell us you and your sister are telepathic? That you communicate with your minds and stuff like that?"

"That stuff's not real . . . ," Lev stated.

"I never said I was telepathic. I said that when my sister's in danger, I know. Kostya, do you remember when we went to the Russian Museum last year with school? My sister wandered off and fell and cut her forehead. I was somewhere else at the time but all of a sudden I had a really strong feeling that something was wrong so I told a teacher . . ."

"Erm. All I remember is you telling a teacher that you were worried because you couldn't find Nadya. You didn't actually know she'd hurt her forehead . . ."

"That doesn't matter. I'm not saying we communicate long distance. But if Nadya were dead, I'd know. I'm sure of it."

"Viktor, you're not thinking straight. I realize it's difficult to accept, but . . ."

"No buts. My sister is not dead. She's alive. I know she is. That's why I have to leave here and go to her."

They all looked at me as if I were mad. Mad enough to be locked up.

"Go to her . . . where?"

"Wherever she is now. The newspaper says train seventy-six was bombed in Mga so that's where I'll go first. Then I'll try to find out what happened, where Nadya ended up. Then . . ."

"But you already know what happened!" Flavio exclaimed. "As well as telepathic, you have to be pretty stupid. We left Leningrad because there's a war on! The enemy has started bombing our trains! You can't go back, I won't help you kill yourself, no way!"

I looked at him. His eyes were as black as marbles. He was serious. And he was right, too. From his point of view.

There was just one small difference.

Nadya is alive.

And because she's alive, because she's near the war, she needs me.

After all, I promised Papa I'd protect her.

I'm writing this at a little before five in the morning. I don't know the exact time but the sun's up and Garayev hasn't come to wake us yet, so I think that's more or less right.

Everyone else in the barn is sleeping. Except for me and Klara.

To be honest, it was Klara who woke me, not long ago.

I was dreaming when she pinched my arm. It was such a shock I nearly screamed but luckily she put a hand over my mouth. "Sssh," she said. "Come outside, quietly. I want to talk to you."

I didn't know why we had to talk at that time of the morning but I was curious. I dragged myself up and followed her outside.

It had stopped raining, thank goodness, but there's so much mud it's like standing in thick soup. We sat astride the fence, she pulled out a piece of paper and handed it to me.

This is it:

KAZAN

Kolkhoz

Barges

New granaries

Volga

"What's that supposed to be?"

"Your escape plan."

"I already know what to do. I'll get out at night so nobody sees me."

"Yeah. And what then? The next morning? When they realize you've gone?" I hadn't thought of that. "I'll tell you what will happen. They'll come looking for you. And you won't have gone far on foot. It won't take them long to catch you."

"What do you suggest?"

"Going up the Volga. We're nearly done harvesting the wheat, another few days and the granaries along the river will be nice and full and the barges will come. They're big, the barges, with engines so they can transport the grain to Kazan. You could steal one to get away undetected."

"Steal a barge? That doesn't sound legal."

"I know, that's why we'll do it at night. If you want to make it back to Leningrad, you need transport. And the barge will help you cover the first leg of your journey."

I looked at the drawing, then at Klara. "How do you know all this stuff about the harvest and the boats?"

"Because I listen, unlike someone else around here."

"And why are you helping me? Does that mean you believe me? Do you think Nadya is still alive?"

She shook her head. "No offence, Viktor, but I don't. I realize you're convinced, that you genuinely believe it. But I don't see how you can 'feel' your sister's presence when she's two thousand kilometres away."

"I don't 'feel' anything. All I know is she's not dead."

"All right."

"If you don't believe me, why do you want to help me?"

Klara heaved an enormous sigh at that point and said, "Because I want to come with you."

I asked her to explain why, she said she couldn't give me an explanation. I had to trust her. That wasn't going to happen. If she wanted to run away with me, I wanted to know why.

She said no. It was too serious. And she was afraid.

I lost my temper and said that I was afraid too, horribly afraid, afraid of not making it, of not getting there in time. Because while I knew Nadya was alive today, she might not be tomorrow. And then I'd regret it for ever.

I thought about walking away.

Klara grabbed my arm.

She hesitated a second then said, "All right."

She added: "I'm German." *S. - !!!*

She could've told me she was a boy and I would have been less surprised.

"What do you mean?"

"That I'm German. Or my parents are. They're communists, from Bavaria, but they moved to Russia before they had me. Like Flavio's parents. Only his family is Peruvian, mine is German. And now . . ."

"Now?"

"Now the Germans are the enemy."

I sighed. "If your mother and father are good communists they'll have nothing to fear. Don't you remember what Comrade Molotov said when war broke out? He said that our enemy is not the German people but the fascists . . ."

Klara sighed too, only her eyes welled up. "Of course I remember, but do you know what actually happened? All Germans living in Leningrad – the ones they managed to find, among which were my parents – were arrested in a matter of days by NKVD agents."

"I'm sorry."

"I wasn't taken because I was at a friend's house that night. Her parents offered to help me. They got me fake papers and put me on train seventy-seven which explains how I got here."

I didn't know what to say. "If they gave you new papers . . . that means . . . you must have a Russian surname now? You're safe."

Klara shivered. She said she'd been working in the fields the other day and, convinced she was alone, had started singing a song to herself, one her mother had taught her. A German song. Garayev had overheard her.

That's why she wanted to escape.

Because she was scared he'd report her. And she'd be arrested just like her parents.

S. – failure to report crime to authorities, Art. 88-2.

*S. – "Klara" is not the girl's real name: none of the children on train 77 had that name. Viktor may have used a code name in the notebooks.
Or did Klara lie to him?*

S. – he's 'sown'?

S. – Viktor and "Klara" plan to run away together. This is unauthorized absence from duty, Art. 245, and inciting a minor to engage in criminal behaviour, Art. 210.

We need the barges to get away.

But the barges only come when the harvest is finished and all the wheat has been reaped.

That will take another ten days so we've no choice but to wait.

In the meantime I work all day, gathering the wheat after it's been cut, my back aching and insects biting.

Something else I do is go to see Khasanov as often as I can.

My running away will get him into trouble, I'm sorry about that.

But Khasanov is the only person who can give me news about Leningrad. He tells me what he's read in the newspaper and, with Klara's help at night, I try to re-create it all on a map.

The fascists took Luga on the 8th of August. Luga is only one hundred and forty kilometres from Leningrad and the enemy is now advancing towards Mga.

"The Germans plan to encircle Leningrad," Khasanov explained. "They need to do two things to achieve this. The first is to take Mga."

"For the railway?"

"Exactly. The second is to take Shlisselburg."

FINLAND

Finnish Army

Lappeenranta

Vyborg

LAKE LADOGA

HELSINKI

GULF OF FINLAND

LENINGRAD

Shlisselburg

Gatchina

Kolpino

Mga

Tikhvin

TALLINN

LAKE PEIPUS

Luza fallen

Luga

Veliky Novgorod

USSR

German army

S. – The fall of Luga was only
announced to the people on 12th August.
So this page (with no date) must have
been written after that.

"What's that?"

"A small but quite strategic village. See? It's at the exact point where the Neva meets Lake Ladoga."

The Neva separates Leningrad's islands from the mainland to the south. The Finnish army is advancing from the north. To the west is the Gulf of Finland, to the east the gigantic Lake Ladoga.

"That's why it's all about Shlisselburg, young man. And if we lose . . ."

"If we lose? . . ."

"Leningrad will be isolated. The siege will be complete. Everything will be lost."

On the map, Mga and the village of Shlisselburg are only thirty kilometres apart.

I don't know what happened to train seventy-six but I hope my sister is nowhere near there.

Hang in there, Nadya. I'm on my way.

I swear I'll find you.

CCCP

PEOPLE'S COMMISSARIAT FOR
INTERNAL AFFAIRS

REPORT FOR INTERNAL USE

End of second notebook belonging to citizens
and siblings, Viktor Nikolayevich Danilov and
Nadya Nikolayevna Danilova, born in Leningrad
on 17 November 1928.

Viktor, one of the accused, has confessed
to the following crimes:

* irregular use of a farm vehicle /milk
  truck/: punishable with up to 1 year
  imprisonment, Article 99-1 Soviet Penal
  Code;
* unauthorized absence from duty /visiting
  Kazan station without permission/: up to
  10 years, Art. 245;
* inciting a minor to engage in criminal
  behaviour /the girl named "Klara" finds
  the courage to escape only after Viktor's
  bad example/: up to 1 year imprisonment,
  Art. 210, Soviet Penal Code;
* concealing crimes against the State
  /failure to report the girl named "Klara"
  to the authorities/: 5 years, Art. 88-2.

The document describes numerous occurrences
of defeatism and unashamed anti-Soviet
sentiment.

The accused's objective /to find his sister, who he believes is still alive/ is egotistic and he appears to be willing to commit serious crimes in order to achieve it.

It is my opinion that this seriously compromises the case of the two siblings.

The final pages of this notebook present a series of photos with no comments or remarks. Some seem to date to a time prior to 1941: I would therefore presume that citizen Danilov found them, or perhaps stole them from the home of Comrade Commander Khasanov, to add them to this diary of sorts and show them to his sister at a later date.

Signed:

COLONEL VALERY GAVRIILOVICH SMIRNOV

Col. Smirnov

NADYA ♡

NOTEBOOK 3

There are inaccuracies
regarding the times and
dates in this notebook. It is
not always in chronological
order.
                    —Smirnov

This place is all sky and marshes, green fields and forests, lakes and rivers. The water is blue because it reflects the sky, and it's always the same yet always different. From up a tree I can see for miles.

"Smoke, black smoke to the west!" I shout.

"That'll be the factories in Leningrad," Anna replies from down below.

"Blue sea to the east!"

"That's Lake Ladoga."

It's so big you can't see the other side and so calm you'd think it were made of glass.

That's where we're headed now, to the start of the River Neva. It comes straight out of the lake, winds its way to Leningrad and flows out into the Gulf of Finland.

A river that springs forth from a lake, could there be anything prettier? That's where I'm going, to a village called Shlisselburg, or so we've been told.

I can't wait to get there.

I wrote the bit above during the trip.

Oh! I wasn't writing while we were walking! It was when we stopped for a rest and Boris was teaching me how to climb trees.

But that's enough about that, I'd better get on otherwise I'll forget what I was supposed to be writing. Which is that it's EFMB (Explanation for My Brother) time!

Dear Viktor, we were stuck on train seventy-six, parked on a siding while we waited to be sent back to Leningrad.

But since there was no sign of the trucks, they decided we should continue onwards by train. Every day they told us we had to be ready, to never leave the train because it could set off at any minute.

But we had had enough and it was too hot to be stuck inside, crammed into the wagons like sardines, so the other night, Mrs. Burova said we could camp outside on the porch of some railway workers' houses.

That's where I was, fast asleep, when someone kicked me.

"Ouch!" I said. As I came to, I heard the thump of feet running around me and voices shouting, "Fire! Fire!"

I got up and it took me a few seconds to work out what was happening, people were shouting, running, and an overpowering, nasty smell of smoke was making it hard to breathe.

"Nadya, this way!" Anna said.

"What's going on?"

"There's a fire! The train's on fire!"

We ran around to the track and I saw the entire train had gone up in flames, burning from the locomotive at the front to the back end. The coal wagon was like a ball of fire, flames were leaping out of the windows and there were clouds of black smoke.

"Help!" we screamed. "Fire, fire!"

The railway workers arrived on the scene at that point and it went a bit mad. We formed a line and passed buckets of water along it while some soldiers aimed fire extinguishers, they weren't working though.

It was exciting and scary, but too late for the train unfortunately. It burned until all that was left was the metal skeleton.

The crucial thing, though, was that no one was hurt because, as I mentioned earlier, we hadn't been sleeping on the train and were quite a distance away. At worst, some of my friends lost their suitcases.

Luckily, I'd taken my notebooks with me, I don't know what I would have done if I'd lost them!

Commissar Bok appeared around dawn.

Hopping from foot to foot, looking this way and that, he was clearly worried about something and decidedly jumpy.

"We don't know . . . we're sorry . . . we don't understand . . ."

"What happened?" Mrs. Burova asked.

"Investigation . . . look into it . . . perhaps it was an accident."

"Trains don't just spontaneously combust."

"No, not trains, but coal can. All it takes is a spark."

That's when Mrs. Esipova from the Mothers' Soviet said, "The train went up in flames all at once, as if someone had doused it in petrol."

"No, I don't think that can have happened."

"Maybe it was a saboteur," Mrs. Burova said. "Or a Nazi."

"I don't think so," the Commissar said again. "The important thing is no one died, but you can't stay here any longer."

"What?"

"Why?"

"Are the trucks finally going to come? Are you sending us back to Leningrad?"

Mr. Bok said no. Apparently there are no longer any trucks and the train, well, even an idiot could see that it wouldn't be taking us anywhere.

"So are we walking back to Leningrad?"

S. – I have no record of this fire in any of my files. Investigate further.

That was a no as well. Too dangerous.

To cut a long story short, they decided to send us all to Shlisselburg (where I am now). It's a small village on Lake Ladoga, about thirty kilometres from Mga.

"There's no time to waste. We must go now."

"What? We don't even know where it is."

"I will lead you."

So we set off almost straight away, in a long column. At the front was a small truck carrying those who were unable to walk (mothers with babies or Anatoly, a friend of my brother's, who fell and broke his leg the other day when he was jumping from a rock). We all walked behind them in a line, two soldiers holding truncheons at the back, shouting at any stragglers.

Anyway.

When we left Mga, it was like walking into the Dark Ages. When we scrambled up a dirt track, we saw peasant women in headscarves, ox-drawn carts, tiny log houses called izbas dotted across the countryside with no electricity or running water, there's nothing modern here at all.

Little by little, our group began to disperse; at one stage, it was just me, Anna and Boris, who knows why I always end up with him under my feet.

Anna and I chatted for a bit. I told her about my parents and Viktor, she told me about her mother – she was beautiful but died when Anna was young.

I asked her about her father next but her face clouded over and she stopped talking.

We walked on in silence.

"Thirty kilometres isn't half a long way," Boris said.

"My shoes are hurting my feet."

"It's so hot!"

S:- The girl is Anna Tereshenkova. Without question.

137

I had the bags, the clothes that Mama had forced me to bring, and a whole lot of other things as well.

"If you ask me, we're lost. Where are all the others?"

He was right, there were only the three of us and there was a chance we'd gone the wrong way. Boris climbed up a tree to be lookout but since I wanted to try it too, he came back down and showed me how to do it. I could see everything from up there, the view was amazing.

We stopped for lunch on the edge of a forest and another group that had been way behind us caught up. There were about twenty of them, I didn't know any of them.

"You-should-get-a-move-on," a pretty girl with glasses said. She spoke so quickly all her words joined together. "The-soldiers-will-be-here-in-five-minutes-hello-my-name-is-Lilya-by-the-way."

"I'm Nadya, she's Anna, and this is Boris."

"Are-you-from-Leningrad?"

I almost laughed. "Why, aren't you?"

"I'm-from-Moscow."

Lilya told us her life story at the speed of light. She went to school in Moscow and had come to Leningrad to stay with her aunt on holiday but the war broke out and she couldn't get back to her parents. She'd hoped train seventy-six would take her home but she'd ended up stuck here with us instead.

Anyway, we set off again while Lilya was still talking and, at around one o'clock, we arrived in the village of Kirovsk, on the River Neva.

I have to admit that the sight of the river, our river, made me and the others feel awfully homesick.

"Maybe-we-should-follow-the-Neva-west-and-go-back-to-Leningrad," Lilya suggested. "No-one-will-see-us-and-on-foot-we-could-be-home-in-one-day-two-at-the-most."

"But isn't Moscow your home?"

Lilya shrugged. "Well-Leningrad-is-still-better-than-here-for-me."

"I'm tired of walking," a boy said.

"And Commissar Bok gave us an order!"

I didn't care about orders, Papa always said I was a bit of a rebel.

Nevertheless, it didn't seem like a good idea to set off on foot on our own, so instead of going west towards Leningrad, we walked east, which was easy, we just had to follow the Neva in the opposite direction and in two or three hours, we finally arrived in Shlisselburg.

Almost everyone had made it to the village before us and Commissar Bok was there, talking into a megaphone, looking extremely agitated.

"Listen carefully," he said. "Since there are so many of you, there isn't room for you all in the villagers' houses. The town soviet has decided to billet you in St. Nicholas's church."

"Is that it over there?" a boy asked, pointing to a very large church with not one but two bell towers.

"No, that's the cathedral. St. Nicholas's church is the other one." He pointed to a much smaller church beside the big one.

The building must've been painted blue and white once but it was all flaking now. The garden around it was knee-high in weeds. It looked abandoned, which is to be expected since religion has been banned since the Revolution.

Anyway, I'm writing this inside St. Nicholas's church, in the Girls' Room to be precise, which is a dusty old place but by the time we've finished tidying it up, it should look much better.

Besides, Commissar Bok said to make ourselves comfortable. It's likely we'll be here a while.

S. — Tendency to disobey orders.

It rained last night and started coming in through the roof at one point. A big wet patch formed on the ceiling and when it started dripping, we all woke up and started screaming.

We ran for buckets so the floor wouldn't flood, but the rain got so heavy we had to evacuate and move into the vestry where the mothers were sleeping.

The next morning, Mrs. Burova went to look for help and came back with three elderly men carrying ladders and some tools to fix the roof.

The chairman of the Shlisselburg town soviet was with them, an old man with thick eyebrows and a big red nose.

"I am very happy to have you here," the chairman said, "but you should know we weren't expecting you so you will all be called upon to make sacrifices. Commissar Bok has had to leave already. Until he returns, I have some instructions you must follow very carefully!"

The chairman nailed a sheet of paper to the church door. It said:

* IT IS FORBIDDEN TO SPEAK TO PEOPLE IN THE VILLAGE

- * IT IS FORBIDDEN TO SPEAK TO FOREIGNERS
- * IT IS FORBIDDEN TO SEND TELEGRAMS OR LETTERS
- * IT IS FORBIDDEN TO SPEAK TO ANYONE ABOUT
  - — THE TRAIN
  - — THE WAR
  - — LENINGRAD

What incredibly stupid rules, I thought. ←

How can they possibly expect us not to speak to anyone?

The chairman said the rules were for our safety but I don't understand why and I certainly don't agree with them.

They're just plain silly.

We train seventy-six survivors just want to go home and the sooner we can, the less bother we'll be to everyone.

S. – insulting a public official. Art. 192.

S. – no date

This morning, Boris and a boy called Sergey decided to go fishing and they invited me and Anna.

"I'm not sure," I said. "Fishing with worms? Do you stick needles through them?"

"They're called hooks," Boris replied. "And there's no other way to fish."

"That's all very well," I replied. "But worms give me the creeps."

"Oh, it sounds interesting to me," Anna quickly chimed in. "Maybe Lilya could come, too."

"I'm-in-for-sure!"

They convinced me to go; we packed some fruit for a snack and set off from the church while the dew was still on the grass. We walked along the Neva and emerged right in front of the lake.

I have to describe how the edge of the mainland has been dug away to construct an artificial canal, so there's this channel of water, then a long, thin strip of land in the shape of a comma.

Boris explained that the channel is called "the ring," it hugs the mainland and stops the smaller boats from being forced back by strong currents. The water is always calm in the ring, even during a storm.

Anyway, here's a map that shows you what it's like. I found it in the church, in the office of the old parish priest.

We walked along a pier and there was an old boat alongside it with an outboard motor (that's the word Boris used).

The two boys jumped in and Sergey untied the mooring rope.

"Come on, get in everyone," Boris urged.

"Are you mad? It's not ours."

"We'll-get-in-trouble-if-we're-found-out."

Boris and Sergey burst out laughing. We did what they said and rowed across the canal ring to the other side.

It was the perfect spot for them to do some fishing while me, Anna and Lilya looked over at the fortress.

Oreshek Fortress (also known as Nöteborg Fortress) is on a small island in the middle of the Neva, right where the river starts from the lake.

The island has high walls around it with an enormous round tower with a pointed roof at each corner. It looks really majestic standing in the middle of the river, and also a bit scary.

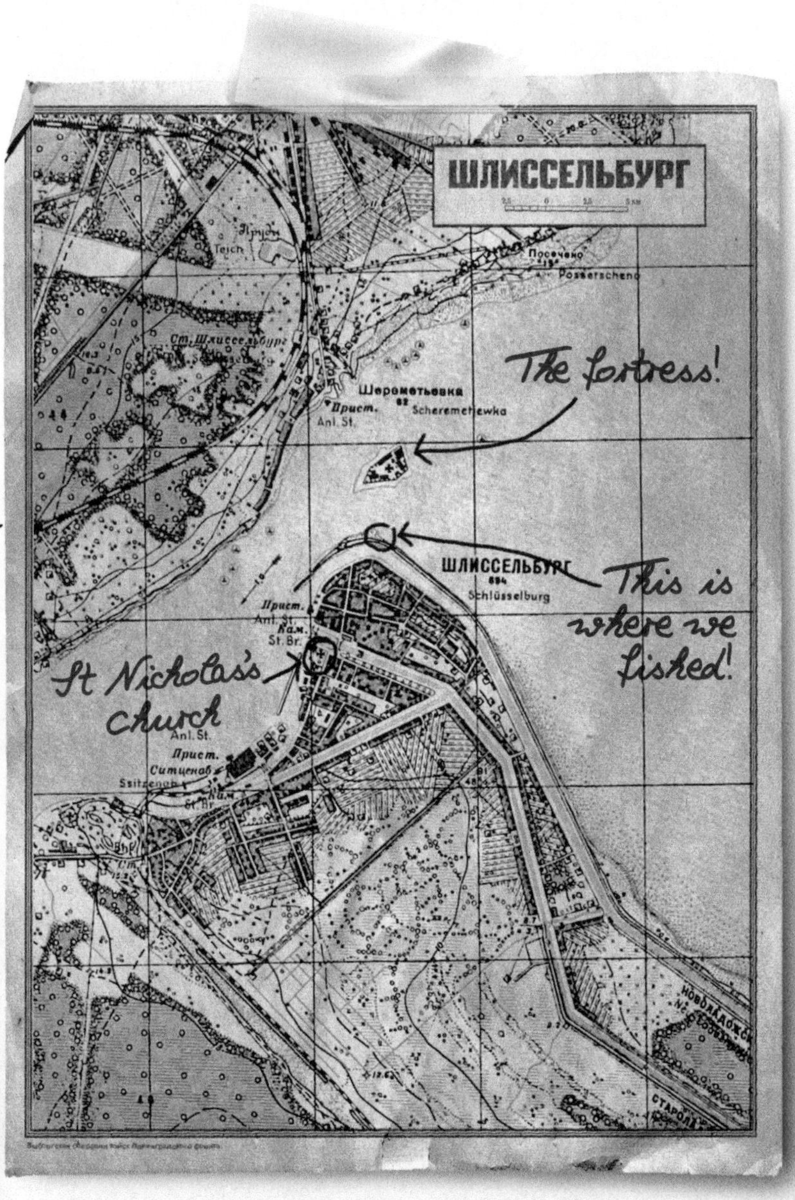
ШЛИССЕЛЬБУРГ
The fortress!
This is where we fished!
St Nicholas's church
Шереметьевка
Scheremetjewka
Schlüsselburg
Posserscheno

Here's a photo I found in the priest's office:

One of his books had the history of the fortress:

It was built by the Prince of Novgorod in the 13th century and named Oreshek, which means hazel-nut, possibly after the many hazelnut trees on the island, or perhaps because the island itself is shaped like a nut – small but hard for enemies to crack. Oreshek was captured by Sweden in 1612 then taken by Tsar Peter the Great in 1702. In the years which followed, the tsar built the city of Saint Petersburg (now Leningrad! The book still had the old name) and the fortress was used as a prison. Many revolutionaries died within its walls.

S. - Hail the Fallen Heroes of the Revolution

"Aleksandr Ulyanov, Comrade Lenin's brother, also died there," Boris said as he fished. "The tsarists hung him right there on the island. His ghost is said to wander the ramparts to this day."

"What nonsense," I commented. "First of all, there is no such thing as ghosts. And I can't believe Lenin's brother was here."

Later I was forced to admit Boris was right. I hadn't found the book in the priest's office at that point, so I couldn't have known while we were still out fishing.

Boris knows lots of things. He also told us that the communists released all the prisoners on the island during the October Revolution and there's now a museum of the Revolution there, although I don't know if you can visit it, because of the war being on.

Gosh, it was hard to imagine there was a war on while we were sitting in the morning sun beside the lake, our feet soaking in the water and the sun in our eyes.

It was so peaceful.

I imagined Mama working in the museum, cataloguing the paintings, Papa in a soldier's uniform, and Viktor playing football with the other boys from his train.

I hope they're all well. I'd really like to be there with them.

Something serious occurred today.

This is what happened: Irina crept out of the church very early this morning with a bucket in her hand.

"Where are you going?" Mrs. Burova asked her.

"For a walk," Irina replied.

"A walk," Mrs. Burova said, "or are you going to see Vladimir?"

Vladimir is a peasant who lives in a log izba just outside Shlisselburg. Irina has made friends with him and visits occasionally. She always has something tasty to eat when she comes back (thank goodness, seeing as all we ever get from the town soviet are never-ending potatoes).

"Who I go to see is my business, no one else's."

"It's not actually, if it means you're breaking the rules," Mrs. Burova proclaimed, tapping the list on the church door. "Life here is hard enough without being reprimanded by the chairman as well."

"Ah, he's quite a guy. He's put the fear of death in all the villagers. They're scared to come near this place and give it a wide berth when they go past. It's like we have the plague. What else could he do to us?"

"Irina . . ."

She huffed and walked off without replying, but when she came back, her bucket was full of eggs wrapped up in an old newspaper.

Anna, Lilya and I were on duty in the kitchen today and when we saw the eggs arrive, we jumped for joy and whisked them away to make an omelette . . .

"Hey," Anna said. "Look here."

She was holding a crumpled page of newspaper.

"What is it?"

"An article from the *Pravda*. It's dated nineteenth of July, that's almost a month ago."

"Let's-see-if-it-says-anything-interesting," Lilya shrieked.

We read it right there and then because we hadn't had any news of the war for such a long time (something else that had been banned by the chairman and People's Commissar). ←

I was only a few lines in when I let out a scream and dropped one of the eggs. It fell to the floor in a slimy, yellow explosion.

S. — violation of orders. Art.239.

dice

p at

iich

ing.

ple

horror.

idents in

t far from

sent reports of

a monstrous attack on one of our

"children's trains" — the convoys

which depart Leningrad daily,

carrying the hopes of our youth

and the pride of the Motherland.

Yesterday, one of these trains,

number seventy-six to be precise,

targeto

it travelled through Mga station.

The bombs destroyed both the

locomotive and the carriages,

resulting in the tragic deaths of

all the young passengers on board.

The soldiers and railway workers

who fought heroically to save the

have been plunged into a prof

state of shock.

But our children, s!

in an a

by the

die

a

"That's impossible," I said. "It can't be. They can't be talking about us."

"Who-can-it-be-then? We're-train-seventy-six."

"I know. But we're alive."

<u>"Bah!" Anna said. "Dead, alive, we are what the Party officials decide."</u>

"Why-do-you-say-that-Anna?"

"It doesn't matter."

"Oh yes it does," I insisted. "They must be talking about another train seventy-six."

"The newspaper is dated nineteenth of July and it says 'yesterday' which has to be eighteenth of July, the very day our train caught fire. We were at Mga station and no other children's trains went through there, we would've noticed."

"But there was no German bombing. And we're not dead. The railway workers weren't in shock, they helped us . . ."

"It's political . . . ," Anna mumbled.

"They-made-us-leave-at-dawn-so-no-one-would-see-us,-remember?"

"Right. So why did they have us come to Shlisselburg? There's not even a railway here. Why didn't they send us to Leningrad, or anywhere else for that matter? It doesn't make any sense."

"And-why-does-Commissar-Bok-seem-so-scared? What-are-those-crazy-rules-on-the-church-door-all-about?"

I have to admit they are all very good questions and I don't have any answers.

In effect, a lot of strange things have happened to us. Then again, it's like the whole world has gone mad since the war started.

Anyway, my friends and I have decided not to tell anyone what we've discovered. For now. We don't want

S. – counter-revolutionary remark, but it is not clear what exactly the girl meant. Investigate further.

S. – it would appear Anna knows a great deal.

to be reprimanded for violating the rules and what purpose would it serve?

There's obviously something very mysterious going on and if we want to find out the truth, we'll have to do it ourselves.

13th August

At dinner time, Shlisselburg citizens all congregate in the People's House to listen to the radio and hear the latest news on the war.

We children know this because we spy on them from a distance but it's never very interesting. Well, not until now.

Me, Lilya and Anna sneaked out of St. Nicholas's church, it must've been around five o'clock.

"I-don't-like-this-at-all-I-remember-my-mum-found-me-once-when-I-was-eavesdropping-on-her-talking-to-Daddy-she-was-furious-and-she-said . . ."

"Don't worry, Lilya, we're not going to spy on anyone. We're just going to listen to the seven o'clock news. They'll never catch us."

We went out for a really long walk and sat down to gaze across at the fortress on the island for a while, then we went back to the village. Some of the locals saw us and instantly vanished, as if by magic, back into their houses.

They were honestly behaving like we had some sort of disease.

This time we actually hoped we did.

We stopped in a small square in front of the People's House and when the coast was clear, I took off my shoes and climbed up a giant tree, the way Boris taught me. Then I hid on a forked branch which was nice and comfortable, quite near the top.

"OH-WHAT-A-HOT-DAY-TOO-HOT-REALLY-SO-HOT-THANK-GOODNESS-FOR-THIS-TREE-AND-THE-LOVELY-SHADE-UNDER-IT . . . ," Lilya babbled.

"YES, HOW LUCKY, LILYA! IT'S SO LOVELY!" Anna replied, shouting just as loud. "WHAT A PITY IT'S TIME TO GO NOW!"

"OKAY-SHALL-WE-GO THEN?"

"YES, LET'S GO BACK TO THE CHURCH!"

My friends wandered off, chatting very loudly, so no one in the village would feel the urge to come outside and wouldn't, therefore, notice that the three girls from before had now become two.

I, on the other hand, hid myself in the branches and waited. And waited. It was very boring.

People finally began to arrive and go into the People's House; it was warm so the windows were open and I could hear fairly well. In fact, I discovered that if I leaned forward a little, I could even get a glimpse of the radio.

It's different from the radio we had in Leningrad. To begin with, it's much bigger, as big as a cabinet you could say, and it's not a cable one, it has an aerial on top.

You couldn't hear anything from it, just lots of buzzing, like bees in a hive.

"Chairman, the radio's not working!"

"Oh, it's just the aerial that needs adjusting a little. There we are. That sounds better."

"Sssh, be quiet. The news is on!"

Well, believe it or not, the first news item was about us, train seventy-six.

"The whole nation is in mourning," the announcer said. "The fascists will soon pay for their heinous crimes. But we must not let the tragedy of train seventy-six weaken our courageous hearts. Citizen comrades, never

S. – Further violation of orders and espionage. Oct. 65.

150

forget: it is your duty to send our city's children to safety. Trains continue to depart daily and the valorous Red Army has taken all necessary precautions to keep the children out of harm's way. We know how difficult it is to say goodbye, but each and every parent must obey the Party's evacuation orders."

"Well, that's rich!" one of the peasants snapped. "Keep them safe. Just like they're doing with those poor mites shut away in the church."

On hearing the woman's remark, the chairman went red in the face, as if he'd just swallowed a beetroot, and started yelling, "Who said that? Who spoke?!" But no one came forward.

Anyway, it means that it's true. People in Leningrad think the Germans destroyed our train and that we're all dead. On top of that, the people in the village don't know we're the children from train seventy-six.

So why aren't Commissar Bok and the chairman of the town soviet telling the truth?

For now, I really don't know what to think.

S. – Why indeed?

20th August

We escaped from the kolkhoz.

We're out.

Garayev came to wake us at five o'clock yesterday morning. But instead of taking us to milk the cows, or to work in the fields, he led us along the path to the river.

There were men in Red Army caps standing guard along the way. One of them had a rifle.

"Wheat harvest important," Garayev said. "Guards make sure no one take grain for himself."

Meanwhile, barges had arrived up the river. There were three of them, all huge, made of wood, lined up along the piers. It was just like a painting I saw in the Russian Museum with Mama. It was called *Barge Haulers on the Volga.* Luckily, these barges had engines.

"You very good work today," Garayev warned us. "Comrade People's Commissar also come for harvest!"

He pointed to a smaller boat. There were four men onboard, wearing headscarves to protect their heads from the sun.

We joined in with the rest of the peasants, loading sacks of wheat onto carts then pushing the carts from

«Бурлаки на Волге»... русского художни...

*S. - Viktor doesn't explain where he got this photo.
Did he tear it out of a book?*

the granaries to the boats. It was sweltering work. The ground squelched with mud. The air scalded with the sound of men cursing and barking orders.

"What's up, Viktor?" asked Klara, coming over to me. "You look worried."

"There's no way your plan can work," I replied. "We can't steal a barge in broad daylight. And they'll all have left for Kazan by tonight."

Klara winked. "Trust me, it will take more than a day to finish the harvest."

She was right. By dusk, we'd only managed to load one barge and it set off back along the river by itself. Khasanov and the People's Commissar went to dinner together and we were given permission to return to the kolkhoz.

"Be ready, Klara. Tonight's the night."

To be honest, I still wasn't sure I could take her with me. It would be much easier to escape on my own. But Klara was smart and I didn't want to <u>betray</u> her just yet.

*S. - the only betrayal here
is the one against the state!*

I sat by myself at dinner and kept my distance, as much as I could, from Lev and Kostya.

At night, I used my haversack as a pillow. There wasn't much in it – just these notebooks, my money, a sweater. And the silver icon of the bearded man, obviously it's just some saint I don't know but it reminds me of Papa.

I wanted to sleep but the others were carrying on, causing a commotion. I heard Klara settle in her bed. I waited. When everyone was finally quiet, I got up, picked up my bundle and tiptoed out of the barn. The night air was clammy. Klara appeared right away, carrying her own small bundle.

We set off without looking back, starting at the slightest noise although there was never anyone there – everyone on the kolkhoz was exhausted and had been asleep for hours.

We'd just gone past the new granaries and had almost reached the boats when Lev jumped out from behind a tree.

"Oh, look who it is, love's young dream!"

"What are you doing here?" I said. "You were sleeping, I checked . . ."

"I was pretending. And I got here before you because we took the shortcut through the ditch . . ."

"We?" Klara asked.

That's when Kostya, Ilya and Flavio appeared, followed by Emma, Marya and Natasha who are Klara's best friends, then even more after them. Around thirty children.

"What are you all doing here?"

"We're just curious."

"We wanted to know why you'd gone out."

"I came because all the others were coming."

I sighed. "Well, thanks, but you can all go away now."

"Why should we?" Kostya asked.

Lev smacked him. "You really are stupid if you haven't worked it out yet. Viktor wants to make a run for it. Isn't that right?"

"What?"

"Really?"

"You want to leave the kolkhoz?"

"Why?"

"Where will you go?"

It wasn't really the time for questions.

"Be quiet," I hissed. "Yes, I have to leave, and I don't want to be found out because of you lot."

"You're going back to Leningrad, aren't you?" Lev said. "You think your sister is still alive and you want to find her."

I didn't reply. There was no need.

"And Klara?"

"Well, she . . . she also has her reasons."

"Uh-huh," Lev said. "I think I'm going to come, too."

It turned out that he was tired of being on the farm, breaking his back toiling in the fields, and nothing could be as bad as the slave labour on the kolkhoz. Flavio concurred. And Ilya. And some of the girls. There was no way I could escape with all of them.

I don't want to describe the argument that took place. But I ended up fighting with someone – we wrestled in the sand, I landed a fair few punches and I took a few as well. The tussle went on until a lantern appeared on the path. Followed by another. And another . . . three of them advancing rapidly together.

"Alert!"

"They're stealing the grain!"

"Saboteurs!"

After that, everything happened very quickly.

In hindsight, what we should have done was stay put and act normal. After all, we were just a group of kids on a path. We weren't doing anything wrong. We possibly shouldn't have been there at that time of night and we *were* planning on escaping, but at that point we were still fairly innocent. ← *S. — naïvety or deceit?*

The truth is that the lights scared us. We ran down to the dock and must've looked guilty because one of the guards started shooting in the air.

I was about to leap aboard the first barge when someone shouted out at me in the dark, "Hey, kid!"

The boat wasn't empty, there were people sleeping onboard, maybe sailors or guards. I didn't hang around to find out.

More people were piling down the path and we were trapped between the sailors on the barge and the men on the shore. In the dark I saw a handful of things at the same time: guards aiming rifles, people shouting, lanterns. My friends.

I wondered what to do.

Diving in and swimming to the other side wasn't an option, it was too far and the Volga was too wide to swim across at night.

In the end I spotted the Commissar's launch which was still anchored at one of the piers just ahead of me. I also remembered that the Commissar had gone to dinner at Commandant Khasanov's house.

I ran, took a huge leap and landed in the boat.

It was only then that I realized it wasn't empty either. A soldier was sleeping in the back. He woke up and started shouting then turned to look at me.

I didn't know what to do.

So I barged him and he fell overboard.

S. — attempted murder of a public official. Art. 191-2.

Flavio jumped into the launch behind me and set to starting up the motor, like he knew what he was doing, then Lev, Klara and Ilya all climbed in as well.

The boat filled up with children in a matter of seconds.

"What are you doing?"

"Let's go!" someone screamed.

"Go, go, go!"

Shots were fired. I saw the guards and realized things were getting serious.

Flavio managed to get the engine running, I unmoored us, and Lev cried, "We're off!"

We raced through the night – well, we went as fast as we could in a motorboat full of people.

A few of the guards tried to follow us for a bit, running along the bank, but we crossed to the opposite side of the river where we were more or less invisible, hugging the riverbank in the dark.

The guards gave up.

"We did it!" Klara said.

"I wouldn't be so hasty!" I exclaimed. "We're in big trouble now. They won't give up that easily."

"So what should we do?"

I thought about it for a second. "The boat will take us as far as Kazan. Once we're there, we'll try to throw them off our trail. Flavio, keep close to the riverbank so if anyone's following us we can jump off. And don't stop until I tell you."

At that point, I demanded to know why they hadn't all stayed at the kolkhoz.

The truth was, they didn't have a reason.

"Eh, I don't know!" was the general reply, or "I heard gunfire and started running," or similar excuses.

We counted how many of us there were: twenty-eight.

Kostya wasn't there, or Natasha, Klara's friend.

S. – Theft of a state vehicle, Art. 89: violation of the rules of military navigation, Art. 254: inciting a minor to engage in criminal behaviour, Art. 210: banditry and piracy, Art. 77.

...eir names, surnames and patronymics.

But Mikhail, the blond kid, and big-ears Yury had made it to the boat.

"Now we know who sounded the alarm!"

"We didn't call anyone," Mikhail said. "We were sleeping but woke at the sound of the others going out. We were curious so just tagged along and heard everything."

"Spying on people as usual."

"You're the one who put us all in danger wanting to run away. And why is it you had to leave?"

"Because he wants to find his sister," Lev said.

Mikhail did something next that took me by surprise.

He looked at Yury. And laughed. "Yeah, of course, his sister . . ."

It was like a red rag to a bull. I put my hands round his neck, convinced I was going to force him overboard. He's not small, Mikhail, but he's a coward if ever there were one.

"What are you laughing at? What do you know about Nadya?"

It had suddenly dawned on me.

He knew something.

I remembered the number on his hand that he'd rubbed out, the things he'd said when our train had just set off from Leningrad. "I had a narrow escape," he'd said.

I kneed him in the stomach and yelled, "You knew, didn't you? You knew train seventy-six was going to be bombed?! Damned fascist spy!"

I shoved him to the floor and jumped on him, throwing punch after punch until Lev and Flavio dragged me off.

Mikhail stood up, his lip was bleeding. "I'm not a fascist spy," he said.

"But you still knew train seventy-six was dangerous!"

"Yes, I knew!"

"How did you know? Why?"

Yury stepped forward at that point. He was shaking. "Leave him alone."

"I'll only let him go if he tells me everything. Otherwise I'll kill him. With my bare hands."

"It was my father. My father told us," Yury blurted.

"Who's your father?"

"He's a major in the NKVD. Okay? See, we're not spies. My father's an agent of the People's Commissariat!"

This is what Yury told me:

The night before we left from Leningrad, Mikhail stayed over at Yury's house so they could go to the station together in the morning. Yury's mother held a sad little party for them. His father wasn't there, he arrived home from work much later. He woke the two boys and asked if they knew a girl called Anna Tereshenkov.

Anna's father also worked for the NKVD, Colonel Tereshenkov he was called, a superior of Yury's father and a real bully of a man. He turned out to be a criminal too, and had just been arrested for a serious crime. S. – *high treason.*

He told Yury and Mikhail to steer well clear of his daughter.

"Don't speak to her, don't go near her, you must pretend she doesn't exist," Yury's father said. "And if you see her get on a train, you wait for the next one. Your life depends on it."

When Yury finished his story, I have to admit I didn't know what to think.

"What does it all mean?"

"That Anna's trouble," Mikhail said. "And anyone travelling with her will be killed."

That's enough of that for now. I'm too tired to keep writing, I can write the rest of what happened really quickly.

S. – so Yury must be Yury Orestovich Fedin. the son of Comrade Major Orest Aleksandrovich Fedin. stationed at the Bolshoy Dom in Leningrad.

We got almost all the way to Kazan in the boat. When we saw the first lights of the city, we left the boat and walked for a bit until we came to some woods. Everyone lay down under the trees and went to sleep. I wasn't tired so Klara shared her candlelight with me and I started writing.

Tomorrow I'll go to the station, get on a train and start heading for Mga.

And when I get there, I'll find out what happened to Nadya.

There's no way I'm taking everyone with me, although Mikhail and Yury can tag along. I need to know if they really have told me everything.

S. – This final section raises serious doubts. Could Comrade Fedin really have known what was going to happen to train 76?

What does the Tereshenkov Affair have to do with Viktor and Nadya?

This whole business could prove to be more serious than previously expected.

20th August

Viktor is coming to get me.

I'm sure of it, as sure as the sky is blue and it's cold in winter.

It's not magic, or the twin telepathy that Viktor has always believed in and is always telling his friends about to impress them.

It's a simple matter of logic.

Think about it. He knows I was on train seventy-six. And he knows the train was bombed by the Germans (he'll have read it in the papers or heard it on the radio: they talked about it for days).

But since he's convinced there's a supernatural force binding us to each other (it doesn't matter if it's true or not, he thinks it is), Viktor will never believe I'm dead. So he'll come. To help. To save me.

It's a really stupid idea, no doubt about it, but I know it's what he'll have thought and I wouldn't be surprised if he were on a truck, a train or a cart right now, heading to Mga. And I can't do anything to stop him!

I beg you, Viktor, if you can hear me . . . don't come. It's dangerous and I don't want you to get caught up in it.

Don't come here.

Please . . .

Something big is going on.

I don't know what it is because it's been raining for days and I haven't been able to get back up the tree to hear the radio. But you can tell by the people going past the church, all deep in conversation, concerned looks on their faces. I saw two families load their things onto a cart yesterday and leave, in the middle of a storm, heading who knows where.

Another family left their home this morning and walked past us – two old people and a young girl. When the girl saw me, Anna and Lilya, she smiled and gave us a wave.

"What do you think that means?" I asked my friends.

"That-she's-not-scared-anymore-of-being-reprimanded-by-the-chairman."

"That she's going away for ever . . . ," Anna added.

"But why?"

Another unanswered question.

25th August

I dreamt about Papa last night. He was dressed as a soldier but wasn't carrying a weapon, there was a battle and he couldn't defend himself. An enemy soldier was pointing a rifle at him and then . . .

I woke screaming and sat up. It was dark outside, no longer the soft glow of the white nights but proper darkness. The days are beginning to get shorter.

For a few minutes I just sat there, not moving, holding my breath, my friends curled up on the floor around me. There was a bolt of bright light then an enormous crash.

Anna woke up. "It's a storm!"

"It's not a storm. Listen. There's no rain."

"It's-bombs," Lilya whispered.

We threw on our clothes and ran outside. Explosions were lighting up the sky, like a fireworks display.

"Let's go up on the roof," I suggested.

"What-do-you-mean-let's-go-up-on-the-roof?"

"When the men from the village came to replace the roof tiles, they left their ladder behind. It's around the back."

All the time I'd spent climbing up the tree had made me realize how much I like heights and I'd been thinking about climbing onto the church roof for a while now, to see the view. Anna was scared, but I said, "Do as you like, I'm going up."

The ladder rungs were still wet from the night before but I raced up as fast as I could, then padded carefully over to the tower over the main door where I finally stopped and turned to look back.

The bright lights were coming from the southwest, the Neva glittered with the reflected glow of the explosions.

A battle was underway over there. But where exactly? In the city of Pushkin? Kolpino? That's just outside Leningrad, so could the enemy have made it to the city already?

I rushed back down from the roof, nearly breaking my neck in the process, and when I jumped down beside Anna and Lilya, half the survivors of train seventy-six were gathered there, the mothers in their nightgowns and the boys half-naked with sleepy faces.

"Where are they bombing?"

"I don't know," I said. "Pushkin, Kolpino."

"So they're attacking Leningrad!"

The words flew from mouth to mouth like frantic flies.

The younger children burst into floods of tears, the older ones ran around in a nervous frenzy. In the end, the Mothers' Soviet stepped in to take control, as usual.

"We have to speak to the chairman of the town soviet," Mrs. Burova announced. "Regardless of the rules on the church door, we have to know what's happening."

"At all costs," Irina echoed.

Five of them made their way over to the People's House, and me and a group of others followed behind them because there was no way we were going to just stand there waiting.

In the meantime, the villagers had poured out into the street, faces turned up to the sky.

The chairman of the town soviet was there too, and when he saw us, he started yelling at us to go away.

"Not until you tell us what's happening."

"What makes you think I know?" the old man spluttered.

"You have a radio, Comrade . . ."

"The radio only plays music, music, music! Meanwhile the war has reached us!"

"We have to leave then, find somewhere safe!"

"No one is leaving! The orders are to stay here. The battle is still far enough away, we'll be safe here!"

I don't think that's true, and the Mothers' Soviet don't think so either, but not having any other option, we went back to the church.

It's afternoon now and while I write, I hear an explosion every now and then. To me it sounds like the bombs are getting nearer.

I hope it's only my imagination.

26th August

The first soldiers have arrived.

There were three of them, wearing filthy uniforms and with boyish faces. One of them didn't even have boots.

They arrived dragging their feet in the mud, and when my friends looked out of the window to watch them go past, the soldiers said, "Can you give us a hand? Where's the town soviet? Our captain's vehicle is stuck in the mud five kilometres from here."

It goes without saying we ran straight outside and led the soldiers to the chairman, firing questions at them along the way. We discovered that:

* The soldiers are part of the 48th Army
* They fought in Luga and other places
* They're from Mga, where the fighting has reached
* There's just three of them at the moment, plus their captain and one more who are back at the vehicle, but a lot more will be arriving soon.

When the chairman saw us, he immediately sent us away and offered the soldiers some tea before summoning his "best men," namely the old guys who fixed the roof, and they all set off on a cart to go and recover the military vehicle.

We tried to follow them at a distance but the chairman threw stones at us and ordered us to stay away.

Anyway, it takes more than that to put us off. Boris and I climbed up some trees on the edge of the village to keep an eye on the situation. We were the first to see the car splutter into Shlisselburg.

The five soldiers (three from before plus the other two) ordered the cathedral right next to our little church to be opened for them. It's their operations base now.

"Do not speak to the children," the chairman told them, pointing to where we were spying on them from behind the wall. "And that's an order . . ."

"That doesn't mean a damn thing to us," one of them

S. – insolent children, like monkeys!

165

replied. "We don't take orders from civilians, Comrade. You'd do better to stick to your own affairs!"

All of us kids gave them a round of applause. To tell the truth, I don't think the army commander is that happy about having a "bunch of snotty brats" running around under his feet. The soldiers, on the other hand, seem quite happy about it, especially with the Mothers' Soviet. In the afternoon, one of them (the one with no boots) brought Irina some flowers. She said thank you and her face went pink like a peach, the soldier said he'd come back again to visit her, if she didn't mind.

I wouldn't mind being courted by a soldier. He might look a bit young but he has eyes as blue as the sky.

27th August

More soldiers finally arrived last night, far too many for me to count.

It would seem that Shlisselburg is now "the rear" while Mga (to think we were there just a month ago) has become "the front."

A lot of the soldiers have already fought in numerous battles, they scare me because they look so grey and sombre. They spit and swear and drink vodka all the time.

There are other nicer ones. They talk to me if I'm polite and make myself useful, for instance by taking them all the cigarette ends I find lying about.

Earlier today, one of them, he might be an officer because he has gold-rimmed glasses and looks quite intellectual, well, he was smoking and writing notes down the side of a map. When I asked him a few things, he was kind enough to let me see it.

I'll try to draw what was on it.

Interestingly, he said that the enemy is not planning to attack Leningrad right away: they aim to encircle it and cut it off.

"For the time being the target is Mga, that's where we're fighting."

"And what happens if we . . . lose?"

"Then they'll advance to Shlisselburg," the officer said. "And if they take that village as well, Leningrad will be surrounded."

He must have seen my face go pale because he forced a smile: "But don't worry, it won't come to that. We soldiers of the Forty-Eighth Army won't allow it."

I do hope he's right, but for now I keep looking at the map and imagining our troops on the move, the enemy advancing, etc. To think I used to get so bored at school when the teacher talked about ancient battles then expected us to recite the lesson word-for-word afterwards! It's different when the war is happening somewhere familiar to you, when you don't know if your father has been wounded or not, when you're wondering where the enemy will attack first: your village or the city your mother works in.

No one can sleep here in the church, we hear the bombs get closer by the minute, and even though we've been taught not to pray, we do.

I have to stop writing now because it's my turn to make the evening meal and they're calling me.

Anyway.

I think that officer was right.

The city of Mga can't fall. It won't fall!

N.B. The events in this chapter take place at the same time as those in the previous chapter.

24th August, don't know where, on a train

We arrived at Kazan station in groups, not all at the same time, like a team of secret agents. ←——————

S. – more like a band of criminals.

There were twenty-eight of us. Way too many. The last time I wrote I said I wanted to get rid of them all, and I did try.

We slept in the forest and I woke up early the next morning. I picked up my things and sneaked away through the trees on my own. But then I turned back. I needed Mikhail and Yury – I had to know what other secrets they were keeping about my sister and train seventy-six. So I went back to wake them, and in doing so, woke everyone else.

"This is where we all go our own way," I announced. "I'm going where I have to go, you can all just go back. Or wherever you like." I walked away by myself but when I looked back, they were all there behind me, following.

I think they're scared. Of the soldiers, of the punishment if they go back.

"What if they shoot us when they see us?"

"What if they don't shoot but arrest us instead?"*

* S. – arrest is a likely possibility.

"There's trouble ahead if you come with me," I said. "It's up to you. Just remember that I'm in charge. You all do what I say."

"You can forget that," Mikhail muttered.

Mutinies have to be nipped in the bud so I dived at him, knocked him to the ground and kept punching until he said, "All right." I don't trust him though, so I ordered Lev to keep an eye on him.

We set off and made it to Kazan around lunchtime, by which time we were all ravenous.

No one had ration cards with them so we couldn't go into a shop. And we had no identity papers because the railway personnel had taken them away when we'd arrived. Maybe they were still being kept at the station?

"If that's where they are, we have to get them back," Klara said.

She threw me a knowing look, as if to say, "Don't forget, I'm German: if anyone checks, they might see my papers are false."

"All right," I said. "I promise we'll get them back."

"But first we need to eat."

"In Leningrad my mother took me to a place where you don't need coupons," I said. "It was in a park."

Lev burst out laughing. "The black market! You went to the black market, you moron!"

No one calls me a moron. I wondered if I should take him down, too. No, now wasn't the time.

"Fine," I replied. "Is there a black market here in Kazan?"

"Maybe. I could find out if you give me some money and some time."

The only ones with money were me and Klara, the others had left their bags back at the farm. We'd have to make do.

S. – a further case of buying contraband goods. Oct. 78.

170

I gave my roubles to Lev and sent him, Flavio, Mikhail and Yury to find food. Klara and I were going to try and retrieve our identity papers. Little Ilya would stay behind with the rest of the group to wait.

"But I don't want to wait!"

"We need someone to keep an eye on this bunch of babies, okay?"

Ilya smiled.

So it was just Klara and me who went to the station. It was an enormous red brick building with a metal roof. It was full of people, almost like Leningrad, and they were all making a commotion. There'd been no passenger train departures for days, with military trains being given priority.

"Just as well," Klara said. "The chaos will make it easier for us."

I led her up some stairs and along the corridor to the office of Commandant Khasanov's friend. The woman with the drawer full of passports.

When we got to the door, we heard tapping on the typewriter so the woman had to be inside. We crouched down in the storeroom next to it and waited.

After what felt like ages, the tapping stopped and I heard the woman answer the phone, grumble a bit, then leave her office and head away along the corridor.

"Fingers crossed she didn't lock the door," I thought.

She hadn't.

We went into the office and Klara said, "You keep watch in case she comes back."

"Oh yeah, why do you get to be the one who looks for the passports?"

She pulled a slip of paper out of her pocket. "Because I asked for everyone's names before we left. And you didn't, so you don't know who you're looking for."

S. — Theft of identity documents. Art.195: violation of special rules regarding passports. Art.198.

It was an excellent reason so I crouched down near the door and waited.

Klara took ages, or it felt like it, but then I finally heard her say, "Done!" and saw her clutching a thick bunch of documents.

I took half of them off her to make it easier and just as we were leaving the office, a surly voice shouted, "Hey you, what are you doing in there? Stop where you are!"

We spun on our heels and started running, the railway worker on our tail. We ran down the stairs, I wanted to head for the ticket office but I must've turned the wrong way because we ended up on the platform.

"This way," I said. "Quick."

I jumped down off the platform and zig-zagged through goods trains, over sleepers and rails. Out of nowhere, this awful noise, like a trumpet, came blasting out of one of the wagons. Klara and I got such a fright we nearly fell over. We realized a long elephant's trunk was sticking out of the wagon door. In the next wagon was a lion, and nearby two chattering workers were carrying a cage full of birds.

"Quickly," one of them said. "This train has to go straight back to pick up another load."

For a second I thought the world had gone mad. Klara and I fleeing with a bunch of passports. A furious railway worker on our heels. Workers up ahead, an elephant, a lion and colourful exotic birds all around us.

An idea came to me: I rammed into the worker closest to me and knocked the cage he was carrying to the ground. It flew open and the birds escaped in a whirlwind of feathers.

"Hey, be careful! Those are rare species!" the two men cried while the railway worker chasing us found himself bang in the middle of a rather irate flock of birds. I grabbed Klara's hand, pulled her into the space between the wagons, through to the other side, then away. We were safe.

We met Lev and the others in a public garden. They had their noses deep in loaves of rye bread as long as your arm. You'd think they hadn't eaten for days.

"Don't worry, you two, there's some for you as well," Lev said, waving another loaf of bread in a cloth bag at me. "We stocked up."

"Excellent."

"What about your mission?"

Klara pulled out the bundle of identity papers.

I said, "That's not all," and showed them my surprise, namely the sheet of paper I'd found on the ground, between the trains, during our escape.

"What is it?" Lev asked.

"An old leaflet for Leningrad Zoo. It would appear that as well as evacuating children, they're also shipping animals out of the city. They're bringing them here, to Kazan, believe it or not, we saw a lion and an elephant today. Seriously. The workers said the train's about to go back to Leningrad to pick up another load."

Lev and the others were staring at me, jaws hanging open. Yes, by a bizarre quirk of fate, I'd found us a lift home. So there you have it.

That's how me and the others ended up on this empty train that stinks of camel droppings.

I wonder if I'll manage to find Nadya and how my parents are doing. More than anything, I wonder if I'll actually make it to my destination. The train keeps stopping and starting. It's been days now. Maybe I should just get out and walk.

"Are you joking?" Klara said. "It's nearly one thousand and five hundred kilometres from Kazan to Leningrad."

She was right, but we're all exhausted and there's nothing to do. The bread is running out. Even finding water isn't easy. Every now and then when the train stops, one of us gets out and runs to the nearest ditch with a bucket, terrified the train might suddenly leave before they get back.

There's no one else here but us.

Well, not counting the train drivers up front, on the locomotive, but we keep well out of their way.

You could say we're in charge. Only it's not that much fun.

We just have to be patient. The important thing is to get there.

Sooner or later.

Home.

S. – travel without permission or a proper ticket. Oct.159.

4th September

I don't have much time, and if they find me they'll make me put the candle out in case the enemy sees the light, which would be impossible given that I'm crouched under the priest's desk which has a sheet over it, hanging down to the floor on all sides, and the room only has a tiny window up high beside the bookcase.

Anyway.

The first thing I have to write today is that Mga fell to the enemy. It happened on the 27th or 28th of August after a fierce battle, and this means the enemy has taken control of the last railway station.

"The Germans thought they could use the tracks," a soldier told me yesterday, "but luckily they can't."

"Why not?"

"Because Nazi trains are narrower than Soviet ones. They say they have a 'narrower gauge,' which means they'd fall off our rails."

The soldier who told me this wasn't the officer with the gold-rimmed glasses, the one who showed me the maps the other time. This was a different one. The officer with the glasses left for Mga and never came back.

I think he was killed.

S. – Hail the Fallen Heroes of the Revolution.

I've seen a lot of dead people recently. It was upsetting to begin with and the first few nights I had trouble sleeping, but now it's just normal. I look away and get on with what I'm doing.

There are soldiers everywhere in the village and a lot of them are injured, so many, in fact, that Shlisselburg cathedral is now being used as both general headquarters and hospital, we even have to share our church, St. Nicholas's, with the injured. People in the village try to lend a hand as much as they can.

I help the doctors and the soldiers.

"Baby nurse, bring me some disinfectant!"

"Baby nurse, help me with these bandages!"

"Baby nurse, would you hold my hand?"

I'm not keen on being called "baby nurse" but I don't say anything, because it makes them smile. There are so few smiles in this place.

So basically I run around nonstop and see so many things I could never put into words.

The worst are the screams from the men who're dying. There was one today and it was terrifying. In fact, it was so bad Mrs. Burova went to have a word with the doctor.

"Can't you do something? It's scaring the little ones."

"What can I do, Comrade? We have no drugs, not even vodka."

Luckily, the sick guy died after a bit and it went quiet again.

I never thought the day would come when I'd say something like that.

Anyway.

After Mga was taken, our soldiers tried to win it back but the enemy had Panzers. I don't know what they are but people sound pretty scared when they talk about them. On the 30th of August, the city fell once and for all.

Since then, Shlisselburg is no longer "the rear" but "the front line" and the Nazis have advanced to the banks of the Neva. Planes with crosses on their wings fly over our heads day and night, they're much bigger than the ones Viktor and I saw from the roof of the apartment building back when we were on fire duty. The soldier who gave me this photo says they're called Junkers Ju 88s and are bombers.

They're on their way to destroy Leningrad, where Mama is, I really hope she managed to escape the museum, that she found somewhere safe to hide.

And what about us survivors of train seventy-six?

Well, to tell the truth, we're in terrible trouble.

It's a strange time of year, the days are bright and shiny like metal. It's getting cooler and everything is white and dewy when we wake up. In Leningrad, Mr. Yashkin always used to say that the gods forged the Russian people from ice and vodka, but it's unusual to see ice here in September. It means the winter is going to be harsh.

I don't know if I'll make it to winter.

I'm scared.

Today we had a meeting in St. Nicholas's church. Or rather, the Mothers' Soviet had a meeting and me and the older children asked if we could listen in.

"We have to leave," Irina said. "It's dangerous, the Germans will be here any day now and all will be lost!"

"That's absurd," another woman replied. "Our boys are giving their lives to save Shlisselburg!"

"They did the same in Mga and what use was it? The enemy has armoured Panzers! And our troops have to face them barefoot!"

"Excuse me," I said.

They all looked at me disapprovingly, including my friend Anna, because no one had ever interrupted an emergency meeting of the mothers before.

"What is it, Nadya?" Mrs. Burova said.

"I think our soldiers will save Shlisselburg. They have to, whatever it takes. This is the last outpost on the Neva – if the Germans take the village and the fortress, they'll shut off access to Lake Ladoga. That means Leningrad would be under siege."

"It's already under siege!"

"Yes, but if they manage to fully encircle it, the city

S. – This is unpatriotic!

178

will be lost for good! Our soldiers will do anything they can to stop that."

I showed them the map I'd drawn a few days ago and everyone gathered around me. It was funny to see so many children studying diagrams like expert army generals.

One of the mothers said, "Do you know all I see in this drawing? Proof that the enemy will attack right here. And they'll be more ferocious than ever! Have you heard the stories, do you know what they do in the villages they conquer? If they find us, they'll kill us all. Or worse than that."

Her words hung in the air like sticky fog.

It was around then that the mothers decided the conversation wasn't suitable for children's ears and sent us away. They talked on for hours before Mrs. Burova eventually went to see the army commander and asked if we could leave.

We eavesdropped obviously; they were talking so loudly it wasn't hard.

"It is not permitted to leave the village," the commander said.

"Why?"

"Because there's nowhere else to go. The roads are closed. The enemy is everywhere."

When Mrs. Burova came back, the Mothers' Soviet had another meeting, but it was pointless.

We're stuck here in Shlisselburg.

5th September

Irina ran away last night. She took her baby son and ten of the younger children with her. She left a note saying they had to go, that if they reached somewhere safe, she'd say we were in danger and ask for reinforcements to be sent.

When the other mothers found out, a lot of them were furious, whereas others said they envied Irina for being so brave.

Not me.

Firstly, I can't leave, not when I know Viktor is on his way here to find me.

Secondly, with the excuse of being a nurse, I've managed to speak to a lot of soldiers and even though there are many things they don't want to tell me, I can read it in their eyes. There's no escape.

I spoke to an officer (you can tell the officers apart from the soldiers because the officers usually have a pistol and the others a rifle; or the officers have a rifle and the others nothing). He told me that a patrol came across some bodies near the river and there was a woman and baby among them. They may have been killed by a bomb, or maybe not. I don't know.

Mrs. Burova went with the officer to identify them.

She's not back yet but I already know what she'll say.

It's Irina. She, her child and their bid for freedom, all dead.

S. – defeatism leads nowhere!

7th September

Shlisselburg has been attacked.

It happened at night.

Our room in the church has been given to the injured, so train seventy-six people were squashed into the vestry, the priest's office, the bathroom and the corridors. Since it was so cramped, me, Lilya, Anna, Boris and a few others had fallen asleep sitting up, fully dressed with our bags beside us, ready to escape.

Around dinnertime, more or less, an officer came to warn us, "Listen, the enemy is closing in. He could strike at any time."

"What about us?" Mrs. Burova asked. "What shall we do? Where shall we go?"

"There's nothing you can do and there's nowhere to go," the officer replied. "Stay here, be ready, that's all."

"But what do we do if there's an attack?"

"That depends," the officer said. "If it's an air raid, run outside as fast as you can. If it's not, stay inside and wait. You're safe here – it's our headquarters so we'll defend it to the last man standing."

Mrs. Burova and the officer took a long, hard look at each other.

In her eyes, you could read the question, "What if we lose?" and in the officer's the silent reply, "Pray."

Clearly they couldn't say things like that out loud, it would be defeatism.✳

We were so scared, my friends and I couldn't sleep.

"Do-you-think-it's-true-the-enemy-will-attack-and-bomb-us-and-we'll-all-die?"

I took Lilya's hand, and Anna's, and thought of Viktor. If I die, I wondered, will he feel it with that twin telepathy of his? Will he give up trying to find me? In that case, maybe my death would be a good thing . . .

But I want to live!

It's like every cell in my body is screaming, "Nadya, live! Live! Live!!"

I fell asleep after a while but the rumble of the planes woke me. Then they were buzzing overhead like swarming hornets. Almost immediately we heard explosions that were so violent, the ground shook like an earthquake.

We jumped to our feet and Mrs. Burova threw the vestry doors open, into the big room with all the injured soldiers, and at that exact second a group of officers came in.

"The Germans! They're here!"

"Be prepared!"

No one suggested running away, maybe because they're soldiers and they're brave. I, on the other hand, was so scared all I could think about was getting as far away from there as possible. But where to?

"Everyone out!" someone said. "Before it's too late!"

"Absolutely not," Mrs. Burova replied. "Did you hear what they said? It's safe here. No one is leaving."

That's when Mrs. Dvorkina from the Mothers' Soviet, a woman who never speaks and is always by herself, jumped to her feet and started screaming that we were about to die and that we should surrender and we were just women and children so they wouldn't hurt us.

Mrs. Burova strode over to her and slapped her, twice, on the face. "Pull yourself together, Comrade. You're scaring the children," she said.

Boris grabbed my elbow. "Come on, let's go into the priest's office. There's a window in there, I want to see what's happening."

I went with him and it was this decision that saved my life.

Me, Boris, Anna and Lilya pushed our way through the throng of children, many of whom were crying, all so squashed together it was difficult to get through but, with some gentle pushing and shoving, we made it to the office which no longer had a desk or filing cabinets because we'd moved them all into the garden to free up space.

The bookcase was still there, a beautiful dark wood cabinet pushed up against the wall. The tiny window is very high up so the only way to reach it was to climb up the bookcase; Boris tried but he's too big and the wood creaked dangerously. "You go, Nadya," he said, "it will hold your weight."

I handed him my haversack and climbed up to the window.

"What can you see?"

I saw the river and the road, both in darkness, lots of trees and huge flashes of light which made the sky glow red. There was also a noise, like a low rumble.

"So, what can you see?" Boris asked me again.

I saw planes, so many they filled the sky from one side to the other, like a swarm of metal insects. Then they banked as one, expelling black eggs from their bellies.

"Watch out!" I said. "Bombs on their way!"

I fell off the bookcase, on top of Boris who was standing below and managed to catch me in time.

There was a huge blast and the vestry was blown away: one second it was there, real, just outside the priest's office, the next it was gone, a cloud of smoke left in its place.

My hearing went at that point, my ears filled with a loud ringing and I can't remember exactly what happened, only disjointed scenes, like a series of camera snapshots.

I remember Lilya covered in dust and thinking she looked like a doll that had been buried in the attic.

I remember Mrs. Burova trapped in the rubble and a boy trying to free her.

I remember a dead girl, and it not seeming right that she'd died before I'd had the decency to learn her name.

I think I may have cried, maybe I didn't, someone took my hand and I was no longer in the priest's office but out in the open, in the dark, while more and more planes appeared in the sky, and a soldier pulled a pistol out from under his jacket and began to shoot at the clouds.

The planes banked again, flew back towards the church, and everything became a wall of flames, everything blown away – bricks, cars, tanks, fences, men.

We started running but I can't remember anything other than the fear, the fires and the explosions. After a bit, we arrived at the river, by a tiny run-down farmhouse.

We went inside.

The sun's up now, the battle's not over and I'm writing because, in all the confusion, Boris remembered to grab my bag with these notebooks.

Unfortunately, I think we're losing the battle: the banks of the Neva are on fire. The village seems to be burning, there are columns of black smoke everywhere. So, yes, we're safe for now, but I don't know for how long.

The explosions are getting closer.

Everything is lost.

Later

There are twenty-four of us here in the farmhouse.

There's me, I'm Nadya Nikolayevna Danilova. With me are Anna, Lilya, Boris and Anatoly, Mrs. Burova and another mother called Galina, then Izabella, Mrs. Burova's daughter, and Mrs. Galina's two children, Nina and Vassily (they're only little).

There's also: Arkady, Bogdan, Grigory, Iosif, Valentin, Kristina, Elena, Eva, Evgeny and Maya.

We've also been joined by an old fisherman called Gennady with no teeth, two peasants who are husband and wife and don't speak to anyone, and the chairman of the town soviet, who has a stomach wound and is bleeding.

There, I've written everyone's name.

If we die soon, whoever finds my notebook will be able to notify our families.

If that happens, please tell Mama and Papa that I love them.

And tell Viktor I know. I know he was coming to get me. I've never doubted it, not for a second.

They're here, they're right outside.

Goodbye . . .

CCCP

PEOPLE'S COMMISSARIAT FOR
INTERNAL AFFAIRS

REPORT FOR INTERNAL USE

This is the end of the third notebook
written by Nadya Nikolayevna Danilova.

It is a vivid depiction of one of the
darkest moments in the Great Patriotic War
which exacted such a terrible toll on our
nation.

I feel it is therefore of vital importance
that I continue my examination of the
notebooks because there have already been
clear signs of anti-Soviet propaganda and
numerous criminal acts committed by both the
accused and their associates.

The two rubber stamps - "Innocent" and
"Guilty" - are still here on my desk, beside
my cigarettes and watch.

There can only be one final sentence.

And reaching it is my one responsibility
in this long affair.

Signed:

COLONEL VALERY GAVRIILOVICH SMIRNOV

Col. Smirnov

Viktor's Journey

NOTEBOOK 4

Viktor Nikolayevich has not given any dates in this notebook and many of the pictures seem to have been added at a later time. This may have been an attempt by the accused to throw the investigation off track.

It is not easy to reconstruct the exact sequence of events and place each one in relation to those of the previous and subsequent notebooks.

This notebook nevertheless covers the period from September to the beginning of November 1941.

—Smirnov

By the time we arrived in Moscow, we could hardly stand we were so hungry.

The train had stopped for such a long time, our provisions had run out. In desperation, Lev went hunting for mice. We roasted them in the wagon but skinned them elsewhere, in secret, so as not to upset the younger ones.

"They're birds," Klara had said.

"But they've got four legs!"

"The birds round here are made like that, didn't you know?"

When we eventually saw the buildings of Moscow from the train, some of the group cried.

Not me. I knew the journey had only just begun.

I told them all to be ready and to gather up their bags so that when the train stopped, we could jump out right away. Someone might come to check the wagons so we certainly didn't want to hang around. We hid underneath the wagon, between the wheels.

Just as well.

Our driver had already climbed down from the locomotive and another man was walking towards him.

"You took your time!"

"They kept ordering us to stop," the train driver said. "Any idea why?"

"Oh, that'll be because the Germans took Shlisselburg."

"Where's that?"

"A village on Lake Ladoga. It means Leningrad is surrounded."

"No, really?"

"Yes. Railways blocked, roads taken, bridges blown up along the Neva."

"Have the fascists invaded the city?"

"No. They haven't attacked yet, but they're tightening the blockade. They want to starve the city to death. Bastards."

"Starve them?!"

"No one from our side can get through to Leningrad. Well, only the odd plane, but it has to get through enemy fire. The people will have to survive on what they've got. And winter is coming."

"What about my train? I have orders to go back to Leningrad and pick up more animals from the zoo."

"Well, you can relax, I think you're going to be here for a while. The people of Leningrad may take your elephants and turn them into meat chops."

They both laughed, whereas I, in my hiding place under the wagon, felt myself die inside.

Shlisselburg conquered? What can have happened to Nadya?

"Are you worried about your sister?" Flavio whispered.

I shook my head. "No, no. Nadya's fine. I'm sure of it."

We were filthy and cold. But the even bigger problem was getting something to fill our bellies.

I gave the last of my roubles to Lev and Flavio and sent them to buy food, maybe pick up some more news. The rest of us waited in a park near the station. And waited. I'd always dreamed of coming to Moscow to visit the Kremlin and Gorky Park, but I was too tired now.

Lev and Flavio didn't come back until the afternoon. With very long faces.

192

"What did you get?"

"Nothing."

"Nothing?"

"It took ages to find the right place. But they didn't have anything. People think Moscow will also be captured soon. Everyone's stockpiling food. On top of that . . ."

". . . Our money was stolen," Flavio continued.

"Are you kidding?" Klara screeched.

"I'm afraid not. We found someone who had bread, maybe even half a sausage, but he wanted to see our money first and when he saw it . . ."

". . . He snatched it."

"They're making it up!" Mikhail spat out between clenched teeth. "I bet you spent the money and had a good lunch behind our backs. Isn't that right?"

"Say that again if you've got the guts!"

They were about to start scrapping so I stepped between them. There was no point us fighting each other.

But we still needed to eat.

We started walking, in no particular direction, a gnawing feeling in our stomachs. After a while, we saw some people queuing. It was a rationed goods store.

"What do you say?"

"I say we don't have cards and our Leningrad papers are definitely not going to get us food here in Moscow."

"But we're children!" one of the younger ones protested. "If we go to the police, they'll take care of us!"

"Yes," I said, "that's a good idea if you ask me. Go, why don't you? The fewer there are of us the better."

With that, I set off again along the pavement. A woman came out of the shop with two loaves of bread in a paper bag. It was a tasty-looking rye. I was just thinking I could almost smell the fresh-baked smell when suddenly . . .

Lev bolted past me. He leapt at the woman, knocked

193

her to the ground and snatched the bread from her hands.
Then took off again at full speed.

"Thief!" someone shouted.

Someone reached out to try and grab me.

So I took off as well, behind Lev, after the bread.

When I caught him, I slammed him against the wall.
He made no attempt to defend himself.

"What on earth are you doing?"

"I'm hungry."

Newspaper clipping

"Do you realize what you've just done?" yelled Klara, who had run after me. "Stealing is a serious crime. We could go to prison."

"If they catch us."

"Well, they didn't catch us, but what about the others?"

Klara turned to look back. Of the twenty-eight who were with us from the start, there were now only seven in the alleyway. Me, Klara, Lev, Flavio, Mikhail. A girl called Marya. And Ilya. He was the only one of the younger ones who'd managed to follow us.

"Where are the others?"

"They're back there, that's where they are! They'll kill them!"

"They don't kill children for stealing bread," Lev said. "And don't forget, they didn't steal anything, I did. They just happened to be in the vicinity."

"Yeah, right," Klara stammered.

"Well, what was I supposed to do? I'm sorry, but I'm hungry. I saw the bread and just sort of snapped."

I punched him. Hard, like a man. On his jaw. I sent him flying across the pavement. He spat up blood.

"What you just did is not the act of a communist," I said.

Lev spat again. He picked himself up and looked me in the eye. There were tears in his. "Oh, so you think you're behaving like a good communist, do you? You don't believe the newspapers, you don't obey orders, and you've run away. And because of you, we've all run away. You stole a boat, you stole passports. You've committed <u>hundreds</u> of crimes. Are these all the acts of a good communist?"

I didn't know what to say.

I wiped my hands on my trousers and picked up the bread from the ground. It smelled divine.

"So what do we do now?" Klara asked.

S. – correct. Attack with intent to steal: 15 years. Oct.146.

S. – according to my calculations. Twenty-one crimes have been committed so far.

"We need to leave Moscow."

"Are you kidding?"

"No, I'm not. The others will have been captured by now and wherever they are, we can't help them. What's more, if they're interrogated, they'll tell where we're from and where we're going."

"Do you mean they'll inform on us?"

"What I mean is, they're just kids, for goodness sake! What else can they do? But it means our only option is to cut the cord quickly if we want to save ourselves. We need to go back to the station and get on the first train. And since we have no money for a ticket, we'll have to do it as stowaways."

"I can't abandon Yury," Mikhail said.

"There's nothing you can do to help him. And I need you, so you're coming with me. Even if I have to force you."

Klara looked daggers at me. But what choice did I have?

"Let's eat," I said. "We need to keep our strength up."

"If we eat, we become accomplices," Klara said.

"You're right," I replied.

We all took some bread, we all ate, so quickly we nearly choked. The two loaves were devoured in seconds.

So that's the story.

It took me a while to write it all down but it's not like I'm short of time here on the train.

Ah, yes, the train.

After the business with the bread, we went back to the station and there were no trains for Leningrad. Which wasn't much of a surprise, given that it's under siege. But we found a group of labourers on their way to Rybinsk, which is sort of on the way.

The labourers are being sent to work in a new factory or something like that. We managed to blend into the group. The girls did their hair and sorted their clothes to make themselves look older, and Lev and Flavio are pretty tall anyway. The big problem was Ilya, but we agreed he could be someone's younger brother. Well, to cut a long story short, we got ourselves into the group. It was easy, all we had to do was join the queue of passengers, give the soldiers our names (false ones obviously!). They didn't even look at our papers. It was a real stroke of luck because in the Soviet Union, <u>everyone</u> looks at your papers <u>all</u> the time.

So we left Moscow, and our friends, behind.

And Klara hasn't spoken to me since.

Girls can be so stupid sometimes.

But why do I feel like I'm the stupid one?

S. – difficult to believe such a breach of procedure could occur. Is there something more to this?

I just wanted to be a good brother.

A good Pioneer.

A good son, a good student. A good friend.

Instead, everything I do goes wrong.

Or maybe not.

Maybe it's the world that's all wrong. And I just hadn't noticed before.

We're stuck in Rybinsk, in the centre of Russia. Six hundred kilometres from Leningrad and from my sister Nadya.

We've been here for three weeks and it's the first time I've managed to write anything in my notebook (it's dangerous! Someone might see me). I've no idea how to get out of here and get on with my journey.

Everything has gone wrong.

To begin with, we were happy. We'd found a train heading north. It was moving quickly and on time, as much as that's possible.

Obviously it wasn't that comfortable. The windows had bars on them. There was just the usual hole in the floor for a toilet. But compared to the trains we'd been on before, you could say this one almost felt luxurious.

Our travel companions, on the other hand, were a different story. I didn't like them at all. There were two

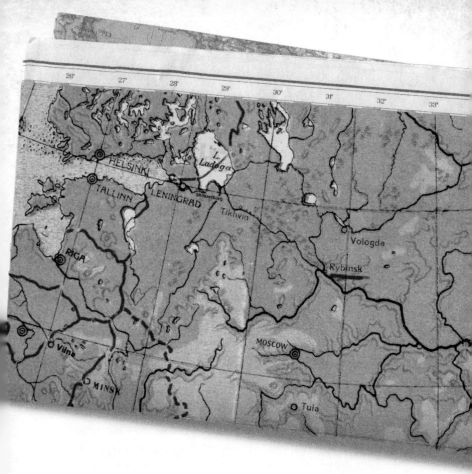

types: those with scars and those with dead eyes. Both equally dangerous.

After the first few days, we had the distinct impression they were watching us.

"Let's just keep away from them and we'll be all right," I said to the others one night.

Klara, who was sitting opposite, heaved a sigh.

"What's up?"

"Lev, please. Would you tell Viktor that what he said is just plain stupid."

Lev spat on the floor. "Klara says that . . ."

"Lev, would you ask Klara why it's so stupid?"

"Lev, explain to him that if we don't speak to the other passengers, we'll never know where we're going and what to expect, so we can't plan anything."

"Lev, explain to Klara that . . ."

"Hey, hey, hey," Lev said. "Would you two just start speaking again. You're giving me a headache!"

A man sitting near us, wearing glasses and with the look of a librarian, glanced up just then. "You want to know what to expect? They make you work until you drop. And then you drop. That's what happens."

"Are you a labourer?" I asked.

"Me? No, I'm a librarian," he replied.

"Isn't this a train for labourers?"

"Ha, ha. That's not funny."

"I'm sorry, but aren't we going to Rybinsk?"

"No, we're going to the GES."

The GES is a hydro-electric power plant which, when completed, will supply power to a huge chunk of the Soviet Union.

Rybinsk is at the crossing point of two huge rivers, the Volga and the Sheksnà. Engineers have built dams and flooded the plain. There's now a thirty-metre-deep reservoir where there used to be trees, houses and fields. They call it the "Rybinsk Sea."

The force of the water pressing on the dams generates electricity. They're going to switch the first turbine on at the end of October.

"Didn't you know?" the librarian asked us. "Are you seriously trying to tell me you have no idea what kind of train this is?"

"Erm, well, actually . . . we didn't stop to ask," I mumbled. "We . . . we didn't really mind what the work was."

"Stop messing around."

We weren't messing around, anything but. I was beginning to get worried. So I pressed the man to tell us more.

That's when he whispered, "This is a train for convicts sentenced to hard labour. They're taking us to the gulag."

Me, Lev, Flavio and Klara, Mikhail, Marya, even little Ilya, had all heard this word before.

Without realizing, we've joined a group of prisoners going to a forced labour camp.← _S. - The notorious Rybinsk camp!_

I felt sick.

This couldn't be happening. It had to be a mistake, a mistake, a mistake.

I went up and down the train looking for someone. To explain our situation.

I came across some soldiers playing cards. Their compartment had an iron grating across the doorway.

"Help," I cried from the other side. "I shouldn't be here! It's all a mistake!"

"Oh, come on. That's not a very original story."

"Can't you come up with something better?"

"But it's true. I'm only twelve years old! I want to speak to someone! Please!"

They weren't listening and carried on with their game. I kept shouting until one of the soldiers finally opened the grating and came out. He lifted his rifle and slammed it into my head. Everything went black and I fell to the ground.

I never thought a single blow could hurt so much.

"If you come around here again, I swear I'll shoot you. One less of you isn't going to make much difference, is it? Who would notice?"

That's when I realized. There was no hope.

We'd become prisoners, too.

"Get out."

"One at a time."

"Give the clerk your names."

"One at a time."

"Hand over your valuables."

"One at a time."

The queue moved at a snail's pace.

"Like heck I'll give them my name and my belongings," Lev whispered.

I agreed with him.

Only Klara and I had bags but we also had nice clothes which was rare among the prisoners. We took out the bundle of identity papers and other things and stuffed them all in my bag which we gave to Ilya. He put it on his back and it made him look hunchbacked. But no one ever pays any attention to children. Klara even took his hand for effect, like an older sister, as they walked past.

We were assigned to a barrack to sleep in.

"I don't want to live in a barrack," Ilya said.

"I lived in one in Leningrad and it wasn't that bad," Lev said.

The barracks here are actually much worse than the ones Lev lived in. There's barbed wire around them and they're overlooked by watchtowers and NKVD soldiers with dogs and rifles.

Klara and Marya were sent to a women's barrack while we were put in with the men. Convicted criminals. They stole our shoes the minute they clapped eyes on us, all except Ilya's that is, because his feet are too small. But it's okay, once you know how it works between the ordinary criminals, you can survive. The political prisoners are guarded night and day, life's much harder for them.

"I'll tell you this once. Every morning you come to me, I tell you the daily work quota, you fulfil the quota, you eat. You don't fulfil the quota, you don't eat."

This is what the foreman told us the first morning in the gulag, it was like being back in the kolkhoz.

Only colder. And nastier. It was raining and there was mud everywhere.

My work quota was to shift ten tons of gravel from one side of the field to the other. That meant loading up the wheelbarrow then pushing hundreds, thousands, millions of stones.

I ripped my hands to shreds and broke my back. By the time night fell, I hadn't even done half my quota but I was so tired I wanted to cry. I'd never felt so hungry.

"No quota, no dinner," the foreman said.

My friends did just as badly as me. No one managed to finish. Lev had gotten the closest but his hands were raw.

I went back to the men's barrack, starving, my stomach cramping.

"Listen," Lev said. "We have to think of something or it'll be the same tomorrow. And the day after. We'll die."

He was right. People die in their hundreds here and the ones still living look like they're not long for this world either.

"Any ideas?" I said.

"I've got one," Flavio replied. "Let's join forces. If we count the girls as well, there are seven of us. There's no way we can finish seven quotas a day. But if we work together, we should manage three. Maybe four. And split the food between us."

"They say that if you repeatedly fail to reach your quota, you get punished."

"Well, we'll take it in turns to finish," I said. "One day we'll do Klara and Flavio's quota, the next day Mikhail and Ilya's . . . and so on."

"Good idea."

It was an excellent idea. But if it was to work, we needed all the girls to agree to it.

I sneaked over to their barracks. I had my doubts because Klara hadn't spoken to me since I'd abandoned all the others in Moscow.

"Hey there," I said. "I . . ."

She threw herself at me and clung on tight. "Viktor, I can't take it anymore. I can't stay here."

Her face was hot on my neck and I could feel my shirt wet with her tears.

"Yes you can, you can do it," I said. "It's not for long. You just have to hold on. We'll get out of here soon, I promise you."

I also think we need to get out of here as soon as possible. But there are a few hurdles to overcome:

- Distance: Leningrad is a long way away and there are no trains. It will take weeks on foot;
- Equipment: winter's coming. We need heavy clothes. Food. Maybe a weapon;
- Escape: NKVD soldiers guard the gulag. We need an escape plan and I don't have one.

I need to come up with something. But what?

Next day

I'd like to know what day it is today so I can write it in here. Nadya will want to know the dates so she can say things like, "Oh, you were working in the gulag when I was resting," or "You were on the train at the same time I was on the train."

The truth is I don't know what day it is, so all I can write is "next day." Nothing more.

The important thing is I have news.

Lev and Flavio have gotten to know some of the convicts from Moscow. They're Article 58s, "political" prisoners in other words.

"You can't trust people like that," I said.

"Think about it," Flavio insisted. "You want to escape and so do they. Who wants to break out more than they do?"

"The problem is they are *proper* criminals. We'd only end up in trouble."

"We're already in trouble. Just by being here. But they have a plan."

"They're digging a tunnel," Lev explained. "It starts below women's barrack five and goes under the perimeter fence and runs west for a bit before it comes up in those woods near the river, remember? They've been working on it for ages. In secret. At night. They've already gone under the fence and it won't be long until they reach the trees where we'll be safe from the searchlights."

"So why did they tell you and Flavio about it?" I asked, a bit suspicious.

"Because when they're digging they end up with a lot of earth under their feet and they need someone to take it out of the barrack without being noticed. So we're helping them."

He turned out his trouser pockets. They were grimy with soil.

"It'll take about another ten days probably," Lev said. "Then we'll escape."

"I don't know," I replied.

It was the truth. I didn't know and will have to think about it.

5. - imprisoned for counter-revolutionary activity.

Lev was right. Joining forces with the Article 58s is our only chance.

I don't want to describe what happens here at the gulag because it's so awful. But the men are no longer men. They turn into something different. Something savage and cruel.

I'm getting thinner and Ilya is like a walking skeleton.

So yes, we have to get out of here.

Before winter comes.

Another day

This morning they made us unload the trucks with supplies for the kitchens.

It's the job everyone wants because the NKVD agents never notice if you take a rest or snaffle something. Not that I'm saying they're kind or anything! They're just too busy stealing what they can for themselves, pocketing dried fish, sugar and as many tins as they can. S. —*sland*

I was put to work with Mikhail. We had to carry heavy sacks between the two of us, him at the front, me at the back. But he kept dropping them.

It was driving me mad because I thought he was doing it on purpose. So the first chance I got, I grabbed him and rammed him up against the wall of one of the barracks.

I'm strong and Mikhail is weak. But it surprised me how light he was. It was like squeezing a bird.

"What's going on with you today?"

"I'm tired and I'm hungry."

"We're all tired and hungry. But if you don't work you'll get us all into trouble."

"And?" Mikhail was crying. Tears squeezed through his eyelashes. "Are you scared the NKVD will start

S. – *interruption of labour in a correctional facility, punishable under Art. 77.1.*

watching you? That I'll ruin your secret plan to escape through the tunnel the convicts are digging?"

I was shocked. I let him go and he crumpled to the ground, flat on his back like a stink bug.

"What, Viktor, did you think I didn't know? Well, I do, because I listen. And I also know you don't want to take me with you."

"So why didn't you inform on us?"

"Because I . . ." He sniffed. "I want to come. If I stay here, I'll die."

"No way."

"You have to say yes because even if I haven't informed so far, I could always do it."

"And I'll kill you," I said.

The threat just slipped out. I never thought I'd say something like that but I did. And I meant it.

"You won't do it because I know things about Anna Tereshenkov and you need to hear them to understand what happened to train seventy-six and find your sister. Me and Yury haven't told you everything yet."

"I could force you."

"If you hit me the guards will come and even then, I could still tell you a lie. But if you let me come with you, I swear I'll tell you the truth." He was so pale he looked almost blue. "Listen, Viktor. There's never been any love lost between the two of us and I was wrong to leave the kolkhoz and . . . well, it doesn't matter now. But I have something you want, and you have something I want. If you leave me here, you're leaving me to die. So let's make a pact."

He held out his hand.

"All right then," I said.

I shook it. The pact was sealed.

S. — in this chapter, the accused, Viktor, confesses to plotting with prisoners to escape from a labour camp. This boy is clearly guilty a hundredfold and events hitherto described are more than enough to sentence him forthwith and be done with it.

Winter is on its way and with it comes the enemy.
He'll sweep everything away.
People, thoughts, my world as I knew it
will never be the same again.
Everything will be destroyed.

But I'm still alive.

I'll wait under the first snow,
like coals
under a veil of ash.
I am Nadya.
And I'm here.

S. – This page must have been
written in September 1941. My
sources report the first real sno
of the year fell on 15th October
Verify.

Klara has made friends with one of the cooks.

I don't like the way he looks at her, and from what I can tell, she doesn't like it either.

"Keep away from him."

"I can't," she said. "He's getting us food for our escape."

Klara is getting thinner and paler. But she's right. When she goes to the cook she always comes back with something.

Lev, on the other hand, is turning out to be a real expert at trading, he managed to procure boots for himself, Flavio and me.

"I want boots too," Mikhail said. "I can give you this in exchange," he said, and showed me an army knife with a serrated blade.

I asked him where he got it and he said he took it from an NKVD officer.

I don't believe that (the NKVD guy could easily have taken Mikhail out first) but it doesn't matter: I promised him I'd find him some boots. Or I'll give him mine and I'll make some cloth ones like the other prisoners do. All that matters is that I'm armed to the teeth. ←

I'm going to make it back to Leningrad. I can feel it.

S. – procuring illegal items. Art. 208; illegal possession of a bladed weapon. Art. 218.

S. - photo of a labour camp. This is confidential
documentation ... How did Viktor get it?

Two days later

We're going to escape tomorrow at the last siren. The
prisoners will line up as usual in front of the kitchens,
but we'll go back to our barracks to get our things, then to
barrack five. That's where the tunnel is that will take us
out of the camp, under the fence and over to the woods.
When we make it there, the prison inmates will go one
way and we'll go the other. As fast as we can. Never to
be seen again.

I'm worried because we haven't finished our prepar-
ations. We don't have coats, gloves or hats. And I don't
know how long my cloth boots will hold up.

There's something else bothering me: Lev and Flavio

have made all the arrangements for the escape but whenever I ask them for details, they're a bit evasive.

Klara brought it up yesterday. "There's something funny going on."

"Do you think we're going to end up in trouble?"

"Trouble? No! We're escaping from a gulag with a group of Article 58 convicts, then we have to cover six hundred kilometres on foot to get to a city that's under siege. What could possibly go wrong?" She smiled and ruffled my hair. It was an unusual gesture. Like something Mama used to do. "You're convinced we can make it, aren't you? That you'll find your sister and everything will be all right."

"Yes," I replied. "I really believe it."

We'll go tomorrow after our shift.

And we'll make it.

Two days later

We're out. ✷

It's pitch black and I'm writing this in a hunter's cabin in the forest. I'm exhausted. The others are all sleeping and the candle has nearly burnt out, but I want to write down everything that happened to make sure I remember it correctly.

I'd like to say our escape went as smooth as oil. But things started going wrong from morning roll call.

"You children, report to the main storehouse."

The storehouse is by the river. It's immense and always crowded. There are steel beams the height of the ceiling and cases of iron bars, bolts and cogwheels.

"At least we'll not freeze to death here," Flavio said.

"Don't you get it?" I said. "We're too far away from the barracks now. It'll waste precious time this evening to get back."

(handwritten in margin:) ✶ S. – escape. Oct. 188.

They had us pushing wheelbarrows back and forth for hours and we were so jumpy no one reached their quota. Not that it mattered, we wouldn't be at dinner anyway.

When the siren went, we dropped everything and dashed away.

I went to get my haversack with the notebooks, shoved our papers in and made sure I had Papa's silver icon in my pocket.

After that we met Klara outside the girls' barrack.

"Everyone ready?"

"Follow me."

We went over to barrack five. So far so good. It was only when we knocked on the door that a voice from inside told us to shove off.

We kept knocking. There was no reply. I threatened to sound the alarm. That's when the door opened and I was yanked inside.

A man punched me hard in the stomach. I rolled on the ground and threw up on the carpet. The man dragged me up and slapped me around.

"So you're going to sound the alarm, are you?"

"He was just bluffing," Lev butted in.

"Huh? Well I don't care."

The guy had a shaved head and no teeth, like an old man.

"Come on, Karl," Lev said. "I'll vouch for him. You can trust him."

"I don't care. What's he doing here? What are you all here for?"

Lev's face went red at that point.

Flavio coughed. "We thought we'd escape, too."

Karl started to laugh. "Why on earth would you think that?"

"We helped you carry the earth out . . ."

"That doesn't mean you can use the tunnel."

"But we earned it!"

"Who gives a toss!" Karl said.

Who knows how it might have ended had we not heard, right at that moment, a scratching noise. It was coming from the bunk at the other end of the barrack, then a bench moved. A dusty face popped out of the ground.

It was a woman.

"Karl, get a move on!"

"We have a problem."

He put a bar across the inside of the barrack door and went to speak to the woman.

I stepped forward. "Sorry to interrupt, but if we don't hurry up dinner will be over and we'll all be in trouble."

"He's right," the woman said.

"We won't be a bother. We'll follow you to the end of the tunnel then we'll go our own way, I promise."

"Really? And where will you go?"

"Leningrad."

They both laughed. "Don't you know there's a war in Leningrad?"

"Yes, but our families are there. And my sister. I prom-ised I wouldn't leave her."

"What a brave little brother."

"Listen," Karl said to the woman. "What should we do? Do you want me to kill them?"

"They're just kids. I have a better idea." She turned to me. "Open that bag and show me what's inside it."

Luckily I'd hidden the important things elsewhere, like the knife and the silver icon, but the woman stole all the rest, including my foot wraps. All she left were the notebooks. She obviously didn't need them.

She robbed my friends as well. "Well, that's your fare paid," she sneered. "You can follow me now. Karl, you bring up the rear and cover the hole. We've wasted too much time already and the others are waiting."

Whoops!

I had to stop writing because the candle went out but I've lit another one now. Or the stump of one anyway.

I was saying . . . We dropped down into the hole below the barrack. The way Lev and Flavio had described it, I was expecting a wide, well-lit tunnel. It was actually so narrow it was like crawling through an intestine, and we had to slither along on our elbows.

It was dark down there. Freezing cold and dark, and difficult to breathe. Like being in a grave.

I stopped to catch my breath and felt Klara's face slam into my feet.

"Disgusting! Warn me before you do that again so I don't have to kiss your manky trotters!"

"Not everyone gets the chance to kiss the feet of Viktor Danilov," I replied.

"Well, tell Viktor Danilov that he should try washing his feet a little more often."

It made me laugh. And Klara and the others behind her, and for a few brief moments the fear melted away. Until the woman barked, "Be quiet. If someone hears us, we're all dead."

That journey through the tunnel was the most horrific thing I've ever done in my life. When I got to the end, I was close to freezing but two hands pulled me out. I found myself in a small copse. There were twenty or so men and women around me, all in prison uniforms.

"What are they doing here?" one of them asked, glaring at me.

"They paid their way," the woman grunted.

"Are you sure they paid enough? Because those look like nice warm sweaters they're wearing."

The man reached out for Klara and I didn't stop to think about it. I kicked him in the groin then turned to the others coming out of the tunnel. "Let's go."

We set off at speed through the woods but we'd only gone a hundred metres or so when we heard a wailing noise, like a slaughtered animal.

The alarm siren.

"They know we've gone!" came a shout from behind.

"Someone informed on us!"

"They'll come after us with dogs! We'll never survive."

The convicts forgot about our sweaters and fled in one direction while we went in the other, in the pitch dark. Our way lit only by the light of the stars.

I hadn't run for a long time and it was hard trying to do it in the mud. My heart was in my throat which was tight with fear.

But I ran, Lev on one side, Flavio on the other, Klara, Ilya, Marya and Mikhail all behind me, while I thought about the dogs. The dogs. The dogs.

The NKVD guard dogs were terrifying: black and big as bears, with shiny teeth. At the camp people said the guards didn't feed them to make them more vicious. Nothing escapes their noses.

"The soldiers will come as far as the forest then the dogs will pick up our trail. They'd find us even in hell," Lev said.

"We need to mask our smell!" Klara cried.

"Yes, but how?" Ilya whimpered.

Two ideas came to me. The first one was the river but it was too far away and, more importantly, it was freezing. If you dive into the Volga at this time of year, you may not come out alive.

The second one was . . . disgusting. But it could work.

"Follow me," I said.

I turned around and headed in the opposite direction. Back the way we'd come. Towards the camp.

"Are you mad?"

"Trust me."

As we raced back towards the fence, I could see everything. The searchlights cutting through the night from the towers. Guards with rifles. Dogs barking.

I veered at the first divide in the path and took the one going to the gulag power plant. But I wasn't aiming for that or the storehouses. I was going to the latrines.

"Oh no," Klara said. "You can't be serious . . ."

"Do you have a better idea?"

I won't describe the latrines building here because it would be too revolting. But, Nadya, when you read this, imagine a place with no windows and a dirt floor with huge ditches dug into it, three feet wide by five feet deep. And imagine that the ditches hold five years' worth of human waste from thousands of prisoners.

The stench was so suffocating no one used it anymore, people preferred to do their business out in the open, even in the dead of winter. I'd heard guards talk about knocking it down and filling the ditches with sand as soon as possible. But it was still there, in all its putridness.

"Viktor, no offence, but I'm not going in there."

"Well, sit back and get captured then."

"But it stinks!"

"I know. That's how we'll save ourselves."

I opened the door of the latrines. The smell knocked me back like a slap in the face. But I steeled myself and we all went in. I shut the door behind us.

The latrine shack was five hundred metres from the camp but there was nothing in between, so we had a clear sight line through the chinks in the wall to what was happening at the main gates of the gulag. Trucks, cars and mounted guards were heading towards the forest.

"I think I'm going to be sick," Marya said.

"If you need to, go ahead. The smell can't get any worse."

I laughed and so did the others. I'd like to think it helped us forget the smell but it didn't, it was just too overpowering. But we held out.

After a while we heard sounds of running and barking. We clung onto each other in a dark corner. Something scratched on the door which, luckily, I'd bolted from the inside. Then a voice. "What have you found, Don?"

The dog barked.

"You want to go into the latrines? Are you mad?"

Another voice. "The escaped prisoners must've had a dump this morning and the stink stuck to them . . ."

"Yeah, you're probably right. But there's no way I'm going in there. Did you hear that, Don? We're not going in."

"You can smell it from here."

The dog barked again then we heard an engine and a screech of tyres. Someone shouted, "Time to head back! We've got them!"

"All of them?"

"Yeah, we got the lot."

There was more running, this time away from us and I peeked through the slits in the wall again. I saw two NKVD officers with the dog and an open truck. The Article 58s were lying in the back in their grey prison jackets.

"They got them," I said. "They'll come for us now."

"No they won't," Klara said. "The smell will have thrown them off our track."

"But when Karl tells them we were with them . . ."

Lev lay a hand on my shoulder. "He won't. Why would he? He'll keep the secret. Anyway, it doesn't matter, we're not really escaping because we'd never been sentenced to be there. We never gave our real papers to the camp commandant: we're just some false names on a list. They'll delete them. Make it look like we died at work or of hunger or fell in the river. It happens, doesn't it? I don't think the NKVD will come after us. If you ask me, no one will ever look for us now."

"And Karl and the others . . . what will happen to them?" Ilya asked.

I didn't reply, it seemed better that way. Better not to think of their fate.

So that's what happened. We waited a few hours then went outside. The air was so cold it hurt our lips. And so pure I cried with joy.

We ran off as fast as we could, and when we were far enough away, we rubbed our faces, necks and hands with mud to get rid of the smell of the latrines.

It wouldn't go away. But we didn't care.

Freedom had never smelt so good.

The island is shaped like a bullet, it's four hundred and fifty metres long and fifty metres wide. The fortress occupies the entire island, the walls reach down to the shore more or less.

There used to be several tall watchtowers but there are only a few left now. The other buildings inside the fortress, like the prisons and the army barracks with soldiers' quarters, etc., are pretty much in ruins.

In the middle of the island there's a church.

Here's a picture.

It's quite a long story why we're here and how we're still alive.

On the night between the 7th and 8th of September, the enemy attacked the city of Shlisselburg, causing the last remaining troops of the 48th Soviet Army to flee.

It all started when I saw the planes out of the window. There was a huge blast and me, Anna, Lilya, Boris and a few others took refuge in the farmhouse by the river.

I don't know how long we hid there but it must've been ages because, in the meantime, the enemy took the village and the air shook so much with all the explosions I thought I'd go deaf.

Then we heard noises outside and were sure the soldiers were coming to get us. But they weren't. They weren't there for us.

Orders were being shouted in a language I didn't know and it was only afterwards I realized it was German. Me, Anna, Lilya and the others were terrified, in our hiding place in the kitchen. Mrs. Galina was holding a hand over the mouths of her young children so they wouldn't make any noise, the chairman of the town soviet was dripping blood on the floor, blood so dark it was almost black, and I knew the enemy would soon find us and kill us.

So, not because I was being brave, perhaps because I was more scared than everyone else, I sneaked out of my hiding place and slithered as quietly as I could across to the window.

I saw soldiers in grey uniforms and coal-scuttle helmets pushing lines of people. At the front were our companions from train seventy-six, crying, then Mrs. Dvorkina and her daughter Raisa, tied up and forced to walk behind, then more people from the village, about twenty or thirty in total, carrying a long steel pole.

The soldiers were shouting and you could tell they

S. – incorrect. The 48th triumphed and strategically ceded ground to the enemy.

220

wanted the prisoners to go faster. They made them plant the steel post in the ground but before they raised it, they attached two more poles in the shape of a cross at the top of it, so it looked like one of those electricity pylons. I had no idea what something like that might be for and since the soldiers were behind the trees, I couldn't really see what was going on.

I'm so glad I couldn't.

Because, just after that, the Germans grabbed four people – Mrs. Dvorkina and her daughter were among them.

They hanged them, one from each of the four arms of the post.

I couldn't stop myself from screaming and Boris put one of his big hands over my mouth.

"Sssh," he said. "Silence, Nadya, quiet. It's okay."

Instead of feeling happy that Boris was there, it made me mad. My face turned red, I think I bit his hand, I wanted to know why he wasn't doing anything when those soldiers had just killed our companions.

"They were civilians," I said, "civilians, not soldiers like them, why . . ."

"Sssh," Boris whispered.

"Why . . .? WHY?"

"Because they were Jews," Mrs. Burova murmured quietly. "I know because Mrs. Dvorkina told me. She was afraid because the Nazis hate the Jews. And now . . ."

I began to sob and Boris pressed my head into his chest, in a rough embrace. It felt like getting a hug from a tree.

I'd like to say that crying made me feel better but it didn't. I would probably have cried for a long time if Mrs. Burova hadn't suddenly said, "Bad news."

What could be any worse than this, I wondered, until I heard another round of gunfire and understood.

"They're searching the village, from house to house."

"We're not Jews," Boris stammered.

"No," Mrs. Burova said. "But we have the chairman of the town soviet here. And, in any case, do you want to be captured by people who have just done *that*?"

I thought to myself, I don't know about Boris, but I certainly don't.

We had to get away.

But where to? And how, given that there were soldiers everywhere?

I went back to looking out the window and I saw the fortress in the middle of the river. With its ramparts and watchtowers.

"Oreshek," I murmured. "We could hide on Oreshek."

"We need a boat," Mrs. Burova said.

I remembered the boat me and my friends had used to cross the canal the day we went fishing. It wasn't exactly close to the farmhouse but it wasn't far either, maybe five hundred metres, a few minutes on foot . . .

"Nadya, that's crazy!" Mrs. Burova said.

"If you have anything less crazy in mind, let's hear it."

I could see she was getting angry, she doesn't like cheeky girls, but it was too critical a moment for good manners.

"I can go," Boris said.

"We'll go together."

"No, you're not coming."

"I certainly am. You'll have to put the boat in the water and drag it here without anyone seeing you. It's too difficult to do alone."

"Nadya's right," Mrs. Burova said. "But she can stay here. I'll go with you."

All three of us went in the end.

Anyway.

Maybe this is a good time to describe Mrs. Burova, given that I've mentioned her a lot but not told you much about her.

Her full name is <u>Natasha Yuryevna Burova</u>, she's thirty-nine and is extremely tall – taller than lots of men – with long black hair and eyes the colour of ice. She has a daughter called Izabella who's just three years old and the best behaved child in the world, but that's to be expected because Mrs. Burova is very strict, and it's no surprise either that she's head of the Mothers' Soviet (or was, given that the Mothers' Soviet no longer exists).

Until that moment, I'd never realized she was also brave, but she took her shoes off, rolled up her skirts so they wouldn't get in the way, and the three of us crawled outside.

The sun was high in the sky. I looked around, worried a soldier might appear from the end of the street and shoot us.

We slipped into the bushes and made our way to the boat. The motor would clearly have made too much noise so Boris and I got into the river, our feet sinking into the mud, and we pushed the launch towards the farmhouse while Mrs. Burova helped by pulling on the mooring rope from the bank.

I stayed with the boat as lookout and Boris and Mrs. Burova went inside. They were away for ages. I was terrified something had happened or that someone would find me, every noise making me jump like a cricket and think I was about to die.

Finally they began to slowly emerge, first Lilya and Anna holding onto each other, then the older children, Gennady the fisherman, the peasant couple, followed at the back by the smaller children, second last was Anatoly, who'd broken a leg and had to hop on his healthy one, then finally Mrs. Burova, who was carrying the wounded chairman. Boris had the haversack containing my diaries over his shoulder. I'd asked him to get them because I could never let them fall into enemy hands.

We all hid in the trees and Gennady the fisherman realized what we were planning. "This boat is only meant to carry eight people," he whispered. "There are twenty-four of us. We'll have to make two trips at least."

"We can't," Mrs. Burova said. "When we get out to the middle of the river, the soldiers will see us and start to shoot. If we're fast enough, we can make it. But a second trip is out of the question."

"There are too many of us," Gennady insisted. "The current is very strong close to the island, it will rock the boat and fill it with water. We'll drown."

"Well, we can tie barrels onto the back and the older ones can hold on to those."

"It's madness," Gennady said.

"If you have a more sensible idea then I'd like to hear it," Mrs. Burova replied. She turned to me and winked.

Mrs. Burova and the fisherman went back into the house and found ropes and some old barrels whose bottoms had half fallen out and which stank of dried fish.

There was no time to lose so we hurried everyone onboard, starting with those who definitely couldn't swim, like the small children and Anatoly with his broken leg.

In the end there were sixteen of us on the boat. The fisherman said we couldn't take any more because we were lying too low in the water. Eight people were left out, namely Boris, the fisherman himself, the peasant man and Mrs. Burova, along with Arkady, Bogdan, Evgeny and Grigory who were all thirteen and pretty strong.

We realized, however, that there was no one on the boat who knew how to steer it so we had to swap – Gennady came onboard and me and Lilya had to get out to make room for him.

"It's-all-right-because-I-can-swim-really-well-I-went-to-the-swimming-pool-all-the-time-in-Moscow," my friend blurted.

"I can swim, too," I said. "It'll be okay, you'll see."

Gennady had secured the three barrels to the boat so that they floated off the back, out of the way of the propeller, like kite tails.

Mrs. Burova then tied the "swimmers" to the barrels with another rope, there were three of us to each barrel, I found myself beside Boris and Lilya.

"Let's go, everyone in the water," Mrs. Burova said. "And watch out, it's very cold."

To say that the water was cold doesn't come close to expressing how freezing it was. The second I stepped in I thought I'd die.

My teeth were chattering as Gennady slipped the mooring and set to starting up the motor.

"Watch out," he said. "This contraption will make a bit of a racket and that could be a problem."

He'd no sooner warned us than the motor began to splutter and spit out black smoke before finally revving to life with a shriek and a roar, the propeller cutting through the water in a fizz of air bubbles. The boat lurched forward, yanking the barrels with it and very nearly strangling me in the rope.

"We're too heavy!" Gennady shouted. "It's too much for the motor! You people on the barrels: swim! Swim for your life!"

But my legs felt like jelly, I was cold and every time Boris and Lilya moved, they banged into me again and again. At one point I even ended up with my head under the water and the others had to flip the barrel over to fish me out.

I swivelled my head round to see how far we'd come and realized we'd hardly moved. We were still close to the shore, the fortress miles away and the current carrying us off in the wrong direction.

We kept swimming though, following Gennady's instructions, and all I could see was the foam around the propeller, the faces of the children on the boat and a brief glimpse of the sun, it was so cold. All of a sudden I heard shouting.

It took me a few seconds to work out it was coming from the shore, and a few more to understand it was in German.

Lilya was the first to say it. "They've-seen-us, they've-seen-us-help!"

She didn't say anything else.

Because there was a blast, deafeningly loud.

And the water turned red.

The barrel spun around like a bullet and Lilya ended up under it. By the time Boris and I managed to get it straight again, she'd gone.

Vanished.

I went under as well at that point, Boris yanked me, I could feel the barrel bucking like an injured horse, there were more shots, I saw someone from the boat topple into the water (only later I realized it was the peasant's wife), I heard Mrs. Burova scream, "We're nearly there, keep swimming!" and Gennady saying, "You're slowing down, you're holding us back!"

From the shore I heard laughter. Bullets pinged off the river like slaps, others hit us.

I cried.

Gennady pulled out a knife, "I'm sorry," he said and cut a rope. One of the three barrels broke away from the boat and floated away, like a stone skimming across the water.

The launch, lighter now, lurched forward and I heard Mrs. Burova scream beside me, "You son of a bitch!" I'd never heard her curse before and it sounded strange, even then.

More shots were fired from the shore and someone in the boat screamed, another body fell into the water, I didn't know who, I hoped it wasn't one of my friends, but who else could it be? They were all my friends now.

The boat was moving so slowly.

The river was so big and bright.

We were like a sitting target for the soldiers on the riverbank. We got it all wrong, I thought, we should've set off at night. We never should have gone now.

There was another huge blast, it almost made me let go of my barrel. I would have died for sure if I had.

Then I heard the enemy shouting on the shore, but this time the voices sounded agitated, and Anna on the boat was shouting, "Cannons! They're shooting from the fortress, they're defending us!"

And so they were. There was someone on the island and they were providing covering fire for our escape.

I swam and swam for what felt like ages, I couldn't feel anything anymore, nothing except shooting pains, like needles, all over my body, and Boris still beside me, his lips had turned blue.

Someone eventually wrenched on our rope and pulled us alongside the boat. Arms reached out to lift us and drag us onboard. I lay gasping on the bottom of the boat, like a landed fish, staring up at the sky, the other children's feet all around me.

Then the boat touched land.

More hands carried me ashore and I heard Mrs. Burova scream at Gennady, "What have you done?!"

Gennady replied, "The folk on the third barrel were already dead. They were holding us back, like an anchor."

"You can't be sure of that."

"I saved our lives."

"Damned coward of a man. You just wanted to save yourself!"

Mrs. Burova was so angry, for a second I thought she might hit him, but instead she whirled around and strode away, dripping water and tears.

I sat and watched her, unable to think about anything except Lilya. She'd come to Leningrad on holiday and wanted to go home, but she never would. Never again. Because the river had taken her.

The end.

Or maybe not.

There's a chance that, despite everything, this could be just the beginning.

The Oreshek fortress hadn't been abandoned after all, clearly, or at least not completely.

A few days ago, the Lake Ladoga Fleet Command sent twelve Soviet sailors to the island on a motorboat to bring back supplies and munitions.

When the German planes launched their attack, the twelve sailors hid in the cellars under the King's Tower, but when they heard the noise of the battle in Shlisselburg, they ran outside to see what was happening. They couldn't do anything though, except sit in silence and pray no one saw them. They didn't have much choice since their motorboat had been sunk during one of the first bombing raids.

But when they saw the Germans hang four civilians, then start shooting at us, they couldn't hold back any longer. One of the younger soldiers called <u>Nikolay</u>

S. - recommend for honourable mention? F. out full name and ran

managed to get an old cannon working and began to shoot, and this is what saved our lives.

When we left the farmhouse, there were twenty-four of us. There are fourteen now.

The ones who made it are me, my friend Anna, Mrs. Burova, Boris, Anatoly, the fisherman, Izabella and Mrs. Galina's two children, Arkady, Valentin, Kristina, Maya and the chairman of the town soviet, although I don't know how long he'll be with us because his wound is getting worse and we don't have any medicines.

All the others died:
My friend Lilya
Mrs. Galina
Bogdan
Grigory
Elena
Eva
Evgeny
Iosif
The peasant couple, whose names I never knew.

There are twelve sailors here on the fortress making a total of twenty-six altogether.

All completely cut off, on this fortress which is like a pebble floating in the middle of the river, the enemy all around us, planes flying over our heads, dropping their bombs night and day.

Trying to break us.

But we'll hold on.

We will resist, for now at least.

On escaping the Rybinsk camp, we roamed for most of
the night. Every now and then we heard the noise of
tanks. Dogs barking. We'd hide behind a bush or in a
ditch, not moving, wet and freezing cold, until silence
returned. Then we'd quietly set off on our way again,
until we heard the next noise.

We came to a river. There was a bridge so we crossed
to the other side.

Klara said we were on the right road. She's the only
one who seems to know where we are.

We travelled constantly northwest, using the stars to
find our way. Mr. Yashkin taught me how to do that. Who
knows what he'd say if he heard I'm using his teachings
to escape from a forced labour camp.

After a bit we came out by the banks of the reservoir.
The night was silent and calm. A church steeple broke
the surface of the water. All we could see was the belfry,
all the rest was submerged.

"That's Mologa," Klara said. "It was a big town once
with a large population but it was swept away when
they built the dam."

"Hush," I said. "Just look."

We stood there for a while, holding hands, admiring
the outline of the submerged city.

S. = he would be ashamed of his pupil!

Today was a perfect day.

To start with, we woke up late. In a cabin we came across last night, just before it started to snow.

(N.B. winter's here. That's a problem we're going to have to deal with.)

I felt warm and rested. I went outside and saw Ilya building a snowman. He'd put the prisoner's jacket on it and used berries as eyes.

"It's nice," I said. "Can I help you?"

We worked together. It was warm. The door of the cabin opened and I threw myself to the ground as a snowball whizzed over my head and hit Ilya.

"Traitors!"

"Let's get them back!"

We entrenched ourselves behind a bush and began bombarding Lev and Klara who were standing by the cabin. Then Marya, Mikhail and Flavio came out. We laughed until our bellies ached and only went inside when we were absolutely soaked through. A fire was lit and we pulled an old fur over us to warm up.

Lev suggested we take it with us. It was a good idea, from now on we'd have to protect ourselves from the cold.

We agreed we should probably take some more things with us and set about looking for anything useful. ←

"Hey, I found a treasure trove!" Klara said.

Up high between the roof beams the hunter had stored some equipment. There were ropes, a lantern, a supply of animal fat for fuel, a pair of gloves, even a sled.

Unfortunately there was no food and we'd worked up a bit of an appetite, having gone without dinner and breakfast.

S = petty theft, Art. 144.

S: = poaching; Oct: 166.

Marya went outside without saying a word. She came back half an hour later holding a hare by the ears.

"Wow! How did you do that?"

Marya let her hair down and showed us the rubber band she kept it tied with. Apparently she'd managed to make some sort of catapult.

"You're quite the sniper," Lev whistled.

"I wish you'd teach me how to do it," Ilya said.

Mikhail stoked the fire and Lev and I skinned the hare. We roasted it on a spit, without salt, and ate it when it was burnt on the outside and raw on the inside. It was the best thing I've ever tasted.

"So what are our plans?" Flavio asked. "Are we going now?"

"Best not to," Lev observed. "It's nearly afternoon already and it'll be dark soon. It's not worth it."

We took a vote on it and decided to stay.

Klara and Marya found an old samovar and made tea from melted snow.

I would've preferred a game of chess because it's been ages since I've played, but there was only a pack of cards in the cabin so we started playing Preferans. No one could remember the rules and we got mixed up right away.

Unfortunately we had to make do with tea for dinner because the hare was finished. But Marya said she'd catch something else tomorrow.

Yes, because tomorrow we're going to wake up early and set off.

The journey home resumes.

I'm happy. I want to find Nadya and find out what happened to my parents. I haven't seen them for so long. Sometimes I worry I've forgotten what they look like.

First day on foot

We walked through fields and woods all day, pulling the sled behind us. We met no one, not until evening when we sought refuge in an empty dacha on the outskirts of a village.

There were other houses nearby so we didn't light any lamps. Or a fire. We found half a bag of potatoes and onions and ate them raw. And got stomachache.

Second day

It rained all day. It melted the snow and we ended up walking in thick mud across a never-changing landscape.

We have no maps to know where we are.

But Klara says we're doing fine.

"We need to keep going in this direction until we get to a city called Tikhvin."

"What's there?" Lev asked.

"Well, the railway line to Leningrad runs through Tikhvin."

That means we could get a train (if the trains have started running again). Or we could just follow the tracks.

While we were walking, I tried to work out how long it will take us to get to Mga, where Nadya is.

Papa says a man walking at a good pace can cover six kilometres in an hour. Given that we have to do six hundred, that will take us one hundred hours. Which is four days without ever stopping or sleeping. Or ten days if we take it easy. And we've done two already. I feel like we're almost there.

Fourth day

It's snowing again. The wind pricked our faces as we walked in the mud. Ilya cried and Mikhail told him stories to keep his spirits up.

I saw a side of Mikhail I've never seen before.

Marya has her catapult constantly at the ready but, because of the storm, there's nothing to catch.

Klara picked some roots which tasted of soil. It's the only thing we've had to eat all day yesterday and today.

It's getting cold and we don't have coats.

Don't know what day it is

I'm writing this inside a hole we dug in the ground, wrapped in the hunter's fur with the others so we don't freeze to death.

"This is how Siberian dogs survive," Lev said. "In holes."

Maybe they do. I don't envy them.

Our supplies are running out and Marya failed to catch anything today. I got angry with her and Klara got angry with me. She said I should have more respect.

Girls.

Another day

I sometimes wonder why they stay with me. All of them: Klara, Lev, Flavio. Little Ilya. Mikhail. Marya.

They wanted to get away from the labour camp. I get that. But why don't they just stop now at the first village and ask for help?

In Rybinsk we gave made-up names. No one can ever capture us now.

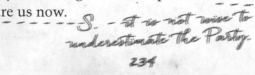

S. — it is not wise to underestimate the Party.

234

Anything would be better than this journey into the unknown.

Is my sister really in Mga? Or has she moved? Maybe she's miles away now. I have no idea.

The last news we had was that Leningrad is surrounded by the enemy and it's impossible to get through. So why do I force myself to carry on? Why do they?

My feeling is that they wouldn't know where else to go. The world has become a dark place and we need to stick together.

I don't know if that's true or I'm just going mad. But it doesn't really matter.

They're with me. And I'm happy they are. I wouldn't stand a chance on my own.

Another day

We're in a village called Mochala, about two hundred kilometres from Rybinsk and another two hundred from Tikhvin.

All this hard work to have travelled so little. I must've got my calculations wrong, or maybe the snow and mud are slowing us down more than I thought.

After all, if the Russian winter stopped Napoleon, what can a bunch of kids in as sorry a state as us hope to achieve?

We had to give up on our plan. I'd sworn we would stay away from people but it's too cold and Ilya is too weak. He kept falling over during the walk today and Lev and I carried him for the last part.

"We need to find somewhere warm and something to eat or he'll die," Klara said, and I knew she was right.

We knocked on the door of the first house in the village.

"Excuse me, ma'am," I said. "Could you put us up for the night?"

I made up a story but the woman didn't ask any questions. She gave us potatoes roasted in the warm ashes. I'd almost forgotten what food even smells like.

Ilya and the others fell asleep in front of the fire.

I wonder if they'll decide to stay here tomorrow instead of setting off with me. I'd understand.

So why am I so afraid?

The next day

We set off again together. Even Ilya. The woman stayed up all night to make woollen capes out of old blankets for us, so now we have coats. She also gave us some bread and a few potatoes. I saw that her pantry was empty, it was probably the last food she had.

Before she left, Klara gave her one of her earrings that she'd managed to salvage from the gulag.

The woman didn't want to know our names.

"That way I can't tell if anyone asks me."

That meant a lot to me.

We began our walk through the snow again. At least there's no wind and the temperature is around zero. Almost warm.

Marya killed a squirrel with her catapult. We were all so happy we hugged her.

I hope we find somewhere to shelter when night comes.

Ilya is dead.

I'm weak and I tire quickly.

Klara says I need to practise. Use my left hand as much as possible.

Dr. Sharapov says remembering will help.

After all, I have plenty of time.

So . . .

The good news is that I'm in Pikalyovo, a village forty kilometres from Tikhvin and less than two hundred kilometres from Leningrad. Not far to go.

The bad news is that Ilya is dead. I'm now left-handed. And all the rest.

The last time I wrote something we'd just left the village of Mochala (one hundred and fifty kilometres from here).

We realized straight away it was a mistake to leave.

The icy rain meant we couldn't see in front of us, our feet kept sinking into the snow. After a few miles we came to an izba and decided to stop there. We bartered the lamp and K's last earring for food and lodging and two pairs of long skis.

The next day we set off again.

Ilya was still weak, so we put him on the sled with the bags.

We skied in tandem. Me, K and M on one set of skis and Lev, F and Marya on the other pair.

S. – This part looks like it was written with great difficulty. There are numerous pauses and breaks.

It was beautiful – bitter cold, but the sky was blue and we made good time with the skis. We must've done around thirty or forty kilometres that day.

When night fell though, it was just us, alone in the wilderness.

"Hey," Lev said. "I can see something down there."

"A pile of wood."

"With a tarpaulin over it."

It was all we had so we used it to build a makeshift shelter.

F and I lit a fire.

It started to snow again.

The temperature dropped to -20.

It was impossible to set off again the next morning. It was too cold. We would've died in a matter of hours. We thickened the walls of our shelter and stayed put.

The next day was the same. And we were running out of food.

"Listen," I said. "Our only option is for someone to go and look for help. Maybe there's a village not too far away. I could go. Try to find some bread . . ."

"Forget it," Klara said. "Either we all go or no one goes."

"No one's going," Mikhail parroted.

"It's too dangerous. I need to think," I said.

That was the day I asked M about train seventy-six. We were outside.

I was using the NKVD knife to cut a branch. He was helping me.

"Tell me about the train," I said.

"Oh." He stared at his shoes.

"Come on! My sister was on it."

"I know." He looked at me. Shook his head. "It's crazy. You really believe it, don't you? That she's still alive.

S. – if Viktor is telling the truth and it was that cold, it was probably late ~~November~~ October.

Even after you heard the radio and saw the newspapers. Even if Leningrad is under siege and the city is starving to death."

"I don't *think* Nadya is still alive. I *know* she is. But she might be in trouble. I have to know why you didn't get on that train."

"Yury's father, Major Fedin, ordered me not to."

"I know that already. But now I want the whole story."

He punched the snow. "Are we friends, Viktor?"

"I wouldn't say so," I replied honestly.

"Well, Yury *was* my friend. My only friend. I can't betray him."

I thought about beating him then. Threatening to leave him outside to die in the snow.

I wanted to. But I couldn't. Not after these past few weeks. Mikhail and I would never be friends but we were comrades. That was for sure.

"I'm not asking you to betray him. Just to tell me the truth."

So he did.

Yury's father is a major in the NKVD. His name's Fedin and he used to work for Colonel Tereshenkov: Anna T's father.

S.

The colonel was very important. He'd received a medal from Stalin. He was a hero almost.

But not long before the start of the war, Major Fedin received a call from Moscow. From Party Official Uvarov.

"Who's that?" I asked.

"Someone from the Party," Mikhail replied. "From high up in the Party."

What Uvarov had to tell him was very unusual. A question of national security.

He said that Colonel Tereshenkov was not the principled person he had led everyone to believe.

240

Before Hitler's betrayal, the Soviet Union and Germany had signed an economic agreement whereby the Soviet Union could sell raw materials and grain to the Germans.

But Colonel T had exploited it. He altered the shipping documents in the Germans' favour and was paid a lot of money for it.✳

By spring, however, secret services across Europe had learned that Germany was planning to betray the pact and attack the Soviet Union. They sent warnings via telegram. Realizing the risk this posed to his dealings, Colonel Tereshenkov hid the messages so no one in Moscow would know what was happening. And he continued to trade as usual.

"Are you serious? Anna's father betrayed the Soviet Union?"

"Yes."

"And Stalin? Tereshenkov managed to hide something like this from the Great Leader?"

"Major Fedin said, when he was a little worse for the drink, that Stalin was scared of Hitler. That's why he signed the non-aggression pact and agreed to sell things to the Germans. To keep them sweet. Stalin preferred not to see what was going on. And Tereshenkov helped keep him in the dark."

Uvarov had proof.

Major Fedin looked into it, carried out investigations. Ultimately, his superior – the colonel – was arrested and sentenced to death only a few hours later.

"You haven't told me yet what train seventy-six has to do with this."

"I'm getting there."

Meanwhile, war broke out. The Leningrad city soviet decided to evacuate all children. Mikhail and Yury were to leave together. After all, they'd grown up like

*S. – aggravated corruption: falsification of documents; theft of State property; high treason.

S. – vile fabrications! Anti-Soviet propaganda.

241

brothers – in the same class, the same Young Pioneers group, etc.

That was when Major Fedin told them everything. And said Yury and Mikhail should stay away from Anna because their lives depended on it.

"Yes, but why?"

The Nazis soon found out that Tereshenkov was dead. They sent secret agents to his house to recover some compromising documents but were unable to find them.

In fact, before he was arrested, Tereshenkov had entrusted the secret documents to his only daughter, Anna.

That was when the Nazis decided the daughter, and any further proof, must be eliminated.

"Did Fedin know this?"

"Yes, or maybe he suspected it. I know he tried to speak to Anna but some traitor friend of her father had hidden her. So, the night before we left, Fedin told us to steer clear of her."

"But doesn't it strike you as odd?" I asked. "If the Germans wanted to get Anna, why would they target an entire train?"

"Well, there's a war on . . ."

"But why didn't they try to kill her while she was in Leningrad? And why did the NKVD let her get on the train? They could have given her protection. Or arrested her as soon as she got to the station. Or . . ."

Mikhail puffed. "You need to ask Yury's father all of this. I don't know anything. But this is what happened, whether you like it or not."

I don't like it, to be honest.

Mikhail seemed sincere, but his story doesn't make any sense.

242

The fact that the NKVD is involved is <u>scary</u>.

I remember once I was walking down Liteyny Avenue in Leningrad with Papa and Nadya. People would cross the road when they got to number six, then cross back again at number two, to avoid going past a big square building with rows and rows of windows across the front.

"What's in there?" Nadya had asked.

"The Bolshoy Dom," Papa had replied.

The Big House. The headquarters of the NKVD, the Soviet Secret Police.

I now know that they come to your house during the night and take you away. *S. - yes. But only if you're a* <u>*criminal*</u>*!*

They guard the gulags. They shoot you if you try to escape!

I hate to think of my sister caught up in a battle between spies . . .

That's enough.

I'm too tired to write any more.

All I know is I have to hurry. I have to get to Nadya, before it's too late.

S. - only those who have something to hide are scared.

I haven't said what happened to Ilya yet.

Nor why I'm writing with my left hand.

Incidentally, I'm finding it quite easy – maybe that means I was already a little left-handed without knowing it. I wonder what Mama will say when she finds out.

Okay, yes, I'm avoiding the issue.

The fact is, it's not easy to write about what happened in the forest.

It's as if me and the others were all of a sudden thrust into a Russian folktale. One of those scary stories about Baba Yaga and her house of bones that walks on chicken legs.

Nadya . . . listen. I really don't know if I should tell you about this part of the journey.

If you think it will scare you, don't read the next few pages. You'd be best not to, honestly. Go straight to the next notebook. Trust me.

But if you want to read on . . . don't say I didn't warn you.

After my chat outside with Mikhail I went back into the shelter, but Klara gestured at me to go outside with her again. She wanted to talk.

"Ilya is running a fever. We need to find a doctor or I'm afraid he won't make it."

It was midday and the temperature was already below zero.

Cold is a dangerous thing. If you're covered up and keep moving, it's not a problem. But if you stop and your sweat freezes, or if you move away from the fire and can't light another one . . .

"It's not long until sunset," I said. "If we leave now and don't find anything straight away, we could end up having to sleep outside. We could all die. It would be far better to set off tomorrow morning."

"All right," Klara said.

That night had to be the worst one of my life.

It was cold. The fire etched deep shadows on everyone's faces. They all looked so thin. Ilya was shaking even though we'd wrapped him in the fur.

I told him a story. Not about Baba Yaga, but a girl called Masha who got lost in the forest one day and met a bear who forced her to cook for him.

"What did she make?"

"Oh," I said. "Ravioli with sour cream and warm buns. Steaming hot cabbage soup, cold roast beef. Bread buns stuffed with roasted onions, kasha porridge. Potatoes roasted in the warm ashes and stuffed vine leaves. A potato omelette. Then cakes, oh yes, she made cheesecake, raspberry cake, apple cake, and . . ."

"Hey," Ilya said. "That bear must've been awfully hungry!"

We laughed.

I think that was the last time we heard him speak.

I prayed all night for a warm sun in the morning. Instead, it was dull and snow fell in tiny flakes. The cold had turned our tarpaulin roof hard as a rock.

"What shall we do?" I asked Klara.

"Ilya still has a fever. If we don't find help, he'll die."

"If we take him away from the fire, he could die anyway."

It was a difficult decision to make but we made it.

We left.

Ilya was on the sled, wrapped in the fur and all the blankets and clothes we could do without. We took it in turns to pull him on the skis, us first then the others.

Snow whirled around us. You couldn't see anything ahead. We were in an icy wasteland. The wind danced inside our clothes and froze the snot in our noses.

Every now and then I'd ask, "Are you okay, Ilya?" and stop to check. He was still breathing but I knew he didn't have much time.

"Klara," I said. "Please, you lead. Find the way."

Covered in a layer of frost, she wrapped a sweater around her face and tried to lead, even though she could see no more than one step in front of her.

Our shelter seemed so far away now. I realized the gamble we'd taken hadn't paid off. There wasn't a soul around. We couldn't last much longer.

After a bit, I pointed to a patch of woodland. "Come on, let's head for that."

"What's over there?" Flavio asked.

"Trees. So there'll be less wind. We could light a fire and rest a while. Then we'll feel much better when we set off again."

I was lying and I knew it.

We'd never set off again. But we didn't have much choice.

Getting to those damned trees was excruciating. I thought every step would be my last one. But I made it and the wind did actually drop once we were under the blanket of trees. As if by magic, we also spotted a house.

It didn't look like a witch's house on chicken legs, but a real log izba, pretty looking, with smoke rising from the chimney.

The only reason I didn't cry was because the tears would've frozen. We hurried towards it and literally knocked down the door as we all fell into the living room, with our skis still on and everything, laughing our heads off. In the main room there was a stove and a fireplace, both were lit. An old man and an old woman were sitting side by side.

When the old man saw us he jumped to his feet. He grabbed a rifle that was as old as he was and pointed it at us. But his wife said, "Can't you see they're just children?"

The fire in the hearth was hot. I explained that we had been on the move but had been caught in the storm. That we were hungry.

"There's no food here," the old woman said. "Our larder is empty and because of the weather, it's impossible to get to the village. We haven't eaten in days."

"No, that can't be possible! Not even a piece of bread, please. We can pay . . ."

"No food."

"Just some hot tea, some water. Let us warm up. Our friend, Ilya . . ."

That's when I realized, in that instant, that Ilya wasn't with us. There was only me, Klara, Lev, Flavio, Mikhail and Marya in the house. Ilya was still outside. On the sled.

I ran outside, the snow hit me hard, I shook him. "Ilya, come on, little one, wake up. There's no food but it's warm inside. You'll feel better . . ."

Ilya was hard. Rigid as a plank of wood. I shook him harder and he fell off into the snow, not like a child falls, but like a branch falling. He was white and immobile.

"Viktor," Klara said. "I'm so sorry."

I took him in my arms. His eyes were open, covered in frost.

The two old people were kind. They helped us put Ilya back on the sled and secure him so he wouldn't fall. They made tea with leaves which weren't actually tea and tasted spicy. They let us sit by the fire, lost in our thoughts.

"I'm sorry," the old man said. "When did it happen?"

We told him that Ilya had been running a fever. He was too weak to walk but we'd decided to leave anyway. Marya started to cry. The old man shook his head.

"If he had a fever, you did the right thing. It was a terrible misfortune."

"Yes," I said.

"Yes," the old woman said. "But often misfortunes can have a silver lining."

She was rocking on her chair while her husband cleaned his rifle. At first, when she said it, I wasn't really paying attention. She said it again. "Some misfortunes can turn out to be a blessing in disguise."

"What do you mean by that?" Flavio shrieked.

"You don't have a crumb to eat," the old woman explained. "Neither do we. We haven't eaten for a week, have we, my dear? We have licked the glue off the furniture. We have scraped the mould from the rafters to make soup. We are starving."

"We're hungry, too."

"Precisely. We would eat anything. And there is something here we could eat. It wouldn't hurt anyone because once you're dead, you can't die again . . ."

I admit I didn't understand.

Not at first. Not really.

But Flavio did. He jumped to his feet, his black curls standing up like lightning bolts on his head.

"Slow down, young boy. Don't do anything you might regret," the old man said.

He pointed his rifle at Flavio.

The old woman whipped an axe out from under her shawl. "It makes sense what I'm suggesting," she continued. "If you think about it, you'll understand. If you don't, well, all the worse for you."

The axe was frightening but I was armed, too. I had the NKVD knife.

I'd hidden it under my clothes.

I didn't stop to think. I pulled it out and leapt straight at the old woman. I knocked her off her chair.

There was a shot. I saw Flavio struggle. Klara screamed. I grappled with the old woman on the floor.

I felt a stab in my hand, like liquid fire, and everything around me became a bright, blinding aura of pain.

We ran outside. I was holding my hand because of the blood pouring from it. "Ilya! We can't forget Ilya!"

Lev and Flavio ran back to get the sled. Then we fled, our feet sinking deep into the snow, without our skis.

"Are they following us? Are they behind us?"

They weren't following, I don't know if it was because we'd injured them. I ran, floundering, the pain in my hand so bad all I could do was run. I was bleeding. I fell into the snow.

After that, nothing.

I woke up here. On a camp bed, in a room full of soldiers. With Klara looking at me, crying, beside Dr. Sharapov who was smiling.

Klara told me what happened.

They were all scared I was dead. They put me on the sled beside Ilya and ran as fast as they could from that cursed house.

[handwritten in left margin: S. – Grievous bodily harm. Art.110: could this be classed as legitimate defence?]

It had stopped snowing and wasn't as cold. More importantly, the old man and woman had mentioned a nearby village and this gave my friends hope.

They found a road and followed it. Not long after, a convoy of army vehicles appeared behind them.

They stopped one of the trucks and pleaded for help.

The driver hauled them up into the cabin beside him, me included. I was still bleeding.

That's when he noticed I was missing three fingers.

He treated the wound. Then brought us here to the village of Pikalyovo where there's a field hospital and I've been given proper medical care.

So that's what happened. I lost three fingers and a friend.

But my journey is not over yet.

S. – lying, no doubt. Oct. 181.

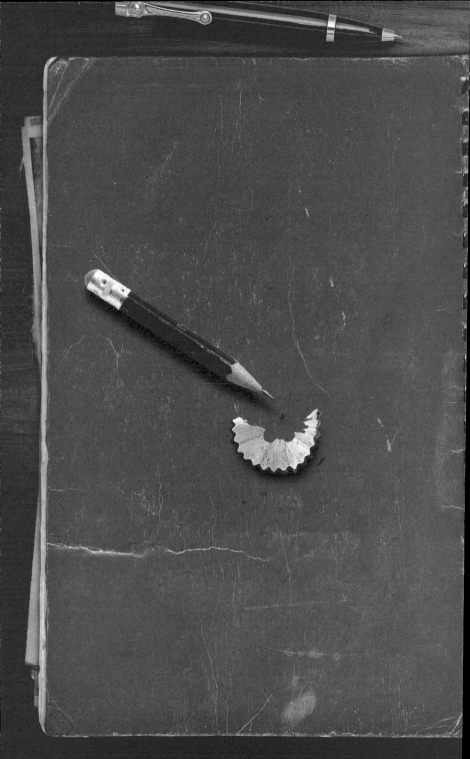

CCCP

PEOPLE'S COMMISSARIAT FOR
INTERNAL AFFAIRS

REPORT FOR INTERNAL USE

The fourth notebook is as ragged as a roll of
barbed wire.
  And the many strands of the investigation
are proving ever more difficult to unravel.

Amongst ourselves, we NKVD officials refer
to the Rybinsk Gulag /the official name is
Volgolag ITL/ as "Hell on the Lake." It is
known to be one of the toughest labour camps
in Russia: one hundred thousand prisoners
are sent there every year and based on the
confidential files I have been able to
inspect, around half of them do not make it
to the next year. The mortality rate is caused
by exhaustion, cold and failed attempts to
escape.
  It is almost impossible to believe that a
handful of children managed to survive it.
  Could it just be pure fabrication?

Even if it were true, from a legal
perspective, the position of the accused is a
complex one.
  Viktor and his companions broke out of a
forced labour camp. Confessed escapees!

Nevertheless, as Lev /surname unknown/ stated, the children were accidental prisoners. They were never sentenced in a court of law and were also too young to be assigned to a gulag. If the camp commandant had requested their papers and performed his duties correctly, they would never have ended up in a barrack for convicts.

The subsequent progression of events - the march through the early winter ice and snow, the firm intention not to abandon young Ilya, the serious injury which disabled Viktor - is also difficult to believe.

Signed:

COLONEL VALERY GAVRIILOVICH SMIRNOV

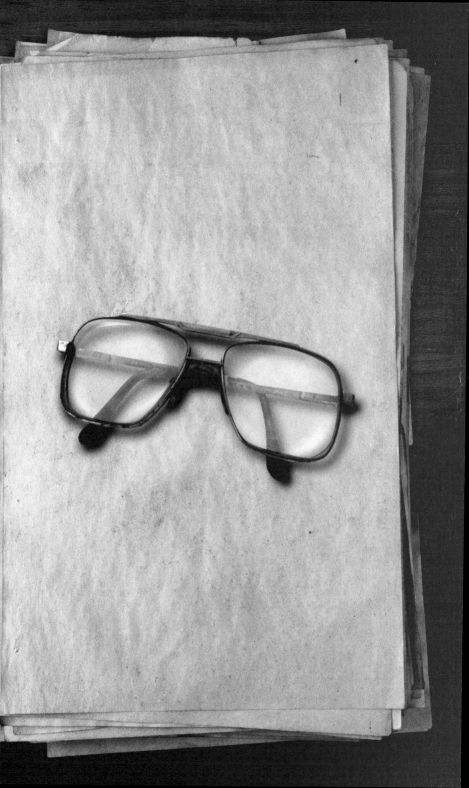

The Queen
of the Fortress

NOTEBOOK 5

The events described herein mostly overlap
with those in the previous notebook (from
September to early November 1941).
    The dates provided are relatively
accurate in this case and it has been
possible to reconstruct the chronology of
events with a degree of precision.

The scraps of paper and photos added
here and there are, as usual, highly
dubious.

                                        —Smirnov

10th September 1941

ORESHEK
FORTRESS

0 10 20 30 40 50

N
W — E
S

1. King's Tower
2. Sovereign Tower
3. Golovkin Tower
4. Watchtower
5. Cathedral
6. Old Prison
7. New Prison
8. Fourth Prison
9. North wall-walk
(covered)
10. River
11. Drawbridge
12. South wall-walk (open)

I live here now. And since I live in the King's Tower, that makes me, officially, the Queen of Oreshek Fortress!

To be honest, I don't live in the actual tower. I'm down below, in the cellars where there are three round chambers (the one in the middle is the biggest and has a giant pillar in the centre that supports the whole tower).

There's no natural light in the cellars and you can feel the cold of the rocks and the river in the air, but we're safe from the bombs and that's the most important thing.

The first few days, Anna and I would try to count the explosions. Hanging onto each other, we'd start, "One, two, three . . ."

"Twenty-four . . . twenty-five . . ."

We've stopped doing that now. I'm not saying we don't notice the explosions. We do, but we don't count them anymore. We've learned to recognize them and can tell the mortars from the shells fired by Panzer tanks. The most frightening of all are the bombs dropped from planes. They start with a whistle and make the ground shake when they explode.

When we first arrived at the fortress, there was a huge church in the inner courtyard called the Cathedral of Saint John. It's not there anymore – it's just a big pile of rubble now.

Luckily, our walls are a lot more solid and can resist any bomb, or at least I hope they can.

There are twelve sailors here at the fortress with us. I have quite a lot to say about some of them but I don't feel like writing about them just now, so I'll tell you about them some other time.

All you have to know is they ended up on Oreshek pretty much by chance. Like I wrote before, they were sent by Ladoga Fleet Command to collect arms and munitions (the fortress is also used as a munitions depot).

But:

1) Their boat was hit by a bomb and sunk
2) The Ladoga Fleet was either destroyed or retreated
3) They discovered that the radio at the fortress was broken
4) The Germans attacked Shlisselburg.

These things all happened more or less simultaneously and there wasn't a lot the sailors could do, not on their own against a whole army. Their only option was to sit tight and hope no one noticed they were there.

But then we appeared, our lives were in peril, and the sailors decided to save us. So now the Germans know we're here.

And they've decided to attack.

They made their first attempt to land on the island a few hours after we arrived. We were still in a state of shock, my clothes were in tatters and I couldn't stop crying over losing Lilya in the river.

A siren suddenly started to wail, the noise was coming from a tower – the Golovkin Tower – on the other end of the island.

"What's happening?" Mrs. Burova asked.

"Alert! Alert! We're under attack!"

"Battle stations, everyone!"

The sailors ran to their combat posts. I looked through a slit in the wall and saw a boat coming towards us, volleys of machine-gun fire bursting forth from it.

Then the Oreshek cannon fired from the Golovkin Tower, there was a huge wave and the Germans went under and never came up again.

I admit I cried tears of joy. I know that's a terrible thing to say because they were people and they died.

Since then the Germans have tried again and again to land, but our sailors have always fought back valiantly and I know you can never let your guard down, but I think *they* are actually starting to fear *us*.

Tsar Peter was right when he called this island the Hazelnut. It has a hard shell and it's not going to be easy to crack!

11th September

I feel like the only things I write in this notebook are war stories. Viktor will find it deadly dull when he reads it!

Lots of other things have been happening, too. Take this morning, for example:

"Nadya . . . Nadya . . . wake up."

"Mrs. Burova, I can't, it's too early, I'm still tired . . ."

"The day's almost half gone. Boris is waiting for you with the pots."

"I don't want to . . . It's a disgusting job."

"That's why we take turns."

"If you don't get moving I'll empty one over you," Boris said.

So I got up.

They were right, it was late. I hadn't realized because there's no light in the cellars. Boris was there, already dressed, waiting in front of the row of chamber pots we had to take outside and empty in the garden.

I hate emptying the chamber pots because the steps that lead out of the cellars are really steep and you always

S. – ambiguous sentiment. unjustified pity for the enemy.

262

end up getting splashed, but at least it's an excuse to go outside. The sky was so beautiful it took my breath away and I got a sudden urge to sing and dance. I was so happy to be alive.

"A lot of bombs came down last night, eh?" Boris said. "I wonder if there are any unexploded ones."

"We should tell the sailors so they can remove them. We don't want any of the younger children jumping on one by mistake . . ."

So we went for a look around the fortress to check. The King's Tower looks onto a small internal courtyard where the Old Prison is located. There's also an apple tree marking where Lenin's brother, Aleksandr Ulyanov, was executed.

Beyond this is a big park with an old barracks (most of which has been destroyed by the bombs), the New Prison building, the Fourth Prison and the church (which has gone too). A little river flows through the park. It comes in through a hole in the outside wall and flows back out a little further down. We can drink water from the Neva without having to go outside the walls.

"Get a bucket and fill it with water. Maybe it will stop Mrs. Burova from grumbling that we've been gone for too long."

"Okay," Boris said. Then he glanced over at the Golovkin Tower: to reach it you have to climb up some steep stone steps then go along an enclosed passageway that runs the length of the northern wall. The steps and the wall-walk are enclosed between two thick stone walls with lots of arched openings, a bit like a castle in a fairy tale.

"Say, do you think we should go over there? To the sailors?"

I did want to go, actually, but since they keep

themselves to themselves so much, we thought better of it and went to the cellars.

There we helped Mrs. Burova with the cleaning. To be honest, there's hardly any point as the place is filthy and most of the space is piled high with boxes of supplies and other army stuff.

"We're going to be here a while and we must behave like civilized people," Mrs. Burova had said.

Then we helped her make lunch. The stew she makes is far better than processed meat eaten straight from the tin.

In the afternoon, I played chess with Anna.

Oh, would you believe it, Viktor? Anna managed to save her book and chessboard with almost all the pieces intact except for the black king (we're using a stone instead). She explained that they're both very important to her so she made sure to slip them under the few bags we brought with us in the boat, like I did with my notebooks.

It was a good thing she did because it's the only way of surviving the boredom here.

Although being bored is better than having bombs dropped on you . . .

12th September

I was tired yesterday and couldn't be bothered writing about the sailors living here with us. But something important happened today and to explain it I'll have to tell you something about our hosts first. So here goes.

(There are twelve sailors at the fortress. I haven't met them all yet so I can only write about the ones I know.)

First and foremost, there's the Chief (that's what all the sailors call him). He has a pockmarked face and wears round glasses. His hands shake constantly. We children get on his nerves and he doesn't seem very nice.

Nikolay, on the other hand, is really nice – he has the same name as my papa after all. He's one of the youngest and since he knows the most about artillery, he's also in charge of the cannon. It was Nikolay who saved us when he decided to shoot at the Germans, although I found out later that he was reprimanded by the Chief because it wasn't of strategic importance. Nikolay replied that strategy could go to pot, he didn't want dead children on his conscience.

Then there's Boris (like my friend Boris), a young boy with black hair and broad shoulders. You can't help but sigh when you see him, even Mrs. Burova. He's so

S. – disobeying orders? Investigate.

265

handsome that we're always saying, "Isn't Boris cute?" to each other. Yesterday Anna and I were talking about it and Boris (my friend) overheard and thought we were talking about him. He went all red, what an idiot.

The other important person in the group is Alina, the only woman. She's a telegraphist, meaning she works the radio, which is broken unfortunately.

Another one of my favourites, as of today, is Ruslan. He doesn't speak much but when he does, he knows what he's talking about. They all treat him more like a commander than they do their Chief.

He's behind the very important thing that happened today.

It all started after lunch. We'd got the quantities wrong and had ended up with too much stew.

"Well, there'll be enough for dinner as well," Gennady the fisherman said.

"You would say that," Mrs. Burova snapped. (After what happened on the boat, she's always very short with Gennady.) "We'll give it to the sailors, that's what we'll do. They'll be thankful for a hot meal and it's a way to say thanks."

What a great opportunity. Anna and I were quick to offer our services.

It's teeth-chatteringly cold today and even though the sun's out, the frost on the ground still hasn't melted. On the bright side, for once we couldn't hear any explosions.

We crossed the park, dragged the tureen up the steep stone steps and went along the wall-walk on the northern wall till we got to the Golovkin Tower. The door at the bottom wasn't shut though, it was slightly ajar.

I shouted, "Hello, is there anybody there?" but no one answered.

"Sssh," Anna said. "Listen, they're having a meeting."

45-мм ПУШКА
обр. 1941 г. (ЗИС-3)

★

КРАТКОЕ ОПИСАНИЕ

1941

That's when I heard the Chief say, "We have to leave the fortress."

"What do you mean by that?" Ruslan asked.

"We were given orders. And those were to collect arms, munitions and food supplies and take them back to fleet command."

"Oh, of course," Ruslan said. "Well let me tell you something, Chief, you can stick your mission up your ★★★★."

(I've written it like that because it didn't seem nice to put swear words in my notebook but that's what Ruslan said, clear and simple.)

"Watch your language," the Chief said.

"Well, you tell me then, how do you plan to see this mission through?"

The Chief was trembling, like a leaf.

"We ended up stuck on this island because we didn't have a boat. But now we do. We have the boat the children came on. We could use it to get to the north bank of the Neva then walk from there to the village of Kokkorevo, or wherever our base camp is now."

"Exactly," Ruslan said. "We don't even know where command is now. And, Chief, you might not have noticed but the Fritzes," (I should explain that the sailors always call the Germans "Fritzes") "have taken Shlisselburg and control the entire southern shore, so if we give up the fortress, we'd be giving up Leningrad as well.★

"You have no way of knowing that!" the Chief stammered.

"The radio might not be working but it's the truth and you know it. The entire fleet has probably been defeated, we're all that's left, so it's our duty to defend the fortress. But we need b★★ls to do that, Chief, and b★★ls are something you clearly don't have."

S. – espionage. Art. 65.

★ S. – accurate analysis but it doesn't lessen the gravity of the rebellion.

I don't know whether the Chief has b**ls or not. I think Ruslan was probably speaking more metaphorically than anything.

With all these swear words flying around, the atmosphere in the room was so frosty even Anna and I, holding our tureen of stew outside, could feel it.

Believe it or not, the Chief then pulled out a pistol and pointed it at Ruslan. "I'm in charge here," he said, "and my orders are to get the arms and munitions out of the fortress."

"Of course," Ruslan replied, not seeming in the least bit concerned. "And what about the children? Will we just leave them here to be slain by the enemy, seeing as they won't be on the boat with us? Do you know what, Chief, go ahead and shoot me because a bullet in the head is far better than leaving the little brats to die. It would be an act of sheer cowardice!"

I'm twelve years old, so I'm not a little brat, but I would still have liked to applaud Ruslan, maybe even give him a kiss.

Alina and Boris the sailor stood up beside Ruslan.

"Chief, if you're going to shoot him, you'll have to shoot us as well because we can't abandon Oreshek."

"Me too," Nikolay added. "I'd rather stay alive for now but whatever happens, I'm not leaving either."

"Me neither," someone else said.

"Nor me," yet another declared.

The Chief was red in the face and twitching furiously by that time. He put down his gun and said, "I thought I was leading a garrison of military personnel in wartime, not a village soviet where everyone wants a say in the decision-making. You don't want to take a vote on it as well, by any chance?"

Ruslan said nothing.

S. — This individual should actually be executed for insubordination.

269

"What you might not have realized," the Chief continued, "is that the enemy is preparing to attack the island. We've managed to keep them at bay so far . . . but only because the Fritzes had other fish to fry. As soon as they've established their control over the village they'll come after us. And how will we stop them? With one cannon?"

"We have more than one," Nikolay said. "The 409 battery is still in the munitions store in the barracks, it's dismantled but still in working order. It just has to be reassembled. In total there are seven cannons, six machine guns and a heap of rifles."

The Chief laughed at that point, "And how will we man all these weapons when there are only twelve of us? The Fritzes will come over here and kill us all. We'll still have failed *and* disobeyed orders."

The Chief was probably expecting Ruslan to respond after such a provocation.

Instead I piped up.

"Excuse me," I said, peeping around the door from the landing. All eyes were instantly on me. Anna very nearly spilled half the stew on the floor.

I was scared the Chief might get his gun out again and shoot me, but I was already on the dance floor and, as Viktor always says, once you're on the dance floor, you may as well start dancing.

"Excuse me," I said. "I couldn't help but overhear and I think I have an idea."

"Ah!" the Chief exclaimed. "Even young girls get to speak in our soviet now!"

"Well," I said. "You're worried that since there aren't many of us, the Germans will attack. Is that right?"

"Right," Ruslan said, giving me an icy glare.

"So maybe the answer is to make them think there are more of us."

"Enough of this nonsense!"

"Chief, let her speak," Ruslan said. "We don't have anything to lose. Young girl, what's your name?"

"Nadya Nikolayevna."

"What are you suggesting?"

"Well, we kids could put on uniforms and march along the walls like real soldiers. We could learn how to use the rifles and stand guard on the turrets. We could also deploy the cannons around the island, and even if they don't fire, they'll look impressive. That way the Germans will be worried that if they get too close, we'll blow them up. They'll be scared and will keep away."

"What a ridiculous idea," the Chief said.

"Yes, you're right," Ruslan admitted. "But it could work."

15th September

I'm sorry I haven't had time to write lately, but some really crazy things have been happening.

The first is that my idea is working!

The Chief is still fairly angry and Mrs. Burova throws me dirty looks occasionally, but only because the grown-ups are too obstinate to admit that young people like me can have good ideas sometimes, and we know how to make them work by being brave and using our brains.

Anyway, this is what happened. The other day, while I was sitting in a corner writing about Ruslan arguing with the Chief, two sailors came down into the cellars, one was Nikolay and the other was an old man they call Sokolov.

It was the first time the sailors had come down to where we are so it caused a bit of a stir, even more so when they went over to Mrs. Burova and said, "Comrade, we are here to see Nadya Nikolayevna."

"Who?"

"Nadya Nikolayevna," Nikolay repeated, then he saw me and said, "her."

It was such a fantastic moment!

Everyone (except Anna) looked at me with an "I can't believe it" look in their eyes.

I stood up and said, "Let's go."

To be honest, I was putting on a bit of an act because I was scared the Chief had decided to punish me. Even Mrs. Burova must have been thinking the same thing because she said, "I'm coming, too."

We went over to the tower together.

"What's going on?" Mrs. Burova asked.

The Chief handed her the binoculars and pointed towards the riverbank. "Look," he said.

I have good eyesight and didn't need binoculars to see that scores of tanks were moving back and forth on the shore, and two huge boats were docked at a pier.

"Do you know what they are?" the Chief asked. "They're assault craft and they're coming to get us."

"But can't you stop them? You managed last time."

"Luck," the Chief replied. "And they didn't make much of an effort. It won't be as easy this time. But it would appear the girl has had an idea and we're going to try what she suggests. We don't have any choice."

Mrs. Burova looked stunned and I heaved a sigh of relief because they didn't want to punish me after all. It was quickly followed by a sigh of concern because the enemy was about to attack so there was no time to lose.

That's when I explained my plan to everyone.

NADYA'S PLAN
TO SAVE ORESHEK FORTRESS

Resources:

12 sailors

+ 2 grown-ups (Mrs. Burova and Gennady)

+ 7 nearly grown-ups (me, Anna, Boris, Anatoly, Arkady, Valentin and Maya)

+ the non-fighters (the younger children and chairman who is very ill and not sure to survive).

Purpose of the plan: to have the enemy believe there's a full garrison at the fortress, armed to the teeth.

We have to look so numerous and so threatening that the Fritzes think it's too dangerous to attack.

If we succeed, we live. If we fail, they kill us.

Plan – phase 1: grown-ups and nearly grown-ups get the 409 battery working again, which will give us seven cannons and six machine guns. Since there aren't enough of us to man everything (or so Nikolay says, and I believe him), they have to be deployed so that:

1) The Germans can see them and know we are well-armed;
2) They can be easily withdrawn when the Germans bomb or attack us, because they're all we have.

Plan – phase 2: we all have to find as many military uniforms as possible and swap them around frequently, so anyone looking at us will think we are each a number of different people. Wearing the uniforms, we must march along the walls, shoot at the sky, sound sirens and stage military exercises, etc., so that planes flying over will report unprecedented levels of activity at Oreshek.

"So, you and your friends want to pretend to be grown-up soldiers and hope the enemy falls for it?" the Chief asked.

"Yes."

"But they have binoculars, they'll see your young faces," he said.

"We'll wear our gas masks," I replied. "At worst we'll look like midget soldiers."

It took a while to agree on the plan, the sailors and Mrs. Burova weren't too keen on it, but at the end of the day, we didn't have many alternatives.

15th September 1941

ORESHEK
FORTRESS

0 10 20 30 40 50

N
W E
S

⊗ ➔ 45 mm cannons
▨ ➔ Machine guns
▲ ➔ Pretend rifles

We gave out the jobs: the grown-ups went to get the crates of artillery and we kids searched the fortress, including the prisons and old barracks, for uniforms and other military props.

Luckily, we found a whole pile.

"Look at these pilot's goggles!"

"And this tank driver's helmet! Don't I look like a real soldier with this on?"

Some of the uniforms were really old though, going back to the Tsars' armies from the 1800s. Hopefully the enemy wouldn't notice.

We got dressed quickly. I chose an officer's uniform with a sword hanging at my hip. It was a bit big for me, although not too much, and I drew a moustache on my face with some boot polish.

Meanwhile the Germans weren't hanging around. We saw them assembling cannons and deploying artillery on the shore.

It was like a race to see who could be ready first. I was beginning to worry but Boris said, "It's a really good idea, Nadya. We just have to look threatening enough."

We climbed up onto the battlements on the southern wall (where there's another wall-walk but not covered this time) and we waved to the soldiers on the Shlisselburg riverbank as if it were a big game. They didn't notice us at first but immediately directed a volley of rifle fire when they did. Luckily they were too far away to hit us.

We went back down after a bit, changed our clothes and went onto the shore to make it look like there were soldiers stationed there as well.

That's when Ruslan appeared. He came running towards us, shouting, "Are you out of your minds, what are you doing?"

"Why? It's part of the plan, to let the enemy see us."

"Yes, but not like this, not out in the open. They have snipers, they could shoot you straight in the head from there. This isn't a game, you know." He stopped to think for a second then added, "Come with me."

We followed him up to the square in the centre of the island, where he asked us to line up in front of him. "If you want to pass for soldiers, you have to behave like soldiers from now on. So, follow the rules, obey orders, and do exactly as I say. Is that clear?"

"Yes."

Ruslan jerked to attention and barked, "It's 'Yes, sir!'"

"Yes, sir!"

"That's a little better," he said. "Now, proper military training takes months. But the main thing is to get started so, listen up."

He then proceeded to explain all kinds of things to us, like how to stay under cover while on the move and what to do if we're attacked, etc. Then he picked up a rifle and taught us how to load it and how to shoot it in the air. He said learning to aim properly wasn't important for now, in actual fact, we could end up hurting each other, but in the event of a battle, at least we could make some noise.

Meanwhile the grown-ups were assembling the heavy machine guns and 45mm cannons. They were originally designed to destroy tanks but at Oreshek they have special platforms to point them at the sky so we can shoot at aircraft.

The sailors, Mrs. Burova and Gennady took up position at their pieces (that's what they call them), while we went back up onto the southern wall with rifles on our shoulders, but being much more careful this time.

S. – from this moment on, Nadya is, to all intents and purposes, subject to military law.

The Germans seemed almost ready to launch their attack, their soldiers were already in the boat and I was amazed they could be so calm before a battle. We jeered and taunted them, as serious and warlike as we could make it.

All of a sudden we heard a distant rumble. Looking up, we saw that planes were approaching from the west, flying very low, and German machine guns began shooting at the fortress.

Mrs. Burova screamed, "Take cover!" and we – well – we took cover. Nikolay, who was manning the anti-aircraft gun, opened fire.

The gun shoots twenty-five rounds a minute (Nikolay told me) so it makes a fast BOOM-BOOM-BOOM noise, almost like a heartbeat. Some of us screamed, then the craziest thing happened: a plane was hit. Smoke started billowing out of it and we shouted, "Hurray!"

The Chief then yelled, "Fire at will!"

One of our heavy machine guns hit the boat that was on its way to attack, opening up a ribbon of holes along its side. It didn't kill the enemy onboard but I saw them dive off into the water.

They stopped attacking us then.

In return, a few hours later a full squadron of planes flew over and we were heavily bombarded, but it didn't matter, we were all safely in hiding.

So that's that.

My plan seems to be going magnificently, for now.

Compared to a few days ago, our life has changed a lot. In the morning, we young people now have to muster in the square where we march, run and do target practice. I can shoot quite well now and Nikolay says if we keep it up, me, Boris and Anna will soon be able to handle a heavy machine gun on our own (although Mrs. Burova has said there's no way she'll allow it because it's too dangerous . . . Maybe she's just jealous because she doesn't know how to).

In short, we're hanging on.

As for me, I'm a little worried about Viktor to be honest. If he's really coming to get me, how will he find me and how will he ever get to the fortress, given that the enemy now controls Mga and Shlisselburg? But one problem at a time. My brother is smart and I'm sure he'll find a way.

S. - chapter 36

16th September

Lots of really awful things happened today.

The first one was that the chairman of the town soviet died. We knew his injury was serious and Mrs. Burova said the poor man had suffered too long already.

I don't think he was that poor a man, to be honest, when I think about those rules he nailed to the church door and all that. There's no doubt he was in a lot of pain, though. That was really sad. I think he regretted some of his unpleasant behaviour too. Yesterday he actually said sorry to me.

I was down in the cellars for something or other when he gestured to me to come over. I did, even though I didn't want to because he spat when he spoke and, to be honest, he had a really unpleasant smell.

"I'm sorry, child," he said. He spoke so quietly at first I thought I'd misheard him.

"Sorry for what?"

"Your father was a good man."

At that point I was sure he must be delirious, he'd never even met my father.

"I wish I'd done more," he continued. "Taken you to Leningrad, spoken to someone . . . but the war . . . I couldn't."

"Don't worry," I said, trying to console him as best I could. "It's all okay."

"I'm sorry for your friends on the train," he mumbled. "Hiding you was the only way to protect you . . . That's what Commissar Bok said . . . That's why he wanted to take you to the village . . . and I . . ." He heaved a huge sigh at that point and said, "Please, forgive me."

I didn't know what else to do so I said it was all right, that I'd forgiven him and that he needn't worry. He smiled.

He died not long after, and I admit it made me sad.

I mentioned it to Anna and she said maybe the chairman had been confused, convinced he was speaking to her when he was speaking to me.

"What does that mean?"

"It means my father really was a good person."

"Well, mine too."

"Yes, but the chairman didn't know yours, whereas he knew mine."

Anna shared a huge secret with me then. She told me her father was a colonel and that he'd devoted his life to fighting the wrongdoings of the NKVD. ←

But some bad people tricked him and had him arrested and Anna thinks he must be dead by now. The same people also tried to harm Anna but luckily someone stopped them, because her father was a nice man who'd helped lots of people over the years, saving them from unfair trials and things like that, and sometimes the people he'd helped had risen to important positions, like a man called General Bagramyan.

S. – daughter's personal opinion. In disaccord with the truth.

S. – Bagramyan was helped by Tereshenkov? This could be significant. Investigate.

Or Commissar Bok.

"What, you knew the Commissar even before we got to Mga?"

Anna replied that she had but she hadn't said anything because she thought Bok didn't want anyone to know.

I sensed, at one point, that talking about this was upsetting her, so I asked if she wanted to play a game of chess instead and she replied, "Do you know why I brought my book with me? Because it was my father's. In truth, he was actually a terrible chess player but he enjoyed it and said that I'd be a famous champion one day. How ridiculous, eh?"

I didn't think it was ridiculous at all, so I gave her the biggest hug I could.

The other awful thing happened at around five o'clock. An icy cold rain was falling but it didn't stop the frenzy of activity among the enemy positions. We heard the rumble of aircraft so Nikolay took up his position at the cannon.

It turned out to be just one plane, flying very low, and Nikolay said, "I'll take this one out easily!" but it just tipped its wings and flew over the fortress, leaving a trail behind it.

We thought they were bombs so we took cover but they turned out to be leaflets. I was the first to leave our hiding place and take one, although it was actually two sheets of paper stuck together.

This was the first one:

It was a page from today's *Pravda*, with the title, "Enemy at the gates."

I read the article with my heart in my mouth. According to the newspaper, the Nazis are laying siege

ЛЕНИНГРАДСКАЯ
ПРАВДА

От Советского Информ
сводки за 22 и 23 ноября (

Постановление Совета
ров Союза ССР о присвое
офицерскому составу Крас

Указы Президиума
СССР (1 и 2 стр.):

Обращение строителей-
строителям (2 стр.).

Обращение ко всем раб
промышленности (2 стр.).

№ 289 (9425)   Среда, 16 сентября 1941 г.   ЦЕНА 20 КОП.

ENEMY AT THE GATES

LENINGRAD — In these times of extreme valour, the Red Army continues its heroic resistance, committed to repelling the enemy metre by metre, enriching our soil with the precious blood of patriots.

The city of Leningrad has risen as one, a single force ready to stop this treacherous attack and break the barbarous siege.

Comrade General Zhukov, supreme commander of the Leningrad front, has reported to Comrade Stalin his proud optimism and firm belief that the tide of this battle is set to turn in our favour.

Our soldiers have, in fact, shown great skill in halting Finnish troops mere kilometres from the city's northern fringes and the German army now lives in fear, encircled on the nearby banks of the Neva, aware that a Russian counterattack could arrive any minute, sealing their fate for ever. Where the Neva pushes through the heart of the city, the enemy has been beaten back to the outskirts of Leningrad, its advance thwarted by the bravery of our soldiers.

Comrade Stalin

The war has only just begun but it is time to put paid to the arrogance of Hitler, an evil invader and piteous imitation of Napoleon. Very soon, he will commit his heinous crimes no longer.

to the city and all citizens are called upon to mount the final defence. After that I looked at the second piece of paper, which was a leaflet with a swastika, the twisted cross the enemy uses as its emblem.

It had terrible things written on it, that the Russian army was disintegrating, that Leningrad would fall within days, and that we have to surrender or there'll be trouble. And that from this moment on, "for every German soldier killed, one hundred Soviet civilians will be killed in retaliation."

Even as I write it here now, it feels like I'm living in a nightmare. Mama is in Leningrad, shut away in the cellars of the museum. Is she all right? What's happening there? Has the Russian Army really been destroyed? Is my papa still alive?

Ruslan ripped the leaflet out of my hands.

"Don't waste your time on this nonsense," he said. "If we'd really lost the war, do you think the enemy would have to drop leaflets to tell us about it?"

"Right," Nikolay said. "It's just a trick to try and scare us. Leave it to me to give them the response they deserve."

Our sailors went to the heavy machine guns and started shooting at the riverbank; the Fritzes all ran for cover and returned fire.

It turned into a proper battle and unfortunately a mortar bomb killed one of the sailors. I didn't know his name. It also wounded Nikolay (just a graze really) and as if that weren't bad enough, it destroyed one of our cannons too.

I know it's not very tactful to mention the death of a man and a destroyed gun in the same breath, but the truth is, without the cannons we're lost.

The others think so, too. The Chief has summoned everyone to a meeting that's going to start in a few

S. — vile enemy propaganda.

minutes' time in the Golovkin Tower to discuss the situation (or rather, "to receive new orders").

I wasn't included, none of the children were, as if he cares about us! But me, Boris and Anna will hide on the landing, to hear what they are saying.

I need to go now.

Later

The meeting has just finished, we're back in the cellars and Mrs. Burova has punished us because we went out during the bombing.

If she knew we'd been spying on the meeting she'd be even more angry, but she doesn't know, and I'm taking advantage of our punishment to write everything in my notebook.

We carried out our plan, just as we'd said. We lay in wait outside the tower, then when the meeting started we climbed up the stairs and crouched down in the shadows so we could hear everything.

The Chief said that, to begin with, he wanted to be briefed on the situation.

Ruslan took out a map and marked the location of the German batteries on the south bank and said that there was no trace of the enemy on the north bank. "The Germans want to surround Leningrad and cut it off completely. We're the only thing keeping them from closing the circle."

He finished his report by saying that our fortress was of crucial strategic importance and that we had to defend it at all costs.

"We'll talk about that shortly," the Chief mumbled.

He then asked for information on the state of our weapons and Nikolay said that the cannon that was

S. – punished?! Spying is punishable with execution!

hit by the mortar will never fire again, but it could be arranged to look like it was still intact from a distance.

At the end of his speech, the Chief asked for a report on our radio.

"It's not working, Chief," Alina the radio operator said.

"I know that. I want to know if it can be repaired."

"If it was possible, I would've done it," the young woman replied.

"Does that mean you don't know how to?"

"It means I need parts," she said, "and we don't have them here."

The Chief smiled and said that was exactly what he'd thought.

At that point he launched into a speech that I don't think I understood properly, about how a garrison of sailors can't be "cut off from the rest of the world" when "the enemy is at the gates."

"Perhaps Ruslan is right and this fortress is important, but without specific instructions from our command, it's impossible to know. We have food, weapons and equipment here that could be vital elsewhere. So, our priority has to be to make contact with the Ladoga Fleet."

"The radio's broken," Alina said again.

"I know. So we'll have to abandon the fortress."

A heated argument broke out, Ruslan said again that he'd rather shoot himself and the Chief accused him of mutiny.

He said that the stupid tricks of a child (that would be me) wouldn't deceive a wily enemy like the Germans, and that sooner or later they'd kill us all.

I don't know how long the argument went on. It felt like ages and it came to nothing, in the sense that the sailors are staying put for now and not going anywhere.

But they left the room muttering and it seems to me that Ruslan, Nikolay, Boris the sailor, Alina and the others are beginning to come round to the Chief's way of thinking, maybe because they're scared of staying here.

Perhaps they'd change their minds if they could really make contact with their command and hear how important it is for them to stay here, or if reinforcements could be sent or something.

What's more, we could ask how the war is going and what's happening in Leningrad, and if the city really is under siege.

I'd like to know about my mama, for example.

But without a radio . . .

Hang on a second, I know where we can get one!

I need to speak to the others about this right away.

26th September

Something I haven't mentioned yet here in the notebook is that we built <u>forty scarecrows</u> a few days ago. You know, the kind farmers put in their fields to scare away crows, except that we use them to keep the enemy away. We dressed them in uniforms, put rifles in their arms and stood them on the rocky spurs on the island's shores, near the windows in the towers or along the southern wall so that it looks like there's a whole army on guard duty.

Anyway, this morning, shortly after dawn, there was an air raid.

"The scarecrows!" I said. "We need to pull them under cover!"

"Why?" asked Arkady, who's a year older than me. "They can hardly die, can they?"

"No, but if the pilots see them standing there like dummies under the bombs, they'll realize we tricked them."

"Or they might think that Red Army soldiers are very brave, ha, ha, ha!"

Arkady can be really stupid sometimes and there was no time to lose. Boris and I ran outside, there was so much smoke and bombs were falling one after the other.

Nikolay was at the cannon, firing at the sky and shouting words that were so bad I can't write them in here. The fact is that Nikolay hates 45mm cannons. He says they're too slow and just make a lot of noise and nothing else, and that it was a fluke that he hit a plane that first time.

Anyway, Boris and I went to get the scarecrows and move them somewhere safe. We were on our way back when a shell exploded very close to us, throwing snow and earth everywhere. I fell and Boris landed on top of me but he got to his feet quickly and said, "We should get back to the others."

We went back down into the cellars under the King's Tower where Anna was handing out gas masks. To tell the truth, the Germans haven't attacked us yet with gas but you never know, and the Chief says they could try to gas us sooner or later.

It turned out that there was one mask missing and I didn't get one.

Anna looked at me with wide eyes.

"How can that be? We counted them last night!"

"Maybe Mrs. Burova took one before going to her battle station," I suggested. "It doesn't matter, we can breathe fine for now."

In truth, it worried me. I sat down and glanced at the door every now and then, seeing the smoke coming in from ground level and wondering if it was gas and if I was going to die.

Kristina, one of the younger children, asked if I'd read her a story, given that I could still read aloud because I wasn't wearing a mask. She handed me her favourite book (the only one we have to be honest) – it was called *Traditional Folktales*.

I could hardly speak.

There was a sudden crash and a cloud of smoke came billowing under the door. It scared me so much I dropped the book.

15

A page fell out so I've stuck
it here for safe-keeping.

I felt a hand touch my shoulder. Boris took off his gas mask and said, "You take it, Nadya."

"What? Are you serious? If there's a gas attack, what will you do?"

"There's no gas," he replied.

"But what if there is?"

Boris turned to me with a serious look, then gave a little smile and said, "Well, we'll just have to take it in turns and breathe for each other."

I didn't know what to say, I ended up taking the mask but there wasn't any gas. The smoke was just dust from a wall that had crumbled.

But I couldn't stop thinking about the look in Boris's eyes and what he'd said.

It's the nicest thing any boy has ever said to me.

30th September

I haven't told you anything else about the radio, so I'll start with that. My idea is actually fairly simple:

1) Use the boat we came to the fortress in
2) Take it across to Shlisselburg
3) Go to the People's House
4) Take the chairman of the town soviet's radio
5) Come back. ✳

It would be so simple, child's play really, if only Shlisselburg weren't occupied by the Germans.

✳ S. - this is madness. The boat was requisitioned by the Chief so is now under military control. Such an action would be absconding from duty without permission. Art. 245; Theft of state property. Art. 91: violation of military sea navigation rules. Art. 254. and given the importance of the boat to the naval personnel. it could also be classed as sabotage. Art. 68.

Apart from the odd scare, like the bombing when I didn't have a gas mask, the situation is relatively stable, by which I mean the Germans try to attack, we push them back, nothing major ever changes. It's like when a game of chess ends in stalemate and none of the players take their opponent's pieces for fear of their own being taken.

But this doesn't mean it will be easy to get to the village. Shlisselburg is a German base now, with artillery batteries pointing straight at us on the riverbank and, worse still, snipers.

"There's one there," Anna said this afternoon.

We were stationed together at the Watchtower on the other end of the island from where we sleep. I call it the Watchtower (that's not its real name) because we use it when we're on lookout duty.

"Let me see," I said, pulling the binoculars off her.

To tell the truth, this business with the binoculars always makes my heart sink because it reminds me of Viktor and when we did fire watch together in Leningrad. Anyway, you need binoculars to be on lookout duty so I pointed them towards the opposite riverbank. "Where should I look?"

"On the roof of the second house from the right. Can you see it? The window's open and you can see the light catch the scope."

Anna was right, I could see blinds half shut and something glinting between them.

"It could be anything . . . maybe a mirror . . ."

"Do you think so?" Anna said. "Watch this."

She gave me one of her cheeky smiles then picked up a soldier's helmet, put it on the end of a stick and waved it in front of the nearest window.

I was looking out through a slit in the wall as she did it. Right away we heard a "Pop!" and a puff of smoke burst forth from the house we were watching. Anna screamed and dropped the stick. There was a round hole in the helmet.

"I can't believe a rifle can shoot from such a distance," Anna said. "I'd like to have one."

That took me by surprise. The idea of Anna with a sniper rifle gave me the shivers.

"What? You'd kill people walking along the street when they were least expecting it?" ←

Anyway, I think we'll have to go and get that radio sooner or later. I just have to wait until the time is right.

Meanwhile I spoke to Alina. She explained that our radio here in the fortress has some broken bits inside it, but the main problem is the headset and microphone. They were both smashed to smithereens, so even if the rest of the radio were to be fixed, we wouldn't be able to hear anything.

I asked her if a normal radio, the kind people have in their houses, would be enough for the spare parts and Alina said yes.

She was sure.

At that point, I was also sure about what we had to do.

15th October

It's snowing!

It started snowing this morning and has been coming down in big, soft, perfectly-formed flakes ever since.

We all ran outside, hugged and spent the morning playing in the snow (which is already pretty deep, about five centimetres!).

Why are we so happy? Well, it's obvious. The snow is

Si - people, as in enemies.
The enemy is to be killed!

our ally! It will be even more difficult for the Germans to attack us now. The Russian cold will freeze their rifles and guns, and we will wait, we will resist, and in the end we will win.

That's why we're so happy.

Viva the snow!

17th October

It snowed for two days and the world around us is now all white. The snow is more than ten centimetres deep and the temperature has plummeted. We'll have to think about how to heat the cellars soon, although the most important thing for now is that there are fewer Germans amassed on the opposite shore, or so it looks. They must be feeling the cold.

It's time to put my plan into action and steal that famous radio. This very night, before it gets even colder and the river starts to freeze over (which would make it dangerous to use the boat).

I discussed it with Anna and Boris because it's obviously too difficult a mission for me to do on my own and the grown-ups would never give us permission.

I'll leave my notebooks here at the fortress, hidden somewhere my friends would find them, should we not make it back.

I'm going now.

Dear Mrs Burova,

I'm sorry. If you're reading this letter, it means we're dead and the boat has been lost.

We went to Shlisselburg. We know there's a radio in the People's House and we want to steal it so that Comrade Alina can call for help.

I know that going there is a reckless idea but I thought about it a lot and was convinced it was worth a try.

You must also know that my brother, Viktor Nikolayevich, is probably somewhere near here and trying to reach me.

Don't ask me how I know, I just do. When you see him, please give him these notebooks and tell him to look after Mama and Papa.

Thank you, Nadya

18th October

Mission accomplished. We went last night and came back with the radio. Alina hugged me and said I'm a hero, Ruslan shook my hand and even the Chief said that it was a significant achievement, although I have to put all ideas of doing anything similar ever again out of my head because I put our only boat in danger and could have ruined it for everyone.

In short, it was a success. Me, Boris and Anna should be over the moon, but . . .

Apart from us, no one at the fortress knows what really happened.

The first part of Operation Radio went according to plan.

The last planes flew over around dusk, dropped a few bombs and then there was silence.

We've learned that the Germans prefer to attack during the day, maybe because they can see targets better. Anyway, we had dinner although we didn't eat much because Mrs. Burova has begun to ration our supplies, since we don't know how much longer we're going to be stuck here.

I stayed up to write while the others went to sleep, then around midnight we crawled outside.

It was freezing and the snow glimmered like a lamp under the crescent moon. The moonlight meant we didn't need a lantern but it also made us more visible.

I wondered for a second if we should call it off, but I decided not to.

We crossed the square, followed the glistening shadow of the frozen canal, climbed onto the northern wall-walk, then instead of heading along it to the tower the sailors use, we turned the other way, towards the Sovereign Tower.

Part of the way along that wall-walk there's an alcove in the wall with a huge wooden winch in it. It's for raising the big iron grille over the entrance to the fortress and, just like in castles, it can be lifted and lowered from above.

"I hope it doesn't make too much noise," I said.

"It doesn't matter, this plan's never going to work anyway," Boris replied. "To get out of the Sovereign Tower we need to get across the drawbridge and that's operated from a room on the first floor." He pointed to the stone ceiling above our heads. "We'll never manage to open it without someone noticing."

"Oh, don't worry, we will," I reassured him.

"You have no idea . . . They'll be onto us before we get the gates open, or they'll hear the boat going across the river. And if our sailors don't, the enemy sure will. One way or another, we're doomed."

I swear I find it hard to believe sometimes that Boris is the same person who, just a few days ago, told me, "We'll just have to take it in turns and breathe for each other."

"We'll be just as doomed if we stay here without a radio," Anna said calmly. "The enemy is at the gates, don't you remember? It's worth the risk."

Anna's words gave us both courage.

We set to work. She went down into the courtyard to stand guard. Boris and I turned the winch by hand, slowly, slipping some fabric between the chains to stop it from creaking too loudly.

I looked down through the arched openings in the wall and saw Anna nodding at us to stop: we'd raised the iron grille by about half a metre, it was high enough now for us to crawl under.

Boris and I then climbed up to the first floor of the Sovereign Tower and went into the room housing the winch that lifts the drawbridge. We turned the crank anti-clockwise to lower the wooden platform.

After that, we joined Anna in the square and, together, crawled under the grille and into the ground floor gatehouse, where the sailors had hidden our boat, motor and oars.

"It shouldn't be too difficult to drag it into the water . . ."

To get out to the drawbridge, we had to open another gate which had a bar across it on the inside. No trouble there.

"We should leave it open for when we come back," Boris said. "But if someone goes out into the courtyard, they'll see we've escaped."

"That's a risk we'll take."

"Let's hope no one comes this way," Anna said.

We opened the last gate and carried the boat across the drawbridge to the pier where we lowered it into the water.

Boris was about to start the motor and we only just managed to stop him in time.

"Are you mad?" I said.

"The noise will have everyone straight down here," Anna echoed.

"So how are we going to get to Shlisselburg then? Swim?"

S. – jeopardizing the safety of a military base, sabotage under Art. 68.

"No, we'll row," I replied. "We can use the oars for a bit, then when we're far enough out and no one can hear, we'll start up the engine."

"Oh, so I guess I'll be doing the rowing?" Boris sighed, setting to work, nevertheless.

Given that we couldn't go past the Golovkin Tower because the sailors on guard duty would see us, we decided to go the long way round, following the island towards the north, passing the King's Tower then out into open water.

"Can we start the motor now?" Boris asked, puffing out great clouds of steam like a horse.

"Yes, it's safe now," I said.

We fired it up and the boat sped across the mouth of the Neva in a wide curve, then we turned and headed back towards the village.

The banks were thick with snow and the lake was dark and calm. You'd never have thought there was a war on.

As we got closer to the shore we switched off the motor and landed close to the farmhouse we'd hidden in the day of the Battle of Shlisselburg. As we climbed out, it was like I could almost smell the enemy and, suddenly, all the terrible things that could happen to us flashed before my eyes. And why? For a radio we didn't even know was still there!

"Nadya, you're shaking," Anna said.

"It's just the cold," I replied. "Let's go."

We pulled the boat up onto dry ground and hid it in the bushes, then started out on foot towards the houses.

Our feet were leaving footprints in the snow, so after the first few metres, I went back to pull off a branch and dragged it behind me to cover up our tracks.

I wondered to myself why we hadn't brought a knife.

It would have been much easier to cut the branch but it was too late now.

Who knows what I thought I'd find in Shlisselburg maybe dead prisoners chained up in the snow; soldiers drinking from bloodstained cups around the fire.

But there was none of that, it was much the same as before: no one around, windows boarded up. The only difference was that many of the houses had burned down, the cathedral and St. Nicholas's church had been so badly gouged by bombs there was hardly anything left of them. Then again, Oreshek had its fair share of scars, too.

We got to the square where the People's House is located and we heard voices. Two soldiers in long coats were standing guard outside the door, smoking a cigarette and chatting.

They didn't look like ferocious wolves, just ordinary people.

I thought to myself that this is what war does: it makes ordinary people do terrible things.

"Trouble ahead," I said. "It looks like the People's House is now the enemy's general headquarters. And the radio, if it still exists, is in there."

"But it's not the only radio in Shlisselburg," Anna replied.

"What do you mean?"

My friend pointed to a building on the other side of the square. A window on the top floor was open and in the dark we could see a wire pole sticking out, like the skeleton of an umbrella without its fabric. It was a radio antenna.

Yes, all right, Viktor, I'll admit it right away, otherwise you'll go on and on about it.

We got lucky.

It happens sometimes and if we hadn't had a little help from Lady Luck, there was no chance three kids like us could have sneaked into an enemy-occupied village, stolen a radio and made it back safe and sound.

So, yes, we were lucky that the tree in the middle of the village was the one I had climbed up in secret thousands of times, and that a few of the branches almost touched the window that the antenna was sticking out of.

It was also an absolutely gigantic stroke of luck that we were out of sight of all of the guards.

And as fate would have it, it was late enough at night that the building was empty and quiet.

There's just one thing I have to add, and it's true. As I sit here writing this, *now*, knowing that we managed to steal the radio, I can admit that we were lucky. But *then*, when I was climbing up the icy tree trunk with Boris behind me, crawling along the branches, practically hanging over the soldiers' heads, Anna down on the ground because she doesn't know how to climb a tree . . . well, *then*, we weren't sure at all that the plan was going to work. We had to be very, very brave.

The fact is, though, we managed to get through the window and into the room. It was a radio-comms room with row upon row of metal radio sets on the table, all covered in indicators and levers.

I picked up a huge headset and a microphone and wound them around my neck like a necklace, before I said to Boris, "Mission accomplished. Alina will be happy with these."

"No," Boris said. "Alina will be happy with *that*."

He pointed to a field radio that had been abandoned in a corner: it was as big as a travel trunk and had straps around it so it could be carried like a backpack.

Boris winked and put the radio on his back. I saw a bar of chocolate on a shelf so I took that, too.

We went back outside, got into position on the window ledge, then jumped across onto the tree. Boris nearly tumbled to the ground because the field radio knocked him off-balance, but at the last minute he managed to right himself.

Anna was as white as a sheet but she smiled when she saw us. We retraced our steps back to the boat, avoiding the guards and also a truck on its way out of the village, spraying snow in its wake. We made it to the farmhouse and the boat.

And that was when it happened.

Our luck ran out.

Well, I suppose we couldn't expect it to last for ever.

A soft, quiet voice called out to us from the bushes. In a language I didn't recognize. I spun around and saw a soldier spying on us in the dark. He was smiling, his face under the helmet glowed in the red light of a cigarette.

He was pointing a pistol at us and held a finger up to his mouth as if to say, "Quiet." He then ran the finger across his throat , as if to say, "Or I'll kill you."

He signalled to us to follow him inside the farmhouse and when the door closed behind us, he lit a lamp on the table, the gun still pointed at us.

So the place which had once kept us safe from the attack on the village had now become our prison.

The windows had all been boarded up so the light wouldn't be seen from outside. The furniture was still the same with some boxes now lined up on the dresser, and there were books on the dining table.

The soldier picked up a rope, handed it to Boris then pointed to me and Anna.

I had to sit down on a chair by the wall and Boris tied

my hands together behind the chair back, then did the same to Anna. The soldier tied Boris to another chair (maybe he preferred to do it himself since Boris is a boy) then checked the knots in the ropes securing me and Anna. Boris had left them quite loose, the soldier pulled them much tighter.

I was so scared, I could feel tears coming. The soldier, on the other hand, was whistling happily. He sat down on the last remaining chair, lit a cigarette and laid the pistol on the table.

"*Gut, gut, gut,*" he said.

He thumped a hand to his chest and said, "Me Franz."

Then he pointed to us and said, "You children island."

He spoke only broken Russian.

He pointed to Anna. "Me see you with . . ." He pretended to point an imaginary rifle at us.

It took a while to put the words and gestures together but I worked out that Franz was the sniper Anna and I had seen on the roof of the farmhouse. He kept watch on the fortress from there and had recognized my friend. Then he'd seen us arrive in the boat and now he'd caught us with the radio.

We were in big trouble; worse than that, we were in the most terrifying situation of my life.

I was shaking and needed to pee. Anna was sobbing.

"You children island. Island soldiers. Soldiers?" he said, counting on his fingers.

Franz was interrogating us. He wanted information on the fortress, the number of soldiers, our weapons.

Why was he doing it on his own instead of taking us to one of his superiors, or to someone who spoke Russian? I had no idea. Maybe he wanted to impress them and be able to say, "I captured three children and discovered the mystery of the fortress all by myself."

Well, he could think again if he thought we'd betray our friends.

"Be careful," I said. "Don't give anything away, not a thing."

"Tsk, tsk, tsk," the soldier said, clicking his tongue.

He lay the cigarette on the edge of the table, stood up, and looked me straight in the eye. Then slapped Boris hard.

It was fast and violent. Boris yelped, Anna screamed and I could hardly breathe.

Boris started to cry, although you could tell he was trying not to. I think Franz had split his lip.

"If you good," the soldier said, and smiled. "If you bad," he said, and slapped Boris again, even harder, sending his head spinning.

"Stop!" I screamed. "You nasty, horrible brute, stop it! Leave him alone. Take it out on me, damn you!"

The soldier ignored me and knelt down in front of Boris.

"You island soldiers. Soldiers?" and held up his fingers, pretending to count.

Boris refused to answer and I can't write down here what happened next. But my friend was very brave, he kept his mouth sealed the whole time and only groaned occasionally when the pain was too much. There were times when it must've been unbearable.

I cried, so did Anna, I would've done anything to help but I was tied up and the rope was so tight I couldn't move.

The soldier got fed up after a bit. He sat down at the table and smoked another cigarette, he seemed to be thinking hard.

He had an idea.

He stood up and came towards me.

"Go on, try it," I thought to myself. "If Boris managed, I'll resist as well."

He slapped me. I'd imagined it would hurt, but not that much. I didn't want to but I cried.

I would never squeal, no, never. But the soldier wasn't looking at me now, he was looking at Boris.

"You boy soldiers island," he said. "You *gut* boy. If not *gut* . . . ," he said, and raised a hand to slap me.

I saw Boris's eyes go wide, like a hare in the headlights. This was Franz's idea. Hit me to get Boris to talk.

"I can take it," I tried to stammer. "Really . . ."

But Boris interrupted me. "Sorry, Nadya, but I can't let him do it."

He looked at the soldier and said, "There are eleven sailors on the island. Do you understand? There were twelve, but one died. Now there are eleven."

"El-ev-en?" The soldier shook his head, maybe he thought he'd misunderstood.

"No, Boris, no! Be quiet!"

"Eleven sailors," my friend repeated.

Franz shook his head. He began counting on his fingers. When he got to ten (holding all his fingers up), he closed his fists and started again. When he got to one, Boris said, "That's it."

"Eleven?"

"Eleven!"

Franz couldn't believe it. He started to laugh. "Eleven!" Cackling. "Eleven."

He'd discovered our secret, namely that there was no garrison on the fortress. At that moment, I'll admit I hated Boris. He'd confessed to save me, but it meant we were all lost now.

Then Franz asked, "Island weapons?"

"Yes, a lot of weapons," Boris replied.

S. – Treason!

"Island . . ." and a word I didn't understand.

"You want to know what they are?" Boris said. "Machine guns and cannons. If you give me paper and pen I'll show you where they're located."

"Pen?"

"Yes, pen. Write. Pen, book." Boris nodded to the table, to a book and pen lying on it.

The soldier's face lit up. "*Gut, gut!*" he said. He untied Boris and let him go over to the table, keeping the gun pointed at his head.

Boris wrote something on a piece of paper. I couldn't stop crying.

The German soldier lowered his gaze to look at the paper. Boris was shielding it with his hand.

That's when Boris picked up the pencil and rammed it into the back of the soldier's neck.

Franz shrieked and Boris jumped on him, knocked him to the ground and threw punch after punch at the soldier's face. I've never seen anything like it. I knew Boris was big (well, obviously, you can see it, Viktor was always saying how massive he was) but I didn't think he could hit someone that hard, he was like a pneumatic drill: POW-POW-POW.

By then I couldn't bear to sit and watch any longer so I rocked back and forward until I fell over onto the floor, still tied to the chair. It really hurt, I thought I'd broken something, but I hadn't, and I managed to get my arms free from the seat back.

"Wait," Boris said. "I'll free you."

He took a knife from the soldier, who was lying motionless on the floor, his face covered in blood, and came over to free me and Anna. Since Anna was crying so much, he gave her a tissue.

"Sorry," Boris said.

"About what?" I shrilled. "You're a hero. I was scared you were going to betray us all but it was just a trick!"

"Well, it wasn't really a trick to begin with," he confessed. "But I soon realized if I could get him to free me, I could attack . . ."

"And it worked!"

I gave him an enormous hug. I might even have kissed him.

"We need to get away from here, as quick as we can, before someone else comes."

"But what about him, Franz, what will we do with him?" *S. - he must be eliminated.*

"Boris," Anna said, "you have to kill him. It's your duty, he knows our secret now!"

"I . . . Yes, but I can't."

"After what he did to you?"

"It doesn't matter. I can't. Punching him is one thing but killing him is a whole different matter. I can't do it," Boris replied. He looked at me, gave me the most disarmingly innocent smile, and continued, "Why, are you saying you could?"

The answer was no. We couldn't kill him either.

There wasn't much else we could do.

We bound Franz with all the rope we could find. Then we took the radio and a few useful things we found lying around the farmhouse (like the sniper's rifle and some tins that looked like food) and loaded it all onto the boat.

It wasn't as easy as it sounds. Franz was a big guy and he kept wriggling and kicking, it took ages and a lot of effort to get him into the boat as well.

It was still dark, thank goodness, I remember the sigh

S. - he must be eliminated!

307

of relief I heaved when I saw the moon because it felt like we'd been shut in that farmhouse for hours.

Boris wanted to row again but he was too weak after the beating he'd taken, so we turned on the motor and zoomed away, as fast as we could. No one heard us.

When we got out into open water, we calmed down a bit and began to talk. We had to decide what to do with Franz.

We couldn't tell anyone – the Chief, Ruslan or the others – that we'd captured the German soldier because they'd definitely kill him, and we all agreed that we couldn't let that happen now. If we'd let him live, then we had to keep him alive.

"We can't hide him," Boris said.

I replied that I thought we could. For a while, at least.

Back at the fortress, everything seemed quiet. The lights were off and no one was up on the walls. We sailed the long way again, dragged the boat onto the shore then put it back where we got it, in the tower gatehouse. We pushed Franz under the grille that was still pulled halfway up and forced him over to the New Prison, where we locked him in an empty cell.

Only after we'd done all that did we wake everyone else. They wouldn't believe us initially but when we showed them the spoils, namely the radio, a real German rifle and all the rest, well, I'm not saying they jumped for joy but there were lots of compliments and pats on the back.

Mrs. Burova kissed Boris and he went bright red. They asked us why we had so many bruises, why Boris's eyes were so swollen and what had happened to his missing teeth, but we just said that to get the radio we'd had to climb up a tree and Boris had fallen. We didn't want to mention the close encounter with the enemy in case

S. – mistreatment of prisoner of war. Oct.268: deliberate falsehood in official statement. Oct. 181: covering up a crime. Oct. 189.

they got suspicious and thought we'd given something away. You never know.

Well, everyone was really happy except the Chief, because we found out he'd been on guard duty and Ruslan said, "Very well done, Comrade Commander. Three kids managed to steal our boat, sneak into the village and get back all by themselves without you noticing a thing."

The Chief was furious, but he couldn't say anything without embarrassing himself even more. So there you go.

What a relief, I've managed to write this all down. It was such a long story, it's taken me for ever!

In short, when the Germans later realized we'd taken one of their men and the radio, they bombed us much more heavily. They even tried to land on the island with two armed motorboats but we fought them off. It was close, though.

"If you ask me, the Fritzes are furious about the note," Boris said one night, after the attacks.

"What note?"

"The one I wrote before I attacked Franz," he replied.

"What did you write?"

"That he could stick it up his ****," Boris replied with a smile.

I don't really approve of swear words but after what we went through that night in the farmhouse, well, Anna and I burst out laughing and couldn't stop.

Oh, well.

It all worked out in the end. But Franz is still in the New Prison and we don't really know what to do with him.

Vorläufige
Beschreibung und Betriebsvorschrift

für das

Tornister-Funkgerät
Torn. Fu. d 2

Ausgabe Oktober 1939

V H/L. Nr. 1298 n

A page from the radio instruction manual!

The village of Pikalyovo lies along the railway line.

It's fifty kilometres from Tikhvin, where the front has advanced to. And where the battle is being fought house-to-house.

The village has been taken over by the military and is a frenzy of activity. Winter has come and these are the final clashes before spring.

Everything has been at a standstill for some time now for me. My world is this hospital ward and the patch of grey sky I can see from the window. The glass will soon ice over and I won't be able to see that either. It's cold. But then again, this isn't even a real hospital, it's just a factory filled up with injured men because they have nowhere else to put them.

The other patients are all soldiers so all they talk about is war. War and girls.

There's a radio set in our room and it broadcasts Radio Leningrad all day, every day. Sometimes a man reads the news. Sometimes there's music. Sometimes there's nothing at all, just the TICK TOCK of a metronome for hours on end.

Leningrad has been under siege since the 8th of September and the news is terrifying. Food has run out and people are dying like flies.

"Did you hear they've cut the rations even further?" said Pavel, the guy in the bed next to me. "Soldiers in the city now get two hundred grams of bread a day. Do you know what that means?"

"No, I don't."

"Two thin slices of bread. A day. And that's soldiers' rations. It's much worse for civilians. I can't bear to think."

I don't want to think either. Mama is a civilian. Who knows if she gets anything to eat.

"How do you think they make bread in Leningrad? They've run out of flour so what do they do?"

"Pavel, stop asking me questions that you keep answering yourself."

"They use sawdust. Chalk dust. Mud!"

According to Pavel, this is the enemy's plan: to leave millions of people in Leningrad to starve to death! Instead of conquering the city with bombs and artillery fire, the Führer, Hitler that is, has decided to let Leningrad slowly fade away and send German tanks to attack Moscow instead.

"It was the mud that stopped them taking Moscow. Russian mud isn't like German mud. It's bellybutton deep here. The Panzers got mired in it and there was no way of moving forward. Then it all froze and it was like they were stuck in a block of cement."

"So we're winning, then," I said. ✳

"Not a chance," he replied. "I'm not sure mud's enough to win a war."

I'm not sure either. It would be good if it were.

My thoughts go back to Nadya, to Mama, her few grams of bread, and to Papa.

I wonder when I'll be able to leave here and get on with my journey.

My right hand is agony. The pain keeps me awake at night.

To be honest, everyone says losing three fingers is only

✳ S. – The first battle for Moscow took place between 13th and 29th October, and Tikhvin fell to the enemy on 8th November. So this page was probably written in early November.

312

a minor injury, and that I'm lucky I'm not a soldier as the army would've sent me back to the front already, to shoot with my other hand. They say they're joking but when they say these things, there are always dark shadows in their eyes.

A postcard of Tikhvin. Pavel gave it to me.

TIKHVIN

Тихвинский Богородичный
Успенский монастырь

Dr. Sharapov says I'm strong and I'll heal quickly. (It'll still take a couple of months though.)

I don't have any time to waste, yet even Klara and the others think the doctor's right. They visit me every day. We play chess and they keep me up-to-date on what they're doing.

They found work in a military depot. They work all day and get food and lodgings in return. Flavio and Marya are in love. (That came as a surprise.)

None of them have any real plans to leave.

Klara helped me to get up today. We walked in the hallway for a bit. Up and down. Up and down.

"There's nowhere to go," she said.

"Of course there is. There's Mga. Leningrad."

She glared at me. "You just don't get it. The road to Leningrad is blocked. It's all enemy territory now. Even Tikhvin is hanging on by a thread, it could fall to the Germans at any minute. I heard talk this morning about evacuating the hospital and shifting everything about a hundred kilometres east!"

"I can't go east. My sister is west."

"Tell that to the enemy."

I was so angry I blurted, "Well, maybe you could. After all, you're one of them."

It slipped out and by the time I realized, it was too late.

Klara's lip trembled. I was afraid she was going to hit me.

Maybe I would have deserved it.

"I am not one of them. I belong to no one. I am Klara and I choose who I want to be and who I want to be with. And someone I definitely don't want to be with just now is you."

She turned on her heel and left.

And hasn't come back.

I could ask someone what day it is instead of writing "another day," "I don't know when," and stuff like that. But I can't be bothered.

Klara didn't come in today but, luckily, Lev and Mikhail showed up instead. Lev handed me a tin.

"It's a present."

"What's inside?"

"Pills," he replied. "Pills for the pain, the same ones they give you here. I thought they might be useful for . . . for when we set off again."

"Oh," I said. "Where did you get them?"

Lev shrugged. ⟵

"Okay, thanks. Where are Flavio and Marya?"

"They'll be around somewhere, kissing as usual."

"And Klara?"

"I think you know the answer to that. She's angry with you. But I have to go now, I have a shift at the depot. Mikhail can hang around and chat with you. I'll see you soon. Be good."

Lev raced off like a squirrel. He doesn't like hospitals, he told me. The fact that he'd come in at all was something. As for Mikhail, well, we might not be enemies anymore but I still don't feel comfortable with him on my own.

"There aren't many of us left, eh?" Mikhail said. "What I mean is, there was a whole trainload of us when we set off from Kazan, then we became a kolkhoz squad, then a handful of fugitives, then Lev did what he did in Moscow and there were even fewer of us."

"Then the Rybinsk camp . . . Ilya . . . and here we are now."

"Yeah."

S. — another theft. And for Viktor it's appropriation of stolen goods. Art. 208.

Mikhail sat down on my bed. We chatted for a bit. About the war mainly. Leningrad and things like that.

"It's a pity the railway is out of use," he said. "There's enough food for everyone here."

"What do you mean?"

"The truck that picked us up was carrying sacks of flour for Leningrad. But all the roads are blocked. The warehouses here are full but we've no way of delivering the stuff. They're talking about recalling the trucks and having them bring everything back from the front. They don't want our food falling into the hands of the Germans."

"Is the situation that bad?"

"Worse. They say Tikhvin is doomed."

I sat in silence.

Partly because my hand hurt. Partly because, honestly, I didn't know what to say.

5th November

When I woke up this morning my hand was hurting.

It's been like this for a week now: I'll be busy doing something then, *POW*, an unbearable pain shoots through my right hand. Luckily I'm left-handed, otherwise it would be difficult to write.

I had sailor Boris take a look at it. Before he joined the Ladoga Fleet he drove an ambulance in Kirishi, so he's become the fortress doctor.

"There's nothing broken," he said. "Your hand isn't swollen . . . Maybe you hurt yourself at the last cannon drill."

Maybe, but the pain can be really bad at times. In fact, that's what woke me today.

Anyway, the other thing I noticed right away is that it's cold now. Like freezing cold. Down in the cellars the children sleep huddled together, snuggling like bunnies in a den, tiny puffs of vapour coming out of their mouths, making them look like mini cigar smokers.

This reminded me of something important, so I grabbed a blanket and ran up the stairs. The door handle had iced over and my hand stuck to it. My eyebrows froze the second I stepped outside. I had to go back inside and put a couple of heavy sweaters on.

Outside the snow was like translucent marble, the trees turned into a lattice of metal spikes. I pulled the blanket tighter around my shoulders and half-ran, half-slid to a slit in the outer wall. It was dark and winter seemed to have swallowed up every sound. The ice had imprisoned the river in its silver, viselike grip. There was only a thin strip of unfrozen water around the island that was still moving.

I crossed the courtyard to the New Prison where me, Anna and Boris have imprisoned Franz.

I have to admit it's not every day you capture someone and have three prisons to choose from. The Old Prison and the Fourth Prison are too close unfortunately (the former is where we are, the latter is beside the Golovkin Tower), so we had no choice but to use the New Prison.

Anyway, I opened the door and the security gates. (When the last people abandoned Oreshek, they left all the keys in the locks so we took them. No one ever comes here.)

When I get to that point, when I open the gates that is, the soldier, Franz, always calls out to me, but not this morning. I hurried down to his cell.

It's not the greatest of accommodation, it's true, but Franz is a prisoner of war so I think he'll just have to put up with it.

I looked into his cell, the third from last.

"Hey, Franz, is everything okay?"

I thought he was dead at first because he was lying motionless on the camp bed wearing all the jumpers we'd given him. Then I noticed he was shaking. It's absolutely freezing in the New Prison because there's no heating and a bomb blew a hole in the roof.

"I brought you a blanket."

Photo of a prison cell
I found in among
the museum things.

I opened the food hatch and chucked the blanket inside.

Franz took it and wrapped himself up in it. His lips were blue.

"You die me."

"No, Franz, I already told you we don't want to hurt you."

"Here much snow."

"Yes, I know it's cold. We'll work something out. I promise."

"Cigarette?"

"I don't have any cigarettes, I'm sorry."

He lay back down on the camp bed. Icicles hung along the side.

I pushed a piece of bread, already like a block of ice because of the cold, through the hatch. He made no effort to catch it and the bread thumped onto the floor.

"You should eat you know. It's important."

Two bright blue eyes looked up at me.

I know it's weird but I feel sorry for him. He doesn't seem like the same person who beat us and who Boris then punched on the farmhouse floor. (Well, apart from the fact that Franz still has loads of bruises, a crooked nose and a horrible wound on the back of his neck where the pencil stabbed him.)

I sometimes wonder how old he is, if he has a family, maybe a girlfriend waiting for him in Germany. Sometimes I wonder if he killed someone with that sniper's rifle. Maybe not. Maybe he's actually a good man: he could've called a superior that night.

I would've liked to talk to him but I don't know a word of German and his Russian isn't good enough for us to have a proper conversation. I try to smile a lot. I hope that's enough.

S. – doubt leads to consorting with the enemy. Oct. 89.

"Franz, I'm sorry. I know you don't want to be here. None of us like it, but we couldn't leave you there, after you learned the truth about us and the fortress."

What would happen if someone were to find Franz in his cell? We could end up in serious trouble. The Chief might call us traitors, maybe even have us shot.

I shut the hatch and ran away.

S. — with good reason.   *6th November*

Anyway, we're going to have to do something for Franz. Yesterday I had a long talk with my friends and Boris came up with the idea of building him a stove.

"You're mad! What will he burn in it?"

"Wood and coal."

"What, you want to steal from our supply? If we get found out, they'll kill us."

"Do you have a better idea?"

I didn't.

"A stove means fire," Anna said. "What happens if Franz sets the prison on fire?"

"There's not much that will burn in there, it's all stone and metal."

"A stove is the only thing that will keep him alive at minus twenty degrees," Boris said. "There's not much to argue about."

So we got hold of an old tin barrel and steel pipe to use as a flue, then fitted them together in the cell beside Franz's. We tried lighting it and it worked quite well, you could feel the heat off it.

"Everyone will see the smoke outside," Boris said.

"Not if the flue points into the corridor instead of out the window," Anna said.

S. — this could be classed as an act of sabotage. Oct. 68.

We tried it and she was right. Out in the corridor the smoke, which puffed out only a little at a time, dispersed into the cells and there was no trace of it in the garden.

Our one remaining problem was how to move Franz from his current cell to the new, heated one. We took a rifle each, and loaded and cocked them like the sailors taught us.

Anna and I locked the gate in the corridor and stood on the other side, rifles pointing through the bars.

Boris stayed where he was and opened the door to Franz's cell. He gestured at him to come out, all three rifles aimed at him, pushed him into the new cell and locked the door again.

We were terrified something untoward might happen, but Franz behaved and didn't attempt to get hold of our weapons. Maybe he knew it was futile.

When he saw the stove in his new cell, he said, "Thank you."

As we left the prison, happy with our work, we saw Mrs. Burova running towards us. "Where have you three been?"

"Oh, just stretching our legs," I replied. "Why?"

"Comrade Alina! Alina has fixed the radio!"

Everyone was standing in the Golovkin Tower, in a circle around the radio. The German one that we stole and also the Russian one. Both were open, half-dismantled, wires running between them.

I don't remember if I wrote this down before: the radio we stole in Shlisselburg was broken but Alina said that, with a little time, she could make one working radio from the two broken ones. After a lot of hard work, she'd done as she'd said.

Anyway, everyone was crowded around her, she had the headset on and was twiddling with some knobs until she announced, "I can hear Radio Leningrad!"

She pulled off the headset and turned the volume up as high as she could so that we could hear as well. It was a piece of classical music with violins and trumpets. It had been months since we'd last heard music. It brought tears to everyone's eyes.

Anna and I hugged. People were slapping each other on the back and that sort of thing. Nikolay took Alina's hand and they began to waltz around the freezing cold room, Ruslan danced with Mrs. Burova, and even I would have danced with Boris (my friend) at that point but he was too much of an idiot to ask me. I got fed up waiting so started jumping up and down with Anna, laughing until we cried.

The jubilations went on for a while, until the Chief said we had to be serious again.

"Comrade Alina," he said. "Make contact with Ladoga Fleet Command."

Alina put the headset on again and went back to twiddling knobs and saying, "Hello, hello," into the microphone. She tried for a long time but apparently our antenna isn't powerful enough to send out a signal or maybe there's no one on the other end to receive it.

It doesn't matter, we'll try again.

The Nazis bombed us more heavily than usual last night. It was like they were trying to make us pay. But our cannons seemed to be exploding with laughter.

I feel happy, even if that doesn't make any sense.

Leaves from the apple tree here in the fortress.

German munitions: stolen!

20 Pist.-Patr. 43 m. E.
1943 aux 14
Nz. R. P. (1,0-0,8/0,2) rdf 1942/6 - 1,68 g
Patrh. (St) 1943 aux versch.   Gesch. 1943 aux 101
Kern: 1943 - a f u   Zdh. 30/40 : 1943 e e m 4 e

A photo I found in the museum: the little girl looks like Kristina.

CCCP

PEOPLE'S COMMISSARIAT FOR
INTERNAL AFFAIRS

REPORT FOR INTERNAL USE

Of all the notebooks, the fifth one raises
the most doubts concerning the veracity of the
facts it presents.

The wild escape from the village of
Shlisselburg may be true. The children
convincing a squadron of Soviet sailors on a
mission to take them into their care may be
true.

But the other things Nadya describes: can
this girl really have invented an imaginary,
non-existent army to deter enemy attack? Not
to mention the nighttime foray into enemy
territory. Or the theft of the radio. Or the
interrogation by the German sniper, Franz. Or
the even more unbelievable capture of said
German soldier and the decision to imprison
him /another act which, in itself, warrants
the "guilty" stamp in red at the bottom of
this file without any further ado/.

The fact is, however, I always recognize a lie
when I hear it, and I believe this notebook
actually speaks the truth.

I can sense it in Nadya's words, and in the
photos and the small objects filling the final
pages of the notebook.

So, what must the sentence be?

I haven't made my mind up yet, but we are almost there. The story is nearing its end. As is the moment of decision.

Signed:

COLONEL VALERY GAVRIILOVICH SMIRNOV

The Long Winter

NOTEBOOK 6

Final part.

—Smirnov

S. - chapter 41
*(no date, although it must be 7th or
8th November 1941: The fall of Tikhvin)*

My name is Viktor Nikolayevich Danilov.

I was born in Leningrad on the 17th of November 1928.

My parents work in the Hermitage Museum. Or rather, they worked there before the war.

I have a twin sister called Nadya.

Nadya and I had to leave Leningrad in July but ended up on two different trains by mistake. Mine went to the Republic of Tatarstan and I lost track of Nadya's in Mga.

My writing is not very good because I'm using my left hand. I'm not left-handed but I lost three fingers in an accident so I can no longer use my right one. My right hand is agony. That's why I'm awake when everyone else is sleeping.

I'm in a truck parked on the road. There's a snowstorm outside and it must be about minus thirty degrees.

It's a miracle I'm alive.

At dinnertime I was in the hospital in Pikalyovo, near Tikhvin.

Our ward was quiet. Some of the injured men were asleep. I was listening to the radio playing the usual metronome: TICK TOCK, TICK TOCK, TICK TOCK.

Sooner or later, I hoped they'd broadcast news about Leningrad, although I was the only one who cared. Everyone else could only think about Tikhvin, where fighting had been fierce for days. (The men on my ward have all come from there.)

There was a sudden commotion outside so I stuck my head into the corridor. Nurses and doctors raced past. A soldier bumped straight into me, almost knocking me over, but he kept going, didn't stop.

"Hey, what's happening?"

No answer.

I tried asking someone else, then I stopped a nurse who told me, "We've lost Tikhvin!"

"What?!"

"The Germans have taken control of the city. What's left of the 48th Soviet Army is retreating to the north, towards Lake Ladoga, the enemy is moving east.

"What, you mean they're coming this way?"

"Yes. We need to get away from here as quickly as possible. Evacuate everyone."

"And where will we go?"

"I don't know. No one has told me that yet. Maybe further east. Far away."

She looked at me. It was only then that she realized she was speaking to a child. "Don't you worry. Go back to your room. Keep calm. We'll come and get you in a bit."

"Okay."

The truth is it wasn't okay. Not at all. I couldn't go east, it would mean going in the opposite direction to Nadya.

(Hang on a second, there's a road atlas in the truck. Klara put it on the dashboard. I'll rip out a page and stick it here, with arrows pointing to Pikalyovo and Tikhvin. — On the other side you'll see Mga and Leningrad, where my sister is.)

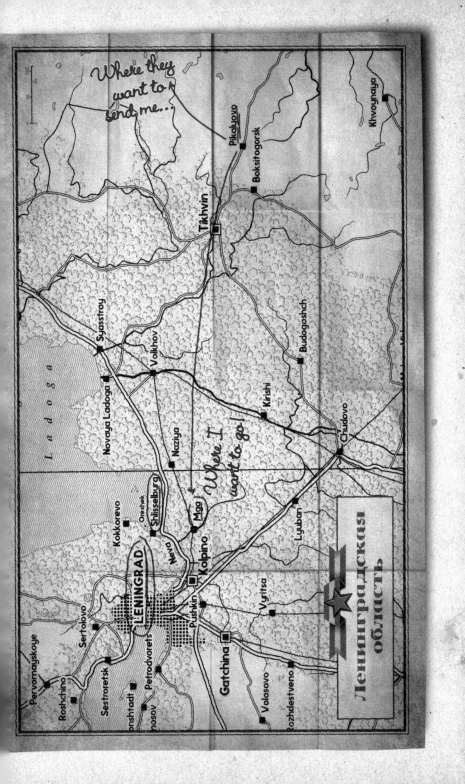

I couldn't let them take me away. Not now that I was so close. In two seconds flat I'd made up my mind.

I went back to the ward.

"What did they say?" Pavel asked.

"Tikhvin has fallen. They're sending us away."

Chaos erupted, which is what I'd been hoping.

I picked up my haversack, which was now almost empty and shoved the notebooks in along with the silver icon Papa gave me. (It's the only thing I have left of his. I've kept it hidden under my pillow here.)

Then I went back out into the corridor. Ice-cold wind was blasting through the front doors. If it was as cold outside as Mikhail had said, I'd need something more than the jumper I was wearing. A heavy coat and a fur hat or something would do.

I thought about it for a few seconds then went into the morgue, that's the room in the hospital where they put all the dead bodies. It's not a great place, as I'm sure you can imagine. But I needed clothes and I knew I'd find them there. They strip any salvageable boots and coats from the dead at the front but the filthiest rags usually get left behind and, well, this was no time to be choosy.

There must've been a few hundred mummy-like figures lying lifeless on the floor. It was creepy but not as bad as you might think. They were like mannequins. I found one man with a tattered greatcoat which I took. Then I found another coat which I put on top of the first one. And a wool cap that smelt disgusting, but I tried not to think about it.

After that, I went back outside, my bag tucked safely under my clothes.

Now. I like the cold, me and the winter get along. But this was *exceptionally* cold. The snow was leaden and the sky a pool of black.

I looked around because it was my first time outside the hospital there in Pikalyovo, but I remembered how my friends had described it and I worked out where their depot was.

The streets were full of peasants fleeing, and soldiers, trucks, shouting, horns. And gunfire.

I ran into the night and found the depot. There was even more chaos there than in the village. It was full of soldiers and labourers. No one seemed to know what to do. I went inside and ran this way and that until I found Klara carrying a huge crate together with another older girl. When she saw me she dropped the crate and said, "What are you doing here?! I wanted to come . . . there's so much to do . . . They said you'd been . . . I thought . . ."

"Forget it," I interrupted. "I'm sorry about what I said the other day. I wasn't feeling well. It was stupid. I don't think those things. But will you come with me now, please? We need to go."

One thing I like about Klara is that she doesn't waste time. "Okay," she said. "Mikhail is over there."

"Excellent. What about Lev? Flavio? Marya?"

"I haven't seen them since this morning."

We found Mikhail almost right away. Who knows where the others were and we didn't have time to look for them. I was sad to leave them behind, especially Lev because he'd been my first ally when he shook my hand in the wagon of train seventy-seven. But I didn't know how long we had until someone noticed us – two scrawny children and a third wearing a stolen coat, with his hand in bandages.

"What do you plan to do?" Mikhail asked me.

"If I tell you, you won't want to come with me."

"We won't come if you don't tell us."

"If you do, we will. I promise," Klara said.

"Okay then. We're going to Tikhvin."

"You're mad!"

"If I'm going to find my sister, I need to go west. And the only road from here goes to Tikhvin."

Having listened to injured soldiers for so long, I had a pretty good idea of the local geography.

"But Tikhvin was taken!"

"I know."

"And it's all enemy territory to the west!"

"I know that, too. But we can head for the centre of the city and join the Red Army as it retreats northwards and towards Lake Ladoga. It will still be better than going back. And, Klara . . ."

"Yes?"

"Trust me."

"I don't know . . ."

"I trust you," Mikhail said. "But Tikhvin is fifty kilometres from here, the lake even further. You can't be thinking of going there on foot in this weather. We wouldn't last half an hour."

"I know," I replied.

That's when I pointed to one of the trucks and said, "We'll take that."

There was so much commotion in the depot that no one paid us any attention. We were able to climb onto a large truck with a long bonnet. The back, under a canvas hood, was stacked high with wooden crates, I had no idea what was inside them. (I do now: tinned food!) ✳

"Do you know how to drive?" Mikhail asked me.

"Yes, but I can't," I said, waving my bandaged hand.

"So who'll drive?"

"You or Klara?"

✳ S. – another case of theft of state property. Art. 89; inciting a minor to engage in criminal behaviour. Art. 210.

"Mikhail would be better," she said. "He's taller and his feet are more likely to reach the pedals than mine."

"Okay, but how does it work?"

I thought back to the time Papa had taken me out in Dr. Orbeli's car. I hoped I remembered or we were in trouble.

"There are three pedals," I said. "The one on the left is the clutch. The one in the middle is the brake. The one on the right, the accelerator."

"What does clutch mean?"

"I've no idea but you have to press it every time you change the gears." I pointed to the gearstick near the steering wheel. "So, press it in and move the gearstick to that sign there which means 'reverse'."

The truck made a CLA-CLANG noise.

"Now, turn the key."

Mikhail did as I told him. The engine spluttered into life.

"And now . . ."

"Get out of my truck, immediately!"

A man grabbed onto the door and thrust his arm through the open window.

"Go, Mikhail, go, go, go!"

I'll say this for him – Mikhail is a pretty good driver.

He revved the engine and the truck did a half-spin backwards. The wheels slipped on the smooth floor of the depot, leaving black skid marks everywhere, but it was enough to knock the shouting man off the door as a soldier pointed a rifle at us.

"What now?" Mikhail asked.

"Put it into first gear . . ."

"No way!" Klara said. "Let's just get out of here before they shoot us!"

So we screeched out of the depot in reverse, I only hope we didn't kill anyone. The road was icy outside and Mikhail lost control. The truck spun around and we crashed into a lamp post.

I shouted at Mikhail to press the clutch and move the gear lever.

He did. The truck moved forwards, in fits and starts to begin with, then lurched onto the road which was full of people. I hope we didn't kill anyone there either.

"Where's Tikhvin? Which way do we go?"

Klara is a genius because she said, "Look, there are the railway tracks, follow them!"

It was a good idea because the roads were jammed full, the truck didn't seem that well suited to driving off-road and the train tracks were fairly empty. Mikhail didn't just follow them, though, he more or less drove along the top of them. We raced along at full speed with our lights off.

"What now?"

"Put it into second gear, otherwise you'll blow the engine, then switch on the headlamps."

"Watch out for trains," Klara said.

"I need to think," I said.

I rummaged around the dashboard of the truck with my left hand and found the road atlas. Klara and I opened it out on our knees.

It was there in black and white. Tikhvin was unavoidable. We'd have to go pretty much into the centre of the town to get onto the orbital road that skirts Tikhvin before finally heading north towards the lake. To go west would be absolutely impossible. As Klara said, that's all enemy territory.

I looked back but there was no one following us. The railway track stretched out before us, straight and dark. The truck bumped over the sleepers. It began to sleet. I showed Mikhail how to turn on the windscreen wipers.

S. – violation of road safety rules for motorized vehicles by unauthorized personnel. Art. 212: breach of driving code for military vehicles. Art. 252.

A train appeared out of nowhere. It had stopped on the track and we very nearly crashed into it. We swerved and the truck skidded over the embankment, thankfully it didn't tip over. We bumped over the ground and managed to get it back onto a road. The road was full of people, mostly civilians, walking in the opposite direction. They were shaking with cold, I wondered to myself if they'd make it to Pikalyovo. I wished I could do something to help them.

"Is it far to Tikhvin?" Mikhail asked.

"No," I replied, looking at the atlas.

We knew right away when we'd arrived at the town – the road suddenly opened out and there were no more trees. Ahead of us fires lit up the darkness. There were explosions, hundreds of them. They made the sky sparkle like a firecracker.

And there was a Panzer, pointing its gun straight at us.

Now. An armoured tank is a big, heavy vehicle, with metal tracks and everything. An iron beast like that crushes everything in its path.

It's slow and noisy.

And also terrifying.

We should have noticed it earlier. But we didn't, maybe because we hadn't been paying attention, well, not until Klara screamed, "Look, a tank!"

There it was, taking up the whole breadth of the road.

I shouted again. Mikhail did, too, and I saw the gun slowly turn towards us, as if it were saluting us.

"Get out of the way!" I yelled and threw my body at the steering wheel. The truck swerved and since the ground was icy, it skidded a fair distance sideways. That's what saved us. There was a giant blast and the

S. – Viktor could've offered to take the displaced civilians on the truck.

road behind us exploded. In front of us, all we saw was earth, snow and stones fly across the windscreen.

Mikhail stepped hard on the accelerator. The truck leapt forward. Someone started shooting at us with a machine gun, puncturing the door with a line of bullet holes, but luckily not hitting any of us. We got away.

We raced through the suburbs of Tikhvin at breakneck speed. There were armoured cars and soldiers in grey uniforms everywhere. I realized I was looking at the enemy: the real enemy.

Klara stared at me, petrified (what an idiot I'd been for saying they were her people). I squeezed her hand for a second before we began to thunder past buildings reduced to rubble by the bombs, the truck lurching dangerously as we dodged the craters. Mikhail was driving like a madman. I had gone past being scared now. It was like I was watching the scene unfold from somewhere else. From a distance.

We found a road that led into darkness so we took it, leaving the bright lights and the explosions behind us. After what felt like ages, we finally managed to catch our breath.

I gave Mikhail a slap on the back and said, "Not bad, partner."

He smiled.

We carried on for another half an hour. At one point, we passed a column of soldiers on foot, but this time they were Russian. They saluted us as we drove past but we didn't slow down, pretending we were on urgent business. They might have seized the truck and who knows what else.

That was probably when we got lost. We ended up on a country road and the truck began to labour in the snow, I was scared we'd get stuck. That would've been a disaster. We found somewhere to shelter, at the side of the road under the trees.

We pulled over.

It was useless trying to talk, we were too tired so we curled up in the cab to wait for dawn when we'd set off again.

Where to? I don't know. To the lake. We've kind of run out of options.

Klara and Mikhail are asleep.

I wish I could sleep too but my hand is throbbing.

I took one of the pills Lev gave me. ← *S. – Illegal administration of medication. Art. 221.*

Swallowing it brought a lump to my throat. We'd made a pact, me and Lev. We'd shaken hands on it. But I'd left him bang in the middle of an evacuation.

What else could I have done? I looked for him but didn't find him. We had to go. He would've done the same thing. And it's better this way. He'll be safe with the warehouse workers. He'll be better off.

But I miss him. I wish I could at least have said goodbye. But life isn't like it is in books. Nothing turns out like it should.

I hope the pill I took starts working soon. I need to get some sleep.

Tomorrow will be a long day.

7th November

I'm starting my notebook with a drawing.

Mrs. Burova drew it, it's Ruslan and Boris the sailor climbing up the Watchtower and raising the red flag. The drawing is a bit made-up because when they put the flag up there weren't any bombs falling, they came later, but I think it's good all the same.

There'd been talk for a while about flying the red flag on Oreshek.

Firstly, a fortress needs a banner, that's been the rule for centuries. It's a symbol of who we are and what we're fighting for (Ruslan said). What's more, the red flag also warns allies we're here. You never know, they might send the reinforcements we badly need.

The only problem was – the Chief didn't want it.

"Raising a flag is playing with fire," he said. "It might anger the Germans when they see it. They could decide to launch a major offensive."

"It is not befitting of you, Comrade Commander, to speak in this way," Ruslan insisted. "It's time for Oreshek to be Oreshek once again."

The Chief had to back down. He said the Germans were setting up camp for the winter so it was okay.

Alina found a piece of red fabric and Ruslan and sailor Boris took it onto the roof and tied it to a mast. Ruslan then turned to us and shouted, "This flag will protect us until the end of the war!"

"And after," Boris added.

"Of course, and after."

The flag fluttered red and furious, like a beating heart. It was a thrilling sight. Down below we all clapped and would have celebrated had we not heard a rumble, then seen planes nose-diving straight at us.

We sprang into action like we'd done hundreds of times before. We pulled the scarecrows dressed as soldiers out of view and trained the guns, the working ones and the broken ones, on the incoming aircraft.

Maybe the Chief was right about the flag. This wasn't an ordinary attack.

S. – commendation for the sailor, Ruslan.

341

I realize I'm not very good at describing the battles. If Viktor reads these pages he might imagine everything very differently from what actually happened.

Because if I write that some bombs exploded and it seems like nothing, well, it's not.

It's terrifying and awful and you know you could die at any moment.

Bombs were raining down, throwing great mountains of snow everywhere. The air erupted with explosions. We all started to scream and the little ones burst into tears. One of the sailors fell to the ground, immobile. Another screeched when shrapnel lacerated his thigh.

Boris (my friend) threw himself on top of me and we rolled on the ice, then got to our feet to see everyone around us fleeing.

Then artillery fire started coming in from the riverbank too so Ruslan yelled, "Combat stations!"

Boris and I went into the Watchtower. He took up position at the heavy machine gun, which is a very long, and therefore very heavy, rifle, so heavy you can't lift it, and it has a stand on the front to keep it in place. He started firing while I fed through the cartridges. The noise was deafening, there was smoke everywhere and I was scared I was going to die.

Across the river on the opposite bank, I could see men running and lines of fires which were actually explosions. There was a huge blast at one point, louder than all the others, and the room fell in on us.

It was dark and Boris and I were buried under a pile of rubble.

"Are we dead?" I asked.

"No, I don't think we're dead," he replied. "Those beams saved us."

When I looked up, I saw some huge beams had fallen over the top of us, forming a kind of ceiling, so that most of the stones were lying on them instead of crushing us.

The battle raged on around us while we were trapped under the beams, squashed up against each other. Boris forced a laugh and said, "Well, we've certainly found ourselves a quiet little spot here."

I replied that it wasn't quiet at all and we could suffocate. I may even have started to cry.

Boris stroked my cheek.

"There's enough air, don't worry, we're safe. Bombs never hit the same place twice."

"How do you know that?"

"I read it somewhere." His eyes shone in the dark like a cat's. "My mum works in a library," he explained. "What I mean is, in a library and in an office and in a hospital, she's a cleaner in all these places. But the library is her afternoon shift so after school I go there. To give her a hand. And every now and then I get to read something . . . anything . . ."

"A lot of things by the sound of it."

"I do it to pass the time. Since my dad went away . . . Don't make that face, he's not dead. Well, I don't think so, not that I know of. They just came for him one night and took him away."

"Who?"

Boris shrugged.

"Since then my mum hasn't . . . Well, she hasn't been in her right mind. So . . ."

I didn't know what to say, he was so close, there by my side, under that pile of rubble. So I hugged him. I'm used to hugging boys, or rather, I'm used to hugging Viktor given that we've slept in the same bed since we were tiny. But hugging Boris wasn't the same as with

S. – Boris: find patronymic and surname. There must be some record of his father in our files.

my brother. I mean, Boris is bigger to start with, and softer, and . . .

He's just different. You get the picture.

"Nadya," he said.

He looked at me, eyes so wide for a second they seemed to fill the whole world.

Then he kissed me.

He kissed me a lot, and I kissed him a lot, too.

(Viktor, if you read this, don't ever try to tease me about it. Never, I'm warning you.)

Anyway, a while later the Chief and Nikolay came to free us. They said the battle had been devastating. Two sailors were dead and also our friend, Valentin, so we now have three fewer people at the fortress, all because of that damned flag.

But when the Chief looked up and saw a bullet had smashed the mast and the flag had fallen into the snow, in shreds, he said, "Hey, Nikolay. Climb up there and put it back up. If it annoys the Fritzes so much, they'll have to come and get it themselves."

I have to say that's the first time I've ever thought the Chief made a fine commander. ✳

Given that we'd missed lunch, we decided to have dinner early. We all gathered in the cellars, sailors and children alike, and Mrs. Burova drew the picture I stuck here in the notebook.

I chatted a bit with Anna (luckily, she wasn't hurt in the battle) but I couldn't bring myself to say anything to her about Boris. Does the fact that he kissed me mean we're together? Does it mean I'm in love?

I have no idea, but kissing him was nice and I'd like it to happen again.

✳ S. – another commendation for the Chief.

344

Something incredible happened.

It's so incredible I still can't believe it and I think I'm going to explode with joy. I can hardly write.

To be honest, until this evening, nothing much had been happening: it's really cold and we've been holed up in the cellars, bored to tears.

You could tell the sailors were bored, too. They came down to have dinner with us tonight, chatting to everyone, and the Chief and Mrs. Burova went to check our supplies.

Mrs. Burova does her best to ration the food and not waste anything, but we won't be able to survive like this for ever. After a bit, the Chief said, "Comrade Alina, we must try again with that radio. If we don't get reinforcements soon, all will be lost."

Alina agreed and went to the tower where the radio is. The Chief and most of the sailors went with her, me and Anna too, mostly because it gave us the excuse to check on our prisoner.

But then something else happened.

Alina turned on the radios but instead of putting the headset on like last time, she turned the volume up as loud as it would go so we could all hear and started saying, "All stations, all stations, all stations. This is Ladoga Fleet, position Oreshek Island. Do you read me?"

There was nothing but *SHSHSSHHSHS* static buzz.

"All stations, all stations, all stations. This is Ladoga Fleet, position Oreshek Island. Do you read me?"

SHSHSSHHSHS.

"This is Ladoga Fleet . . ."

SHSHSSHHSHS.

This went on so long I started to get bored and tugged Anna's sleeve to ask if we could leave. But that very second, a gruff voice crackled out of the headset, a man's voice, and it said, "Position Oreshek Island? Say again, Oreshek?"

"Affirmative! Affirmative!"

"But . . . I mean, who is this? Sir! There's someone here says they're calling from Oreshek . . ."

We looked at each other for a second, then, in the stunned, astonished silence, I jumped to my feet and screamed, "They heard us! Hoorah, someone answered!"

In the silence that followed, another voice came forth from the headset on Alina's lap.

". . . Nadya? Is that you?" it said.

I realize this is utterly crazy and incredible.

But the voice that said my name was Viktor's.

My brother.

He'd done it!

I'd been right all along. He's alive and he's coming to get me.

We woke up in an ice trap. The windscreen on the truck was covered with a thick, shimmering layer of crystals.

Me, Klara and Mikhail had curled up beside each other under the same blanket and my back was hurting. But much worse than that was my hand. The pain burned so hot it felt like my hand was on fire.

"Does it hurt?" Klara asked.

"It's killing me," I replied.

"Maybe you should change the dressing."

"Yes," I said. "But this is a truck, not a hospital."

I made do with another pill.

After that, I forced open the door of the truck which had iced shut and ventured outside. That's when I had my first nasty surprise of the day, and by that I mean that the truck was half-buried. We shovelled away the snow and lit a fire under the bonnet to defrost the engine. Then Mikhail climbed back behind the wheel. He tried moving forward and reversing but the wheels span and it just made things worse. We were gouging ourselves into a hole.

"That's not going to work."

"So what shall we do?"

"Let's go for help. We need to find some planks to put under the wheels. And maybe some rope."

Mikhail agreed. Klara disagreed. So we decided that she would stay to guard the truck and we would go for help.

"And how will you convince them to help us? You don't have anything to offer."

I pointed to the truck. "There's loads to bargain with in there."

I climbed into the back, prised open one of the crates and filled my pockets with tinned sardines.

Mikhail and I traversed the forest and made our way back onto the road. We came across a column of soldiers on foot. Many of them were injured and I felt like one of them. A survivor.

"Hey, boy, what did they do to your hand?" asked a man with a long, snow-covered beard.

"I lost three fingers," I replied.

"Ouch. Shell?"

"No. Axe."

He gave me a look as if to say, I know what you mean.

"Which way is the lake?" I asked.

"Do you mean the village of Novaya Ladoga? It's along this road. That's where we're all headed."

"Have you come from Tikhvin?"

"Yes. What's left of it."

Mikhail and I walked with them, listening to their battle stories, how they'd fought for every single building. In half an hour, we arrived at the village. It's where the River Volkhov flows into Lake Ladoga. Except that it's frozen over now obviously.

Lake Ladoga was a white desert glittering in the sun. You couldn't see the end of it. It was like the pictures of the North Pole Mama often showed us in books.

"It's immense!" Mikhail gasped.

"You're right, it's huge," one soldier said. He pointed to the horizon with his left hand and said, "Leningrad is that way, on the other side of the lake. In summer, you can go on the ferry. It's a long crossing."

"Could it be done now on a sleigh?"

"Only when the ice is strong enough. But you have to be sure it's thick enough as it could crack and you'd fall straight through. It's a dangerous place this."

"You're right," I replied.

It definitely felt like it.

The village of Novaya Ladoga is a little like Pikalyovo – a quiet place that's been converted to a military base.

The streets are backed up with trucks. Part of the forest was razed to the ground and filled with tents. Fishermen wander around with a lost look, while commanders, doctors and soldiers rush between houses which have become outposts, carrying dispatches, barking orders, receiving instructions.

A group of soldiers who'd survived the front were cooking on a field stove. Village peasants were selling baskets of eggs.

I asked if they knew who might have some planks and rope. They wanted to know why I needed them. I replied that we were helping some soldiers whose truck was stuck.

"It's full of soldiers here," the peasants replied. "They'll be happy to help their comrades."

We thanked them for the excellent advice and moved on. We offered our sardines to the next man we met. He offered to help without asking too many questions.

A soldier appeared behind us at that point and said, "Who are you? You don't look like local children. And what happened to your hand? Show me your papers."

For a fleeting second I thought about running away, but there was nowhere to go. Mikhail pulled out the passports and gave them to the soldier, who said, "You're from Leningrad?"

"We've come from Tikhvin," I replied. "We're cousins, and our parents sent us there when the war broke out. To stay with an uncle. But then . . ."

"So you and this boy here are cousins, eh? Your papers don't say that and neither do your faces. I think you should come with me."

What else could we do?

We went with him.

We ended up in a big room that looked to all intents and purposes like a command centre. At the back of the room were three radio operators sitting before huge metal boxes, twiddling with the dials and babbling into the microphones.

The soldier walked off with our papers. We had no choice but to stand and wait.

For hours.

By lunchtime, Mikhail and I were hungry so we pulled out some tins. This attracted a bit of attention, the soldiers were hungry too, and wanted to barter with us. The only thing we wanted were our papers but they wouldn't hand them over.

An officer finally appeared to ask us some questions, then told us we'd still have to wait where we were.

So we waited.

By sunset the barracks emptied and we're still here like a pair of idiots. I'm tired and my hand hurts. I just want to get back to Klara. She'll be worried by now and probably freezing to death.

Mikhail has fallen asleep with his head on my shoulder.

I'm tired, too. The radio operators on the other side of the room are still talking into microphones, faces buried under their headsets, speaking in monotone voices that are beginning to sound a bit like a bedtime lullaby . . .

CRASH!

I'd just about dropped off to sleep on this wretched bench when a chair tipped back and clattered to the floor with an almighty crash.

One of the radio operators had sprung to his feet and whirled around, as if possessed. He ripped off the headset and shouted, "Sir! Sir! There's someone here saying they're transmitting from Oreshek . . ."

He flicked a switch and all of a sudden, from a huge speaker, came the voice of my sister Nadya. "They heard us! Hoorah, someone answered!" she cried.

I shot to my feet so quickly it was like I'd had an electric shock.

"Nadya?" I shouted. "Is that you?"

She didn't reply. I wanted to say something else but I couldn't because the soldiers pushed me back. But an officer took over and started bellowing into the microphone, "This is Fourth Army Command, in Novaya Ladoga. Identify yourself. Over."

A woman's voice, not my sister's, boomed out of the speaker. "This is seaman Alina Aleksandrovna Voronina, Oreshek Garrison, Ladoga Fleet, under the command of Comrade Commander Ilyazov. Over."

The officer gripped the microphone so tight he was in danger of crushing it.

"Say again your position."

"Oreshek Fortress, sir, over."

"The fleet has no position there! The fortress fell into enemy hands two months ago."

"What? Oh no, sir, negative. Negative. The fortress has always been in Soviet hands, sir. The garrison here is led by Comrade Commander Ilyazov. We were sent here and came under German attack. But we resisted, sir. The red flag flies over the fortress."

She pronounced the last part with a note of pride.

The officer took a step back and put a hand over the microphone. He turned to the radio operator. "Can you locate where they are transmitting from?"

"No, sir. Not with this equipment."

"Well, send someone to call the colonel . . . I can't take responsibility for this . . ."

I was tired of their useless chatter. I jumped to my feet and shouted. "Give me the microphone! My sister's there!"

And there it was again. Nadya's voice. "Viktor, is that really you?"

"Nadya!"

"Viktor! I knew you'd come and get me!"

"I promised you, didn't I?"

"And I waited for you! If you only knew everything I've been through . . ."

"Me too! Where are you?"

"The fortress on Oreshek, in the Neva, at the edge of Lake Ladoga . . ."

"I'm on Lake Ladoga, too. But a village on the southern shore! I'm coming, Nadya, wait for me, I'm on my way . . ."

That's as much as we managed before a soldier yanked my shoulder, lifted me from the seat in front of the radio and said, "That's enough, son. You're under arrest."

Okay.

So that's not actually true.

They didn't arrest me. It was just something they said to get me away from the radio and out of their way.

It doesn't matter. Nadya's alive, she's well, and I know where she is now!

I never doubted it for a minute, but hearing her voice was…

Oh, my word, Nadya!

Nothing else matters.

The soldiers took me into a room, an officer came in and asked me a lot of questions. Who I was. What my name was. Who the person I'd spoken to on the radio was. If I was an enemy spy. Things like that.

I told them what I could, which is the truth minus the illegal parts. I gave them my name (it was on my papers anyway) and explained that I'd been separated from my sister when we'd been evacuated, so I'd gone back to find her.

"You escaped from one of the children's trains?"

"Yes."

"Which train were you on?"

"Number seventy-seven. My sister was on train seventy-six."

The soldier gaped. "You're not fooling me. Train seventy-six was destroyed by the Nazis at the start of the war. Everyone knows that."

I wondered if I should tell him what I knew about Anna's dad the colonel, Major Fedin from the NKVD and Party Official Uvarov in Moscow. But I realized it would only raise a whole new set of questions, so it was best to just keep quiet.

failure to report crimes against the State, Art. 88-1.

"Apparently the train is still fully intact, the proof being that my sister is alive and well on Oreshek."

"Or you're lying and it's all part of a plot."

"To do what?"

"I don't know. You tell me."

It went back and forth like this for a long time.

Until, I'm ashamed to admit, I fainted.

I regained consciousness in the shack they use as a hospital. It's where I am now and where I wrote the last part of this story.

When I opened my eyes, I saw Mikhail standing beside me. And Klara.

"Oh, what did you expect? That I was going to stay by myself all night in the truck?"

They explained that the soldiers had rushed me here because I'd fallen face down on the table in the interrogation room and they'd had to call a doctor.

To be honest, me fainting was an excellent move. While I was being looked after, Nadya, or the people with her, had managed to convince the soldiers that Oreshek had held out and that the sailors there weren't Nazi spies but one hundred per cent Russian, which means I'm no longer under suspicion either.

They haven't given us our papers back yet (a very big problem) but at least we're no longer under arrest.

"Great," I said. "Because we're leaving tonight."

"For where?"

"For Oreshek Fortress. Where else? I haven't come all this way to give up now."

My friends exchanged glances. Sighed. Then Klara pulled out a sheet of paper – yet another map ripped out of the road atlas.

"We knew you'd say that. But to get to Oreshek we need to get through enemy territory and across the front. It's impossible."

"We won't cross enemy territory. Our route will take us to this village here, Kobona," I said, pointing on the map. "Then we'll make our way to the fortress across the frozen lake."

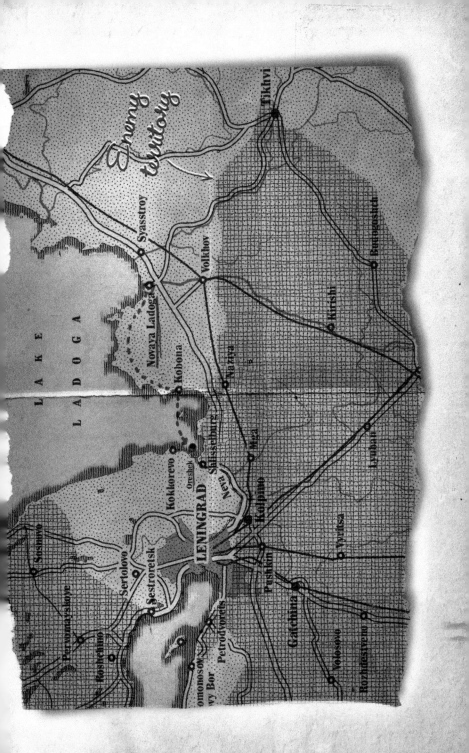

Silence.

"I'm serious."

"You mean you want to walk over the ice from Kobona to Oreshek? It must be thirty or forty kilometres! In the open, with nowhere to hide from enemy planes, at thirty degrees below zero. And your hand in that state. You won't last half an hour!"

I shook my head, "That's why we're going in the truck."

Mikhail erupted. "Have you forgotten what that soldier said this morning? The ice is still too thin. All it takes is the smallest crack and *BAM!* we're dead."

"Mikhail's right. Think about it. If trucks could cross the lake then why isn't there an ice route into Leningrad already, getting food and medicines into the blockaded city? If the army hasn't tried it, it must be impossible."

"Until a few hours ago, the army thought Oreshek had fallen, that they faced the enemy on the opposite bank of Lake Ladoga. Whereas we now know that my sister's on the fortress, defending it. That's why I need to go and help her." I looked at them before I continued, "Today was bitter cold, tonight will be even worse. I bet the ice is solid. We'll empty the truck, make it as light as we can. But if you don't feel up to it . . . it doesn't matter. I'm still going."

I was shaking as I waited for their reply.

"If you're going, I'm going with you," Klara said.

"You'll need a driver," Mikhail added.

They both smiled. They weren't the stupid smiles of people embarking on a dangerous adventure just for the sake of it. They were the smiles of people willing to risk their lives for a friend.

Something I'll never forget.

*

We made a pact. I stayed here in the hospital (I'm taking advantage of it to write all this down) while they went to get the truck ready, or rather, to make it as light as possible.

"This afternoon, while I was waiting for you, some woodsmen came past," Klara said. "In return for one of our crates, they dug out the truck and got it back on the road."

"How on earth?!" Mikhail asked. "Weren't you scared they'd steal everything and not help you?!"

"Well, that's what they planned to do but I pointed out that if I reported them, the crates would go straight back to their rightful owners, namely the army, and the only way we could all gain from the situation was for them to do what good people do and lend a helping hand."

Klara really does excel at this kind of stroke of genius.

"And?" I asked.

"So Mikhail and I will get them to help us again and, in return, they can take all the crates, not just one."

I agreed it was a good idea. We said goodbye and I've been waiting here ever since.

They should be here to collect me soon.

And we'll be leaving.

All going well, the next time I write in this notebook, I'll be with my sister Nadya.

S. – It's banditry and contraband. That's what it is: Articles 77 and 78.

We didn't make it.

We're not at Oreshek.

Where we are is in the middle of nowhere. In a desert of ice.

Mikhail and Klara are asleep here beside me, on the seats of the truck.

These words might be my last.

I'm writing with my left hand, in the dark, so I hope it's legible. But it's important to write this down. Because if we don't make it, I want Nadya to know what happened. That I tried until the very end.

I'm scared.

For the first time since this journey started, I'm honestly scared that this is the end.

To fail when I'm so close to reaching my destination would be a cruel twist of fate.

Klara and Mikhail came to get me at around two o'clock in the morning. They came inside the hospital shack where everyone was asleep. Without making a sound.

"It's time," Klara said.

I went outside, the truck was there, engine still running. It was like a plucked chicken – the doors had gone, there were no bumpers, the bars over the trailer had been dismantled and the spare tyre removed. It looked more like a skeleton on wheels than a truck.

"Won't we be cold with no doors?" I asked.

"If the ice cracks it will be easier to get out," Klara explained.

Mikhail nodded. "To be honest, the woodsmen offered us a trade: the truck in exchange for a sleigh . . ."

"But we thought the horses would be too slow and with your hand in that state, we haven't got any time to waste."

In short, they'd been offered a lightweight, manoeuvrable sleigh but had turned it down. For me. The idea that their thoughtfulness could end up killing us all makes me shake as I write this.

"What about the cold?" I asked again, because it was minus thirty and the skin on my face was turning as stiff as steel.

"We found some extra blankets," Klara said. "We'll manage."

I couldn't argue with her reasoning and the quicker we got away the better. I hopped up into the cab. Mikhail sat in the driver's seat; he'd found some gloves which would be useful since he had to keep his hands on the steering wheel.

"Wait," I said. "The petrol gauge is broken." I tapped the broken dial on the dashboard with my fingernail.

"I know, but don't worry. We filled the tank."

"Well, not completely full," Klara said. "Diesel is heavy. But the woodsmen gave us, let's say, enough to get where we're going."

"Here's hoping."

"Ladies and gentlemen, tickets at the ready. We're off!"

Mikhail threw the truck into gear. We drove through the village and no one saw us. No one stopped us. We took the road heading west out of the village until we came to a crossroads. One way was a wide, open road and a sign indicating Shlisselburg. It led straight into enemy territory. To the right was a mule track that led into a clump of trees as thin and scraggy as skeletons.

Klara checked the map.

"This path runs around the coast to Kobona."

"That means it follows the curve of the lake which will take us longer," I commented.

"But we'll be out of the way of the enemy," Klara replied.

"And there'll be no roadblocks by our own troops," Mikhail added.

We opted for the mule track.

We followed it for a couple of hours through the forest, keeping a safe distance from the anonymous clusters of houses scattered along the lakeside. They were fairly dilapidated and all deserted. Kobona was as well – just a few ramshackle huts hidden between the trees.

Mikhail ventured along paths that got narrower and narrower until we ended up on the banks of a frozen canal. Up ahead of us, beyond the trees, glimmered the surface of Lake Ladoga.

Now came the difficult bit. "Let's test the ice here," Klara said. "On the canal."

"Why not on the lake?" I asked.

"Because if it's too thin and breaks under our weight, it's better to be in water where we can still get out."

"Is Lake Ladoga very deep?"

"More than two hundred metres."

"Fine. We'll try here first."

"Agreed," Mikhail said. "Hold on tight."

We drove down towards the winding white serpent that was the canal, yelling to keep our spirits up.

"Not too fast, Mikhail. Nice and slow, slow, slowwww!"

The truck crept forward onto the ice with one wheel, then another, then with all four. There was a slight *SCHRIP* but we didn't go through. The ice was holding. Somehow or other, it was holding.

"Keep going like that, slowly."

We followed the canal for a few hundred metres then it opened up like a fan and we found ourselves looking out into an immensity.

"Lake Ladoga, ladies and gentlemen," said Mikhail, whose bus driver act was beginning to get on my nerves. "Passengers are kindly informed that, for the time being, the ice appears to be solid."

"Yes," Klara said. "But remember to stay in sight of the lakeside."

S. – photo clearly added afterwards. Shows a truck driving across frozen Lake Ladoga.

"Didn't you say the shore was under enemy control?"

"We'll drive with our headlamps off. It's risky, but better than the alternative – if the ice breaks and we're too far out . . . Well, you know, I think you get my drift."

"What way?"

"The fortress must be straight ahead of us."

"Speed?"

"Mikhail! Give it a break with the stupid questions!"

He glared at me. "It's not a stupid question. I was serious. Is it better to go at full speed or extra slow? For the ice, I mean."

I had no idea, so he put his foot down. We were speeding along when suddenly something caught under our wheels, who knows, a rock maybe. The truck bounced over it and landed back down on the ice with an almighty thud. A crack opened below us and freezing water sprayed into the cab.

I was about to throw myself out when the truck made it back onto solid ice just in time, leaving a web of cracks spreading out behind us.

"Careful! We might not be so lucky next time!"

We kept moving, but so slow it was almost walking pace. Mikhail had to concentrate because, although from a distance the lake looks like an expanse of smooth, white ice, up close it's actually a mass of frozen boulders, spikes, cracks, and pools of water hidden under layers of sleet.

"Enough," said Mikhail, after a while, "we can't go on like this. We could end up face down in the lake without even realizing it."

"So, what do we do?" Klara asked.

"I have to turn on the headlamps to be able to see."

Stupidly, I said, "All right, but go a bit further out from the lakeside. We don't want some Nazi on the shore to see the light."

Mikhail did what I said. We left the dark line of the coast on our left and moved out towards the middle of the frozen lake. As sailors say, we sailed "into open water."

Once there, we turned on the headlamps and Mikhail drove carefully, trying to dodge any obstacles in our way; I stuck my head out of the cab every now and then to look at the sky, seeking out the moon to navigate by. The immensity of the lake began to feel oppressive. The sky was an enormous blanket of black smoke. It was as if it were saying to us, "Look at you, so small, trying so hard, I could crush you whenever I choose."

It's difficult to describe what it feels like to be in a truck advancing through an infinite nothingness of ice and snow. Every noise swallowed up in the immensity. We were just a dot of light in a dead and frozen world.

I don't know how long we travelled like that. None of us spoke, Mikhail strained at the wheel, Klara had curled up beside me, under the blanket.

We had to stop every now and then to scrape ice off the windscreen, it was impossible to see out otherwise. During one of these stops I happened to look up and realized something was wrong. The moon we'd been following (or rather, that I'd been following) was in a completely different position.

"Klara," I said. "Shouldn't we be heading that way?"

"No, we have to go this way."

"But the fortress is west. All we have to do is follow the moon."

"Are you sure?"

"No, it's the sun that sets in the west. The moon does the opposite."

"Are you sure?"

Klara thought about it for a second. "Maybe it rises in the north and sets in the south . . . or maybe it changes . . ."

We realized that each time either she or I had put our heads out of the window, we'd been following a different course. Who knows how many zig-zags we'd done across the lake.

"Land is on our left though," I said. "So, Mikhail, head a bit to the left now and keep going until we see the coast."

"Fine," he said.

We carried on for a bit.

Then Klara told Mikhail to stop. "What are you doing?"

"What you told me to do. I'm going left."

"Yes, but if you keep the steering wheel pulled hard to the left, you'll end up driving in a circle. We are literally going around in circles."

"No."

"Yes!"

"What about the moon?"

"I've no idea how to navigate by the damned moon!"

To cut a long story short, we were lost.

Fear began to set in, it was getting colder and colder and who knows how much fuel we had left.

Even a German plane over our heads would have been a blessing at that point. But we were absolutely alone. As if that weren't bad enough, the ice suddenly *CRACKED* and a back wheel gave way.

The three of us jumped out. The right wheel was jammed in a crack.

"We need planks to get it out," I said.

"We don't have any planks. We took them all out to lighten the load," Mikhail said.

"So what do we do?"

"I don't know."

"Neither do I."

"I say Mikhail should turn the steering wheel all the way to the left, then slowly reverse while we try to push," Klara suggested.

We tried it and it worked. But I had to use my injured hand and it hurt so much I thought I was going to faint.

After only two minutes back in the truck there was another *SCHRIP* noise and we realized we were in trouble again. I don't know how but we'd ended up on a patch of thin ice.

"What shall we do?" Mikhail asked. I think he was crying.

"We'll wait for dawn," I suggested. "We all agree that the sun rises in the east, so by then we'll finally know what direction we're going in."

"But it will be warmer when the sun's up and the ice will melt," Klara said.

"I know, but when it's light maybe we'll be able to spot the thinner patches and get ourselves out of this mess."

"Okay," Klara said.

"Okay," Mikhail said, but only because they were too tired to argue.

They went back inside the truck and fell asleep.

I didn't. I can't.

Klara's right.

As soon as the sun is out, the temperature will rise so we can't hang about if we want to get out of this alive.

So this is my job tonight.

To stay awake. And watch for the sun.

10th November 1941

Chained to an oak tree on a curve of shingle,
There lives a prowling, walking-talking cat,
Who strains his golden chain-links till they jingle
As he sneaks night and day, this way and that.
When he goes right he sets the woodland warbling,
When he goes left he tells tales by the sea.

O magic world! Here comes a forest goblin,
And there's a mermaid halfway up a tree,
And unseen paths across the forest floorway
Are streaked with freaky tracks from freaky paws.
And here's a little cabin with no doorway
Or windows, yet it moves on chicken's claws.

Forest and vale swirl with fantastic fancies,
And with the dawn a salty swell advances
To overflood the wilderness of sand,
And thirty men, brave heroes, knights and courtiers,
March forth in single file from crystal waters
And follow their sea captain up the strand...

This is a poem by Pushkin we learned at school.
I recite it in my head as I probe the night with the binoculars, from the top of the Watchtower.

I start scanning from the south: along the German-occupied bank and the houses of Shlisselburg, now barracks and artillery posts. To the west is the Neva, now completely frozen. In the north, the free shore which, thanks to us, the enemy has been unable to conquer. To the east is the tree from the poem, on the shores of the Ladoga (*Chained to an oak tree on a curve of shingle*), then beyond that, just the vastness of the frozen desert, like a sweeping stroke of white painted across the horizon.

It's difficult to see anything in the dark so I'm relieved when enemy planes fly over – they drop their firebombs and light up the sky.

I take advantage of them to search for Viktor.

Since I spoke to him on the radio I can do nothing else, think about nothing else. The Chief agreed to put me on sentry duty more often and even Mrs. Burova says she understands.

I don't care about being understood: I'd still come up here to the top of the tower, every day and every night.

When will my brother get here? Will he come by sleigh, foot or plane? There are Germans everywhere . . . He really needs to fly!

The hours go past and there's no sign of Viktor.

The sun pushes over the horizon. Ladoga is a rainbow of pink and I want to cry because Viktor's not here.

Boris and Anna brought me some hot tea.

"How did the night go?" Anna asked.

Boris didn't say anything. Actually, after what happened that night under the rubble of the tower, he hasn't spoken to me much. It's as if he's embarrassed. I think that's pretty stupid of him but I've got other things to think about now.

I'm not hungry and I'm really tired but I don't want to sleep. I just want to stay here and wait.

It can't be long. I know it can't be long now.

So why isn't he here?

VIKTOR!

Viktor's here! He's finally here!

He came!

Viktor's here with me now!

Oh, it was just like in a fairy tale!

Like Pushkin's champions striding from crystal waters!

It happened this afternoon, around three o'clock.

I'd been up in the Watchtower all morning but by lunchtime I was beginning to feel sick with exhaustion. Anna convinced me to go down to the cellars to eat something. It was such a quiet day, not even one explosion and no sign of movement on the opposite bank.

After lunch, I was so exhausted I could hardly stand and I thought about having a nap, just five minutes before I went back to the Watchtower, but we had to take Franz his food and

Who's Franz?

(Argh, Viktor! Let me finish! You'll find out for yourself when you read all my notebooks.)

Anyway, I was saying.

I took lunch to Franz and I'd just come out of the New Prison when I heard the siren wailing on the Golovkin Tower. That's the tower that looks out onto the river and the enemy's forward positions, so when the siren sounds it means there's a battle underway. I ran to my combat post which is the machine gun on the Watchtower.

Boris was kneeling by the opening in the wall, sweeping the horizon with a long barrel, back and forward, ready to engage the enemy, but there was nothing to see, just ice and the river. Still, the siren wailed and wailed.

"What's going on?"

"I don't know, but it's odd. Can you hear planes?"

"Not a whisper."

"So where are they attacking us from?"

They weren't attacking us, it was Viktor! He'd arrived!

I knew right away and it was like an electric shock to the spine. I could feel that my brother was near. Maybe twins are telepathic after all . . .

Anyway, I left Boris where he was, flew down the stairs and across the courtyard. Mrs. Burova was making her way to the Sovereign Tower, and Alina was running that way, too. She saw me and said, "A truck! A truck has just driven out from the trees on the north bank! There are three children inside it, and Ruslan says one of them looks like you!"

I didn't stop to hear any more, I dashed across the snow, skated along the frozen river that runs through the courtyard and made my way to the tower. The metal grille and gates had been opened already and me, Mrs. Burova and the Chief rushed outside.

That's when I saw it.

A beaten-up truck with no doors, no fenders and a blond boy behind the wheel.

And my brother waving out the other side, shouting, "Don't shoot! Don't shoot! We're Russian!"

"I know you're Russian, stupid Viktor Nikolayevich!" I yelled, the words catching in my throat.

I gulped for breath. Then added, "You took your time getting here . . ."

I didn't know it was possible to laugh and cry at the same time, but it is.

The truck came to a stop with a creak and a half-spin on the ice – I was scared it might overturn – then Viktor jumped out and ran towards us. I noticed his hand was bandaged up and I wondered why.

My brother has grown taller, he's very thin, his face is gaunt and his expression has changed – it's much harder-looking.   ←   *S. - the look of a criminal!*

"Sorry for taking so long," he said, stopping on the ice just a few metres from the shore.

I smiled from where I was standing on the pier, tears streaming down my face, and replied, "It doesn't matter. We were just defending an entire fortress here while you were taking your time."

I started to laugh.

Viktor took another step towards me and finally I regained control of my legs. I jumped down from the lakeside, slid over the ice, and threw myself at him.

I squeezed him tight and we both fell into the snow.

Later

So many times I've wondered what I'd do when I saw Viktor again. I thought I'd talk and talk and talk. And listen to everything he had to tell me!

Instead we didn't say anything.

The truth is, maybe we don't need words.

Before I was only half a person. Now I'm whole again.

Nothing else matters.

So I just clung to his side as the other two children with him climbed out of the truck. That's the blond boy who'd been driving and a girl with gingery hair and freckles, quite pretty. I wondered if she was his girlfriend.

Stop it.

Meanwhile Ruslan and the other sailors had joined us.

"What shall we do with the truck, sir?" Ruslan asked the Chief.

"Better park it on the north bank. Hide it under the trees. It could come in handy."

"Yes, sir."

"Now I'd like to speak to these young people."

"Nadya's brother looks wounded," Mrs. Burova noticed. "Perhaps the interrogation can wait?"

I looked at Viktor's hand (he still hasn't told me what happened but it must be awfully painful).

Anyway, the Chief changed his mind and agreed to postpone his questions until tomorrow. All of them except one. He wanted to know about the crossing. Crossing Lake Ladoga.

Give the diary here, sister. This is my story.

And it won't take long anyway to describe crossing Lake Ladoga.

That last night was awful. We didn't think we'd make it. I woke Klara and Mikhail at dawn. In the early light it was much easier to see where the ice was thinner – the lake was darker there, almost blue under the snow.

The main problem was we couldn't see land anywhere.

"But we can get our bearings from the sun now," Klara said.

It was a struggle to get the truck to start but we managed and set off westwards, in the direction of the lakeside.

We made it to Kokkorevo, a village twenty kilometres north of here.

The look on the villagers' faces when they saw a truck drive across the lake! To be honest, they were a bit concerned at first, scared we might be the enemy. But when we greeted them in Russian – oh, the celebrations! They didn't have much to eat but they gave us some tea and fuel to fill our tank.

They said they'd been waiting for reinforcements for months but Leningrad had sent nothing. We explained that they were coming. That the 4th Army had lost Tikhvin but was moving to Novaya Ladoga and now that the lake was frozen, they'd find a way to bring reinforcements, and food too.

Then Mikhail said, "Ladies and gentlemen, tickets ready! We're off!"

I punched him. This bus driver business was really wearing thin. But we were in high spirits so we both laughed. We set off along the side of the lake and after a bit, we saw this island, with walls around it and the red flag at the top. We'd arrived.

I wish Papa could hear me now because I'd tell him, look, no need to worry.

I kept my promise.

The end.

Or maybe not.

I actually still have a question. Who's Franz?

So, I took Viktor to Franz.

We waited until everyone was asleep then ran across the garden to the prison.

A plane flew overheard right at that moment. I grabbed Viktor and pulled him to the ground; a few seconds later a burst of machine gun fire erupted into the snow around us and Nikolay responded with a couple of rounds of cannon fire.

"Is this the kind of thing you've gotten used to?" my brother asked, seeing me through new eyes.

I could've shrugged and said, "Yes, of course." But this is Viktor. He deserved the truth.

"You never get used to it," I replied. "Every time you

think it's the last time. But it's war. We have to keep fighting."

"I hardly recognize you. You were the one who always seemed against it. War, that is, and weapons and battles . . ."

"I still am."

"But you've learned to shoot."

My brother's right. I hate weapons, but I shoot, and if need be, I can man the guns. Maybe I've even killed someone: you can't see much out of the openings in the walls. Boris and I usually shoot into the bushes and the snow, to make noise more than anything. But what if there were someone there? What have I done? What have I become? ✳

*S. — simply a good soldier.

I pulled out the keys, opened the gate and we slipped inside.

Going inside an abandoned prison is strange because even though there's no one there, it's as if the air is heavy and the cells are still occupied by the shadows of the prisoners.

"Is this where Lenin's brother was imprisoned?" Viktor asked.

"I don't know," I replied. "The whole island was a maximum security prison. Did you see the apple tree, the one covered in snow by the King's Tower? That's where he was shot."

"Yep."

I opened the last gate and we entered the final corridor.

"Do you come down here often?"

"When we have to."

"I would never come."

"I don't have much choice."

We got to the cell, I opened the hatch and the prisoner lifted his head to look up at us.

I have to say Franz no longer looks like the sniper who smoked cigarettes and beat Boris in the village. After his time here, he's become painfully thin, his skin is ashen, his thin face all beard and eyes.

"Excellent!"

"It's not excellent. He's a person and we're responsible for him now."

"Responsible for a swastika-loving monster?"

"Swastika?" Franz asked.

"Yes, you heard right, you damned Nazi!" Viktor replied. Then he said, "Did you interrogate him? Did he tell you how the Germans planned to starve us all to death?"

"Starve to death?"

"Oh, I forgot, you've been cut off from everything for months. Leningrad is about to be annihilated, there's nothing left to eat and people are dropping dead on the streets. And it's all because of this monster and his mates."

"But . . . but . . . ," I stammered, "why don't our troops try to break the blockade?"

"The enemy is stronger. We've just lost Tikhvin."

"So why don't people flee Leningrad, across the lake, like you did today?"

"That," Viktor said, "is an excellent question. One I might have the answer to."

S. - consistently lying to a public official. Alt. 181.

12th November

In the end, the Chief got his way and for most of yesterday, my brother and his friends were given the third degree. He wanted to know where they'd come from, what was happening outside, the general situation and if we're winning the war.

Viktor responded to every question with the calm of a grown-up but I know him well enough to realize he wasn't always telling the truth.

By the time night came, my brother looked so tired and pale I thought he'd want nothing more than to go to sleep.

After all, it's not easy getting used to life here at the fortress: bombs fell almost all day today and one of the towers was brought down, leaving only a stump in its place.

At every explosion, Viktor and his friends turned chalk white.

"I've tried to get you a more comfortable bed," I said. "It's over here . . ."

"Forget bed," he replied. "I want a quiet place where I can talk to you and your friend Anna. Some of the others can come too, but only people you trust. Anatoly?"

"Anatoly is your friend, not mine. I trust Boris."

"Ah, what is he, your boyfriend?"

"Stop it."

"If he's your boyfriend, I swear I'll give him a good punch. But whatever, bring him if you want. Where shall we meet?"

"The New Prison, where Franz is?"

"No, I don't like that place."

"All right, let's go to the winch that moves the metal grille at the entrance to the fortress."

"How do I get there?"

"It's at the end of the north passageway. From the square, go up the stairs by the Sovereign Tower. They lead up into a kind of corridor. If you go straight, you end up at the Golovkin Tower, but if you go the other way, you'll come to an alcove with a winch in it. We'll be safe from the bombs and no one ever goes there, so we'll be able to talk."

"Agreed. I'll go and get Klara and Mikhail. We'll meet there in an hour."

The passageway was dotted with arched openings which let in a bitter cold, but my brother brought a blanket and I brought a small stove to heat water for tea.

We huddled together against the wall, backs resting against the wooden winch.

"We'll freeze to death up here," Mikhail muttered.

"But we're out of danger," I replied. "What do we have to talk about?"

I was sure Viktor had something surprising to say, it was the only reason for so much secrecy.

The last thing I expected, though, was that he would turn to my friend Anna, and say, "We're here to talk about her." ←

S. - Finally.

"About me?"

"Yes. You are Anna Tereshenkov, which means your father is Colonel Aleksey Tereshenkov. Am I right?"

The blood drained from Anna's face. In the dark her eyes glowed like mountain lakes. "It's no secret."

"Where is your father now?"

Anna lowered her eyes. "He's dead, I believe," she finally said.

"To be precise, he was killed," Viktor continued. "Your father was an NKVD officer. He plotted against the Soviet Union to help the fascist enemy invade our country. That's why he was arrested and sentenced, towards the beginning of the war."

"That's not true."

The blond boy, Mikhail, butted in at that point. "Oh yes it is. I spoke to the man who arrested him. He's a major in the NKVD, Fedin. I know him."

"You know a major in the NKVD?" I asked.

Mikhail shrugged. "He's my friend's dad."

Viktor nodded. "Major Fedin worked for another guy, someone in the Party based in Moscow. A high Party official. His name's . . ."

"Uvarov," Anna said.

Viktor smirked, as if to say, "So I was right."

"Precisely. Party Official Uvarov ordered Major Fedin to arrest your father." My brother was speaking in undertones, the words clicking between his teeth like seeds. "But that's not all. Fedin received another order. And that was to find you."

I jumped to my feet on hearing that. "What are you talking about? What's all this about?"

"It's unbelievable, it took Mikhail and me ages to piece it all together. But there's one piece still missing. That's why we're here tonight."

Not long before the war, Party Official Uvarov discovered that Colonel Tereshenkov had committed sabotage against the state.

In particular, he had learned that Tereshenkov:

1) Was trading with Germany for huge personal gain
2) Had received foreign intelligence that the Nazis were preparing to attack the Soviet Union
3) Had chosen not to alert Soviet High Command in order to continue his business.

On making this discovery, Uvarov notified Major Fedin of the NKVD in Leningrad and asked for justice to be done.

Fedin worked fast. In a single night, he had Anna's father arrested (then executed), leaving Anna all alone.

Normally, when the NKVD arrests someone, their friends keep a very low profile and pretend they've never met the person, for fear of being investigated and arrested themselves. ← *S. – Tendentious remark.*

But Tereshenkov must've had a long list of favours to call in because Anna wasn't abandoned. In fact, she went to stay with friends of her father who later decided to send her away on the children's trains.

Meanwhile the Nazis had discovered everything from their spies. They also knew that Anna's dad held compromising papers outlining some of their plans to invade enemy nations. It was vital that these papers did not get into Soviet hands.

The Nazis feared that, before his death, Tereshenkov had given the dossier to his only daughter.

For this reason, they decided to attack and destroy train seventy-six.

"What?!" said Boris. "That's ludicrous!"

"It's all true," my brother replied.

"If you believe that, you must have rocks for brains."

The two of them stood up, close to punching each other, my brother's injured hand the only reason he held back from hitting Boris.

That, and the fact that I forced myself between them.

"Stop it!" I said. "Viktor, Boris didn't mean to insult you. He's just very surprised because your story . . . well, it's not true."

"What do you mean?"

"The Germans never attacked train seventy-six. Sorry, I should've told you before but there was no time. Anyway, that's the way it is. We were never bombed. Our train was simply stopped for days on the tracks. Then there was a fire, we don't know who caused it, but I definitely don't think it was the enemy."

"If they wanted to destroy us they would've dropped bombs, just like they wrote in the newspaper," Boris said.

"But that didn't happen," I continued. "It was just an ordinary fire. After which Commissar Bok came to tell us we couldn't stay in Mga station any longer and that we had to come here to Shlisselburg."

"Maybe he wanted to save you from the Germans," Mikhail protested.

"How could he have known that they were after Anna?" Boris said.

"He couldn't," Anna chimed in. "Bok was actually a friend of my father's. And he knew the Nazis had no desire to target me. For one very good reason: my father never collaborated with the enemy so the enemy had no idea who he was. My father is innocent." ✳

"You're wrong," Mikhail said.

"I'm not," Anna replied. "My father would never

✳ S. – as before. This is the opinion of a daughter. Although it is true the train was never bombed.

380

have done what you think. He was a good person. He devoted his life to fighting corruption, he would never have become one of them."

"You obviously *would* say that. He was your father. But evil people often manage to hide their true natures," Viktor remarked.

"Not him. In all these months, you've always known Nadya was alive, right? Even if no one else believed you. Now I'm begging you to believe me. My father was an honest man."

We sat in silence for a long time until Viktor sighed and said, "All right. Let's pretend for a second that you're telling the truth. Then why did someone set train seventy-six on fire?"

"That's not the only mystery," I added. "Why did the chairman of the town soviet apologize to me before he died? Why couldn't we speak to anyone when we were in Shlisselburg? And why has no one ever come to see if Oreshek Fortress really is controlled by the enemy? It's almost as if they'd rather forget we exist."

Until then, my brother's friend Klara had been sitting to one side in silence. "I think I have the answer," she said.

"What?"

"The guilty party is not Anna's father. It's Major Fedin."

KLARA'S STORY   *S. - ??!*

Just before the war, Colonel Tereshenkov found out that a high Party official in Moscow called Uvarov had committed sabotage.

In particular, he learned that Uvarov:

1) Was trading with Germany for huge personal gain
2) Had received foreign intelligence that the Nazis were preparing to attack the Soviet Union

3) Had chosen not to alert Soviet High Command in order to continue his business.

On making this discovery, Tereshenkov planned to arrest Uvarov, but the wily official had a lot of contacts and found out about the investigation. He decided to get rid of Tereshenkov first, before it was too late. That's why he alerted his friend, Major Fedin in the NKVD in Leningrad, and asked him to take care of his enemy.

Fedin worked fast. In a single night, he had Anna's father arrested (then executed) leaving Anna all alone.

But Colonel Tereshenkov also had a lot of friends and they took it upon themselves to protect his daughter. Firstly they put her on the children's train, then, when they realized Fedin was still on her trail, they decided to save her by faking a fire on the train and hiding her in Shlisselburg.

S.

"Wait a second. Do you mean to say the fire on the train was a hoax?"

"No, I'm saying the fire was real. But it probably wasn't started by the Germans. It may have been an attempt by Commissar Bok to make people think all the children on train seventy-six had been killed. It was a way of protecting them," Klara explained. "That must be why, once the children had been hidden in the village, he ordered the chairman of the town soviet not to tell anyone they were there."

"But why?" I said.

"Because otherwise Major Fedin would've come looking for you again."

"But why would he come looking for Anna?!"

Mikhail stood up. "The major said Anna had some papers with her! And that's why the Germans wanted her dead!"

S. – commissar guilty of sabotage?

382

S. — yes. There must be proof!

"Yes," Viktor said. "But now it looks like it was Fedin who wanted her dead. That can mean only one thing . . ."

My brother smiled. "Anna, you must have proof somewhere, that your father was innocent."

We all stared at each other, bewildered.

"That's impossible. My father didn't give me anything before he . . . before he . . ."

"There has to be something," Viktor insisted. "If Klara's reconstruction is true, it means someone may have intentionally neglected to send reinforcements here to the fortress . . ."

"Why?"

"Think about it. Isn't it strange that in all these months command didn't send a single Russian plane to check if the fortress had been captured? They might even have tried to take it back, especially considering how strategically important it is. But they didn't! If you ask me, when Commissar Bok went back to Leningrad he was captured by Fedin, who realized that Anna might still be alive. To be safe, he chose to keep everyone away . . ."

"These are serious accusations . . . ," I said.

S. — it means Soviet officials are partly responsible for the siege of Leningrad.

"Without proof, this is nothing but a great story."

"But I don't have anything," Anna stammered. "My father didn't give me anything!"

"Could he have hidden it? In your bags?"

We raced down from the tower, into the gardens and down to the cellars where everyone had been asleep for hours.

Anna picked up her few belongings and brought them into one of the other rooms where we had to light a candle to see everything properly.

There was nothing much in her bag:

- summer clothes
- a jumper

- a fur cap
- the chessboard with all the pieces except for the black king
- the book of chess games.

"Do you play?" Viktor asked.

"Anna's really good," I explained. "She could easily beat you."

"I don't believe that – but if you carried the board and book all the way here, you must be fond of them."

Anna nodded.

"Did your father know you would never have left these things behind?"

"Oh definitely! Even during our escape in the boat," I reminded her.

Klara picked up the book and began to flick through it, page by page. There were drawings of famous games, annotations pencilled in the margins here and there, notes, suggestions and diagrams. It wasn't Anna's hand-writing, but that of an adult. I wondered how I'd never noticed it before.

"Maybe there's a secret code hidden between the lines."

We passed the book around again and again, but no one understood a word, and there weren't enough notes in the margins to contain proof of international sabotage.

"Maybe there's something written in invisible ink!" I suggested, moving the candle closer to see if anything would miraculously appear on the paper.

Nothing.

"Argh!" Boris said. "If you ask me, Anna's secret isn't in the book!"

Before we could stop him, he grabbed the chessboard, our beloved chessboard, the one thing that had provided endless hours of respite from the war, and smashed it against a stone.

The *CRACK* it made was so loud I was scared it would wake everyone up.

Anna screamed.

Wooden splinters flew everywhere.

Not just splinters, pages, too.

Lots of pages of very fine paper that Anna's father had typed up and concealed in the false bottom of the chessboard before he'd been arrested!

Evidence that highlighted Uvarov's guilt and cleared the colonel's name, or his memory at least.

They'd been with us all the time.   *S. - !!!*

13th November

We gave ourselves a few days to mull it over.

In reality, we already knew what needed to be done:

- go to Leningrad
- find Red Army HQ
- tell our story and show our evidence
- have Major Fedin and Party Official Uvarov arrested
- request reinforcements for Oreshek
- organize a convoy of trucks across Lake Ladoga to take food into the starving city.

But there are still a lot of questions that need answering:

- Who should go to Leningrad?
- What vehicle should they go in?
- How to get into the city?
- Who is the right person to show our evidence to?
- How can we get him to listen to us?

Leningrad is under siege. German Junkers bomb the city around the clock. There will be enemy and Red Army roadblocks everywhere.

Crossing defensive lines would be difficult even if we had the written permission of a general!

But the main problem, the one we really can't agree on, is the first one: Who should leave the fortress for the city?

"We need to speak to the Chief, let the sailors take care of it," Boris suggested. "They're trained military personnel, in uniform, and maybe the Chief can give them some sort of pass."

"The sailors need to stay here to defend Oreshek. There are so few of us in the first place, if the island were to be attacked . . ."

"That's the Chief's problem, he should decide. Maybe he'll send Mrs. Burova and Gennady."

The idea of the two of them making their way to Leningrad made us all laugh.

In the end, Anna said, "I have to go. This is about my father and the proof that he's innocent is mine. What's more, I know a lot of his colleagues. They'll listen to me."

Anna has been very pale and serious since we found her father's papers in the chessboard, she has dark ghostly shadows under her eyes. That said, she also seems more confident than before, and stronger.

"Of course, Anna has to go," Viktor said. "And I'll go with her."

I butted in at that point. "I won't hear of it."

"Always interfering."

"I am not interfering. But I can't let you go away again, not after it took so long to find you this time. And you're injured, your hand needs a lot more time to heal!"

Travelling across the lake to get here was crazy enough.

I won't let him do this.

We spent another day debating and arguing over it, and it very nearly ended up in a fist fight like when we were children.

Last night, I had it out with him again, just before we went to sleep. I grabbed him by the shoulders and pushed him up against the wall.

He's usually the bossy one but only because he's never made me this angry before.

It must've been obvious because he didn't try to defend himself.

"I'm sorry, little sister," he said.

"You're not sorry. You've only just arrived and already you want to leave."

"I have to finish what I started."

"No. You found me, you've already kept your promise. You can stop now."

"But if I don't go to Leningrad, everything I've done will have been in vain: you'll still be here in the fortress, the fortress will still be under attack by the enemy, and there still won't be any sign of reinforcements. We need to break this stalemate. Anna's papers are the perfect opportunity."

"All right, I understand that. But why do you have to be the one to go? Why can't someone else do it?"

"I've already proved that I can hold my own. The others trust me. But, the real reason I have to go is because I want to. I want to go where Mama is. I want to save you."

I really blew my top at that point. "I don't need saving!" I shouted. "I've already saved myself, getting here to the fortress, stealing the radio, fighting off the enemy!"

"I know. That's why I need you to be here, holding the fort, so to speak, while I'm away. Covering my back and making sure Oreshek doesn't fall now, at this late stage. Before the war, Leningrad had a population of almost three and a half million! But if the stories I've heard are true, well, the people there are dying of starvation. And we have the chance to do something for them."

"But why you?!"

"Because it's up to us! And because, even though we're twins, we've always been different, it's what makes us strong, it's the reason no one will ever be able to stop us. If I find someone in Leningrad willing to listen to me it will only be because you've stayed behind and done the impossible. Some people are heroes because they go out and fight to save the world, others stay behind and are heroes because they resist."

15th November

So, three of us are going.

Me, Mikhail (the only one who can drive the damned truck) and Anna.

Klara will stay at the fortress with my sister and Boris.

It might seem obvious but it's taken us three whole days to reach this decision.

The only one who didn't make much of a fuss was Boris. He folded his arms and said, "I go where Nadya goes. If she stays, I'm staying too."

Nadya went as red as a strawberry. Those two are so sickly sweet it would turn your stomach.

Mikhail was pretty clear where he stood from the beginning.

The hard nuts to crack were Nadya and Klara, for opposite reasons. My sister because she wanted me to stay, Klara because she wanted to go.

In the end, I managed to reason with both of them.

I really need it to be me who sees this mission through, because it's my mission. I made it this far and I have to see it through to the end.

As for Klara, Leningrad is too dangerous for a German girl. We don't know what could happen to her and I can't bring myself to take her into the heart of the NKVD.

So, it will be me, Mikhail and Anna. No one else.

Since me and Mikhail don't have papers (we left them in the barracks at Novaya Ladoga), we borrowed some from Boris and Anatoly.

S. – Theft of documents. Art. 195.

As for all the rest – we hope the proof Anna is bringing with her will be enough.

It's our only option. I'm also taking a gun, Nadya showed me how to use it, although I'm not sure how reliable I'll be aiming with my left hand. Anna is armed, too.

The truck should still be hidden among the snowy shrubs on the lakeside.

Our plan is fairly simple: tonight, my sister and Boris will help us to open the fortress gates, we'll cross the frozen river, retrieve the truck and set off in it. We could follow the frozen Neva into the city, but the river takes a wide curve to the south from here so it would take too long. That's why we'll try to find the old motorway and take that instead. It's less than fifty kilometres. With a bit of luck, we could be there and back before dawn, and before anyone here at the fortress notices we've left.

"If it were that simple," Nadya said, "don't you think the sailors would have gone into the city lots of times by now?"

"They didn't have a truck before," I replied. "Just wait and see, Nadya, it will be a piece of cake. I'll be back before our birthday."

We'll celebrate together.

* S. – Theft of army weapons. Art. 89; carrying a weapon without a licence. Art. 219.

16th November
Outskirts of Leningrad, middle of the night

We're in a block of flats, or what's left of it.

Half of it has been blown away by bombs. From the outside you can see the living rooms and kitchens, like an open doll's house.

There's no heating. It's deserted, with the exception of a few dead occupants on the floor below ours, left behind because no one had the time to move them.

We're somewhere to the south of the city. In a neighbourhood I've never been to before. But you can see the river, and if we follow it we'll get to the Hermitage. The army headquarters are right opposite there.

On foot, in normal circumstances, it would take us three or four hours to walk it. Whereas now it feels like an impossible distance.

This isn't the city I knew.

It's not the place I grew up in.

The Leningrad I see now is a city of monsters.

We set off from Oreshek last night, everything went according to plan. We were convinced it would be easy. I told Nadya I wanted to be back for our birthday. As if that mattered. As if there'd be a tomorrow.

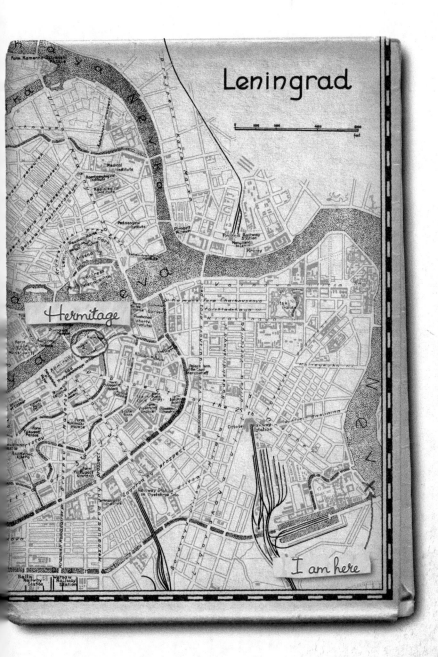

Leningrad

Hermitage

I am here

To begin with, Mikhail and I were even happy. We were going to save the city! We'd be given a hero's welcome, right?

I was getting itchy feet in the fortress. Living underground with bombs raining down on your head constantly is not for me. I've seen a lot of horrific things on my journey. The Rybinsk camp was like hell on earth. But it can't have been easy for Nadya either.

Mikhail and I guided Anna through the trees. The truck was in worse shape than I remembered. The seats and dashboard had a layer of ice on them.

We set to work, or rather, Anna and Mikhail set to work. I couldn't because of my hand. It took a couple of hours, then the truck wouldn't start and we feared we'd have to give up.

Thankfully, we finally got it going. The wheels kept slipping in the snow, it wasn't terribly cold but we were shaking all the same, maybe because we'd gotten used to the stoves at Oreshek the past few days.

We drove along a country lane that wound its way north towards Kokkorevo. Then we turned at a couple of junctions until we eventually got onto the motorway.

It was more a ribbon of snow that cut the forest in two than a motorway – a dirt track full of potholes.

But at least it was straight, more or less, and after a bit, Anna spotted a sign pockmarked with bullet holes that said LENINGRAD. She hugged Mikhail and we all laughed.

"Nothing can stop us now!" Mikhail said. "We'll be in Leningrad in no time!"

"Yes!" I said. "Hurrah!"

In truth, there wasn't much to celebrate. With trees on either side, the road was littered with the empty shells of cars. There was even a beauty of a GAZ-M1, the bodywork ravaged by fire.

Then there were the bodies.

The first one I saw seemed like a rock in the middle of the road.

"Watch out," I said, and Mikhail swerved out of the way at the last minute, nearly driving us into a ditch. He managed to straighten out the truck, but one of our wheels went over the snow-covered mound and it wasn't a rock. It didn't make the sound of a rock.

"Mikhail," Anna screamed. "We've just killed someone!"

"Calm down," I said. "Lying out on the road like that, under a layer of snow, whoever it was definitely wasn't alive."

"But we drove over them!"

"I know. Mikhail, can you be more careful, please?"

I've seen dead bodies before, enough to have nightmares about them for the rest of my life, but they were always somewhere I was trying to escape from – the labour camp, the hospital, etc. Now the horror is here before me. In my home.

I don't know how long we drove but, a while later, the road was blocked halfway across with sandbags and barbed wire. They'd been lined up diagonally so there was just enough space at the end for the truck to get past.

Mikhail had to slow down almost to a stop, and as he did, rifle shots crackled from the trees at the sides of the road. I don't know if they were our soldiers or the enemy but we heard the blasts and saw the yellow flares light up the night.

"Go, Mikhail, go!"

Mikhail accelerated, the truck skidded and hit the sandbags. A bullet hit the windscreen and we could no longer see anything. Bullets whistled around our heads through the cab. There had to be an artillery post hidden somewhere.

Mikhail flung the truck suddenly left. I thought he'd gone mad until I realized whoever was shooting at us had hit one of our tyres. The truck rattled over the furrows of a ploughed field, sending snow flying everywhere, before shuddering to a halt.

The shots kept coming. At this distance they were flying wide, but the truck was caught in the deep snow and we couldn't move.

"Is everyone all right?" I asked.

"No," Anna replied.

I turned around and saw she was holding her leg. The army trousers she was wearing were soaked with blood.

"A bullet or a splinter," she said. "Do you think it's serious? Argh, it really hurts." She'd gone pale and was shaking.

Mikhail said, "Let me have a look at it."

He got out of the truck.

To go round to Anna.

Climbed out of the truck with no doors.

Just climbed out.

And the second his foot touched the ground, Mikhail exploded.

He became a blinding light, a star, then all that was left was the noise. I fell onto Anna and very nearly pushed her out the other side of the truck.

"What happened?"

"Mikhail!"

. . .

"Mikhail!"

Mikhail was gone. The truck had ended up in a mine-field and he'd stepped on a mine hidden by the snow. One second he'd been there, a second later he was gone.

Blond-haired Mikhail. Mikhail the traitor I'd called him.

Mikhail who I'd punched. Mikhail who'd asked me to take him away from the gulag, who'd slept beside me in the mud, who'd come to visit me in the hospital when Klara refused. Mikhail who'd learned to drive the truck. Mikhail who'd all of a sudden turned to smoke.

When the shooting had petered out, Anna and I tried to get away as best we could and it was awful, every step we took could have been on another mine and it could have killed us.

She couldn't walk so we had to kind of shuffle along. I picked up stones and threw them in front of us, hoping they'd set off any mines in our path before we walked on them. I knew it was just for show, for Anna's sake.

So I prayed, one step after another, and Anna hobbled behind me, holding her injured leg. What a rescue party – one with a mutilated hand, the other with a maimed leg. Sorry, Nadya, if I don't make it. Sorry, Nadya, for going away.

We came to the end of the field – still alive – and made it back onto the road. I bandaged Anna's leg with a scarf and found a stick to use as a splint. We limped along the edge of the road, staying low so no one would see us.

When dawn broke, the trees thinned out and the forest turned into city. In the distance we could see the first buildings, desolate factories and empty fields, like a black and white film.

We heard a whine and a formation of planes appeared in the sky. Anna was frightened and started to cry, grabbing at her hair. She looked like she'd gone mad.

I dragged her into one of the wrecked cars at the side of the road. I opened the door and pushed her inside.

*S. – probably PMS 40 cannon or anti-personnel mines which detonate at weights of at least 30kg. A stone wouldn't be enough.

"Easy does it," I said. "Easy, easy, easy!"

I waited there for the planes to go away and for Anna to calm down. Then we set off again, dragging our feet in the snow. The scarf I'd wrapped around Anna's leg had turned black with blood.

Much later in the morning, we encountered our first roadblock. It was another sandbag barricade. A motorcycle was parked beside it, one of those with a sidecar, and soldiers were lounging next to machine guns, smoking.

They were Russians, no doubt about it, but I decided to hide first anyway, to work out our best course of action. I'd stupidly risked my life too many times already.

Just as well, because after a bit someone came from the direction of Leningrad. He wasn't wearing a uniform and the soldiers sent him back, yelling after him, then one of them pulled out a gun and shot him. Just like that. From my hiding place, I couldn't see why but they all looked like they'd gone mad.

I was scared.

I pulled up Anna and we retraced our steps for a bit. We left the road and started following a long barbed-wire fence. At one point, I lifted it up so Anna could get under it. She looked at the snow-covered field and the burnt-out cars on the other side.

"Will there be mines?"

If there are, we're dead, I wanted to say. But I didn't.

With that, we kept plodding on, slowly. Further ahead, there were more roadblocks. We saw some long wooden huts so we headed towards them.

It wasn't Uncle Dmitry's hut but barrack people tend to be friendly in general, and we were exhausted. We hadn't slept all night and we'd just seen Mikhail die. I wanted to ask someone if they could put us up. Time to catch our breath. Even just for a few hours.

S. — a deserter? A saboteur?

396

I'd always thought of barrack-huts as gloomy, whereas now they looked so welcoming, with solid walls to keep the cold out. But the place was eerily quiet.

The first hut had no doors, the furniture inside had been knocked over, and the stove was off. We were hungry (why didn't I think to bring something to eat with us?) so I rummaged around for food but there was nothing. Not a crumb.

We were about to go into the second hut when the door opened and a woman appeared. I'd never seen anyone like her in my life before – like a skeleton with skin. She stared at us without saying anything. Then took a step forward, slowly, as if her legs were filled with lead.

I don't know what I was thinking but I reached out to her, "Are you all right?" I asked.

The woman slipped something into her coat, ration cards I noticed. She must've been going to look for food for the family.

"Excuse me, do you need help?"

She screamed and darted back inside, bolting the door behind her in her panic.

The same scene played out each time.

People are so thin you can count their bones. They look like cadavers wrapped in coats, and they walk so slowly. They're scared of everything. They scream at you if you get close, and they have nothing to eat.

Has hunger turned them into monsters?

Not long after the huts we began to encounter the dead. No one buries them, they're just left there, along the roads. Sitting on pavements.

Like broken toys.

At this time of year, the sun sets early and as dusk fell,

the streets filled with soldiers. That's why we decided to stop in this block of flats where we are now.

I managed to break a chair and use it to light the stove. Anna's sleeping but she's still shaking. Maybe she has a fever. She reminds me of little Ilya. Her leg seems to be getting worse – it's swollen and at this rate, I'll have to find a way of carrying her because she won't be able to walk.

How will we manage, I wondered to myself, just the two us, trying to cross this nightmare that the city has become?

Tomorrow's my birthday and I'll be home.

I was so sure it would be amazing.

Instead, I'm terrified of what I might find.

17th November
Leningrad suburbs, morning

Anna's health deteriorated during the night. She can barely stand now.

I'll have to find a way to move her and it'll have to be quick. But first, I decided to write these few lines because something happened that gave me a little hope.

At first light, I went out to look for something to eat. I'll admit I was feeling pretty desperate. My feet sank deeper and deeper into the snow and I wondered how I could carry on. My stomach hurt and my hand even more. I was scared of falling down into the snow because I wasn't sure I'd have the energy to pick myself back up.

I sat down under the grey sky to catch my breath, and out of nowhere a man appeared. He was wearing an overcoat with an astrakhan collar and had a spider's web of wrinkles around his eyes. And a long, scruffy beard like a creature of the forest.

"Child. Do you need help?"

He spoke in Russian but you could tell he was foreign.

There was nothing menacing about him, though. He was actually smiling. It was like he was the first human being I'd seen for a long time.

"I'm just resting," I said.

"What happened to your fingers?"

"A witch cut them off. But not here and not today. It's a long story."

"Oh," the man said. "I like long stories."

"Well, I don't. And I don't have time. I have to find something to eat for my friend. She's injured. And she's very hungry."

"Yes," he replied. "Many people are hungry here in Leningrad. It's the war." He rustled in the pocket of his overcoat and pulled out a piece of dry, grey bread. He handed it to me. "Take it," he said. "Take it to her. I hope it helps."

I stood up right away to go back to Anna but I felt something wasn't right. I couldn't accept the bread without offering something in return.

I stuck my hands in my jacket pockets and suddenly it was there in my hand. The silver icon. The one Papa had given me before we left, my last memory of him. I'd sworn to myself I'd never let it go. But silver is dead. And the bread is alive. Anna is alive.

I gave the icon to the man. I felt immediately better.

"There you are," I said. "You can remember me by it."

"Yes, child, I will. I promise."

18th November
Leningrad, Smolny Institute

So many things happened yesterday. I wish I could just shut my eyes and go to sleep. But I have to write everything down, to tell Nadya when the time comes.

Okay, let's begin. Dear sister, here are Viktor's adventures on the day of his thirteenth birthday.

After speaking to that unusual foreign gentleman, I raced back to Anna with the hunk of bread.

"Good news! I found something to nibble on!"

Now, I don't know what exactly that concrete-coloured block was made of. There might have been flour in it somewhere, but it tasted of mud and it was all pasty when you tried to chew it. There also wasn't enough of it.

I collected our things together, by that I mean my notebook and Anna's secret papers, and said, "Are you ready?"

She looked at me with wide eyes and I realized the answer was no.

I pushed her chair into the light. I tried to take the scarf off to check her wound but it was impossible. The fabric and the wool were stiff as boards because of the dried blood. Her leg seemed even more swollen than the day before.

Does that mean something bad? I thought it probably did but I'm not a doctor so I smiled.

"Come on, Anna, don't worry. We just have to focus on getting there, then they'll get you a doctor and everything will be fine."

It felt like a flat-out lie. I didn't even know if there were any doctors left in the city. But we had to try.

I gave her a pill for the pain. One of Lev's pills. Then I went back outside alone, wandered up and down a few blocks until I found a children's sled, the flat plastic kind you can pull behind you on a string.

It had been left outside by the front door of a house, half-buried in the snow. It felt like stealing, but there was no one to ask so I took it and left. ←——— *S. - looting.*

I helped Anna to walk down the stairs and to get herself onto the sled, then I wrapped her in a blanket.

"Now be sure to tell me if there's anything wrong or when you've had enough."

She said she would, and she reminded me again of little Ilya, when we'd loaded him onto the sled like Anna, but he'd died.

No one was going to die this time.

"Ready?"

"Ready."

Looking down, I saw a leaflet on the ground. I unrolled it, smiled.

"We'll just cross the road, is that okay, Anna?"

She said yes.

We set off.

And so the last part of my journey began, with Anna on the sled, me pulling her.

I walked along roads I didn't know. I saw buildings destroyed. Bodies abandoned. Planes flew overhead every now and then, dropped their bombs. Occasionally I saw someone but no one came near us.

I had to rest a lot because pulling Anna was hard work. Other times we had to stop to avoid roadblocks, or to get round buildings that had collapsed and were in our way, things like that.

I was scared we'd get lost. I only really know our neighbourhood and the city centre where the museum is (and the palace of the General Staff of the Armed Forces).

Everything seemed different, hostile. The statues had been boxed up. The buildings were draped in camouflage nets. There were military trucks and patrols.

The war had left Leningrad deeply scarred.

I climbed up the embankment of the Neva then down onto the frozen river.

I walked on, pulling the sled behind me, until I felt almost faint with exhaustion, and when the river finally opened out to reveal the front of the Hermitage, I nearly dropped to my knees in the snow.

Mama was in there, maybe. A few more steps and I'd be able to see her again.

"Do you recognize me? It's Viktor."

I could ask her for help.

I pushed myself over in that direction but had to stop. No, I couldn't do it.

Of course I was anxious to see her again. But what if she wasn't at the Hermitage anymore? What if she'd been sent somewhere else? What if she was . . . dead?

I'd used up every last scrap of energy I had. A disappointment like that would kill me.

So I gave the museum a silent nod and walked on. I scrambled up the embankment and onto the road then crossed the massive Palace Square, now just a grey, desolate space.

On the other side of the square were the headquarters of the General Staff.

My destination.

The enormous building was dark and silent. An icy wind blew out of the huge monumental archway, as if a hand were trying to push me back.

I saw some soldiers in greatcoats on patrol. They were gathered around a jeep. Until then I'd been careful to steer clear of soldiers but I couldn't put it off any longer.

So I walked over to them, pulling Anna on the sled behind me.

"Excuse me," I said. "Comrade soldiers."

They didn't bother with me the first time. I moved closer.

"I'm talking to you. Excuse me!"

They weren't that much older than me and were very thin. Compared to them, I looked fat.

"Who are you? What do you want? Papers!"

I gave them my documents (or rather, my friend Anatoly's) and Anna's (they were actually hers).

"This says you live in Leningrad but were evacuated for the war. What are you doing here?"

"It's a long story," I said. "We need to speak to General Zhukov."

The name just slipped out, without thinking. It was the only one I knew, having heard it a thousand times on the radio.

"Who?"

"Zhukov," I said.

One of them laughed. "Listen to him!"

"Don't you know the general was summoned back to Moscow where he now commands the defence of the city?"

"Don't you know that even if he were here, in this square, he wouldn't deign to give you so much as a glance?"

They laughed loudly but I was in no mood to be made fun of. I walked over to the one who seemed to be enjoying it the most. If he'd been just a little bit smaller, I wouldn't have thought twice about taking a swing at him.

"Listen carefully," I said. "Do you see these fingers? Someone cut them off. And it wasn't fun. And do you see that girl on the sled? You've just read her name on her papers, so you should know she's the daughter of a colonel in the NKVD. One of the most powerful men in Leningrad. I risked my life a hundred times to bring her this far. She's injured, has important information with her and, if we don't hurry, she could die, putting the whole of Leningrad in danger. That'll make this girl's father very angry and he'll want to know whose fault it was. It won't be mine. And if he asks me what happened, I'll tell him how I nearly made it but some soldiers, instead of helping me, laughed at me like I was some snotty-nosed kid."

I don't know if it was because I was so furious, or my bandaged hand, or Anna's teary eyes. Or the fact that she really was the daughter of an NKVD colonel, albeit one who'd been dead for a few months, but whatever it was, the soldiers suddenly took me seriously.

"We . . ."

"You're going to take me to someone at General Staff. Now."

I heard Anna mumble something. I leant down. It was a name.

"If Zhukov isn't there, General Bagramyan will do!" I said, repeating the name Anna had just whispered in my ear.

This general had to be a big shot because the soldiers sprang to attention.

"The general! I don't think you'll find him here . . ."

"Where is he? Do you know?"

"The Smolny Institute – the old Party headquarters. High Command has been transferred there."

"That's too far for a girl in this state . . . She's injured."

I glanced over at the jeep. "Well, what are you waiting for? Jump in and start her up," I said.

The soldiers, believe it or not, did as I said.

The next few hours were hard but also extremely boring. I'm so tired. So I'll try to sum them up quickly.

The soldiers raced us over to the Smolny Institute, which is an enormous building that looks like a Greek temple, nestling in a park that stretches down to the river.

We had to get through checkpoint after checkpoint. Each time they asked for my papers, Anna's, even the soldiers', I would repeat my story and they'd let us past.

We went inside the Institute. Checkpoint. We went into an office. Checkpoint. Another office. Checkpoint. Each time, the person looking at me from behind the desk was a little older. A little fatter. The uniform a little shinier. More bars on their shoulder pieces.

After getting through level after level, one of the officials suddenly froze when he read Anna's ID papers. "There's something not right here. I fear the girl's father is no longer, ahem, in service."

I'd been waiting for this to happen so quickly replied, "Yes, but his reputation has just been restored. We have important documents that General Bagramyan needs to see immediately!"

"I would also like to see them."

"Our orders are to deliver them to the general. On pain of death."

The official sent us through to another checkpoint. Then another. At the third one, they requested to see the secret documents. I asked Anna to give them to me.

The man read them and the blood drained instantly from his face.

He disappeared. A second later he returned and said, "The Comrade General would like to see you in his office."

It really happened.

Anna and I, filthy and injured like two war veterans, were shown into a warm, opulent room, with rugs on the floor and crystal chandeliers. The air was blue with cigarette smoke, a bald man sat behind a solid wood desk.

The desk was piled high with papers.

The man was the general.

He greeted Anna like an old friend. But his face looked serious, as if to say, "I can't help you."

It was time for Anna to speak.

She talked about her father, the enemy's scheming, the evidence that exonerated him. She mentioned train seventy-six, the garrison holding out at Oreshek, and all the rest.

The general listened without interrupting. Then, when Anna had finished her speech, he asked, "Anything to add, young Anatoly?"

"Erm, in truth, I'm actually Viktor," I explained. "Viktor Nikolayevich Danilov. I borrowed a friend's passport . . . because . . ."

"Where is your passport?"

"In a military base in Novaya Ladoga," I said. "That's where I was ten days ago."

The general shot to his feet. He pulled a map out of the hundreds of things cluttering his desk and said, "You were where?"

I pointed to the village north of Tikhvin.

"But Tikhvin was conquered by the enemy!"

"Yes, that's why I had to retreat with the 4th Army to Novaya Ladoga. From there, my friends and I came across the frozen lake. In a truck. That we, erm, borrowed."

"You crossed Ladoga in a truck?"

"Yes, sir. We drove to Kobona first and made the crossing from there."

"And the ice held?"

"Yes, sir."

At that point the general turned yellow, like a lemon. He lit a cigarette, stood up, walked across to a telephone hanging on the wall and said, "This is the general speaking. I have several urgent orders and I want them carried out immediately. Firstly, find Major Fedin from the NKVD and have him arrested. Secondly, call Moscow and have Uvarov located. I think he is Kremlin staff. Arrest him as well."

The general paused, as if someone were responding to his list of instructions. Then he said, "I don't care! He can go to hell as far as I'm concerned. I have proof of what I am saying, so do it quickly. And I want a team of military engineers here immediately. The ice on Ladoga is apparently thick enough for trucks to drive across. So I want someone to go to the village of Kokkorevo, on the banks of the lake, and start mapping out an ice route to Kobona. Then I want another team of horses and sleighs ready to leave the city in two hours to go straight across the lake to Novaya Ladoga. Today is Monday. I expect them back here with a cargo of food by the weekend."

Another pause.

"No, that is not all. Get a company of soldiers ready and send them to Oreshek without delay, to help those heroes who have held the fortress so far, alone, in the face of the enemy. Yes, you heard right. Oreshek never fell. But they need us, so get to work. Now!"

The general slammed down the phone so hard he nearly pulled the whole thing off the wall.

Then he turned to me and Anna and said, "I will need you later. But now you may rest."

"To be honest," I said, "I think we need a doctor first."

So that's what happened.

They took us into another room. Thirty minutes later, three doctors arrived, real ones, in white coats carrying doctors' bags. They examined Anna (they said the wound had become badly infected but it will heal, she shouldn't lose her leg) and me (they said my hand is getting better but I have to rest it for the next few weeks).

After that, they brought us some food: real food, that had been cooked. And they gave us a bedroom here at the Smolny.

I felt a little guilty being so comfortable and well-fed when the city outside was starving to death and my sister at the fortress was facing all kinds of danger. But then I thought to myself that I'd done my best, which made me feel better.

I was just dropping off when the final thing of the day happened. The best thing.

There was a sudden knock at the door, then it opened. I looked up and saw a woman standing quite still in the doorway.

I have to admit I didn't recognize her straight away, she was so thin, her hair so brittle, with cheekbones that seemed to be pushing through her skin.

But the eyes, I would've recognized those eyes anywhere.

"Mama," I said.

"Viktor. Viktor? Is it really you?"

I don't think she recognized me either. She faltered as she made her way over. I got out of bed and went to meet her.

When I reached her, she squeezed me tight. Her arms were as thin as toothpicks.

I was about to tell her to let me go. A soldier was watching us from the corridor and, well, you know, I'm not a child anymore.

But then I had second thoughts.

I remembered when we'd said goodbye at the station, a lifetime ago.

So I said nothing.

Because that hug wasn't just for Mama.

It was for everyone.

18th November

So, I ended up spending my birthday in prison. They arrested me along with Boris and Klara. It happened on Saturday morning at dawn, right after everyone in the fortress woke up and realized my brother and the others were gone.

They wanted to know why.

Maybe I was a bit naïve, but I told the truth. In part, at least.

I explained that they'd gone to Leningrad to summon reinforcements. That the fortress couldn't afford to lose three adult sailors when three children could go in their place. That they'd be back soon with a rescue squad.

I don't know why but the Chief was livid.

"A fortress is not somewhere a bunch of kids can come and go from as they please! This is a military base in wartime and those three have risked the safety of us all!"

He went on and on like this for quite some time and, surprisingly, everyone else, including Mrs. Burova, agreed with him.

A few hours later they discovered that Viktor had taken two pistols and a rifle. There were so many here at the fortress, I didn't think it was such an issue, but

S. - undoubtedly.

they said it was theft of military supplies, that the punishment for a crime like that is execution by firing squad.

Given that my brother wasn't here to take his punishment, they contented themselves with throwing us into jail.

Luckily Klara and I were put in the same cell, we're in the Old Prison, not the New Prison where our German guest is.

They haven't discovered Franz yet and who knows what they'll do when they find out. On top of that, it's now our fourth day in prison which means that poor wretch hasn't had anything to eat or wood for the stove for four days.

When they eventually let us out, he might be dead and it would be our fault.

This thought makes me feel worse.

"To be honest," Klara said, "there's no guarantee they'll let us out at all."

"No, we won't be in here for ever," I replied. "Just until Viktor comes back to save us."

"You really trust him."

"Yes," I replied. "But it's not trust. I *know* he'll make it."

"It might not be that easy."

"He'll find a way."

Klara said nothing, just smiled, and that was when I realized she was in love with my brother.

So I started talking about him, when we were young, and tried to find out something about her.

It didn't take long for it to come out. Klara is German. What I mean is, she was born in Leningrad like me, but her parents are German. My first thought was that this makes her just like the sniper Franz, in his cell in the other prison, like the soldiers who had been attacking us for days on end. Like Hitler.

I felt . . . I don't know how to describe it. I didn't know what to do. I was angry, but I didn't know why. I felt like hitting her.

I realized she had nothing to do with everything that had happened to me, with Lilya who'd drowned in the river, with Irina who'd run away from the church, with Leningrad under siege, and Mama and Papa who could be alive or dead for all I knew.

Yet it was her people who had done all this to me. So it's her fault, too, right? Even if just a little?

But she said, "I might be German because my parents are, but that doesn't mean the Nazis are 'my people.' There are Germans fighting against Hitler as well. Did you know that?"

"Not many though."

"That's not true. My father told me. And as for 'your people' – Russians put Viktor and me in a gulag. The old woman who nearly chopped Viktor's hand off was Russian. Do you feel guilty because a Russian hurt your brother?"

"No, I don't."

"So neither do I," Klara concluded.

We made peace.

I don't know if we'll ever be friends, she's an odd girl, but if she and Viktor get together, I think we'll be able to get along.

I feel bad for poor Boris though, he's in a cell at the other end of the corridor so we can't talk to him. It's a pity because I would've liked his company, to know how he's feeling. I'll have to wait . . .

Later

Big news! Very big news!

Alina has just come to see us and she said they're going to let us out!

Klara asked why, but I already know.

It means Viktor, Anna and Mikhail made it! I knew it! I KNEW IT!

19th November

Yesterday, we were eventually freed. Boris the sailor came. "Come on, move, get out of here," he said.

"Why?" Klara asked again.

He didn't seem in the mood to chat. "The Chief will tell you. I just obey orders."

We went to the Golovkin Tower.

"What a pleasure to see you again, Chief," I said.

"Less of your cheek if you don't want trouble," he replied. "The fact is it's your lucky day today. We have just received a message from High Command."

My brother really had made it, he'd spoken to a general and they're sending reinforcements. They should be arriving today – soldiers, weapons and vehicles to make sure the fortress remains in our hands until the end of the war.

"That's not all," the Chief continued. "The Leningrad People's Militia Army has decided to open a supply route across Lake Ladoga, following the one your brother took in the truck. That way they'll be able to get the remaining civilians out of the city and get food and medicine in."

"Are you serious?"

He was serious.

As I write, thirty-five horse-drawn sleighs are already making their way across the lake, en route to the village of Kobona where food and other essentials are being gathered together.

Leningrad High Command said that this is only possible because of what we've achieved here at Oreshek.

We stopped the enemy from travelling along the Neva and completing the blockade. Gosh.

It would seem, therefore, that we've been successful.

Of course, the war's not over. We don't know if we'll win. The outlook is pretty bleak. But I feel as happy as when you reach the end of a long journey and can finally go home. Although my journey didn't actually take me very far from where I'd started.

But before I can write – THE END – there's one more thing I have to do.

Franz.

When me, Klara and Boris finally went to see him, he was more dead than alive – frozen and hungry; for all the time we were locked up he'd been drinking melted snow and nothing else.

What should we do with him? We discussed it, the three of us, and considered our options:

✳ 1) Kill him. But we hadn't been able to do it originally and didn't think we could do it now either.
✳ 2) Hand him over to the Chief or the new soldiers who'll be arriving soon. But this meant leaving them to kill him, which takes us back to point 1.
3) Leave him where he is now. But the fortress is going to fill up with soldiers, maybe forty or fifty people, and there are bound to be guards and inspections, maybe the discipline that the Chief says he so sorely misses will be reintroduced. Franz will be discovered sooner or later, which takes us back to point 2, then to point 1.
4) Free him. Let him go back to his people, on the south bank of the Neva.

S. – 1 or 2 acceptable.

"Free Franz? Are you mad?!" Boris exclaimed. "We can't do that."

I sighed. "Why not?"

"Because as soon as he gets to his people, he'll tell them there are only ten people here and that they can attack!!"

"But there aren't just ten people anymore . . . Re inforcements are on their way!"

"What if they don't get here right away?"

"We can't wait too long to free him. We might not have another chance."

"It's too dangerous," Boris insisted.

"There's also the ethical dilemma," Klara said, with the seriousness of someone who knows words like "eth ical dilemma." "If we free Franz, sooner or later he'll be back behind his sniper rifle and will use it to kill someone. So, if you think about it, by freeing him we'll be responsible for those future deaths."

It's true. Klara was right.

There was an ethical dilemma.

Aside from all this, was it right to let Franz go? An enemy? We'd seen him hit Boris, he'd hit me as well. Would he do it again, after we freed him? Yes, of course he would. It would be expected of him.

"That will be his decision," I said. "I can't do anything about that. But I have to decide for me. And I want to free him."

We took a vote on it, we talked, and in the end we made a decision.

I decided for me.

We couldn't wait for nightfall because the reinforce ments would be arriving any minute. There was no other option but to act now, and to do it out in the open, in the light of day. When it would be more dangerous.

S. — To let a prisoner go is an act of high treason.

416

"We'll do it at lunchtime," I suggested. "Boris will offer to help serve up and will do it as slowly as he can to keep everyone underground in the cellars. While Klara and I free Franz."

"I'm a man and Franz is strong. Don't you think I should be with you, too?"

"Possibly, but there are only three of us and I need Klara."

Boris seemed disappointed. He asked me why but I didn't answer.

The fact is I didn't want to lie to him and I didn't want to have to explain that, since Klara is German, she can speak to Franz in his own language.

The plan went off fairly smoothly. The two of us went over to the New Prison. I had a gun and some handcuffs that must've been about a hundred years old.

We opened the peephole in his cell door and Franz looked up.

"Tell him to put his hands through the hatch, the one we use for his food," I said to Klara.

She translated and Franz replied.

"He wants to know why."

"Tell him we're going to free him."

There was another exchange between Klara and Franz.

"He wants to know why."

"Because it's the right thing to do."

Franz didn't believe us, so through the peephole I showed him the gun and had Klara say that if he didn't obey, I was sorry but I'd have to kill him.

He put his hands through the hatch and Klara put the handcuffs on him. They were ancient and thick with rust, and we don't have the keys but it doesn't matter. When he gets back to his people, he'll find a way to get them off.

We let him out of his cell, Franz at the front, me and Klara behind him, the gun in his back so he wouldn't do anything silly.

"Klara," I said. "Tell him what we're doing. Explain that we're freeing him because reinforcements are on their way to the fortress. Say that they'll be here in a few minutes and we've decided to save his life."

"Okay."

"Tell him also that we have sentries in all the towers. If he wants to get out alive, he should hide in the trees on the north bank, which is Soviet territory. He should wait until it gets dark before crossing the river and going back to his base camp on the south bank. That's my advice."

Klara began to translate and as she spoke, Franz stared at me with his bright blue eyes. I couldn't see his mouth under the bushy beard he'd grown, so I wondered what he was thinking, if he understood that we really did want to save his life.

From our hiding place in the anteroom at the entrance to the prison, we heard Boris ring the lunch bell (which is actually a ladle you bang on sheet metal). The sailors in the fortress began to make their way down, Klara and I stood and watched. I counted them one by one and when all of them had gone past, we left our hiding place and pushed Franz through the garden.

First we scrambled up to the covered wall-walk, and from there to the winch. With Franz's help (who despite being handcuffed, was still stronger than us) we turned the crank to raise the first grille, just a tiny bit.

Then we did the same thing again to lower the draw-bridge.

After that we went down to the main entrance to the fortress but that's when I got a nasty surprise. Someone had put a padlock on the outer gate.

"You fire," Franz said, gesturing that I should aim the gun at the padlock.

"I can't shoot," I replied. "Someone might hear."

It was a quite a problem. We thought about it for a bit, Klara went away then came back with a stone and a huge iron nail.

"I'll try to break it."

"But they'll see the padlock's been broken."

"Yes, but they won't know it was us. And what can they do to us anyway? Put us back in prison?"

She was right. She hit the padlock but it didn't budge. Franz said, "I try."

He knelt down in front of the lock, grasped the nail with both hands while I pointed the gun at him, and started battering it, once, twice, three times, until it fell to the floor.

We were able to go outside, then, into the snow which came halfway up our legs. I pointed to the sheer surface of the frozen river.

"Tell him to go. To hide and wait for nightfall."

Klara translated but Franz didn't move.

He just stared at me, no one else, just me.

Finally he said something.

"It means thank you," Klara said.

"Say you're welcome." I smiled, without meaning to, then became serious again. "Tell him I think he's a bad person. What he did to me, Boris and Anna in the farmhouse was cruel. I'll never forget it. I think that's why I decided to free him, because I want him to remember everything. And to tell people. And to make sure horrors like this don't happen again."

Franz listened carefully and gave a quick nod.

Then he said simply, in Russian, "Goodbye."

He pulled his greatcoat around him and jumped onto

the river. He slid, picked himself up then started to walk, then run, staggering this way and that, towards the north bank.

Klara and I stayed to watch our exhausted enemy escape. We didn't take our eyes off him until he'd reached the trees.

Franz turned around to look at us one last time. He flashed me a smile, a wolf's smile, then disappeared between the tree trunks and branches. Seconds later he was gone.

In his place all that remained was the snow, the sun and the blinding light of the frozen lake.

DECEMBER / 1946
N° ..... 973 ... / ..B....

CCCP

PEOPLE'S COMMISSARIAT FOR INTERNAL AFFAIRS

FINAL REPORT

The Judicial Authority has completed its examination of these documents in the case against the accused:

* <u>Viktor Nikolayevich Danilov</u>; born Leningrad, 17 November 1928;
* <u>Nadya Nikolayevna Danilova</u>; born Leningrad, 17 November 1928.

The events described herein cover the early months of the Great Patriotic War, from June to November 1941. Events after these dates are not described, namely the heroic resistance of the Soviet Union and the final victory, when the enemy was valiantly repelled, forced to retreat and forcefully pursued into German territory.

Soviet troops liberated Berlin from German tyranny and forced Hitler to take his own life when his secret bunker was surrounded.

To achieve such an epic victory, the people of our country had to overcome the most gruelling of challenges. That of Leningrad was, without doubt, the worst. The Nazi dictator's plan was to sentence the city's

inhabitants - soldiers, civilians, men, women
and children alike - to a brutal death by
starvation.

The siege of Leningrad lasted almost nine
hundred days, until the city was finally
liberated on the 27th of January 1944. Over
these long and arduous months, 650,000 people
died.

No doubt this number would have been
significantly higher without Military
Highway 101. The so-called "Road of Life"
opened across Lake Ladoga which enabled
almost 1,500,000 people to be evacuated to
safety, and 360,000 tons of food supplies
to be brought into the city, thanks to which
those who remained in Leningrad were able to
survive.

The accused, Viktor and Nadya, never saw the
fruits of their endeavours.

On the 20th of November 1941, the survivors
of Oreshek were transported to Kobona on a
convoy of horse-drawn sleighs, and onwards
from there to safety.

According to the documents in my possession,
Viktor and Nadya, along with their mother and
their companions, were taken back to Kazan,
to their assigned kolkhoz and remained there
until the end of the conflict, at which time
they returned to Leningrad.

Unfortunately the twins were never reunited
with their father, Nikolay Ivanovich Danilov.
This brave citizen, who served in the People's
Militia, is recorded as having died in battle
as early as September 1941, only days after
arriving at the front. No further information
is held about him.

<u>I come now to the difficult task I face.</u>
   I have been asked to examine the evidence
against the accused and determine the fate of
the two young people, who have only recently
come of age.
   Both have confessed to the numerous crimes
of which they stand accused.

In particular, Viktor Nikolayevich Danilov is
accused of breaching Articles 89 ; 82; 257;
78; 99-1; 245; 88-2; 210; 245; 191-2; 254; 77;
108; 195; 198; 159; 146; 181; 239; 77-1; 208;
218; 188; 144; 166; 110; 212; 252; 221; 174;
88-1; 98; 219 of the Soviet Penal Code.

Nadya Nikolayevna Danilova is accused of
breaching Articles 89; 82; 257; 78; 192; 163;
239; 65; 245; 91; 254; 68; 268; 181; 189; 64;
219; 58-1b /high treason/.

Of their many crimes, aiding and abetting
the enemy in times of war, in the persons
of "Franz" and "Klara", is of the highest
gravity. Investigations are ongoing into the
case of Klara; it would appear the young
woman managed to escape a second time from
the kolkhoz in December 1944, perhaps aided
by Viktor and Nadya, and since then has
apparently vanished. No further trace of her
was ever found.

In reaching my judgement of the accused,
several mitigating circumstances must first be
considered, namely their young age at the time
of the events, the exceptional circumstances
in which they found themselves and the
incredible benefits their actions had for the
Russian people.

For the latter, at such a dark time in history for the whole of humankind, the Viktor and Nadya Affair tells of the blazing light of two red stars.

One further element must also be considered.
My investigation found that senior Party officials and officers of the NKVD at the very highest level and in the uppermost ranks were implicated in the Tereshenkov affair, and that they bore serious responsibility for Russian defeats suffered in the early months of the conflict.

For reasons of national security, however, the entire affair has been classified a State secret. All documents were destroyed. All information censored.

Every trace of the corruption of Party Official Uvarov and Major Fedin has been redacted from official history and, by extension, also the worthy conduct of Comrade Colonel Tereshenkov.

As Officer in Charge of the People's Commissariat for Internal Affairs /NKVD/, my primary task is to protect the secrets of the State, the Party and its illustrious representatives.

It is therefore my belief that this particularly dangerous dossier, referred to as The Story of Viktor and Nadya, must be classified.

NON-COMPLIANT

NOT TO BE READ

TO BE DELETED

Therefore, in accordance with protocol
regarding State secrets and the special
procedures of the NKVD, these notebooks
and the information they contain must be
considered as never having existed. On
the orders of the Judicial Authority, the
situations described herein did not take
place.

Consequently, train seventy-six never
stopped outside Leningrad and was never,
subsequently, set on fire; no group of
passengers was secretly moved to Shlisselburg;
no civilians sought refuge in Oreshek when the
village was taken by the enemy; no civilians
were ever hosted by the garrison in residence
at the fortress; no radios were stolen
nor prisoners taken; the garrison followed
procedure and awaited reinforcements which
arrived only a few days after Shlisselburg
fell.

Likewise, no passengers on train seventy-
seven escaped from their assigned kolkhoz;
no clandestine passengers boarded a train
for Leningrad Zoo; no young children joined
a group of prisoners in the Rybinsk gulag;
nor did they escape weeks later nor were they
admitted to the field hospital in Pikalyovo;
nor did they subsequently escape by stealing
an army vehicle nor reach the base in Novaya
Ladoga; moreover, no civilian was the first to
travel the Road of Life which was proposed,
planned and established by members of the Red
Army.

Since none of the above ever took place,
the crimes for which Viktor and Nadya stand
accused cannot be verified. It is for this
reason that I hereby declare:

Citizen VIKTOR NIKOLAYEVICH DANILOV
has been <u>acquitted</u> on all counts.

Citizen NADYA NIKOLAYEVNA DANILOVA
has been <u>acquitted</u> on all counts.

The case is closed.
Glory to the Party!

Signed:

COLONEL VALERY GAVRIILOVICH SMIRNOV

Col. Smirnov

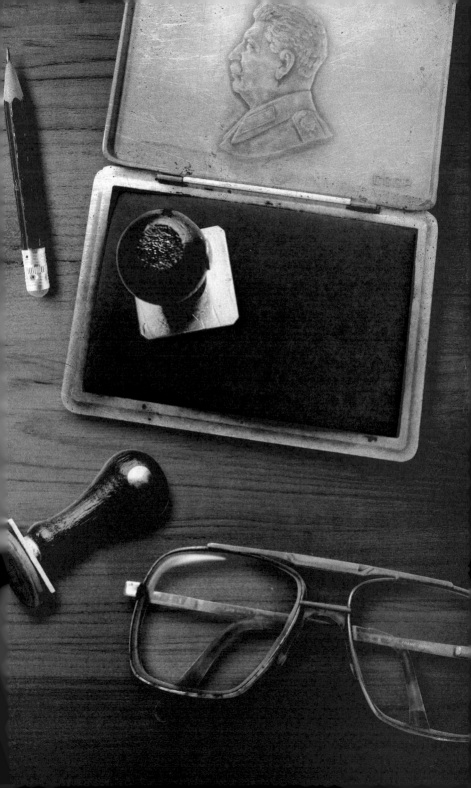

Author's Note

This is a quasi-historical novel, in that it has some characters who were real people and others whom I made up; it mentions truths so far-fetched they seem pretend and pretences so real they could have taken place.

The images adorning the pages of the book are presented out of their original context. Paintings and drawings have been modified for the purpose of the unfolding narrative and historical photographs have been used to represent imaginary characters.

For everything concerning the story proper, I tried to be as accurate as possible but some errors may have slipped through nonetheless, and I apologize for this. At other times, I chose not to be wholly faithful to the *big* story, the historical one, because it was important for the telling of my *little* one.

Generally speaking, everything in the novel reflects real historical events, with the exception of the things which happened to Viktor and Nadya, their friends and the mysterious Tereshenkov affair.

Luckily (in a manner of speaking), by the end of the book, Colonel Smirnov determines the "official version" of the truth.

One last thing before I leave you.

I am Italian, and during the Second World War, Italy fought at Germany's side against the Soviet Union.

Both my grandfathers were conscripted to fight in the conflict, and one of them ended up in the Italian Army in

Russia, a unit of 230,000 soldiers. Barely half of them made it home alive.

I grew up listening to my grandfather's stories about Russia – for him it was a huge, cold and terrible place, where nature itself became your enemy.

Now that I have finished writing this book, my thoughts go to my grandfather and the thousands of people who were forced to leave, and to die, for the sake of a senseless dictatorship.

The twentieth century was a period of madness in which humankind attempted to destroy the very things that make us human.

So to come back to the book. I have always believed in the power of stories and the importance of reading. And, as Nadya says in the story, we have a duty to remember the past. And to ensure it is never repeated.

Acknowledgments

My thanks go to all my friends, colleagues and fellow adventurers at Book on a Tree: to Pierdomenico Baccalario, Lorenzo Rulfo, Christian Hill, Tomaso Percivale, Sarah Rossi, Lucia "Lilya" Vaccarino, Barbara Gozzi, Guido Sgardoli, Giuseppe Festa, Daniele Nicastro, Gianna Tarditi, Mirco Zilio, Martina Sala, Silvia Genovese, Davide Calì, Alessandro Gatti.

Thanks to all the team and my friends at Mondadori: to Alessandro Gelso, Chiara Pontoglio, Fernando Ambrosi, Stefano Moro, Sandra Barbui, Marta Mazza, Giulia Geraci; and thank you Enrico Racca.

Thanks to Viola Gambarini for her editing; to Francesca Mazzurana for reading the drafts; to Francesca Poli for advising on medical issues; to Denise Silvestri for her help on language issues; and to Mila Crippa for consulting on cultural issues; to Federica Colombo and Alessandro Nicodemo for lending a pen to Nadya and Viktor; to Yuliya Plaksina and Vladimir Orlov for being my guides all the way to Oreshek.

Thanks to my family, and to Laura, my partner in life and in travels . . . even in Russia.

A special thanks to Pushkin Press and Daniel Seton for bringing my book to the UK, to Denise Muir for her great translation and to India Darsley, Alex Billington and Hannah Featherstone for their work in production.

As always, dear reader, my final thoughts are for you. This is a book I felt I had to write. Thank you for having stuck with me this far.

Image Credits